LONDON AFTER MIDNIGHT

Alice was surrounded—zombies to her left and right, a zombie in the cab ahead of her, and a brick wall behind. No doorways to dodge into, no stairs to climb. Nowhere to flee . . .

"Get away!" she screamed at them. "Get away from me!"

A shot cracked through the fog. The head of the zombie woman exploded like a ripe melon. An awful smell washed over Alice as the body dropped to the sidewalk. Alice gaped. A horse rode up—two horses, no, four—their iron shoes clattering on the cobblestones. One of the riders rushed at Alice, stomping over the zombie woman's corpse.

"Up you come," the rider said, hauling Alice up behind the saddle. Alice barely had time to register the fact that her rescuer was a woman in leather trousers before the horse wheeled around and cantered back the way it had come.

"Who are you?" Alice demanded. "What's going on?"

"We're here to help," the woman said.

THE
DOOMSDAY
VAULT

A NOVEL OF THE
CLOCKWORK EMPIRE

STEVEN HARPER

A ROC BOOK

ROC
Published by New American Library, a division of
Penguin Group (USA) Inc., 375 Hudson Street,
New York, New York 10014, USA
Penguin Group (Canada), 90 Eglinton Avenue East, Suite 700, Toronto,
Ontario M4P 2Y3, Canada (a division of Pearson Penguin Canada Inc.)
Penguin Books Ltd., 80 Strand, London WC2R 0RL, England
Penguin Ireland, 25 St. Stephen's Green, Dublin 2,
Ireland (a division of Penguin Books Ltd.)
Penguin Group (Australia), 250 Camberwell Road, Camberwell, Victoria 3124,
Australia (a division of Pearson Australia Group Pty. Ltd.)
Penguin Books India Pvt. Ltd., 11 Community Centre, Panchsheel Park,
New Delhi - 110 017, India
Penguin Group (NZ), 67 Apollo Drive, Rosedale, Auckland 0632,
New Zealand (a division of Pearson New Zealand Ltd.)
Penguin Books (South Africa) (Pty.) Ltd., 24 Sturdee Avenue,
Rosebank, Johannesburg 2196, South Africa

Penguin Books Ltd., Registered Offices:
80 Strand, London WC2R 0RL, England

First published by Roc, an imprint of New American Library,
a division of Penguin Group (USA) Inc.

First Printing, November 2011
10 9 8 7 6 5 4 3 2 1

Copyright © Steven Piziks, 2011
All rights reserved

ROC REGISTERED TRADEMARK — MARCA REGISTRADA

Printed in the United States of America

ACKNOWLEDGMENTS

Many thanks to the members of the Untitled Writers Group (Cindy, Christian, Diana, Erica, Jonathan, Mary Beth, Merrie, Sarah, and Steve) for their endlessly patient critiques—and gourmet snack supply.

PART
I

Chapter One

The zombie lurched out of the yellow fog and reached for the door on Alice's hansom cab. Alice Michaels shied away.

"Driver!" she shouted.

"I see it, miss." The driver leaned down from his seat above and behind Alice and cracked the zombie smartly across the forearms with his carriage whip. The zombie groaned. Its face was a mass of open sores, and its skin had worn through in places, exposing red muscle beneath. Old rags barely covered its body. Fear and adrenaline thrilled through Alice's veins as the zombie's festering arm reached through the open sides of the cab. She pushed herself away from it, but there wasn't much room in the little two-wheeled cab, and The Dress hindered her movements. The driver lashed down with the whip again. The zombie abruptly let the cab go, and the driver smacked the reins across the horse's rump. Alice clutched a handle inside the cab as it bounced across the cobblestones, the wheels pounding as hard as her heart. Despite herself, she turned on the leather-covered seat and looked out the rear window. The zombie was already fading into the night and mist.

A particularly rough bounce jolted Alice to her teeth. "You can slow down now," she called. "It's gone."

The driver obeyed, and Alice resettled The Dress about her. The Dress was a deep violet affair with multiple flounces, fashionably puffed sleeves, and a short matching shawl to ward off the damp spring chill. The layers formed a heavy shell around her, concealing her pounding heart and shaking knees beneath a veneer of smooth satin. It had cost Father an enormous sum, and Alice realized she had been more afraid of the zombie's tearing The Dress than of the creature's touching and infecting her.

"You all right, miss?" the driver called down from his seat.

"I'm fine. Thank you for fending it off."

The driver touched the brim of his high hat, and Alice realized she was required to tip him extra. She made a mental inventory of the coins in her purse and decided she could do it, but only if the driver on the return trip would be willing to wait while she ran into the house for tuppence. It would make her look foolish, but there was nothing for it.

Yellow gaslights lit the London evening as the horse clopped through winding streets, the driver keeping carefully to the better-traveled avenues. Other carriages and cabs pulled by horses both living and mechanical joined them. Overhead, Alice heard the faint *whup-whup-whup* noise of a dirigible's propellers, and its massive, blunt shape made a black spot among the misty stars. Restaurants and pubs kept their doors open and their windows lit—lights kept the zombies at bay. Smells of coal smoke, manure, and wet wool permeated the air. People strolled in couples or groups on the sidewalks, heading to or from concerts, plays, parties, celebrations, and other social events. It was a Saturday evening in May, and the London spring season was in full swing. Alice watched the men in their dark trousers and coats, and the women in their skirts that belled and swayed with every step, and she wondered what flaws each one was hiding beneath sartorial perfection.

Mere clothing wouldn't hide Alice's shortcomings. A new dress couldn't smooth over the fact that she was still unmarried at the age of twenty-two, or that twelve years ago, her mother and brother had died in the same outbreak of clockwork plague that had left her father a cripple, or that three years ago, Alice had become engaged to Frederick, heir to the Earl of Trent, only to watch the clockwork plague kill him as well. After that, no one wanted anything much to do with the Michaels family. Their fortunes, both monetary and social, had declined sharply. Alice would gladly have found some kind of useful work, but traditional society had long ago decreed that the daughter of a baron was expected to be a lady of leisure, no matter how badly her family might need money, and her family's history with the clockwork plague precluded her from trying to find a position as a lady-in-waiting. This dance was her last chance to redeem the Michaelses' social graces.

The cab drew up to a large three-story town house with a cobblestoned courtyard and fountain out front. Electric lights, the new fashion, blazed in all the windows, and a short line of cabs and carriages snaked around the courtyard. Alice checked the pocket watch inside her purse. Nine fifteen. She had arrived late, but not fashionably late—all part of her strategy. The majority of the guests would arrive after ten, and Alice hoped her arrival to a nearly empty ballroom would allow her lack of an escort to go unnoticed, or at least unremarked. Alice's mother would have been her first choice as escort, of course, and her brother second, but neither of them was available.

While they were waiting in line, Alice paid—and generously tipped—the driver so she wouldn't have to do so in front of her hosts. The daughter of a traditional baron didn't handle financial transactions, but Alice didn't have much choice, sitting in the shabby cab she had hired herself.

She couldn't help but notice that many of the other conveyances were richly appointed private carriages or, at a minimum, hired cabs of a better class than hers. A few were pulled by steam-snorting mechanical horses. The couple directly behind Alice arrived in a rickshaw pulled by a brass automaton shaped roughly like a man. Alice stared thoughtfully at it, trying to trace how the gears underneath its smooth metal skin would be put together, where the pistons would be placed, how the boiler would deliver proper power. It would be so much more interesting to spend the evening pulling the automaton apart and putting it back together than—

The woman in the rickshaw glanced at Alice's little hired hansom, cracked open her fan, and whispered something behind it to her male companion. They both laughed. Alice's cheeks burned, and she sat rigidly upright in her seat, determined to brazen this out. Father had used up his final favors among certain business contacts to get Alice this invitation, and she wasn't going to fail him.

At last, Alice's cab came to the front door. A footman in gold livery helped her down, but she had to walk through the double doors into the house by herself. Light music—all sweet strings in a major key—drifted from the house's interior. Inside was a large, marble-floored foyer, where a starched servant girl took Alice's shawl and pointed her toward the main ballroom. Alice, back straight, pleasant smile on her lips, swayed toward the door, where Lady Greenfellow, the hostess, had stationed herself to greet her guests. She was a heavyset woman whose wrinkled face belied her jet-black hair, and her dark green dress wrapped her high and low. Alice extended a gloved hand.

"Thank you so much for inviting me, Lady Greenfellow," she said earnestly.

"Of course," Lady Greenfellow replied. "My husband was quite insistent that you should come, on account of your father. And how *is* dear Arthur these days?"

"He's well," Alice said.

"Wonderful to hear." The warmth in Lady Greenfellow's tone was as false as her hair color. "How time flies. I still remember that day I found you on the street with those adorable urchins. How long ago was that?"

For a terrible moment, Alice's hand moved to slap Lady Greenfellow's wrinkly cheek. Instead, she opened her fan and waved it idly. "My impetuous days are long behind me."

"Of course. And you do look lovely tonight."

Alice hoped that was true. Her honey brown hair was pinned up in the latest style, leaving a single stream of curls trailing down the left side of her face, and her cosmetics were artful enough that no one could tell she was wearing any at all. She had a triangular chin and pert nose, and The Dress hid the fact that her legs and body had grown rather thin in recent months. Her shoes had no heel to conceal her height. "Thank you," she said.

"But, my dear"—Lady Greenfellow peered over Alice's shoulder at the foyer behind her—"you didn't even bring a maid! You're not here on your own, are you? I didn't think Arthur would allow his daughter to become one of those new Ad Hoc women."

"Not at all. Bridget tripped and sprained her ankle just as we were leaving," Alice said, giving her prepared lie. A trickle of sweat ran down her back. "It was too late to engage another maid, so here I am."

Lady Greenfellow clicked her tongue. "Misfortune does follow you. Well, the ballroom is through there, and sitting rooms are that way. Our supper buffet begins at one."

Approved and dismissed, Alice nodded with relief and stepped into the main ballroom. The main hurdle was over.

The ballroom was a two-storied affair, with a balcony that ran around the upper half. Lush arrangements of fresh red and white roses covered the balcony rail and hung nearly to the floor below, filling the air with the sweet smells of nectar. The string players were stationed upstairs, their rubber-tipped fingers weaving a soft, melodic tapestry at odds with their hard metal faces. High windows looked out on the city, and an enormous electric chandelier—the showpiece of the house—provided bright light. Refreshment tables and sitting areas ringed the polished oak dance floor. Barely twenty people wandered among them, every one much older than Alice, who at twenty-two was fast becoming an old maid. She handed one of her name cards to the elderly butler stationed at the door.

"The Honorable Alice B. Michaels," he announced over the music.

Reflexively, everyone in the room turned, nodded at Alice, and went back to their conversations. Alice allowed herself a moment of relief—her unescorted entry hadn't caused even a ripple. Expression pleasant, she drifted toward a refreshment table and found herself falling back into a rhythm she hadn't felt since Frederick's death had cast her from the social rolls: pluck a dance card from the tray at the table, tie the ribbon to her fan so she could flash it at eligible gentlemen or conceal it from less desirable ones, select a glass of champagne from the arrangement, let her gaze wander about the room to see who else had arrived. So far she didn't recognize anyone, which made things awkward—women could converse only with other women, and only a man could ask for a dance. She made herself pointedly available for approach, either for a dance or for conversation.

No one came near her. After a bit, she went up to the balcony to look at the orchestra. A dozen faceless automatons played violin, viola, cello, drum, and other instruments. No music stands or music stood before them, and no conductor waved a baton. Their brass skins gleamed in the light of the chandelier, and Alice was surprised at the sweet precision of the music they produced. Their movements, however, jarred. The fingers moved with quick grace, but the torsos remained motionless, in stark contrast to human musicians, who played with their entire bodies. This orchestra were really nothing more than a giant music box, and Alice decided she'd much rather let a set of live musicians sweep her away.

The cello player faltered. Its bow squawked across the strings, and the dissonance tore through the delicate music. The other musicians continued to play as if nothing had happened. On the floor below, several dancers winced and faltered in their steps. Without thinking, Alice reached in and plucked the bow from the cello player's fingers. The cello went silent, and the waltz continued with a missing instrument. The cello player jerked in its seat, fingers twitching spasmodically over the strings.

"What's going on up here?" demanded Lady Greenfellow, skirts still swirling from her indignant scurry up the staircase. "What on earth are you doing to my musicians?"

Alice suppressed a desire to hide the bow behind her back. "I think something went wrong with your cello player," she said, ignoring the accusation. "I took the bow away before the noise could ruin the dance. Do you have an automatist on staff?"

"No." Lady Greenfellow's face flushed. "And we'll never find one at this time of night. Now what do I do?"

Alice hesitated, then plunged ahead. "I could have a quick look," she offered. And before Lady Greenfellow could object, Alice scooted around behind the players, stripped off her gloves, and leaned in to pop the rear panel off the errant cellist. The musicians played mechanically on as Alice peered inside one of their number. Gears whirled, oil dripped, and the wheels of an analytical engine spun merrily, trying to direct a body that refused to obey properly. A fascinating little world, where everything was connected to everything else. Alice found herself drawn in, searching for the patterns and for the flaw causing the problem. Her heart quickened a little, and she had to admit she was showing off a bit for her hostess. It wasn't correct ballroom behavior for a traditional lady, but Alice had been shunned so far. What did she have to lose?

"I don't think this is quite—" Lady Greenfellow began.

"There's your problem," Alice said. "One of the drive pistons has become disconnected, and it's throwing off the machinery. Easy enough to fix." Without thinking, she drew back her sleeve to midforearm and reached inside. Lady Greenfellow huffily turned her back and spread herself as wide as she could to provide cover. Alice reconnected the piston and snatched her hand free as it started up again. She put the panel back on, delicately wiped machine oil from her fingers with a handkerchief, and handed the bow back to the cellist, who rejoined the song in progress.

"All fixed," Alice said, donning her gloves.

Lady Greenfellow turned around and stared. "I . . . see. Thank you." Her words were stiff, more ice than gratitude.

"Not at all," Alice replied, feeling her heart sink. Clearly, having a woman—or perhaps this particular woman—rescue the mechanical musicians wasn't going to provide the social coup Alice had been hoping for. Perhaps this would be a good time for her first swearwords.

Alice went back downstairs as more guests arrived. She began to recognize people—girls she had gone to school with, attended dances with, discussed weddings and social outings with. They were all married now, attending the dance with their new husbands. And they all ignored Alice. When she approached, they glided away. When she stood still, they kept their distance. None of the men asked Alice for a slot on her dance card. Couples young and old whirled and glided across the dance floor. At first, Alice felt self-conscious and embarrassed, sitting at a small table by herself. Then she felt angry. Then she felt desperate. This was supposed to be her reentry into society, and—

"Not going well, is it?" A woman in a startlingly low-cut

blue gown plunked down in a chair opposite Alice's at the table. "What a bunch of bores."

"I'm sorry," Alice said. "I'm afraid I—"

"Louisa Creek," she said, extending a hand. She looked quite a few years older than Alice. Artful cosmetics couldn't conceal a bad complexion or a beaky nose, though her thick black hair was coiled in a complex braided bun. Alice tried to guess at her age, but she could have been anywhere from her early thirties to her late forties. The dance card hanging from her fan was as empty as Alice's. "You're Lady Michaels—or you will be, once your father dies. We've never met, but I've heard of you. Terrible situation. The clockwork plague hits your family twice, and everyone treats the survivors like lepers. An apt simile, I suppose."

"I suppose," Alice said. She found Louisa's forthrightness shocking, but also a little thrilling. Daring. "Aren't you afraid everyone will see you talking to me and begin to treat you the same way?"

"It doesn't matter who *I* talk to." Louisa cracked her fan open and waved it nonchalantly. "See that . . . gentleman over there in the badly cut jacket? Ash-blond, a little short, talking to the bald fat man?"

"Yes."

"He'll eventually ask me to dance. And so will that man over there, the one hovering near the ice sculpture."

"How do you know they'll ask you?"

Louisa grinned. "They're second sons, dear. No inheritance prospects. But I have pots of money, which makes *me* an enormous prospect, even if I'm that much older than they are. That's why I can have a less-than-beautiful face and talk to lepers." She smiled and patted Alice's hand to show it was a joke. "Are you an Ad Hoc lady?"

"Good Lord, no. Are you?"

Louisa waved her fan. "I haven't decided. Wouldn't it just shock these stuffies? It's been legal for us to vote for three years now, thanks to the wonderful work of the

Hats-On Committee in Parliament, but if we take advantage of it, certain people act as if a cow wanted to recite Shakespeare."

Alice gave a weak smile in acknowledgment. Three years ago, the same wave of clockwork plague that had killed her fiancé, Frederick, had also incapacitated several prominent members of Parliament, threatening to cripple the entire government. In a surprise move, their wives took over their affairs, writing letters, giving speeches, and even voting in their husbands' names while the emergency lasted. They created the Hats-On Committee, so nicknamed because the members didn't remove their hats indoors. Rumors abounded of an anonymous benefactor who provided the committee with money and other resources, though nothing was ever proven. By the time their husbands died from the plague, this "ad HOC" group had gained enough power and support to push through one important piece of legislation: suffrage for women. Females could now vote and hold office, just like men. Legal sanction, however, didn't always grant social acceptance, especially among the upper classes.

"My father would have a fit if an Ad Hoc lady turned up in the family," Alice said. "I wouldn't do that to him. It would certainly ruin my chances here."

"How did you get invited in the first place?" Louisa asked.

"Father called in a final favor." Alice set her mouth, not sure whether she was going to laugh or cry. "This was to be a step forward for us. I would comport myself well, attract the eye of the gentlemen, and Father's business contacts would start turning up again."

"Good plan," Louisa said. "A damned pity it's not working. Word has it you came unescorted in a cab."

"My maid twisted her ankle—"

Louisa waved this aside with her fan. "It's a good lie, but it fades when you repeat it. Be brazen! No one likes a beggar, even an invited beggar, so don't act like one."

"But I need them," Alice said, gesturing toward the couples on the floor.

"Less than you think. You're pretty and you're smart, and that's a deadly combination. Nice job repairing Lady Greenfellow's cellist, by the way. Very Ad Hoc. If it had been anyone but you, the old bat would have been grateful. Oh look—here comes my first."

The ash-blond man in the badly cut coat Louisa had pointed out earlier came around the dance floor to the table. "May I have the honor of a dance?"

"Let me check my card," Louisa said, doing so. "I seem to be free. Shall we?" She gave Alice a final wink as her new escort led her away while the women who weren't dancing murmured to one another behind their fans. Chagrined, Alice watched Louisa go. Perhaps it was time to slip away and go home. There was nothing for her to—

"May I have the honor of a dance?"

The man was older than Alice, nearly thirty, tall and lean, in a stylish Fairmont waistcoat and shining black silk coat. His brown hair and muttonchop whiskers were neatly trimmed, and his dark brown eyes looked pleasantly down at her. His features were attractive though not quite handsome.

Alice was so startled, she forgot she was supposed to check her dance card. "I would be delighted, sir," she said, taking his hand and rising. "But I don't know your name."

"Mr. Norbert Williamson, at your service," he said instantly. "And you, I believe, are Miss Alice Michaels. I've done some work with your father, Lord Michaels."

The orchestra ended the waltz and swept into a gavotte, precise and perfect as an ice sculpture. Norbert guided Alice to the dance floor and put his hand on her waist. Several couples gave them sideways looks, but most ignored them.

"Everyone is talking about how you repaired the cellist," he said as they moved across the polished wood. "Your father says you have quite a talent with automatons, Miss Michaels."

"That's kind of him," Alice replied, surprised. "I suppose it's because I find automatons more interesting than people."

"Oh."

An awkward silence followed, and Alice mentally kicked herself. "But not tonight," she added hastily. "I haven't been out in so long, I'd forgotten how enjoyable it is. Dancing is so much fun, especially with a talented partner like you, Mr. Williamson."

She couldn't quite bring herself to bat her eyes, but the flattery had its intended effect. His arms relaxed a little, and he smiled.

"What do you think of the orchestra?" he asked. "Now that it's working."

"They play very nicely," she said, and let herself sway a little more with the rhythm. "I love music of all sorts, but I have no talent at making it. Do you play an instrument?"

"I'm completely tone-deaf," he said, and Alice was surprised at how deeply the admission disappointed her. "Lady Greenfellow's players need to be serviced more often," he continued, oblivious. "The cellist wouldn't have seized up like that if I were in charge of it."

"Are you an automatist by trade, Mr. Williamson?"

He shook his head. "My company makes machine parts. Automatons are a bit of a hobby. I think that's why your father is trying to fling us together."

Alice's heart quickened despite her earlier disappointment. This was the main reason she was here, then. Norbert Williamson was a marriage prospect. He swung her around, and Alice smiled up at him. Her job was to be winning and witty.

"He shouldn't need to fling anything, Mr. Williamson," she said. "If you enjoy automatons, we have a lot in common. What are your views on the idea that Charles Babbage took credit for Ada Lovelace's work with the analytical engine?"

"I do enjoy automatons," Norbert said. "But for the moment, I'd prefer to dance with a beautiful woman."

It was empty flattery, but it was nice to hear. They danced three dances before Alice pleaded the need to rest; Norbert immediately guided her back to the side tables and went off in search of refreshments. The moment he was gone, Louisa all but hurled herself into a neighboring chair.

"Norbert Williamson?" Louisa said. "How interesting."

"What do you know about him?" Alice demanded. "Quick!"

"Very little. He's new to London. No title, so he's not a peer. He bought a factory, and it's making good money. He seems to have a lot of male friends, and for a while rumors were circulating that he runs with the bulls, if you know what I mean."

"Louisa!"

"Oh, as if you've never come across the type." Louisa laughed. "But lately he's been showing himself at a lot of social events and sniffing around some heifers. He's a traditional man, not Ad Hoc, and probably interested in your title."

"He wouldn't get it," Alice said. "It'll come to me, and then only because Father has no male relatives. After that, it'll go to my first son, never my husband."

"Close enough for us mere commoners," Louisa replied. "Puff up your chest, dear. Here he comes with the petits fours."

Two more dances followed, and Norbert accompanied Alice to the buffet supper at one o'clock. Alice was starving, but she restricted herself to proper ladylike servings of veal escalopes, carrots Vichy, and gooseberry fool. Norbert, for his part, remained attentive and charming. Alice liked his company well enough, though she didn't feel any of the pounding, heaving, or poetic emotions referred to in any of the poetry or . . . less literary work about romance she had read over the years. Norbert certainly seemed interested in her, and Alice did find that both heartening and satisfying. It was nice to know someone found her desirable.

They were just moving back to the dance floor when a delicate brass dove fluttered into the ballroom and landed on Norbert's shoulder. With a surprised look, he opened a small panel on the back, removed a slip of paper, and read. Alice took the bird from him and examined it. The delicate work on the feathers was particularly fine. The glassy eyes were bright and alert, and it moved realistically in her gloved hands.

"I'm sorry, Miss Michaels, but a situation has arisen at my factory and I must leave," Norbert said. "And here I was hoping to see you home. Do forgive me."

And then he was gone, the dove fluttering after him.

"Everyone's talking about you," Louisa said, appearing at her elbow like magic.

"Is that good or bad?"

"Hard to tell. Norbert Williamson is the joker in the pack. No one knows what he's really about, so they don't know how to react to him—or to you, now. But they're still not talking to you. The men are afraid of the clockwork plague, and the women are afraid that anyone who talks to you won't be asked to dance by anyone good."

Alice sighed, suddenly tired. "Except you."

"There are advantages to having one's own money," Louisa said without a shred of self-consciousness. "Patrick Barton—the ash-blond one in the bad coat—is seeing me home tonight. And he'll probably have breakfast."

It took a moment for the meaning to sink in. Alice snapped open her fan, scandalized. "Louisa!"

Louisa laughed again. "You need to have more fun, Alice. Call on me, darling. I should mingle." And she left.

Exhaustion settled over Alice, and the ballroom air was loaded with heat from dancing bodies. She decided it was time to go. Lady Greenfellow hadn't stationed herself near the door yet, which meant Alice didn't need to bid her an official good-bye, though she would have to write a long thank-you letter later. She retrieved her shawl and allowed the manservant to open the massive front doors for her. The cool night air woke her a bit as the servant waved at one of the cabs for hire that waited in the circular drive. It was an old-fashioned one, with four wheels instead of two and a driver who sat up front. In the distance, faint music played—a haunting, compelling melody from a flutelike instrument Alice couldn't quite identify. To Alice's surprise, the servant handed the driver a sum of money and told him to take the lady home.

"Courtesy of Mr. Williamson, ma'am," the servant said, helping her in.

Alice knew she should feel delighted that Norbert Williamson was expressing a continued interest in her, but now that she wasn't dancing, the champagne was catching up with her and she felt only sleepy. At least Father would be pleased. The cab clattered and rolled through gaslit London streets with Alice dozing in the back. The faint music she had heard earlier grew louder, irritating rather than pleasing. Far off, Big Ben tolled the time with his familiar bells—two a.m.—and the carriage came to an abrupt halt. Alice roused herself and turned to look out the side of the cab.

Facing her was a crowd of plague zombies. The first one reached for the door.

Chapter Two

Gavin Ennock let the last long note slide from his fiddle and fade away. He lifted the bow from the strings and cocked a bright blue eye at Old Graf, whose own eyes were obscured by heavy brass lookout goggles.

"Ah, that puts heart into a man." Old Graf sighed. His magnified gaze, however, never left the cloud-flecked sky ahead of them. A thin wind blew at their backs, not quite able to penetrate the pale, supple leather of the jackets and trousers they both wore. Overhead, the ever-present bulge of the airship's gas envelope blotted out the sun, though in à few hours, the sun would sink behind them, and the decks would grow uncomfortably warm. The netting that hung from the envelope creaked in a familiar rhythm, and the ship swayed beneath it. A faint vibration from the engine propellers came up through the soles of Gavin's boots. Far below, the Atlantic Ocean lay calm and flat and blue.

Gavin inhaled the sea air. His hair, a pale blond bleached nearly white by the sun, fluttered against his forehead like feathers. Gavin's face had lost its boyish roundness and acquired the more squared look of a man, but he was a little short for his seventeen years and had no hint of facial hair, two facts the airmen teased him about mercilessly. Old

Graf never did, which was one of the reasons Gavin had come up to the lookout post at the front of the airship.

A seagull coasted past with a thin cry that started on an E-flat and descended to a gravelly A. Gavin echoed the bird's call on his fiddle, matching the pitches exactly. The gull cocked a beady eye at him, then dived away.

"'Blind Mary'?" Old Graf said.

"How is *that* a song for a man on lookout duty?" Gavin countered with a grin.

Old Graf continued to scan the air ahead of them. They were on the forecastle, the foremost section of the ship. An airship like the USS *Juniper* didn't have a crow's nest—the cigar-shaped envelope precluded one—which meant the lookout had to be as far forward as possible.

"It's a taste of home," Old Graf said.

Gavin set bow to strings and played. "Blind Mary" was an old Irish song, one of hundreds he'd picked up as a kid in Boston. In his head, he saw an old woman feeling her way along a country lane, and he let his fingers slide along the strings, playing her sadness and age. Gavin heard every note perfectly in his head. Each note, each chord, each song had its own unique sound, and it seemed impossible to him that anyone couldn't tell them apart. A and A-sharp were as different as red and blue.

Gavin let himself play with the melody the second time through, wandering with it as if Mary had lost her way, stumbling, frightened, but finding her place again at the last second. Yet, in the end, the song still left her blind and alone. Behind them on the main deck, some of the airmen paused in their work to listen until the song ended. Old Graf fished in his pocket for a handkerchief and blew his nose.

"How is it that a seventeen-year-old cabin boy plays like an immortal angel?" he blurted out, then flushed slightly and coughed.

"It helps to have a fine listener." Gavin clapped him on

the shoulder. "My gramps gave me the fiddle, but he said the music is a gift from God. And Captain Naismith says I'll be a full airman soon enough."

Old Graf's weathered face went pale. "Dear Lord."

"My being an airman isn't such bad news, is it?"

"Gliders. Straight for us." Old Graf flicked the lenses of his goggles up and reached for the alarm bell. Gavin grabbed the spare lookout helmet from the rack, jammed it on his own head, and looked through the lenses as Old Graf yanked the cord. Bells sounded all throughout the *Juniper*. Through the helmet lenses, Gavin saw ominous birdlike shapes zipping toward the airship he'd been calling home since he was twelve. They were painted blue and white to better hide in the sky, and part of Gavin was impressed that Old Graf had seen them even as the rest of him tightened with fear and dread. He counted eight, and there were probably more that he couldn't see.

"What's out there, Graf?" demanded Captain Naismith's voice through the speaking tube at Old Graf's elbow.

"Pirate gliders, Captain," Old Graf yelled back, flipping his lenses back down. "I mark at least a dozen."

"Which means probably twice that. Shit. Shit, shit, shit. Can you see the main cruiser?"

"Not—yes! Welsh privateer, probably with a letter of marque." He squinted through the lenses. "Gondolier class. Semirigid."

"All hands prepare for battle!" boomed the captain. *"Drop ballast compression and take us up to fifteen hundred feet. We have two dozen gliders coming in. They'll try to get over the netting to attack the decks, so I want everyone who can swing a sword or fire an air pistol up in the ropes! Mr. Thomas, prepare to jettison the cargo. Master Ennock, get your ass down to the gondola, and I mean now!"*

"Better hurry, boy," Old Graf said as Gavin pulled the helmet off. "He won't appreciate it if you're slow."

Gavin shoved his fiddle into its case and ran for it. He

skittered down the ladder to the main deck, which swarmed with activity. Airmen boiled out of the hatchways, rushing to ready the ship for battle. Ports flipped open along the hull, exposing flechette and harpoon guns. Men in white and gray leather manned the pumps that forced ballast air out of certain ballonets inside the *Juniper*'s envelope and inflated other ballonets with more hydrogen, allowing the ship to rise. Other men swarmed into the netting, climbing toward the envelope with compressed air pistols and cutlasses of tempered glass—only a fool used gunpowder or sparking steel near several tons of explosive hydrogen.

Gavin ran to the center of the deck and slid down the rails of another ladder polished by years of use, pausing only to drop his fiddle off in the crew quarters, where he stuffed it under a blanket and prayed no pirate would find it. Then he ran back to the ladder.

The *Juniper* was an American ship of American design. A web of wrist-thick ropes hung from an enormous, cigar-shaped envelope of gas and cradled what looked like a sailing ship with the masts removed. Fastened to the bottom of the ship and looking a bit like a glass bubble with a wooden bottom was the navigation gondola, where Pilot and the captain spent most of their time. Gavin dropped past two decks and out the bottom of the ship into the gondola.

The floor was solid wood, but the sides of the gondola were made of glass to give a good view in all directions, and now Gavin could see the gliders skimming ominously toward the *Juniper*. Speaking tubes sprouted from every cranny, and pigeonholes held rolled-up charts and instruments. Captain Naismith stood at the helm, his fingers white on the wheel spokes and his plain features tense. His dark blue captain's coat with its gold buttons and epaulets rustled not at all, and his hair remained hidden beneath his cap. Captain Naismith was a young man, not yet thirty, and he dealt with the grumblings of the much older men put under his command by expecting strict discipline from everyone, including himself.

Beside him stood Pilot. Gavin had never learned his name—the pilot of an airship was always just called Pilot. He was perhaps forty, with a shock of wheat blond hair. At the moment, he was bent over a tableful of charts, his sextant clutched in one hand.

"Sir," Gavin said.

"Master Ennock," Captain Naismith said, "you were thirteen years old the last time we were attacked by privateers."

"Fourteen, sir. Two days after my birthday."

He waved this aside. "You wanted to fight, but I ordered you to hide in the cargo hold."

Gavin nodded. That had been a dreadful day. He remembered crouching among the crates and barrels with the rats, hearing thumps and screams and other noises he couldn't identify. Part of him wanted to help, and part of him was glad for the captain's order. The *Juniper*'s crew had managed to beat the pirates off and escape, but there had still been blood to scrub off the deck afterward, and Gavin had accidentally stepped on a severed hand that rolled beneath his boot. Only Old Graf had seen him throw up over the side.

"Only full airmen carry weapons," Captain Naismith continued, "but today we have special circumstances. Old Graf's been teaching you, hasn't he?"

"Yes, sir." Gavin's heart was pounding now.

"Take what you need from the arms master and get up in the netting. Defend my ship, Master Ennock. She's only a merchant vessel, but she's all we have."

"Sir!" And Gavin rushed up the ladder. He found the arms master belowdecks, and the man handed him a tempered glass cutlass and a heavy brass pistol that fired glass flechettes using compressed air. On the main deck, Gavin could see the gliders were less than a hundred yards away, and in the distance coasted the ominous shape of a pirate airship, emerging from the clouds like a killer whale rising from an ocean trench. Although the *Juniper* was gaining altitude, leaving the ocean far below, the pirate ship was matching them. The gliders drew nearer. Each held a pirate suspended beneath a wide wing of oiled silk on a light frame painted blue. A bottle of compressed air fizzled behind each one, propelling it forward. The bottle didn't have enough propulsion in it for a return trip. It wasn't meant to.

"Fire!" shouted First Mate Lightman.

A hiss snaked through the air, followed by a pop. Four of the side guns spat a barrage of deadly metal darts. Two of the gliders evaporated in a cloud of blood and silk. The wing on one of the others was clipped, and it spiraled out of sight, the pirate's shouts of terror thinning away as it went. Gavin grabbed some of the heavy netting, climbing upward and outward, nimble as a monkey.

The netting comprised heavy rope tied in foot-wide squares that slanted outward like a giant V, with the narrow ship in the bottom and the wide envelope at the top. Halfway up the netting were gaps and wooden platforms that allowed the airmen to work on both sides of the netting as needed, and these were the gliders' targets—the pirates could slip through the gaps, drop down the inside, and land on the deck to attack the crew.

"Fire!" The big guns hissed once more below.

Gavin skittered farther up the slanted ropes. Here he felt at home, with nothing but free-flowing air rushing above and below him. He felt every creak and sway of the ship as if the ropes were his own tendons, the envelope his lungs, the deck his body. He loved this place, this ship. And now the *Juniper* was under attack.

He was out of the envelope's shadow, and the sun glared down from a clear sky while the damp wind pushed steadily from his left. He reached one of the gaps and perched on the heavy horizontal rope at the top. On the outer hull below whirled the propellers on their engine nacelles, and farther below that, blue ocean filled the horizon. Other airmen were taking up positions in other gaps and on various platforms, while the gliders closed in.

A guy rope was tied to the netting. Gavin flicked it free but lost his grip on it. Another hand snatched the rope before the wind could swing it away. Airman Tom Danforth grinned at Gavin through a great deal of dark hair, and his brown eyes sparkled with excitement as he tossed the guy rope to Gavin. The captain had promoted Tom from cabin boy to airman only a few months ago on his eighteenth birthday, but his and Gavin's friendship had survived the change in rank. Gavin sometimes envied seagoing cabin boys, who often became full sailors long before they turned eighteen, but the feeling never lasted long—he couldn't imagine being stranded on Earth forever, an eternal prisoner of gravity.

"Ready for this?" Tom asked.

Gavin tried to wet his lips but had no spit. "Ready as I can be. You scared?"

"Yep." He gave a nervous smile. "But I'm not going to let them take our ship."

As if on cue, the flock of gliders rushed silently upward past the gunwale, out of range of the big guns and toward the netting gaps. Still clinging to the netting with one hand, Tom drew his pistol and fired down at them, but the shot went wide. An airman a few yards away—Stanley Barefield—fired more carefully, and one of the pirates went limp. His glider yawed and veered away. The *Juniper* continued to rise, which meant the gliders appeared to be dropping toward the gunwale. The gliders needed enough altitude to gain the gaps in the netting and land on the deck before their air bottles gave out.

Gavin drew his pistol, fired, and missed. The ship's guns spoke one more time, but Gavin doubted they did any good. More than two dozen gliders were swarming like wasps around the *Juniper* now, and the enormous bulk of the privateer airship was less than half a mile away. Its design was similar to the *Juniper*'s, but its envelope was thinner, built more for speed, and painted blue to blend in with the sky. It was also larger than the *Juniper*, and no doubt better armed. Air pistols hissed, and glass flechettes zipped through the air. When the pirate ship got close enough, she would send a full force of fighting men to overwhelm the crew and capture the *Juniper* entirely. Gavin swallowed.

"We're in trouble," he said.

"I know." Tom's face was pale. "But we can win this."

A glider whipped close to Tom and Gavin. Tom brought his pistol around, but before he could shoot, the pirate fired his own weapon. The shot caught Tom in the forehead, and Gavin saw the shiny flechette exit the back of his friend's skull in a burst of blood that spattered across the netting. Tom didn't make a sound. He simply fell away from the netting and vanished into the blue void below.

Gavin heard a terrible scream and only vaguely realized it was coming from his own throat. He didn't remember dropping his pistol or drawing his cutlass, but he leapt from the netting and his blade swept a gleaming arc. He had a tiny moment of closeness, when he came eye to eye with the bearded pirate. He smelled fish on the other man's breath and heard him swear in Welsh. Then Gavin's cutlass took the man's pistol arm off at the elbow. The pirate howled in pain and veered away in a scarlet spray. The guy rope Gavin had grabbed earlier swung him back toward the ship, but another glider was already speeding toward him. Gavin tightened his gut and bent himself upward into a tight ball just in time to let a barrage of flechettes pass beneath him. His arm, the one holding the rope, burned, and his shoulder felt ready to come apart. He slammed into the netting and managed to get his feet into it, release the rope, and grab the netting without losing his cutlass. He sheathed the blade and climbed, trying not to think of Tom's spattered blood or ruined head.

Although the airmen had managed to fend off a few, most of the pirate gliders had dived through the gaps and down toward the main deck. Cursing the loss of his pistol, Gavin flipped over the top of the netting, grabbed another guy rope, and slid down as fast as he could. All around him, the rest of the crew followed suit, sliding down ropes like pale spiders to defend the decks.

The pirates disengaged from their gliders. They wore mismatched, ill-fit clothes, and a few were barefoot. Most were unshaven. All were armed with glass cutlasses and air pistols. And the huge dark bulk of the pirate airship was barely two hundred yards off the starboard bow, not quite within firing range. The airship had also taken altitude, remaining level with the *Juniper*.

Gavin landed near a group of airmen that included Old Graf, and suddenly he was very busy. The world dissolved into a whirlwind of glittering glass blades, hissing air, screams, blood, and severed limbs. He became aware that he was standing beside a group of grim-faced airmen. The deck was overrun with pirates and discarded gliders. Bodies lay everywhere—some still living; some dead. And less than forty yards away loomed the bulging blue shape of the Welsh airship. Gavin could hear her propeller engines buzzing over the sounds of combat around him. His arms were growing tired, and he was panting now. He swung at the pirate in front of him. The man laughed and ducked.

"You're a fine, pretty lad," the pirate shouted in a Welsh accent. "I'll teach you some tricks with my blade."

There was a heavy thud, and a crash shook the *Juniper*. Everyone stopped fighting for a moment. The pirate ship had fired an enormous barbed harpoon. The tree-sized spear had penetrated the *Juniper*'s hull, drawing with it a hawser at least a foot in diameter. A faint cheer went up from the pirate ship. The two vessels were now joined like beads on a string.

The fight started again, but something had shifted. The *Juniper*'s airmen were losing. Gavin saw Captain Naismith standing at the gunwale, a foot-long crossbow in his grip. A yellow flicker danced in his hands, and Gavin's stomach went cold at the sight of a small open flame, the absolute bane of every airship in existence. The captain lit the end of his crossbow bolt and raised it, but no crossbow that small had the range to reach the pirate ship. A nauseating horror swept Gavin as he realized that the captain was aiming not at the pirate ship, but at the *Juniper*'s own envelope.

The distraction allowed the pirate to swat Gavin's cutlass. Pain stung Gavin's hand, and the glass blade spun away, distorting light as it went. Gavin jumped back in time to avoid the pirate's second swing, then fled. The airmen who fought beside him, caught in fights of their own, barely had time to give him a glance.

"Come back, love!" the pirate yelled. "You need to dance for me!"

Gavin all but flew across the deck to Captain Naismith. Already he could imagine the blazing bolt piercing the envelope, ripping into the ballonets of hydrogen to create a fireball that would incinerate the ship and drop the charred remains into the ocean. The detail was sharp—Gavin could see Naismith's finger tense around the trigger. Heart pounding from both exertion and terror, Gavin lunged and grabbed Naismith's arm.

"Captain!" he shouted. "No!"

"Let go my arm, Master Ennock," he said through gritted teeth. "They won't take my ship."

"We can't get revenge if we're dead," Gavin said.

A dull clanking noise vibrated the deck beneath Gavin's boots. The pirates were operating a winch that pulled the two ships closer together. Fear fought with pale determination in Naismith's expression.

"It's ransom or slavery for us, Master Ennock," he said. "I can't condemn my men to such a life." He wrenched his arm free and raised the crossbow again. The dreadful little flame flickered like a demon.

Gavin hesitated, uncertain. It would be so easy to let him. Naismith was the captain, and Gavin was duty-bound to follow his orders, orders that would destroy Tom's killer. But Gavin wasn't ready to die, and burning to death was the secret horror of every airman.

In that moment of hesitation, Naismith's finger tightened on the trigger. Then he made a small sound and collapsed face-forward to the deck. The crossbow fell also, the bolt extinguished. An enormous scarlet stain spread across the back of the captain's blue coat. Behind him stood the pirate Gavin had just been fighting, air pistol still in his hand. He holstered the weapon.

"Looks like I reloaded just in time, love," he said with a grin. "Got me a captain."

Hot rage overcame Gavin. He snarled and flung himself at the pirate. The pirate's eyes widened in surprise, but only for a moment. His fist lashed out and caught Gavin squarely in the face. Pain exploded through his head, and he went down to the hard deck.

Gavin awoke to pain. Someone was dabbing at his cheek with a cloth. He opened his eyes and sat up. Light hurt his eyes and sitting up made him dizzy, so he shut his eyes and put his hands to his head. He shivered with cold.

"You're all right, son." It was Old Graf's voice. "Bump on the head, some bruises. You'll survive."

Gavin risked opening his eyes again. He was sitting on the deck in the same place he had fallen. For a moment it looked as if everything had returned to normal. Airmen in white moved about the deck and climbed in the netting. Then he saw the stacks of dead bodies, the pools of blood, the gashes in the wood. The two ships were still tethered together, though now they were both moving off, continuing the *Juniper*'s original eastern course. The airmen weren't the crew Gavin knew. They were the pirates. Gavin's own leathers were gone. He wore nothing but undergarments and chilly skin. Old Graf himself wore a ragged shirt and torn trousers.

"What—?" Gavin said.

"The pirates took our good white leathers for themselves," he said. "Keep your voice down. You don't want to call attention to yourself. Here." He gave Gavin a dirty brown shirt, a pair of loose trousers, and an old pair of shoes. Gavin quickly pulled them on, though they did little to blunt the ever-present wind. The pain in his head continued to throb, and he was thirsty.

"A third of the crew dead, and Captain Naismith," Old Graf said, unprompted. "Captain Keene—the pirate captain—put some of the 'dangerous' survivors off the ship in life balloons already so we wouldn't try to raise a mutiny." He handed Gavin a canteen, and Gavin gulped down stale water. "The rest of us are expected to help run the ship until we get to London."

"London?" Gavin echoed stupidly. "We're supposed to go to Madrid. I was going to see the castle."

"Tell that to Captain Keene," Old Graf growled. "When we get to London, he's going to sell the cargo and hold us and the *Juniper* for ransom to the shipping company."

Outrage cleared Gavin's head a little. "That's illegal! We're not at war with England! That's—"

"Part of his letter of marque. Keene's been charged with keeping the airways safe for British ships, and we fired on him first."

"No, we didn't!" Gavin said hotly.

"Shush!" Old Graf made a sharp gesture. "Who do you think a British court will believe, son? Just be glad you didn't get tossed over in a life balloon."

"Why wasn't I?" Gavin asked bitterly. "I'm just a cabin

boy. The company won't pay a ransom for me, and my family doesn't have any money."

"He spoke for you." Old Graf jerked his head toward one of the pirates, who was wearing stolen airman leathers and inspecting the hydrogen extractor on deck not far away. "Name's Madoc Blue. Said he was going to teach you to dance or something."

Gavin's gut knotted. Madoc Blue was the pirate who had killed Captain Naismith. As if Gavin's thought caught Blue's attention, the pirate turned and met Gavin's eye. He winked broadly and went back to what he was doing. Gavin fought to keep his face impassive. He had a pretty good idea of what Blue had in mind for him, and the thought made him want to throw up.

"So what do we do?" Gavin whispered.

"We run the ship," Old Graf said. "And when we get to London, we sit in whatever cell these bastards lock us in and hope the company pays our ransom."

Three days passed. Gavin fell into a stupor. His body mechanically went through his normal daily tasks under the watchful eye of armed pirates, but his mind was filled with a blessed fog. He scrubbed decks and sewed seams and spliced rope and ran messages for the new captain, all without truly thinking about what he did. At night, he slept fitfully in his hammock, dreaming of his family back in Boston. Sometimes he saw Tom plummeting into an abyss, but he wore Gavin's own face. Then the pirate first mate would be shouting them awake, and a new day of captive work began. At least Madoc Blue kept his distance. Bernie Yost, the *Juniper*'s hydrogen man, had been killed in the original raid, and Captain Keene had given the job to Blue. Even the most tightly sewn ballonets leaked a little, and without continual replacement, the ship would eventually sink to the ground—or into the ocean. An efficient hydrogen extractor was therefore key to the survival of any working airship, and the job of hydrogen man carried the same status as ship's carpenter or pilot. The job also took up a lot of time, which meant Blue was too busy to pay Gavin any heed.

At the end of the fourth day, Captain Keene, a red-faced man built like a brick, assembled the captive airmen and his pirates on the *Juniper*'s deck and announced a celebration for his crew. The pirates cheered. The airmen, less enthusiastic, were to be locked in the brig so the pirates could enjoy themselves without keeping an eye on their captives.

"And who plays this?" Keene demanded of the assembled airmen. Gavin's entire body jerked. Keene was holding Gavin's fiddle. Gavin hadn't even looked at it since the raid. One of the pirates must have found its hiding place. "Come on now—we'll need music, and one of you American turds can provide some, right?"

Gavin didn't move. The thought of playing for cavorting murderers turned his stomach greasy and sour. He could feel the other airmen carefully not looking in his direction, but he himself couldn't take his eyes off his beloved fiddle. Keene's hand was pressing the strings into the neck, his fingers leaving oily prints on the red-brown wood. Gavin felt violated, as if Keene had laid hands on his soul.

"No one?" Keene said. "Too bad. It must belong to one of the men we killed or put off the ship. No point in keeping it." He turned and drew his arm back to throw the fiddle overboard.

"Wait!" Gavin said.

Keene paused and turned back.

"It's mine," Gavin said miserably. "I'll play."

Keene handed Gavin the fiddle and ruffled his hair like an uncle greeting a favorite nephew, even though Gavin was nearly eighteen. "That's a good lad. Do you sing, too?"

Gavin thought about lying, then decided he didn't want to know what would happen if the truth came out. "A little," he hedged.

"Then what are you waiting for, boys?" Keene boomed. "Lock up these miserable bastards and have a party!"

An enormous cheer went up. Gavin watched while his compatriots, including Old Graf, were herded belowdecks to the brig. The crew members were already looking haggard and thinner than just a few days ago. Gavin tried not to shiver in his ragged clothes, and not for the first time he wondered which of the pirates had originally worn them. The sun was setting behind the tethered ships, and the engines continued their implacable rumble as the propellers whirled unceasingly. Somewhere below lay Tom's body, food for sharks and other sea creatures. Gavin glanced at the envelope overhead. If he hadn't stopped Naismith, none of this would be happening right now. He wouldn't be sad, wouldn't be upset, wouldn't be thinking at all.

The pirates rolled out several casks of rum and lit the blue-green phosphor lamps that hung about the ship to provide flame-free light amidships. A heavy arm dropped around Gavin's shoulders. He tried to twist, but the arm held him.

"Looking forward to hearing you," said Madoc Blue. "Maybe tonight I'll teach you how to dance."

And then he was gone. Gavin's hands shook so hard, he could barely tune up. Someone brought a crate for Gavin to stand on. He forced himself to remain steady, set bow to strings, and play.

Once the melody began, things became easier. It felt good to use his talents again, and he hadn't realized how much he'd missed his music. He closed his eyes and tried to pretend he was playing for his family back in Boston. They had two dark rooms in the slums, and both were filled with comings and goings. Ma was always at the stove, trying to stretch what Gavin's four brothers and sisters brought home, or at the kitchen table madly basting shirts for the tailor up the street. Gramps sat in the corner, trying to watch Gavin's younger siblings with his failing eyesight. The place was never quiet, except when Gavin played fiddle in the evenings. He played in the dark because they couldn't afford lamp oil or gas jets. He played away their hunger, the cold Boston weather, and their fear of bill collectors. But when Gavin turned twelve, Gramps had taken him down to the airfields outside Boston, where a dozen giant airships stood tethered to their towers like clouds staked to the ground, and introduced him to Captain Felix Naismith. The next day, he'd sailed off as a cabin boy.

It had started as a job, a way to send money home to his family. But after a few weeks in the air, Gavin found himself unwilling to touch the ground. The *Juniper* quickly became his home, the sky his backyard, the clouds his city. When he worked, he helped send the ship across Infinite. When he played, he sent songs into the blue and white like a sacrifice. Now, both work and music served a different master.

The pirates, including the captain, laughed and danced and drank all around Gavin's crate while the sky darkened and the lamps shed their familiar eerie glow over the gunwales, turning his pale hair green. He closed his eyes so he could play in the dark. Music rippled off his fiddle and vanished into blackness. The pirates called out songs for him, and he played "Highland Mary," "The Irish Washerwoman," and "Sheebeg, Sheemore."

"Play 'Londonderry Air,'" shouted one pirate.

"That's a sissy song, Stone," yelled another. "We don't want to hear that."

"I'll show you a sissy song," Stone yelled back, holding up his fists. "Two of 'em."

Quickly, Gavin played the requested song, a slow, sad piece. He put everything he had into it, echoes of green Irish hills floating in fog, sad cemeteries with tilted gravestones, and stone cottages warmed by peat fires. The belligerence died away. The pirates fell silent. When the music ended, Stone wiped his nose on his stolen leather sleeve and acted as if he weren't also wiping his eyes.

"Nice," he coughed. "Very nice." And the other pirates cheered.

"Sing for us, boy!" "Sing a song!" "A dancing song!"

"Sing us," called out a too-familiar voice, "'Tom of Bedlam.'"

Gavin's head jerked around. Madoc Blue was staring up at him, thumbs hooked in his belt near his glass-bladed knife. A lump formed in Gavin's throat. Had Blue learned Tom's name and chosen that song on purpose? It might have been coincidence—"Tom of Bedlam" was the unofficial anthem for all airmen, and it wasn't an unusual request.

"Go on, pretty lad," Blue said. "You can't tell me you don't know it. Lie to me, and I'll tie one of those fiddle strings around your balls until they turn . . . blue."

The pirates roared with laughter. Gavin swallowed the lump in his throat and firmed his jaw. He wouldn't give Blue any satisfaction. He set bow to strings and sang.

> For to see Mad Tom of Bedlam, ten thousand miles
> I'd travel.
> Mad Maudlin goes on dirty toes for to save her shoes
> from gravel.
> And still I'd sing bonny boys, bonny mad boys, bed-
> lam boys are bonny,
> For they all go bare, and they live by the air, and they
> want no drink nor money.

The pirates stomped and drummed on the deck for the last two lines—the chorus was the reason the song was popular among airmen. Want, in this case, meant lack, and the idea that airmen were more than a little insane but also naked, drunk, and rich held great appeal. The song had endless verses, and Gavin settled in to sing them all, his voice pounding at the men like a weapon, letting his anger and fear come pouring out. The men clapped and sang along, oblivious. Blue, however, simply stared at Gavin, his thumbs still hooked in his knife belt. Without thinking, Gavin sang the verse:

I slept not since the Conquest. Till then I never waked,
Till the naked boy of love where I lay me found and
    stripped me naked.

Every pirate burst out into raucous laughs and cheers. Blue smirked and gave Gavin a pointed look. Gavin flushed bright red and sang the chorus as if he had no idea what anyone was laughing about, but quickly switched to a different verse.

My staff has murdered giants. My bag a long knife
    carries
To cut mince pies from grown men's thighs and feed
    them to the fairies.

He met Blue's gaze straight on at the last line. The original words ran *children's thighs*. The pirates were drunk enough that they didn't seem to notice the change, but Blue ... Blue nodded slightly and turned away. Message understood. Gavin breathed a mental sigh of relief, sang one more verse, and called for a break. The pirates clapped him on the back and congratulated him on his skill, as if he were one of them, as if they hadn't killed his best friend, his captain, and a dozen of his compatriots. Gavin forced a smile to his face, pretended to accept their accolades, then slipped away from the men, moving toward the lookout post. Overhead, the envelope blotted out the stars, but they formed a field of shining diamonds in all other directions. Ahead, the pirate airship was outlined in its own blue-green glow. A skeleton crew over there had the misfortune to miss the party. The air was cooler, crisper now that he was away from the press of bodies amidships. Gavin blew out a breath, glad to be apart from them for a moment, however short.

As Gavin passed the man-high bulk of the hydrogen extractor, a figure appeared from the shadows. Before Gavin could react, the figure grabbed Gavin by the shoulders, swung him around, and shoved his back against the extractor. Gavin's heart lurched, and he barely kept hold of his fiddle.

"Wandering alone, love?" said Madoc Blue, the rum strong on his breath. "I'm ready to teach you how to dance."

Fresh fear spurted through Gavin's every vein. His breath came in short gasps and his fingers went cold around the neck of his fiddle. The bow clattered to the deck. Blue pressed his body against Gavin's, his weight shoving Gavin harder against the extractor's warm brass wall with his forearm across Gavin's throat. Blue leaned in, his beard scratchy against Gavin's face. Gavin choked, barely able to breathe.

"You think I'm stupid and ugly, pretty boy?" Blue growled. "You think I can't get women? *Do you?*"

Gavin tried to answer, but he couldn't get enough breath. His free hand flailed uselessly, looking for something, anything that might help.

"When there aren't any women on deck," Blue snarled, "a man's gotta use whatever he can get his hands on." He grabbed the string that held Gavin's trousers up and snapped it with a sharp, one-handed jerk. Gavin tried to yell, but Blue's forearm prevented him. The lack of air made him dizzy. "Got three or four friends who've had their eye on you, love. Once I break you in, I can show you around, collect a little money for your services. What do you think of that, hey?"

And then Gavin's flailing hand found the hilt of Blue's knife in his belt. He snatched it out of the holder and slashed downward. Gavin felt warm blood spurt against the thin cloth of his trousers. Blue screamed and instantly let Gavin go. He staggered back, clutching his upper leg. A loose flap of meat the size of Gavin's hand hung there by a hinge of skin.

"You little shit!" Blue howled. "I'll fucking kill you!"

He lunged for Gavin, who didn't even think. He stepped aside and swung the knife again. It plunged up to the hilt into the side of Blue's neck. Blue's eyes flew wide-open. He made a terrible choking noise and clawed at the knife hilt with curved fingers, then fell twitching to the deck. The air filled with the stench of blood and bowel as he died.

Gavin didn't have time to react, or even think. Blue's screams summoned the rest of the men, who were only a dozen yards away. In an instant, Gavin found himself surrounded by angry pirates. Blood covered his hands and spattered across his face, and he was holding his trousers up with one hand. The other still clutched his fiddle.

"It's the fiddler boy." "He killed Blue!" "Cut his balls off!" "Throw him overboard!" "String him up!" "Shit! There's blood everywhere!" "The captain!" "Make way for the captain!"

Captain Keene, short and stocky, shouldered his way through the crowd. He took in the scene, including Gavin's torn trousers, with a glance. "What the hell happened?"

"He killed Blue!" someone shouted.

"I'm not asking you, Biggs," Keene bellowed.

Gavin looked at the men. His mind froze. He couldn't think. It was all too much. "I—I . . . ," he stammered.

"Did you kill him?" Keene asked.

"He . . . attacked me," Gavin said. It was hard to talk. He wanted all those eyes to go away. "He—he shoved me against the extractor. He said he wanted . . ."

"Ah," Keene said with understanding. "Well, you ain't his first, but it looks like you're definitely his last." This got an uneasy chuckle from a few of the pirates. Gavin let himself hope that everything would be all right. Then Keene said, "But you're a prisoner, boy, and you killed one of my men." He raised his voice. "Saw his hands off and throw him overboard."

Shock numbed Gavin. He barely felt the fingers that snatched his fiddle away, barely noticed that he was being hauled toward the crate where he'd been playing merry music only a few minutes earlier. One of the pirates drew his cutlass. It gleamed green in the phosphorescent light. Gavin's hands were yanked down to the crate and laid across the rough wood, wrist up. The pirate raised the blade.

"Captain!"

The speaker was Stone, the pirate who had requested "Londonderry Air." The pirate holding the cutlass halted. Keene folded his arms across a broad chest. "You got something to say, Stone?"

"He's still a boy, Captain," Stone said. "You called him one yourself. It don't seem quite right to give him a man's punishment, sir." He held up Gavin's fiddle. "And he plays so nice. Be a shame to lose that because he fought back against the likes of Madoc Blue. Sir."

The hands holding Gavin down were tight enough to leave bruises, though Gavin didn't have the strength to struggle. Above him, he could see distorted stars through the pirate's clear cutlass. Keene looked at Gavin for a long moment, surrounded by silent pirates.

"Fine," he grumbled at last. "Boy's punishment. Twenty-four lashes."

The hands suddenly shifted from holding Gavin down to wrenching him around. His mind spun, unable to take it all in. He caught a fleeting glimpse of Stone still holding his fiddle, another glimpse of two men covering Blue's body with a piece of gray canvas, and then his wrists were being strapped to the heavy netting. Someone ripped the shirt off his back. Cold night air washed over his skin, and that broke the stupor. He shouted and struggled against the bonds, but they were too tight. The first mate swung his whip around. It slashed the air, hissing like a snake.

And then Stone was beside him, his hand on Gavin's shoulder. "Don't worry about your fiddle," he whispered urgently in Gavin's ear. "I'll keep it safe."

He backed away and the first lash tore a red stripe of pain across Gavin's back.

Chapter Three

The lead zombie pulled the cab door open. Behind it, half a dozen other zombies groaned in an eerie chorus. Alice Michaels gave an unladylike yelp, jerked her violet skirts away, and kicked the opposite door. It banged open, and she flung herself out of the cab to the sidewalk, stumbling over crinolines and hoops. The zombie climbed into the cab, moaning and muttering. Alice slammed the door shut and twisted the cheap handle so hard it broke. The zombie fumbled with the latch but couldn't get it to work, and the possibility of simply climbing through the open sides of the cab didn't seem to occur to it. It reached for Alice with bloody fingers. Heart pounding, she backed away until she flattened against a rough brick wall. The cab driver, meanwhile, leapt from his seat and fled down an alley. A pair of zombies shambled after him. The coward hadn't even stayed to help her. Alice flicked a glance at the foggy street and stared.

Plague zombies in various stages of deterioration filled the byway. They were—had been—men and women, boys and girls. It looked to be every zombie in London. They limped and hobbled and dragged themselves through the mist, skin sloughing off their muscles, open sores festering in the dim gaslight. The hackney horse snorted in fear. Terrified, Alice pressed herself against the wall. A tiny whimper died in her throat. It was every nightmare she'd ever had come to life. The plague had taken her mother, brother, and fiancé. Now it was lurching toward her in a crowd of mottled, oozing flesh.

Screams from frightened horses and shouts of panicked people filled the air. Alice stayed perfectly still, trying to remain as inconspicuous as a woman in a ball gown could. Her breath came in quick, short pants as she tried to overcome her fear and make sense of what she saw in the street. The crowd of zombies oozed around night-delivery carts, rocking them, shoving at them—they were working together. It was impossible. Plague zombies suffered from an advanced case of the clockwork plague, a disease that attacked both body and brain. It separated skin from muscle and opened up holes in the dermis. It attacked neural tissue, creating dementia, palsy, and paralysis. Nine times out of ten, it killed. The plague was highly contagious, but only after initial contraction, when the victim was asymptomatic, and toward the end, when the victim looked more monster than human. At this stage, the victim's eyes also became sensitive to daylight, forcing a nocturnal existence that might last for a year before death finally claimed them, though most died of starvation or exposure long before then. Ironically, it was the contagious aspect of the disease that allowed plague zombies to exist within London—the police and other authorities were afraid to get too close for fear of contracting the illness themselves.

But for their contagious nature, zombies were usually harmless scavengers who looked more frightening than they actually were. They didn't have the mental capacity to work together in their final months. Yet this mob was doing exactly that.

There was a crash, and the street flooded with ale as the zombies tipped over a beer delivery van. Drovers scrambled away and fled, abandoning lorries and teams of horses alike.

And then she heard the music—low, eerie music that reminded her of a flute or an oboe. Intricate and strange, it wove in and through the crowd of zombies. She remembered hearing it earlier, as she left the dance. It chilled her blood. Alice tracked the sound to a figure standing in the middle of the plague zombie crowd. The figure wore a long brown coat with tarnished silver buttons, and a battered top hat. A white mask covered the upper half of its face. It grinned almost wider than any human should be able to grin. In its hands, the figure held a strange device that looked a bit like a set of bagpipes, but without the mouthpiece, and with a number of strange and tiny machines attached. The figure grinned and grinned, white teeth shining in the dim light. Its fingers moved across the device, and the music grew louder. The zombies jerked in unison and tipped over another truck.

"A clockworker," Alice whispered with understanding.

Every so often, perhaps one time in a hundred thousand, the plague gave even as it took. Instead of destroying the victim's brain, the disease made it work with a wondrous efficiency. Mathematics, physics, biology, chemistry—even some forms of art—became mere toys to these rare and particular plague victims. They created amazing, impossible inventions. Every automaton in existence, for example, owed its mechanical brain to Charles Babbage catching the plague and almost overnight perfecting the analytical engine. Jean-Pierre Blanchard came down with it and swiftly designed not only the light, semirigid framework used by most airships, but also the engines used to propel them and the hydrogen extractors that pulled the necessary gasses out of thin air. Alexander Pilkington discovered how to temper glass so it would keep an edge without shattering, allowing the creation of glass blades and electric lights that didn't break.

Unfortunately, such geniuses became notoriously unstable as the disease continued to devour their brains. They went completely mad in the end; for all that they showed no other physical symptoms. Due to their penchant for complicated machinery, many people called them clockworkers. People also called them lunatics, bedbugs, fireflies, and any number of less-flattering names.

Alice grimaced. This particular clockworker seemed to have discovered how to control his plague-ridden brethren through hypnotic music. She had no idea where he'd come from or what he hoped to accomplish. At the moment, she didn't care. All she wanted, with every fiber of her being, was to get away and find her way home without touching a zombie. The ones on the street might or might not be at the infectious stage, but Alice had no intention of finding out.

Her original cab was not a possibility—that zombie was still inside it. The cab horse snorted again and tossed its head but miraculously remained where it was. The blinders no doubt prevented it from understanding everything that was going on.

The grinning man continued to play the eerie music, and two zombies shambled around the cab, one from each side. They limped toward Alice, ragged clothes seeming to fade into the yellow fog, as if they wore the mist itself. Alice was surrounded—zombies to her left and right, a zombie in the cab ahead of her, and a brick wall behind. No doorways to dodge into, no stairs to climb. Nowhere to flee. Desperately, she cast about for a weapon or a distraction, anything. The zombies shuffled closer. One was a woman in a torn housedress. Alice fumbled under her heavy skirts in an attempt to wrench off a shoe, but the buttons were done up too tightly. Tears streamed down her face.

"Get away!" she screamed at them. "Get away from me!"

A shot cracked through the fog. The head of the zombie woman exploded like a ripe melon. An awful smell washed over Alice as the body dropped to the sidewalk. Alice gaped.

A horse rode up—two horses, no, four—their iron shoes clattering on the cobblestones. One of the riders rushed at Alice, stomping over the zombie woman's corpse.

"Up you come," the rider said, hauling Alice up behind the saddle in an awkward sideways perch. Alice, clutching for purchase and fighting The Dress, barely had time to register the fact that her rescuer was a woman in leather trousers before the horse wheeled around and cantered back the way it had come, leaving the two remaining zombies behind. Alice noted the pistol at the woman's belt.

"Who are you?" Alice demanded. "What's going on?"

"We're here to help," the woman said. "Down you go. Stay safe, love."

Before Alice could register the shocking familiarity of the address, the woman deposited her on the street. The other horseback riders were shooting at the zombies and working their way toward the grinning clockworker. He continued to play, then abruptly turned, caught Alice's eye, and winked. Alice took a backward step, uncertain. She was clear of the zombie mob now. She could run. But the tableaux tugged at her. Now that she was out of immediate danger, the scene turned more fascinating than frightening, and she wanted to stay. She could help somehow, *should* help. They had helped her. Still, she was half turning to flee when another thought whipped through her mind.

Louisa wouldn't run.

With that, Alice turned back, and the clockworker threw her a wide grin as he played and played. The music scraped over Alice's bones with the edge of a butcher's knife. She was the only person left on the street besides the mysterious horsemen—and horsewomen. Another rider was pushing his way toward the sea of zombies, lashing out with a truncheon and using his horse to shoulder his way through the crowd toward the clockworker. But the clockworker seemed to glide away without effort, still surrounded by a zombie mob. Their screeches and groans half threatened to drown out the ever-present music. Yet another rider was forced to abandon his horse and leap atop the overturned beer truck. The horse disappeared, screaming, beneath a pile of ragged, half-dead plague victims.

"I could use a bit of help over here!" the rider shouted as three zombies clawed slowly up the side of the truck toward him. He kicked at one, a male in a tattered opera cloak, and the zombie lost its grip.

"On the way!" the woman rider shouted back from the edge of the zombie crowd. She drew her pistol and shot one of the other zombies crawling up the truck. Blood sprayed. The zombie fell backward, dead. Alice put a hand to her mouth.

A cart careened around the corner on two wheels, its horses in a lather. It skidded to a stop not far from Alice. A young man in a dark topcoat, work boots, and twill trousers dropped the reins and leapt to the back of the cart, where he whipped a canvas cover off an enormous . . . thing. It looked to Alice like a calliope that had lost a fight with a steam engine. Some of the pipes had come loose, and the young man was thrusting them back into place. Alice watched with fascination. The clockworker continued pouring out demonic music that drowned out the voice of God.

"Hurry with that, d'Arco!" the rider on the truck shouted, still kicking at zombies. The woman and the other riders circled the zombie mob, shooting where they could and trying to find a way to reach the clockworker.

D'Arco sat down at the machine, pumped at a few pedals, and slammed the ivory keyboard with both hands. A chord tooted from the pipes. The sound was jarring, almost dissonant. It was also barely audible over the clockworker's music. Alice heard d'Arco say a word she wasn't supposed to know. He pumped the pedals harder and tried again. The chord came out louder this time. Several of the zombies paused. So did the clockworker. He stared across the cobblestones at d'Arco. For a long moment, the two locked eyes. Then the clockworker changed his melody. With a blood-chilling sound of dozens of bare feet slapping stone in unison, every zombie on the street turned smartly to face d'Arco—and Alice.

"Uh-oh," d'Arco said.

The clockworker snapped out notes in a quick tempo, and the zombies marched forward, straight for the cart. D'Arco nervously played his chord again, but he'd had little time to pump up the bellows attached to the pedals under his machine, and the sound came out differently. The clockworker laughed and continued to play. Alice backed away, then climbed into the wagon beside d'Arco, not sure what to do, but determined to do *something*. The other riders tried to slow the zombies like sheepdogs working a flock, but the zombies largely ignored them, even when they got trampled, and the three riders left on horses couldn't hope to stop more than a hundred zombies on their own. What did the grinning man *want*?

"You're doing it wrong!" Alice shouted at d'Arco. "It's not affecting them!"

He ignored her, pumped furiously, and tried again. The ugly chords came out still louder this time, and the clockworker winced in the middle of his shambling army, though his playing continued. He added a new element to his tune, and one of the zombies picked up a chunk of wood from the overturned truck. It threw the piece straight at Alice. With a gasp, she ducked, and the piece of wood smashed into the machine. There was a *pop*, and hot steam hissed from the interior. The machine groaned and fell silent.

"Shit!" d'Arco said. The zombies were only a dozen paces away. His face pale beneath dark hair—he seemed to have lost his hat—he jumped down to the cobblestones and pulled an enormous rifle from a rack strapped to the side of the wagon. A cable ran from the stock of the rifle to another machine, the size of a Saint Bernard, bolted to the wagon floor.

"Pull that lever on the rear of the power pack!" d'Arco yelled.

Alice saw the lever he meant. It was pointing down. She yanked back her skirts and gave it a kick to shove it upright. Lights glowed and dials flickered across the pack's surface. Alice smelled ozone and wondered what Louisa would think of all this.

"That weapon hasn't been tested!" the female rider called out.

"No time like the present!" d'Arco yelled back. He aimed the rifle at the advancing row of zombies and pulled the trigger.

A hum rose from the power pack. It grew louder and more intense. A bolt of lightning cracked from the rifle barrel and struck one of the zombies full in the chest. The zombie, a boy who couldn't have been more than twelve, sparked and danced in place, then collapsed. The others continued forward.

"All that to hurt one zombie?" Alice said. "A real rifle would do more!"

D'Arco said nothing, but fiddled feverishly with several dials on the rifle, aimed it, and fired again. This time the electric bolt went wide and encompassed most of the zombies in the forefront. They froze, paralyzed but upright, as electricity poured from the strange rifle. The clockworker continued to play while the zombies behind pushed at their immobilized brethren, trying to knock them over. The electric field, however, seemed to be shocking them as well and pushing them back. The clockworker changed his tune yet again, and the zombies shoved harder, even as they groaned in pain. Several dials on the power pack drooped, and Alice had the feeling the electricity wouldn't last much longer. A bead of sweat ran around d'Arco's temple.

"To hell with the directive!" he shouted. "Shoot the damned clockworker!"

"We're trying!" the woman shouted. "We can't get a clear shot with all these zombies in the way."

Alice's eye fell on the calliope. Quickly, she pulled the piece of wood out and tossed it aside. At first glance, the throw seemed to have staved in the side of the machine and broken a steam pipe, but when she looked closer, she could see that one of the fittings had simply popped loose, depriving the calliope of its high-powered steam. She knelt next to it and reached in, but heat from the pipes threatened to sear her hands through her thin evening gloves. Damp steam swirled around her, condensing on her face. A glance down at The Dress told her it was already torn, either from her unexpected ride on the horse or from the moment she had jumped into the wagon. Quickly, she used the tear as a starting point to rip a chunk of thick cloth loose so she could protect her hands. Reaching inside, she managed to push the fittings back together and slide the lock back into place.

D'Arco was still trying to hold the zombies back with the rifle, but already the electricity was weakening. The zombies were starting to move again, and they were nearly close enough to grab d'Arco. He was panting, either from fear or effort; Alice couldn't tell which. She scrambled to the bench at the strange calliope and, thanking God for the music lessons Father had forced on her, pumped the pedals that worked the bellows.

"I have repaired your machine, Mr. d'Arco," she called down to him. "What should I play?"

He glanced over his shoulder at her, utter surprise written across his face. Clearly, he'd forgotten all about her.

"I hardly suppose they want to hear 'God Save the Queen,'" she prompted, still pumping. "But they *are* getting closer, sir, and that rifle of yours is nearly played out."

The electricity sputtered and went out, then started up again, weaker than before. The zombies jerked forward. The grinning clockworker played his jaunty tune.

"A tritone," d'Arco said. "Play a tritone!"

Alice put her fingers on the keys, still pumping. She could feel the pressure building in the machine. Tiny jets of steam spurted from the calliope's seams. "Which one?"

"Any one! Just play!"

The rifle spat once more and went out. The zombies lurched forward, reaching for d'Arco. Alice set her fingers on the keys for C and F-sharp—an interval called a tritone because it consisted of exactly three whole steps—and pressed.

The machine roared.

Every zombie in the area clapped hands over its ears and howled. Several collapsed to the ground. The clockworker screamed. He dropped his instrument and the music stopped. Alice pumped the foot bellows and hit the chord again. The clockworker fell to the ground amid the zombies and vanished from her view. Alice played the awful chord again and again. It pounded the air like an angry train whistle. The calliope throbbed beneath her fingers, and her thighs grew tired from the pumping, but she kept going.

At last, she became aware of a hand on her shoulder. She looked up into the face of the female rider. *You can stop*, she mouthed.

Alice stopped. The calliope groaned to silence, and Alice sat on the bench, panting and sweaty despite the chilly night air.

"Are you all right?" the woman asked. She had a pleasant, round face, chocolate eyes, and light brown hair pulled into a French braid. The nails on her hand were bitten to the quick, and she still wore the leather trousers, though the puffy blouse with the lace at the throat was distinctly feminine.

"I'm . . . I'm fine," Alice said. "What happened? Is everyone else all right?"

"Everyone's fine, thanks to you, love," the woman said.

"You were a wonder! How did you understand Mr. d'Arco's machine?"

"It was obvious," Alice replied, "to anyone with a bit of sense. What happened to the zombies?"

"Some are still unconscious, and some have wandered away. Without the clockworker to guide them, they reverted to their normal behavior, poor things." She gestured at the street behind her. It was empty but for the wreckage of the beer truck and the people on horseback. A single zombie slunk into the darkness, dragging one leg.

"Good heavens," Alice said. She put a palm to her mouth as elation threatened to overtake her and swell her corsets. A sudden urge to jump up and down and clap her hands like a little girl swept over her, and she barely managed to contain herself. "We did it. We actually did it!"

The woman laughed. "Indeed we did."

"What about the clockworker, then?" Alice asked.

"He got away." The woman grimaced. "There was a sewer cover directly beneath him, and he dropped down into it right after you began to play. It was almost as if he'd planned it that way. Perhaps he did."

Alice blew out a long breath, her elation somewhat deflated. "I'm sorry."

"It wasn't your fault, love," the woman said. "You did far better than we did."

There it was again—that familiar form of address. It should have bothered Alice, coming from a commoner, even from someone who was probably an Ad Hoc woman, but in the aftermath of the fight, she found it endearing instead, as if she'd been welcomed into a circle of tight-knit friends.

"But what did the clockworker *want*?" Alice demanded. "What was all that *for*?"

The woman shrugged. "Clockworkers live in a world of their own. No doubt gathering an army of zombies to tip over beer vans made perfect sense to him. Did they touch you?"

"No." Alice glanced down at her ruined gown. "But I don't think I'll be wearing this again. And it was my only one."

The woman clucked her tongue. "I'm sorry about that."

"How does that machine work?" Alice asked, suddenly eager to change the subject. "And why did Mr. d'Arco need me to play a tritone?"

"Ah. I'm afraid I can't go into that here," the woman said. "But listen, love, there's clearly quite a lot to you, far more than that dress can contain. If you ever need help, or if you find you need a change in your life, write to me, all right?"

She handed Alice a card. On it was written:

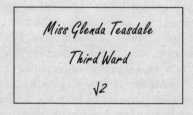

Miss Glenda Teasdale

Third Ward

$\sqrt{2}$

"Are you an Ad Hoc woman?" Alice blurted.

Glenda smiled. "Of course. There should be no other kind, if you ask me."

At that moment, d'Arco rode up on Glenda's horse, his dark eyes inquisitive beneath mussed black curls. Alice noted for the first time how handsome d'Arco was. His features were even, his jaw long, his smile wide. His body was long and lean beneath his topcoat.

"Did you thank her?" he asked. "Did you tell her she was wonderful?"

"I did, Simon," Glenda said. "And I'll thank you to give me Roulette back. *You* can drive the cart back to headquarters."

"Your cab is still sitting over there," d'Arco told Alice as he dismounted. "I'd offer to see you home, but we simply can't leave the machinery. Can you drive it? What am I saying—a woman of your talents could probably shoe the horse." And Alice had to laugh.

The drive home was uneventful, and Alice was surprised at how little fear she felt. She should have been jumping at every shadow, but she felt perfectly calm, even a bit thrilled, as she guided the horse through damp streets. The Dress was in violet tatters, her hair was coming down, and anyone might see her in the driver's seat of the shabby hansom, but she didn't care in the slightest. She allowed herself a little whoop of glee.

This, she decided, must be how Louisa felt all the time.

When she arrived home, she climbed down from the hansom cab and, not knowing what else to do, left it in the street. The horse would no doubt eventually return to its stable on its own, or its owner would remember Alice's address and come looking for it, or someone would steal the beast. Alice had to admit she didn't much care at this point. She retrieved her pocketbook from the cab floor and wearily climbed the short steps to the run-down row house she shared with her father, Arthur, Baron Michaels. When she entered, a clockwork cat leapt down from the windowsill with a light clicking of iron claws. It peered up at her, segmented tail switching back and forth, lamplit eyes glowing with unearthly green phosphor.

Alice reached down to pat the cat's head. "Hello, Click. I'm glad you waited up for me."

The cat made a rumbling noise that sounded nearly like a purr, batted at her tattered sleeves, then abruptly scrambled to his feet and rushed out of the room. Alice shook her head and suddenly realized she was starving. She tiptoed past her father's study-cum-bedroom and slipped into the tiny kitchen, where she threw together a sandwich, her dress bulging inconveniently about her. Click jumped up on the counter to watch, his phosphorous eyes casting small circles of light over the bread and ham. He swatted at her hand, and she tapped his nose with the knife handle with a thin *clank* in admonishment.

"You don't even eat," she said.

Click meowed at her, somehow managing to sound a little huffy. He looked as if he wanted to say something, but actual speech wasn't part of the codex that ran the tiny analytical engine in his head, and for this Alice was wryly grateful—a talking clockwork cat would be dreadfully obnoxious.

She put sandwich and tea on a tray with a candle and bustled upstairs, not wanting to awaken Father. The thought of having to explain the condition of The Dress to him filled her with dread.

The yellow fog continued to shoulder itself against the windows as Alice entered her room. Her candle provided only a little light, but putting on a gas jet would cost too much. Like Father's study, Alice's room lacked much furniture, but Alice had learned to weave rag rugs, and they added warmth to the floor. Under the window stood her workbench—a tall table with several drawers under it and a stool to sit on. Several wooden shipping boxes were stacked on the floor, all of them with Alice's address on them. Cogs, flywheels, and tiny barrels for analytical engines littered the tabletop, and an array of tools hung neatly on hooks from the wall above. Standing incongruously nearby was a dressmaker's stand for The Dress.

Alice flung open the wardrobe. "Out, please," she said. "I need help."

From the wardrobe flittered, crawled, and scampered a dozen small machines, automatons of brass and copper. Some skittered on half a dozen legs; others buzzed about beneath whirling blades. All of them possessed tiny, intelligent eyes and long-fingered hands.

"I need to get ready for bed," Alice told them.

The automatons instantly set to work. They zipped about the room, their tiny hands tugging Alice out of The Dress, or what remained of it, clicking and squeaking to themselves all the while. Petticoats and lacings and corset all fell away, layer by layer. The automatons unfastened dozens and dozens of buttons. One of the automatons, a flier, seemed to be having trouble staying aloft. It labored, then dropped toward the floor. Alice caught it, halted the others in their work, and took the little machine to her workbench. Standing in her petticoats, she popped the key from the windup mechanism, deactivating the automaton, and swiftly disassembled it.

Alice hadn't built her automatons, of course. They had arrived in pieces at Christmas, her birthday, Easter, even Guy Fawkes Night, along with complicated instructions for assembly and activation. And always at the bottom of every box of parts lay hidden a small pasteboard card with a handwritten scrawl: *Love, Aunt Edwina.*

The little automatons had started off fairly simple and had become more and more complicated over the years. Assembling them had given Alice quite an education in mechanics, engineering, and basic physics, and sometimes she wondered if that was the purpose Aunt Edwina had in mind.

Alice barely remembered her aunt Edwina. According to her father, the last time he had spoken to her was after Alice's ninth birthday, just before the clockwork plague struck the Michaels family. It had killed Alice's mother and older brother, forced her father into a wheelchair, and marked the Michaelses as socially undesirable. Aunt Edwina had withdrawn to her small estate outside London, snubbing the society that was trying to snub her and living her life as she liked. She wore trousers instead of skirts, talked to strange men without a proper introduction, and supported suffrage years before the Hats-Off Committee appeared in Parliament. In order to wheedle his way back into the social graces of the traditional folk, Arthur Michaels publicly repudiated his sister's behavior and declared her a bad influence, though he didn't refuse the little automatons she sent to Alice.

Click jumped up on the workbench, and Alice briefly touched the cat's smooth head before going to back to work, her stiff petticoats hitched unbecomingly around her knees. Click had arrived fully assembled as an engagement present from Aunt Edwina three years ago, when Alice was eighteen. Father had arranged a marriage to Frederick Trent, a business associate. Knowing she had few other prospects, Alice hadn't protested. In a stunningly unfortunate series of events, however, Frederick Trent himself contracted the clockwork plague from an errant beggar and died a week before the wedding.

What few social and business contacts had been left to Arthur Michaels quickly dried up. His investments went bad, and he'd been forced to sell the family home. Debts and bad business moves had decreased their fortunes further. Now they couldn't even afford a girl to come in and sweep. And the daughter of a baron was socially forbidden from finding paying work, no matter how many useful skills she might have. Even Ad Hoc ladies would find the idea of a baron's daughter laboring for mere money horrifying. More than once, Alice had considered disguising herself somehow and finding a job, but the only skill she had was assembling and repairing automatic machinery, and since most automatons were owned by nobility, she stood a good chance of being recognized. The possibility of being caught out made her too nervous to try it.

Alice donned a jeweler's loupe to magnify the tiny machinery and saw one of the propeller gears was missing several teeth. Alice plucked a replacement from a drawer with a pair of tweezers, dropped it into place, and tightened the tiny bolt. She had already sold several of Aunt Edwina's gift automatons without telling Father, and she wondered how long it would be before she ran out of machines to sell. Her greatest fear was that she might have to sell Click.

Deftly she finished reassembling the little automaton, unable to help but admire how its smooth brass surface hid a number of greasy, whirling bits of machinery. Her quick fingers rewound the brass key, and the automaton whirled to life. Its eyes snapped open, its blades spun it aloft, and it flew, chittering, across the room to join the others. They caressed it and squeaked among themselves.

"Enough of that now," Alice told them with mock sternness. "I want my nightshirt."

The automatons scampered and flew to obey. They removed the remainder of Alice's petticoats and helped Alice pull the worn nightshirt over her head. The undergarments, at least, were undamaged. She kicked The Dress into the corner before wolfing down the sandwich. One of the automatons picked up a bit of pasteboard from the floor and handed it to Alice. It was Glenda Teasdale's card, the one with the square root of two on it—a mystery indeed. And what on earth was the Third Ward?

If you find you need a change in your life, write to me, all right?

Alice frowned as she finished the last bite of sandwich. Miss Teasdale was an Ad Hoc woman, wearing trousers, riding astride, calling a peer of the realm *love* as if they were related. Earlier, Alice had found it exciting, but now that she'd had time to calm down, she realized how ridiculous the entire affair was. And she had sacrificed an extremely expensive dress to this Third Ward for barely a thank-you. Glenda Teasdale and her Third Ward could go hang.

Alice Michaels tossed the card onto her workbench, blew out the candle, and dropped into exhausted, righteous sleep.

Chapter Four

"Here you go, son." Stone hunkered next to the pallet and set the pewter plate on the deck near Gavin. His phosphorescent lantern cast a low circle of green light on the wood and shoved the shadows backward. "I got you some beans this time. They even have some salt pork in 'em."

Gavin pushed himself into an upright sitting position on his pallet with deliberate slowness. Each movement pulled at his back, sending demon twinges up and down his body. Around him, the dark hold smelled of tea and cinnamon, silk and paper. Bundles, boxes, and crates created chunks of deeper shadow all their own. He carefully took up the plate and shoveled salty beans into his mouth. The chain around his left ankle clanked.

"Have we moved yet?" he asked.

Stone shook his head. "Still tethered. Not much to see out there but a hangar, my boy. Wellesley Field's a good three miles from London. You can't even see the city now that we've landed, so you ain't missing anything."

"I've made the Beefeater run a hundred times," Gavin muttered. "Seen London."

"Right."

Gavin finished the beans and shoved the plate aside. It felt odd to be on board ship with her engines silent. Two engines had turned up damaged from the pirate fight and had shut themselves down not long after Gavin's whipping. Repairs had taken more than a week, and in that time both the *Juniper* and the pirate ship had drifted about as playthings of light and wind. Correcting their course and getting to England had taken another two days. A medium-sized dirigible normally made the run from New York to London in three days, two with favorable winds, but the *Juniper* had arrived in London as a captive more than ten days late. Gavin wondered if she and her crew had been reported lost. Had anyone notified his family? The telegraph offices ran regular messages, but he had no idea if the Boston Shipping and Mail Company would go through the expense for a mere cabin boy. The image of his mother slumped across the kitchen table, a crumpled telegram in her hand and tears on her face, made his throat grow thick, and he found himself hoping the BSMC was too miserly for common courtesy.

He swallowed the tinny taste of beans and made himself ask the question he'd been dreading. "Will we be ransomed soon?"

Stone shrugged. "Probably. Captain hasn't said, but he can hardly keep you all locked in the brig for another week, can he?"

"Is he going to ransom *me*?"

"He'll ask. The real question is"—Stone leaned forward a little—"will your company pay it?"

Gavin's mouth went dry. The fears he'd been trying to suppress all the long days he'd spent lying on his stomach in the *Juniper*'s hold while fevers wrenched and tore at his healing body came roaring back. The BSMC always paid ransom for ships. It usually paid ransom for officers. It often paid ransom for airmen. It never paid ransom for cabin boys—not even for cabin boys only a few weeks away from their eighteenth birthdays.

"That's what I thought," Stone said, reading the expression on Gavin's face. "Listen, boy—Captain Keene ain't cruel. He only beat you instead of throwing you overboard for killing Blue, didn't he? And he let that old man tend your back, right?" When Gavin didn't answer, he went on. "I think he likes you. If I talked to him, I bet he'd let you stay on with us. You'd be a proper privateer instead of a milksop merchant. Load better'n being sold to the East End whorehouses."

"Is that what he'll do?"

"Most like. He has to make money off you somehow to pay for everything you ate."

Gavin wondered on what sort of scale a few cans of beans outweighed the lives of Tom and Captain Naismith and the lashes that had landed on Gavin's back. He wanted to be angry, but he was too tired. The skin over his spine felt tight.

"So those are my choices," Gavin said. "Join you or spend my time doing . . . doing what Madoc Blue wanted."

"Think so." He scooted closer to the gunnysack pallet and perched on its edge, close enough for Gavin to feel the heat of his leg. "Anyway, I'm ready."

With stiff, reluctant movements, Gavin leaned toward Stone and retrieved his fiddle from its battered case on the floor. Once it was under his chin, he gave Stone a resigned look. It was the price for extra food—and for Stone speaking up so Gavin would keep his life.

"'Tam Lin,'" the man said, his eyes glowing green above the phosphorous light. His white leathers, those he had stolen from one of Gavin's crewmates, took on the same sickly hue.

Gavin played. The ancient song's minor key meshed with the unearthly cold fire within the lantern as his bow and skittering fingers cast dreadful shadows over the bulkheads. Every note was a curse, but the iron chain around Gavin's ankle siphoned his strength, and the music seemed to fall away into the darkness, its art and beauty flat and dead. Stone didn't notice. He nodded his head, tapped his fingers, and grinned with green teeth.

When Gavin finished, he said, "I lied, son. I'm sorry."

The bow jumped in Gavin's hands and screeched across the strings. "What do you mean?" he asked, straining to keep his voice level even as his heart jerked hard.

"The captain already ransomed the crew, and the company's wired the money. Except for you. They drew the line at a cabin boy."

Gavin's mouth dried up and tension tightened his chest. "They're gone? Everyone's gone?"

"On their way back to Boston. You're the only one left. The captain talked to a woman what runs a little backgammon house, and she was all happy to hear about a boy who can fiddle in the evening and handle instruments at night. I'm supposed to bring you up. The captain'll give me hell for taking so long, but I had to get another tune of you, didn't I?"

Gavin hit him with his fiddle. The instrument's edge caught the underside of Stone's chin, and he went down with a grunt, eyes glassy. Gavin went through his pockets with chilly fingers and came up with a key. It fit the lock on his ankle chain. He released it, fastened it around Stone's ankle, and tossed the key into the dark hold.

"Bastard," he whispered, then shoved the fiddle into its case and made his way toward the ladder out of the hold, abandoning the pretense that his wounds made him a near invalid. He just wished they didn't still hurt. At the last moment, he ran back to strip Stone's white leather jacket and put it on himself. It was overly large and still warm from Stone's body heat.

Gavin threaded a path through the dark hold, finding his way by touch and memory, until he came to the rear ladder. He crept upward to the hatch, fiddle case strapped to his back, and listened. No voices. With aching care, he edged the hatch cover up until he could peer out onto the deck. Dim light; no people. He eased the cover higher, set it aside, and froze as it scraped against the wooden decking. The sound vanished into the distance as if swallowed.

Heart thudding in his rib cage, Gavin slipped out onto the deck. He had the sense of great space all around him, but there was no sky. Overhead, he heard the faint creak of the envelope straining against the thick netting that tethered it to the ship, and the deck swayed only faintly. Behind the ship lay a huge archway of cloudy light, a doorway so big the *Juniper* could coast straight through it. She was in one of the hangars at Wellesley Field. Gavin had seen the *Juniper* into Wellesley any number of times, but this was the first time she'd arrived as a prisoner. He wondered where the pirate ship had gotten to—and the pirates, for that matter.

As if in answer, a voice from below shouted, "Stone!"

Gavin's heart jerked again, and he scrambled to the thin cover of the gunwale.

"Stone!" called the voice again, and Gavin recognized Captain Keene. "Bring that boy down now, you lazy fuck! The lady wants to have a look."

Gavin risked a peek over the edge. The *Juniper* was anchored only a few feet above the hangar floor, lashed down with a series of guy ropes that ran through a complex system of gears and pulleys, which were, in turn, held down with flyweights and levers like those found backstage in a theater. Gavin could almost feel the ship straining against her bonds, longing to burst free and sail the clouds again. Several rope ladders trailed to the ground, and a loading ramp with a block and tackle mounted atop it had been rolled up, ready to unload cargo into Captain Keene's pockets. Below, Captain Keene himself waited with his arms crossed. A dumpy woman in a simple dress and hat stood beside him. No doubt she owned the house Stone had mentioned. Both woman and captain were looking up.

"Stone!" Keene bellowed. "If I have to come up there, you'll scrub decks for a month!"

Gavin realized he was holding his breath. Keeping low, he moved across the deck to the other side of the ship and found a guy rope that angled down to the ground. He slipped between a gap in the netting, wrapped his knees around the rope, then slid downward hand over hand. His arms and legs, weakened and stiff from weeks of inactivity, screamed murder at him, and his back joined in. Gavin ignored them. The tar coating made the rope a little slick. He was halfway down now, and picking up speed.

"He'd better not be playing with the merchandise," said the woman on the far side of the ship. "You said the boy's unspoiled, and I'm holding an auction for his first."

"Don't worry your little head," Keene said. "Stone's not that sort. He only has a soft spot for music, and he's been making the boy play for him. Bugger thinks we don't know."

Gavin dropped to the ground and peered around the hull, which hovered a scant foot above the hangar floor. The captain and the woman stood between him and the huge hangar door. He might or might not be able to outrun Keene if the captain spotted him, but Keene would raise the alarm, and who knew how many other pirates might be sitting around outside? There were other exits from the hangar, though. All he had to do was—

"Who's this, now?" A pair of hard hands grabbed him from behind. Gavin yelped with surprise and automatically elbowed the man in the stomach. The grip relaxed, allowing Gavin to wrench free. He caught a glimpse of white leather— a stolen leather jacket—before he fled. The man gasped once or twice, then bellowed for help.

No time to think. Legs and back afire, Gavin ran for the shadows at the hangar wall even as Keene bolted around the hull, followed by more pirates. They must have been stationed outside. Keene spotted him and shouted orders. Gavin reached the wall that housed the levers and flyweights. He yanked each lever, sending the weight stacks soaring. Each pull released a guy line holding the *Juniper* in place. Ropes snapped and hissed in the air like angry snakes. The pirates pounded toward him. Several bore glass cutlasses that gleamed in the dim light. Gavin pulled another lever, and a slashing rope caught a pirate full across the torso and swept him aside like a toy. He thudded against the *Juniper*'s hull and slid to the ground, his eyes glassy as his cutlass.

"The bastard got Billy!"

"You little shit!"

"Chop his hands off for real this time!"

The *Juniper* was now free of the ropes. She floated upward and bumbled against the smooth ceiling, probing hopefully for a way out. Gavin yanked a final lever, and with a clatter of gears, the enormous front door of the hangar ground open. A stiff, cold breeze whipped through the building, which had become a large tunnel. The wind pushed the ship away from Gavin, toward the opposite door, the one already open.

"No!" Keene shouted.

Gavin ran for it. Fiddle still strapped to his back, he bolted toward the pirates and, a prayer on his lips, he leapt with all his strength. One hand caught the trailing end of a rope ladder that dangled from the gunwale. He forced himself to grab a second rung with his other hand and pull himself higher until his feet found a perch just as the *Juniper*'s forward movement carried him over the pirates' heads. The envelope slid across the hangar ceiling with a high-pitched noise that sounded like laughter. Gavin looked down at the startled and angry faces of the pirates as he coasted above them. Keene pulled a flechette pistol from his breast pocket and fired. The dart skimmed past Gavin's shoulder.

"Shit!" Gavin swung on the ladder to make himself a more difficult target. Keene fired again and again, but the light was bad and the ship was picking up speed. Gavin caught a glimpse of the woman's stark and startled face just before the *Juniper* cleared the hangar doors entirely and shot upward. A whoop of laughter burst from Gavin's chest at the rush of movement, but in a split second he realized he wouldn't be able to pilot or land the ship by himself. He made an instant decision and leapt off the ladder to the hangar roof the moment he came level with it, stumbling a bit but keeping his feet.

The *Juniper* soared upward into a cloudy sky, and Gavin watched her go with satisfaction. She might be recaptured, but in his mind, she would soar forever, gliding among the mists and the stars. People would tell stories about the ghost airship with the pirate chained inside her cargo hull. In any case, Keene wouldn't have her.

Captain Keene and the pirate crew boiled out of the building. As Gavin hoped, Keene and the pirates seemed to assume Gavin was still on board the ship. Keene uselessly fired his flechette pistol at the diminishing *Juniper*, screaming incoherently about his lost cargo, his lost ship's ransom, his lost reward. Gavin used the noise of Keene's tantrum to cover the sound of his footsteps as he scuttled to the far side of the hangar roof and slid down a drainpipe. Almost instantly he became just another white-jacketed airman among the crowd of them running to see what all the fuss was about at this particular hangar. A few moments after that, he had made his way to the edge of the airfield, out of Keene's sight and reach. The *Juniper* was a tiny speck high in the sky that eventually vanished into the clouds.

Gavin ducked behind another hangar, one among dozens, and paused to catch his breath. Now that he wasn't in immediate danger, his legs had gone rubbery and the scars on his back burned again. He sat down with his head between his knees, wondering what the hell he was going to do now. An airmen or cabin boy who had been refused ransom was considered worthless. It didn't matter that the pirate attack wasn't Gavin's fault or that the Boston Shipping and Mail Company's refusal to ransom him had nothing to do with Gavin's ability and everything to do with money. All that mattered was that Gavin was an unransomed cabin boy. No one would hire him.

He could take a false name, lie about his age, and apply for work as an airman on a different ship, but that option offered little hope as well. Word traveled fast among airmen. By now, everyone knew or would soon know that Gavin Ennock, cabin boy for the *Juniper*, hadn't made ransom in London, and his reputation, however unfairly, was already ruined. A "new" airman who nosed around the city looking for work would be painfully obvious. Gavin's only option was to somehow earn enough money to buy passage back to America and beg a job on another Boston Shipping and Mail airship. BSMC knew it wasn't his fault he'd lost his position, and he technically still worked for them, anyway. He just needed another ship.

Gavin breathed hard. How would he earn that kind of money? The only trade he knew floated high in the air above him, untouchable as a star.

Sorrow for his friends from the *Juniper* crashed over him, and the realization that he would probably never play for Old Graf again forced a choked sound from his throat. He swallowed hard and swiped at his eyes. He wasn't going to cry. Not down here, in the dirt and mud of the airfield. He wouldn't give Keene the satisfaction. Besides, he had his life; he had his freedom; he had his fiddle. He was in much better shape now than he had been an hour ago.

So get to your feet and do something to help yourself, he told himself. *No one else will do it for you.*

Gavin got to his feet, shifted his fiddle case on his back, and trotted down to the rail line that ran between Welles-ley Field and London proper. He knew from previous Beefeater runs that a train ran every ten minutes on the dot, shuttling passengers and airmen to and from the city.

Airmen, identifiable by their white leathers, rode free. Luck was with Gavin—a train was pulling away just as he arrived at the platform, and he hoisted himself into an open-topped third-class car jammed with men and women alike before it picked up too much speed. He wedged himself into a corner, unable even to sit. The locomotive coughed harsh-smelling cinders over them, quickly covering everyone's clothing with a patina of ash and dulling Gavin's coat to a dirty gray. At least it wasn't raining.

Gavin flung a last look over his shoulder at Wellesley Airfield. The hangars had already receded into the distance, and a moment later, a series of row houses flashed by. His old life was gone. Sometime later, the train pulled into Paddington station, and Gavin climbed out of the car, feeling battered and sore. He made his way away from the swirling crowd and screaming whistles of the platforms until he could find a quiet corner to take stock. First he checked his fiddle. By a miracle, it wasn't broken or even cracked. He must have hit Stone under the chin just right. He spared a moment's thought for the pirate, chained in the *Juniper*'s hold and soaring high above the earth while Gavin roamed the ground below, free but unable to fly. Which of them was better off?

In the jacket pockets, Gavin found a few small coins and a used handkerchief. He also had the jacket itself, which would keep him warm. He could sell that, if it came to it. And he'd eaten today. So he had a few resources.

He left Paddington station and vanished into the dirty, swirling throng of London. Horses, carts, cabs, and carriages clogged cobblestoned streets. Women in bustled skirts and men in waistcoats and hats rushed up and down the walkways. A spidery automaton clicked over the stones, ignoring the piles of horse apples it stepped in. Smells of urine, coal smoke, and roasting meat washed over Gavin beneath a heavy gray sky. A ragged little girl begged to sweep manure aside for pedestrians who crossed the street. Everything was dirt and noise and oppression.

An idea occurred to Gavin. Hope bloomed, and he trotted off down London Street until he found an omnibus heading in the right direction. It cost him a precious penny, but he was able to find his way to the pillared building that housed the London office of the Boston Shipping and Mail Company. He had forgotten they had a headquarters here. Inside, an enormous open-floored wooden space sported rows of desks, each with clerks scratching in ledgers or poking at enormous engines that clacked and spat out long lines of paper. In the corner, a huge multi-armed automaton sorted mail and telegrams. Its arms blurred as it flung bits of paper into bins or thrust them into the hands of waiting errand boys. Voices rose and fell, and footsteps clattered ceaselessly across the worn floorboards.

Gavin snagged a mail boy, who pointed him toward a set of desks in the back. A small freestanding sign read EMPLOYMENT. Easy enough—BSMC knew his qualifications and would give him a job on another ship. His heart beat faster as he approached one of the desks.

"We're not hiring," the balding clerk said before Gavin could even take a breath.

"I already work for BSMC," Gavin said. "I'm from Boston. The *Juniper*."

"Oh yes." The clerk opened a letter and scanned it. "The cabin boy. We don't ransom cabin boys."

"Uh . . . I don't need to be ransomed," Gavin said. "I need a position on another ship."

"What are your qualifications?"

Gavin stared at him. Hadn't he just said? "I'm a cabin boy. Six years' experience. In a few weeks, I'll qualify for airman."

"Can your captain vouch for you?" the clerk asked.

"He was killed in the pirate attack," Gavin replied around clenched teeth. "Along with my best friend. Then a pirate tried to . . . to take my trousers down, so I killed him, and the pirates beat me bloody for it."

The clerk took dispassionate shorthand notes. "Why didn't they kill you?"

Gavin blinked. This conversation was becoming more and more surreal. "I played fiddle for them. They liked my music and decided not to kill me. One of the pirates especially enjoyed my playing, and I escaped when he let his guard down."

"I see." More notes. "So you're saying your captain can't vouch for you, you had illegal carnal knowledge of an enemy airman, and you deliberately collaborated with and gave comfort to the enemy?"

Gavin's face burned. "It wasn't anything like—"

"In any case, we have no positions for cabin boys on this side of the pond," the clerk finished with a dismissive wave. "Check with the Boston office."

"What? How am I supposed to get to Boston?"

"You should have thought of that before you decided to fiddle for pirates with your trousers down."

For the second time that day, Gavin hit a man. This time it was with his fist. Even though the blow had to travel across the clerk's desk, it landed with enough force to knock the clerk ass over teakettle. The entire floor went silent except for the clatter and hum of the sorting machine in the corner as everyone turned to stare. Gavin stood at the desk, panting, his fist still outstretched.

"Get out!" the clerk bawled, scrambling to his feet. His nose dripped blood on his spotless white shirt. "Get out! You'll never work for us again! Police! Police!"

Gavin turned on his heel and stomped out.

An hour or so of mindless walking later, he managed to calm down, and anger gave way to fear. He forced himself to think. Money was the main issue. He needed it for the short term, and, unless he wanted to risk a life of crime, there was only one way to earn it. Eventually he found his way to Hyde Park.

Hyde Park wasn't simply a park—exhibition halls, gazebos, outdoor auditoriums, carnivals, and other attractions peppered the place, and thousands of people visited every day. It was late spring, and many of the bushes were in full bloom, scenting the air with sweetness. Couples with chaperones, groups of young people and families, and schoolchildren on outings trod the roads and footpaths beneath green trees, some wandering aimlessly, some scampering with glee, some walking to a specific event. Food sellers with trays around their necks or pushing small carts hawked their wares. Gavin found a likely corner, got out his violin, dropped two of the small coins from his pocket into the open fiddle case at his feet for seed money, and set to playing.

He had done this before, busking street corners in Boston as soon as he'd been able to scratch out a tune on his grandfather's fiddle. Being hungry had provided a certain amount of impetus to learn music faster; people didn't give money to bad players, even when they were little boys with big blue eyes. He had done some busking again on three or four other occasions when he'd been caught short in other ports and needed some quick money, but it had never occurred to him that his livelihood might once again depend on his music. He smiled with all his might at passersby and nodded his thanks whenever someone dropped a coin into his case.

It felt better than playing for pirates.

Sometime later, he had several farthings—quarter pennies—and a few pence in his case, enough to buy half a loaf of bread. He kept on playing. A woman in a wine red velvet dress, unusual for spring, paused on the path to listen. Gavin knew from experience that if he met her gaze for long, she would feel awkward and move on, so he avoided looking directly at her, though he studied her out of the corner of his eye. She was tall for a woman, slender, and old enough to be his mother. Her hair was piled under a red hat, and the buttons on her gloves and shoes were actually tiny gold cogs. She carried a walking stick, also unusual. Behind her came an automaton, a stocky brass mechanical man with a boiler chest and pistonlike arms and legs. It carried a large shopping basket. The woman practically screamed wealth, and Gavin swept into "O'Carolan's Argument with the Landlady," a particularly difficult tune with complicated scales and turns. The woman stared at Gavin as if she were a lion and he a gazelle. Gavin felt uncomfortable, and he looked elsewhere so he wouldn't make a mistake. The song rippled from his fiddle, and when it ended, applause fluttered about the park. A small audience had gathered. Gavin smiled and bowed. Several people tossed farthings into his case and went on their way. The woman in red velvet was nowhere to be seen. Gavin scooped the coins out of his case to avoid tempting thieves, and among them he found a shilling. He stared at it. This was enough to feed him for two days. Had it come from the Red Velvet Lady? It seemed likely—she had been the only one in the crowd who looked wealthy enough to throw that much money into a busker's case. He went back to his fiddle. Maybe he *could* do this. He could earn enough money for a ticket back to Boston, where he could plead his case to BSMC in a country where he knew the people and where—he hoped—they wouldn't have heard about Gavin punching a clerk in the face.

The rest of the day Gavin earned very little, though he played until his fingers burned and his feet ached from standing in one place. When darkness threatened and the automatic lamplighters clanked from lamp to lamp, he bought a day-old roll from a vendor who was on her way out of the park and searched the area until he found a hiding place between a bush and a boulder. Safe from night marauders and patrolling bobbies, he wrapped his ashen coat around himself and curled up to sleep.

Gavin jerked awake with a yelp of pain. His body was so stiff he could barely move. His back howled with pain when he sat up, and he hobbled about with old-man steps in the damp morning air, breathing sharply and heavily, until his body relented. In the interest of saving money, he skipped breakfast. At least the sun drove the plague zombies into hiding and he didn't have to worry about them for the moment.

Hyde Park was largely deserted in the morning—no point in playing—so Gavin spent the time looking for a better place to spend his nights. Public buildings such as train stations were bad because the bobbies would make him move on, possibly with a crack on the head first. He considered looking for a job, then discarded the idea. The factories were almost all automated and hired few human workers. His reading and writing were decent for everyday use but not up to scratch for an office. And the thought of manual labor that required him to strain his half-healed back made him shake. The main trouble was, he had no real skills except music and flying.

He was wandering aimlessly around side streets, fiddle case on his back, and eventually found himself taking a dogleg through an alley. Brick walls broken by windows and ragged doors rose up to a narrow strip of sky, though the alley itself was quite clean—trash attracted plague zombies, and people rarely left it out. Still, human refuse might show up at any moment. Gavin hurried his steps, then paused. A trick of the light brought his attention to a ground-level window. It was supposed to be boarded over, but he could just see that the wood was coming loose. Gavin glanced around to ensure he went unobserved, then pushed the boards aside, crawled through the opening, and risked a drop into darkness.

A damp, echoing room of stone lay beyond. The only

light crept in through the window he had just violated. Rats scattered as Gavin came to his feet, groaning with reawakened pain. Then he cut the sound off. What if this place was used by plague zombies as a daytime hiding place? He froze, listening, until his eyes adjusted to the gloom. The cellar room was small, maybe ten feet across. A pile of crates jumbled up in one corner, and a door loomed opposite them. No zombies. Gavin heaved a relieved sigh and examined the door, which had no knob and had been nailed shut from the other side. A real piece of luck at last—no one would enter from the main building. It wouldn't be safe to leave anything valuable in here, but it would be a place to sleep.

He piled the crates under the window as a makeshift staircase and crawled cautiously back into the alley. His stomach growled, reminding him that he hadn't eaten at all that day. Furtively, Gavin moved the loose boards back into place and hobbled away. He deserved lunch, at least.

Gavin spent the next two weeks playing Hyde Park for farthings in the afternoons and evenings. After nightfall, he spent a precious penny to ride an omnibus to the West End, where he played for people entering and exiting the music halls and theaters. He arrived in his cellar long after dark, feeling his fearful way down the alley away from the gaslights and toward potential plague zombies. Fortunately, he didn't encounter any. Unfortunately, even this frugal lifestyle didn't allow him to save much. Some days he didn't earn the two pennies it cost him to get to the theater district and back. Some days it rained, preventing him from playing at all. The dampness in the cellar finally forced him to buy a blanket, which ate up several days' money. He had to buy food, of course. And sleeping in the cellar seemed to stop his back from healing completely. Every afternoon he jerked awake, stiff and sore, every muscle on fire. He never woke slowly or peacefully anymore, not since his encounter with Madoc Blue and the first mate's lash. One day he spent nine pence at an apothecary's, and the medicine helped with the pain, but only for a time, and then he was right back where he started. Gavin was beginning to feel desperate. Eventually, spring and summer would end, bringing the chill winds of winter. He would be in deep trouble then.

One soft afternoon in Hyde Park, he had managed to wash up a bit in one of the ponds and was feeling a little better. Gavin's skin itched terribly under his clothes—he hadn't even rinsed them since the *Juniper*. Maybe today he would catch sight of the Red Velvet Lady. She had shown up twice more with her automaton to listen to him, and both times he had found a shilling in his case, though she never said a word. If she came today, maybe he'd use the money to visit a bathhouse and have his clothes laundered to boot.

A fog rolled in from the Thames and mixed with the ever-present coal smoke from the chimneys and streetlamps, creating a thick yellow mist that covered the park in a sulfurous cloak. Gavin sighed as he walked. So much for optimism. Fewer people would be out in weather like this—the chill kept people indoors and lack of sunlight let the plague zombies roam. The damp also worsened his back. *Clip-clop* hooves and quiet voices mingled with the mist, seeming to come from everywhere and nowhere. Men in coats and women in wide dresses ghosted in and out of view. The itching under Gavin's coat was growing worse, and he pulled his jacket off to scratch vigorously once he arrived at his usual corner.

At that moment, a commotion broke out somewhere in the distance. A woman squawked in fear or outrage. Voices shouted, and a pistol shot rang out. Gavin froze. Footsteps pounded down the walkway toward him, and out of the yellow mist emerged a boy a year younger than Gavin. With a start, Gavin realized he was Oriental and dressed in a red silk jacket and wide trousers. He tore down the footpath with angry voices coming behind him, their owners still hidden by fog. The boy skidded to a halt in front of Gavin and grabbed his elbow.

"Help me!" the boy begged in a light Chinese accent. "Please!"

Gavin didn't pause to think. He pushed the boy to the ground in a crouch and flung his filthy jacket over him. Then he sat down on the boy's covered back and opened his fiddle case just as half a dozen angry-looking men came into view, sliding out of the mist like sharks from murky water.

"Where'd the little Chink go, boy?" one of them snarled. He brandished a pistol.

Gavin could feel the boy shaking beneath him. "That way, sir," he said, pointing down a random path.

The man flipped Gavin a small coin as the others tore off. Gavin caught the coin and pulled his fiddle from its case as if nothing interesting had happened. The boy didn't move. Once the noises of pursuit died away, the boy shifted a bit.

"Don't," Gavin murmured. He set bow to strings and played as if he were simply perched on a rock covered by his jacket. Not much later, the men materialized out of the mist again.

"Did the little bastard come back here?" the man with the pistol demanded.

Gavin shook his head and continued playing a bright, happy tune, though his fingers felt shaky. The men conferred a moment, then rushed off in another direction. When their footsteps and voices had faded completely, Gavin whipped his jacket off the boy, who leapt to his feet.

"Thank you," he said, pumping Gavin's hand. "Thank you so much."

"What happened back there?" Gavin demanded.

"A misunderstanding with the lady," he said.

Gavin squinted at him. "That usually means the man did something he shouldn't have."

"No, no." The boy put up his hands. "She kissed *me*. But then her husband jumped out of the bushes with friends. I didn't even know she was married. She screamed, he fired that pistol, and I *ran*. You were wonderful." He fished around in his pockets and thrust something into Gavin's hands. "Take this."

Gavin looked down. He was holding a tiny mechanical bird no bigger than a pocket watch. Its silver feathers gleamed in the pale light. Tiny sapphires made up its eyes and tipped its claws.

"It's beautiful," Gavin breathed. He touched the bird's head. It opened its little beak and trilled a miniature melody, a perfect replica of a nightingale's song, then fell silent.

"I can't accept this," he said. "I don't even know your name."

But when he looked up, the boy was gone.

Although a carriage horse clopped in the distance, crowds in the park were nonexistent, so Gavin put his fiddle away, perched on a bench, and examined the bird. Its wings were etched with tiny Chinese pictograms, and more tiny gems were hidden among the strange icons. Whenever he pressed the head, it trilled the same song over and over, without fail. The first few times, it was beautiful, but after a while Gavin realized it was really nothing more than a music box—very pretty, but lacking the soul of real music. Still, the bird was immensely valuable. The money he'd get from a pawnshop or fence would be five times the cost of a ticket home, though it would be only a fraction of the bird's true worth.

Gavin stroked the nightingale's smooth feathers again. It seemed a dreadful shame to sell something so beautiful for so little money.

Footsteps shuffled through the yellow mist. Gavin

stuffed the nightingale in his pocket and leaned casually back on the bench as two well-dressed young men strolled into view. They were engaged in an animated discussion that involved a great deal of hand waving. Gavin whipped out his fiddle and set to playing—no sense in losing a chance. The men stopped just in front of Gavin and continued their discussion.

"This is the best time to invest in China," the first man was saying. "War always makes money. That little tiff they had over the opium trade proves that—I made a mint. And now it's flaring up all over again. When the conflict ends, China will become much more open to foreigners, and those of us with money on the inside will make our fortunes."

"The Treaty of Nanking was an unequal proposition," the second retorted. "Why do you think the locals are in revolt again? Once Lord Elgin puts the Chinks down, he'll do something dreadful to Emperor Xianfeng to ensure this never happens again, and that will send your speculations into a downward spin."

"You're always a pessimist, White," the first man said. "Tell you what. Let's ask this enterprising young man what he thinks."

Both men turned to Gavin, who stopped playing, startled.

"A street player?" White said. "You can't be serious, Peterson."

"Completely. We can make a bet of it." Peterson fished around in his pocket. "Young man, would you like to earn a sovereign?"

Gavin's eyes widened. It seemed to be a holiday for flinging enormous amounts of money at him. "A sovereign? For doing what?"

"For failing to pay attention, I'm afraid," Peterson replied.

"I don't understand," Gavin said. "What's—"

A cloth bag flipped down over his face and hard hands grabbed him from behind. The bag had a sweet, chemical smell. Gavin struggled and tried to shout, but the hands held him firmly, and the fumes made him dizzy. Soft cloth filled his mouth, muffling his voice.

"Sorry, my boy," said Peterson. "We'll try to make this painless."

The man's words swooped and swirled and faded. Gavin felt a pinprick on his upper arm just before he lost consciousness entirely.

Time stretched and bunched. Voices rushed at him and slid away. Hands prodded him, then forced him upright. Tones and chords burst into his ear, and a voice demanded that he give each one a name: C, B-flat, D-sharp augmented. The voice ordered him to sing, and he sang, the notes falling from his lips in an uncontrolled torrent. He sang songs and changed keys in midmelody as the voice ordered. It never occurred to him to disobey. In fact, he was only vaguely aware of his surroundings. He seemed to be sitting on a soft chair, and he had a vague impression of stone walls. Twice, he caught a flash of wine red velvet. The mysterious lady? Then he fell asleep.

Gavin awoke with a dry mouth and a vague headache. He sat up with a groan and put a hand to his forehead for a moment, then looked around. The stone room was round and small, but brightly illuminated by the light from two electric lamps fastened to the curving walls. A carpet covered the floor. The bed he was lying on felt springy and comfortable, and the blankets were thick. A single narrow window looked out on a darkening sky. Gavin decided he must be in a tower. But why? Slowly he got to his feet. A nightstand near the bed bore a pitcher of water and a glass. Gavin poured and drank, too thirsty to care if the water was drugged. When he bent his arm, he noticed the bandage on his left bicep, and he remembered the needle pricking him in the park. He checked underneath and found a tiny red wound, nothing more.

"Hello?" Gavin called. "I'm awake! Is anyone here?"

No response. Nervously, he searched the room more closely. The heavy door was locked, no surprise. The lights could be turned off by means of a switch near the door. Interesting. He knew a little about electricity, but only a little. Why give something so expensive to a prisoner? Against one wall stood a radiator, which heated the room and drove the dampness away, another odd luxury. He turned his back to it and let the heat soak in.

Hanging off the foot of the bed was a set of clothes—blue work shirt, black trousers, socks, boots. His airman's jacket was gone, as were the coins he had saved. Gavin looked at the filthy rags he'd been wearing since the pirates took the *Juniper* and stripped them off. With a cloth he found near the pitcher, he gave himself a sponge bath. Being clean made him feel amazingly better. The new clothes fit perfectly. A part of him felt he should rebel, refuse gifts from people who had kidnapped him, drugged him, and held him prisoner. But the more practical part of him said it was stupid to wear rags when perfectly good clothes were sitting right there. The window swung outward over a dizzying drop to a cobblestoned courtyard several stories below. Beyond that lay a high wall with gargoyles on it, then green fields scattered with trees. The sun wasn't visible, but the gathering dusk told Gavin it was near night. He looked down at the smooth tower walls. No ledges or gutters to climb down on. What the hell was he doing here? He tried to remember more about the park. The men—Peterson and White—must have been a distraction for someone sneaking up behind him. But why would someone go through all that trouble for a street musician?

A pang went through him. His fiddle! What had happened to his fiddle? A moment later he found its case under the bed. Inside was the instrument, undamaged, along with a fresh supply of rosin for his bow, and the little silver nightingale. Gavin touched the bird's head, and it sang. That they hadn't taken it had made it clear he could keep it.

A clatter brought his head around. A cleverly fitted piece of the door slid upward, allowing just enough room for a mechanical brass spider to click through. It towed a covered tray on wheels behind it. The door piece snapped shut, and the spider tugged the tray around to the foot of the bed, where it whipped off the cover with one spindly leg. Gavin's mouth watered at the smells of beef, potatoes, bread, and gravy. He snatched up the fork and knife provided and ate quickly while the spider gathered up Gavin's discarded clothes and vanished out of the little door hole with them. Gavin, still chewing, wondered if he could fit through it. He also remembered the flash of red he had seen while he was half out of his mind from . . . whatever it was that had happened to him. Was the Red Velvet Lady responsible for all this?

"Hello?" he shouted again. "Can anyone hear me? What do you want?"

No response. He tried the door again. Still locked. He pushed it, then rattled the knob. Frustration poured out of him, and after a moment he realized he was screaming and pounding on the door with his fists, kicking at it with his new boots. He forced himself to stop and backed up, panting. A drop of sweat trickled from his white-blond hair, and the room suddenly felt small and stuffy. He opened the window and perched on the edge with his fiddle. It occurred to him that he had no idea how long he had been here. It could have been hours or days or weeks.

It was time to breathe, take stock. From a certain perspective, he was better off than he had been before. He had good clothes, good food, and a good bed. Whoever had captured him clearly wanted him alive and in good condition. Eventually, the Red Velvet Lady or whoever it was would show up and tell him more, and he would deal with the situation then. In the meantime, he could enjoy comforts such as those he had never known and he could play his fiddle.

He set the nightingale on the windowsill next to him for company and played to the empty night.

Chapter Five

"Miss Michaels? I say, Miss Michaels, are you all right?"

Alice came to herself with a start and shook her head. "Oh my goodness!" she trilled. "My mind went wandering for a moment, Mr. Williamson. How rude! What were you saying?"

"I was observing how the mist seems to both muffle sound and extend it," said Norbert Williamson. "One can hardly tell if we're in Hyde Park or on a country estate."

"True," Alice observed. "It's very eerie. I'm glad you're nearby to keep me safe."

"Now that was blatant flattery, Miss Michaels," Norbert pretended to scold, "however much I enjoyed hearing it."

"You've caught me, Mr. Williamson," she replied with a small smile. "I'm a dreadful person."

The open-topped carriage moved sedately over the gravel pathways of Hyde Park, currently obscured by thick yellow fog. Norbert had suggested cutting their afternoon drive short, but Alice wouldn't hear of it. It gave them a chance to enjoy the park with fewer people about, and, with a set of lap robes covering them, they could remain perfectly comfortable. It also gave Norbert the chance to be shockingly daring by pressing his muscular thigh against hers under cover of the robes. Alice made herself blush, but let her leg remain for quite a long moment before shifting away. Norbert's expression didn't shift as he changed the subject.

"I hear the Hats-On Committee is proposing more legislation regarding child labor in factories," he said. "As if I don't have to deal with enough regulations. I already can't hire children under the age of ten, and they can't work more than ten hours per day. Now they want to cut the time back to eight hours and institute a minimum wage."

This time Alice was ready for him. "Why hire children at all?"

"They work for less than adults. And their hands are smaller, which makes them better at assembling certain machines."

This time as he talked, Alice was careful to pay attention so she could insert the proper comments in the proper places. It was a bit audacious of them to be out without a chaperone, but they were in public and both of them were older, so Alice found it acceptable. The driverless carriage wound through the park, the automatic horse that drew it clopping with mechanical precision. Steam snorted from the horse's gleaming muzzle at regular intervals. Then another sound caught Alice's attention. She laid a hand on Norbert's arm to interrupt.

"Was that a pistol shot?" she asked.

He cocked his head. "I didn't hear anything."

"I'm quite certain I heard a shot."

"In Hyde Park in broad daylight? You must be mistaken. The mist is playing tricks. But we could leave, if you're fearful of your safety."

"Certainly not," Alice replied. "I won't—"

The high, sweet sound of a violin slid through the fog, now close, now far away. Unable to help herself, Alice fell silent to listen. The melody was complicated and quick, happy with a hint of something else. Uncertainty? Fear?

"That's lovely," Alice breathed, entranced. The music pushed all fear of the phantom pistol from her mind. "Like a spirit asking to be set free."

"You have a delightful turn of phrase, Miss Michaels," Norbert was saying. "Truly."

Alice sighed. "He sounds festive and frightened at the same time. How does he—" The music stopped, and Alice felt crushed. Her face fell. "Oh. How disappointing."

"We could try to find him, if you like," Norbert offered gallantly. "I'm sure he'd play if you asked."

She almost took him up on it—but no. What would she do if she found the musician? Fawn on him with Norbert looking on? "You're very kind, Mr. Williamson, but we'd never find him in this mist." She patted his hand. "Best to leave it a fond memory. Still, I'm finding it a bit chilly."

Norbert took the hint and leaned forward to flip levers and twist dials on a control box set into what would be the backward-facing seat of the carriage. The mechanical horse paused, then set off at a brisk trot. In a short time, the conveyance arrived at the small row house Alice shared with her father. Their little meetings were taking on a regularity. Each one involved a simple activity—a drive through the park, a walk in London, a picnic at the river—and each one lasted no more than two hours. This was exactly the case today.

Norbert helped her down from the carriage, his almost-handsome features brightened considerably by a fashionably cut waistcoat and fine wool jacket and a high hat. His clothes and his outrageously expensive carriage only made Alice's neighborhood seem even shabbier, but as always, he pretended not to notice, and Alice pretended not to notice he was pretending not to notice.

"So good of you to join me, Miss Michaels," Norbert said, his usual farewell.

"So good of you to invite me, Mr. Williamson," she said, her usual reply.

Their eyes met for a moment, brown to brown. Alice held her breath. Now was the moment. It would happen. She would feel a catch in her throat, a flutter in her breast, a weakening in her knees.

She felt nothing.

Quickly, she lowered her eyes and released his hand as if a bit overcome, turned, and fled into the house. Once inside, she peeped through the drawing room window in time to watch Norbert's carriage pull away.

"All London is astir, darling. You have to tell me everything!"

Alice spun around so quickly, her skirts swirled to catch up with her. Louisa Creek was sitting in a wingback chair, an open book in her hand and Click in her lap. She wore a soft green dress with a stark white hat and matching white gloves.

"Louisa!" Alice gasped. "What are you doing here?"

"You never called on me after the ball." Louisa idly stroked Click's brass back with her free hand. "I was deeply wounded and came to see about your apology. Your father— a very nice man who was quite pleased to discover his close-mouthed daughter actually has a friend—invited me in and offered to let me sit until you came home. We had a nice chat until he retired for his nap. I'm surprised he didn't recognize me, but he *has* grown nearsighted."

"Why would he recognize you?"

"We ran in the same circles years ago, darling. I'm surprised he never mentioned me."

"Oh. Yes. Well." Alice hung her jacket on the coatrack to regain her composure. Finding Louisa in her drawing room was like discovering a kitten in the cupboard—not necessarily unwelcome, but still startling. "I see you've met Click."

"Indeed. He's charming." She stood up, dumping the affronted Click off her lap and tossing the book aside. "Let's go upstairs. I'll help you change, and you can beg my forgiveness while you tell me all about this tempestuous affair with Norby."

In an instant, Louisa was up the steps and disappearing around the turn. A pang touched Alice's stomach. "Louisa! Wait!"

She gathered her long skirts and hurried up the stairs. In the tiny hallway, Louisa was already opening Alice's bedroom door. Before Alice could stop her, she strode on in. Alice halted. There was a long, long silence.

"Alice!" Louisa called. "Really!"

Alice sighed, straightened her back, and marched in. "Yes?"

Louisa stood in the middle of the room surrounded by Alice's little automatons. More than a dozen of them scampered, climbed, crawled, and flitted about her. Louisa stared at them, her mouth agape.

"I'm so sorry," Alice babbled. "I usually shut them away when company comes, but I didn't know you were—"

"These are astonishing, darling." Louisa put out her hand, and one of the whirligig automatons landed on it. "The work of a true genius. Are they gifts from Norby?"

"No."

"Did you make them yourself, then?"

"I assembled them. They came in pieces as gifts from my aunt Edwina."

"She sounds a fascinating woman! I *must* meet her sometime."

Alice edged closer. "You're not upset?"

"Upset? Why would I be upset?"

"Women aren't engineers," Alice said.

"Yes, they are," Louisa said. "You of all people must have heard of Countess Ada Lovelace, and she isn't alone in the field."

"Ada Lovelace didn't work for money. She had the wealth to flout convention."

Louisa flipped the automaton into the air and leveled a

hard gaze at Alice. "You honestly thought someone who flouted convention would bother *me*?"

"Oh." Alice felt she was rapidly losing more and more control of the situation. "I mean, we haven't known each other that long."

"Now you owe me two apologies," Louisa sniffed. "Let's get you changed. You smell like machine oil from that dreadfully overstated carriage your beau drives. Do you keep your wardrobe locked?"

"No, of course not." Alice straightened again and clapped her hands. "I need an at-home dress. My blue one, please."

The automatons rushed to open the wardrobe and bring out Alice's dress, which glided through the air like a ghost. Another automaton dashed up to pry open Alice's shoes while a flier zipped around behind to start on her back buttons. Inscribed on the flier's side were the words *Love, Aunt Edwina*.

"I'll do that. Thank you." Louisa brushed the whirling machine aside. "So this is how you got ready for the ball without the help of a maid. They're so well designed, darling. The work of a genius."

"You said that." Alice stepped out of her shoes and carriage dress, and Louisa set to work on the stubborn crinolines. "They make Father uncomfortable. That's why I usually keep them up here."

"A shame. Lift your arms, darling. Why have I never heard of this aunt Edwina?"

"She lives like a hermit on a small estate on the edge of London."

"Did she make these automatons so you could put them together? Is she a . . . clockworker?"

"Louisa! Certainly not! She's been sending me automatons since my teenage years. If she had contracted the clockwork plague back then, she would have died years ago."

"True, darling, true. I didn't mean to offend. What was she like? I'm dying to know."

"I barely knew her, to tell the truth, though in some ways I feel I know her very well." And she found herself telling Louisa the entire story, including the death of her brother, mother, and fiancé, even though Louisa doubtless knew most of it.

"I'm so sorry," Louisa said when she finished. "It's unfair."

"It *is*." Alice pulled the last crinoline layer off and tossed it aside with a vehemence that surprised even herself. "Sometimes I think the worst of it isn't that everyone died—I've learned to cope with that—but that, though I'm good with machines, as a woman of quality, I can't do anything with my talent. My only hope for a decent life is to persuade Norbert Williamson to propose marriage, and I don't even like him very much."

"Oh dear. So the lovebirds rumor . . . ?"

Alice dropped onto the bed. "I *should* love him, Louisa. He's rich. He's intelligent. He's not bad-looking. He seems utterly smitten with me—or with the family title; I'm not sure which. But I feel nothing. Nothing at all."

"You hardly need to," Louisa pointed out. "You said you can't look for work, but it sounds as though you're interviewing for the position of rich man's wife."

"You make it sound so mercenary."

"I'm not judging you, darling. But let's talk about something more pleasant. Tell me what this is." She picked up a bit of pasteboard from the workbench. "*Miss Glenda Teasdale, Third Ward*, and the square root of two. What on earth?"

"Oh, er . . ." Alice flushed again. Louisa had an absolute genius for ferreting out awkwardness. "On the way home from the ball, I had an unfortunate encounter with a plague zombie or two. Miss Teasdale and . . . and some friends of hers rescued me."

"*What?*" Louisa's squawk sent the automatons skittering about the room. "Now listen here—I pride myself on knowing everything of interest that goes on in London. Heaven knows I have nothing else to do. But in one afternoon I learn you have a brilliant aunt who managed to escape my notice, and we add to that a zombie attack? Alice!"

"It's all right," Alice said, rushing to reassure her. "I wasn't hurt." She found herself telling yet another story while Louisa sat rapt on the bed. It felt oddly palliative to relate even these scandalous events out loud.

"What a fascinating adventure! Shouldn't you write this Teasdale woman?" Louisa asked when Alice finished.

It was such an unexpected question, though Alice realized she should be used to them from Louisa by now. "It's not a proper thing for a lady. I'm only glad no one found out about the entire sordid affair. Mr. Williamson would no doubt drop his suit immediately."

"There *are* worse things," Louisa sniffed.

A dreadful thought struck Alice. "Louisa, you must promise you won't tell anyone. This is all in strictest confidence. It would ruin me."

"Not a word, I promise," Louisa said, raising her right hand. "Besides, who would believe that an up-and-coming baroness single-handedly defeated a clockworker and a horde of zombies?"

"Stop that! I did no such thing."

"That's not the way I would tell it," she said, then added hastily, "If you let me. But I won't. Well, darling, I really should go. Visiting you delivers a number of shocks to the system, and I find myself in need of a lie-down." She smiled. "I have to say I find it quite refreshing. Quite Ad Hoc. Call. On. Me."

And she left.

Nearly a fortnight later, Alice was bringing morning tea into her father's study, where he was reading a letter.

"I was just going to call you in," he said. "We've something to discuss."

"Tea first, Father," she said, setting the tray next to him. "The doctor said you've been losing weight. I want you to eat everything on this tray."

"Yes, my dear." He set the letter on the desk with a spidery hand and reached for bread and butter. Alice, who knew his every gesture, noted how slow and heavy the simple movement had become, however much she didn't want to admit it. How much longer did he have? The thought of his absence made her throat thick, and she forced herself to look elsewhere. A bit of paper on the desk caught her eye—a business letter across which someone had scrawled *Final Notice* in red ink. Alice bit the inside of her cheek. Tonight she would slip down to the study and see which bills were the worst. Tomorrow she would take two or three of the little automatons into town and sell them to stave off the creditors for a few more weeks.

And when those weeks were over?

"I'm worried, Alice," Arthur said, echoing her own thoughts.

She sank onto a low stool next to his wheelchair. "About what, Father?"

"You. I need to know you're taken care of before I pass away, my dear."

"Father." She took his light, thin hand. "You'll bury us all."

"I don't want to," he said almost peevishly. "I'm tired, Alice. I'm tired of worrying about money and about this dreadful little house and about your future. I can't . . . go until I know someone will be able to take care of you."

"I can take care of myself, you know," she said.

"There's care and there's care," Arthur replied with a small smile. He sipped his tea and continued. "I just received an important letter. Our Mr. Williamson has expressed a deepening interest in you, and he has invited you to his town house for luncheon today. He's sending his carriage for you."

"Luncheon?" Alice asked. "Unchaperoned?"

"Oh no," Arthur said. "Norbert—Mr. Williamson—said there will be a chaperone, and I believe him. He and I have exchanged several letters and held numerous conversations about you, and I believe his intentions honorable." His face remained expressionless, but Alice caught the tremor in his hands. "You might change your dress."

"Oh?" Alice said, then realized what he meant. "Oh!"

Sometime later, the ostentatious automatic horse and carriage pulled up to Norbert Williamson's London town house on Hill Street not far from Berkeley Square. Alice, seated alone within the machine, looked at the four-storied brick structure and tried to hide her awe. She had never visited this place. Even being here now made her uncomfortable, and she glanced up and down the wide, busy street to see if anyone was taking notice of her. The mechanical horse halted neatly at the front door, responding to a command it must have been given previously, and for a moment Alice was distracted by an inappropriate urge—not her first one—to take the horse and carriage apart to peer inside. The machine was so sleek and fine, hiding its secret workings and machinations beneath a coating of bronze and copper.

The front door opened, and two men in their forties emerged, donning high hats and smoothing their jackets like second skins. Their movements were brisk and businesslike as they strode down the short flight of steps to the street and turned to leave. Alice watched them go, trying to figure out what their presence meant, and failing. Unease made her shift in her seat. An Ad Hoc lady might enter a bachelor's home unchaperoned and eat a meal there, but Alice came from a traditional family. Were other men besides Norbert still in the house? People might think Alice had come to—well, who *knew* what they would think? Alice sat in the carriage, uncertain about what to do.

An automaton followed the men out and approached

the carriage. It was dressed in gold footman's livery, and its face had been painted with human features that didn't move. It looked eerie.

"Miss Michaels," it said, extending a hand. "The master and his other lady visitor are expecting you. May I help you down?"

The mention of the other visitor flooded Alice with relief. She shook off her initial reaction to the automaton and accepted its hand down from the carriage. Talking automatons were nothing new—the many improvements made to the Babbage and Lovelace analytical engines over the years saw to that—but they *were* extremely expensive. Using one as a mere footman showed even more wealth than Alice had imagined. She felt more and more intimidated in her outdated dress and aging hat.

Stop it, she admonished herself sternly. *You are the daughter of a baron, no matter how poor, and he is a commoner, no matter how wealthy. He's asking for your hand in—* She stopped that line of thought, not wanting to bring a jinx. *He's begging you to grace his home with your presence, so act like a proper woman of your position.*

The footman led Alice up the steps and held the door open for her; she swept past as if it didn't exist. Here she halted again. The house's interior was stunning. High ceilings, marble floors, electric lighting, a grand staircase that swept upward from the entry foyer. Then Alice regained her composure long enough to let the footman take her coat and gloves and lead her through the house. They passed a number of large rooms—a ballroom, a conservatory, a library, a dining hall—all of them spotlessly kept, with up-to-the-moment furnishings. What tugged at Alice's attention was the army of automatons. They were breathtaking, even thrilling, in their numbers. Machines of all shapes and sizes scampered, flittered, and crawled everywhere. They waxed floors, dusted shelves, and folded linens. A few were human-shaped, mostly feminine and dressed in a variety of maid uniforms, which Alice found odd—most people required their servants to dress alike. One of the maids wore a scandalously low- and high-cut dress that Alice imagined was meant to be French. Well, once she was mistress of this house, that would—

No, no. Best not to get her hopes too high.

The footman brought her to a sitting room where Norbert Williamson was waiting at a small table laid with linen, crystal, and china for two. He rose when she entered.

"Miss Michaels," he said, bowing over her hand with exaggerated formality. "I hope your journey here was pleasant."

"It was, Mr. Williamson." Alice found her heart beating a little more quickly as he moved suavely to seat her. Did that mean she felt what she thought she was feeling? How did one know one was in love? Perhaps it was possible to only *think* one was in love without truly being in love. More importantly, did it matter?

"And this is Mrs. Leeds." He gestured toward an armchair in the corner, where an old woman dressed in black sat knitting. A pot of tea occupied a low table next to her. Mrs. Leeds inclined her head and kept knitting as Norbert introduced Alice. "Mrs. Leeds is the mother of my factory manager, and she kindly agreed to be our chaperone today."

"Pleased to meet you," Alice said.

Mrs. Leeds nodded again.

"She's already eaten, so it'll be just the two of us at table." Norbert spun a crank on a box sitting on a nearby sideboard, and a gentle, harplike melody emerged, played with overly exact precision. "I know how much you enjoy music. I hope you like this."

"Thank you," Alice lied. "I do."

One of the mechanical maids—not, Alice was relieved to see, the one in the French outfit—rolled in a cart and served poached salmon followed by an endive salad. Alice ate without tasting and responded to Norbert's conversation automatically. Throughout, Mrs. Leeds knitted without a word. Finally, Alice laid down her fork.

"Mr. Williamson," she said, "I have to say I don't feel entirely comfortable. Mrs. Leeds seems to be very nice, but I don't know her, and I'm not sure it's proper for—"

He held up a hand to interrupt. "I apologize. We can make it more proper." He pressed a button on a control box that sat on the table at his elbow. Instantly, the maid stepped forward. A small trapdoor at her stomach opened and an arm telescoped from the cavity within bearing a little velvet box. The arm laid the box on the table in front of Alice and sucked itself back into the maid's body. Before Alice could react further, the box popped open, revealing a gold ring with a large emerald stone.

"I've already discussed matters with your father," Norbert said. "If you will accept this small token, we can be married next summer. I was thinking June or July."

"A year is a good engagement," Alice said, picking up the ring and slipping it on her forefinger. "How large a wedding do we want?"

"I'm not much for ceremonies," Norbert said. "I have no relatives—or rather, none I'd want to invite. You?"

"Just my father. And Louisa Creek, I suppose. She could be my maid of honor." The emerald made a heavy weight on Alice's finger. "I wouldn't mind a small ceremony."

"Splendid!" Norbert rubbed his hands together. "I'll draw up the announcement for the *Times* and handle the other details, and you can eat all your lunches here without distress—or Mrs. Leeds. A fiancée doesn't need a chaperone."

"True," Alice said dazedly. "True."

Mrs. Leeds continued to knit.

"And, just so you know, once we're married, you needn't worry about your father's debts. You will, of course, move here afterward and take over running the household. It's so difficult to manage both the factory and this home. You *can* manage a large household, can't you?"

"I can look after household accounts, entertain, and supervise servants, yes," Alice said. "I did attend the correct schools. But are all your servants automatons?"

"At this house they are. Your skill with machines is one reason I pursued you, after all. I can hire a hundred engineers at my factory, but in my private home"—he leaned forward—"certain aspects of my life require delicacy and privacy."

"I see," Alice said, though she didn't. The maid didn't move.

"My country estate, on the other hand, is staffed with living servants—the villagers mistrust automatons. We'll spend autumns and winters there, and when our first son is born, he will inherit both your father's title and my lands, meaning the Michaels family will once again be landed nobility. Is that satisfactory?"

"Perfectly, Mr. Williamson," Alice said.

"You must call me Norbert," he replied with a smile. "We are engaged."

"Oh!" she said again. "It's still sinking in. Norbert. And you must call me Alice."

"Alice. Dear Alice." He reached across the table and took her hand. "You've barely responded. What do you think of all this?"

A dozen responses flicked through Alice's mind. She had accomplished her goal, that of persuading Norbert to propose to her. Father would be elated that he wouldn't have to worry about her fate, and those horrible, crushing debts that had dogged them for a dozen years would vanish with a flick of Norbert's pen. She should feel ecstatic, or at least happy. And she *was* happy. Quite glad. Relieved. Well, relieved wasn't the same as glad, and glad wasn't the same as happy, but she did feel this was a positive step. With a start, she realized Norbert hadn't actually *asked* her to marry him and she hadn't actually said she would. Yet here they were discussing banns and estates, children and heirs, business and machines. It certainly wouldn't be politic to point out the omission.

"It's so much to take in." Alice squeezed his hand. "But I'm thrilled, Norbert. Absolutely thrilled."

"Congratulations," Mrs. Leeds said. Alice started. It was the first word the woman had spoken, and Alice had quite forgotten she was there.

"We must celebrate!" Norbert said. "It's a bit early in the day for a mixed drink, but it's never too early for champagne, eh?" He pressed another button, and the footman arrived with a dark bottle in a silver ice bucket. Behind trotted a familiar figure.

"Click?" Alice said. "What on earth are you doing here?"

Click jumped up to the tabletop, nearly upsetting Alice's salmon plate. He opened his mouth, and a man's voice said, "'Dear Miss Michaels: I hope this letter finds you and your father in good health and good spirits. I am solicitor to your esteemed aunt Edwina, and I must request your presence at a most urgent meeting. It is with great hope I request that you come to my office with all haste at your earliest possible convenience. Your dutiful servant, Harold Stoneworthy.'" An address followed, and Click closed his mouth. Alice stared in mute astonishment.

"Extraordinary," Norbert murmured.

"I didn't know he could do that," Alice said, curiosity and surprise both warring for supremacy in her breast. "Norbert, I'm sorry, but this appears to be an emergency and I must leave. Can your footman call me a cab, or—"

"Nonsense! I'll accompany you in my carriage."

"Thank you," Alice said, "but I think this is a private matter, and although you're my fiancé, we aren't yet married, and I suspect Mr. Stoneworthy won't speak with you. It would be silly for you to ride all the way down there and then sit in his waiting room, darling."

"Hm. I suppose you're right," Norbert said, apparently mollified by Alice's use of the word *darling*. "But I shall send you in my carriage, nonetheless. And now that I think of it, I should have one built for you, as a wedding present, perhaps."

"Oh! I'm overwhelmed." Alice got to her feet, and Norbert leapt to his. Mrs. Leeds finished a row and unwound more yarn. "And I really must go."

"Do I get a good-bye kiss?" he asked, moving around the table.

"My goodness, I suppose you do. Darling."

Her first kiss. Norbert cupped her face gently in both hands and leaned in. Alice waited, not knowing what to expect. She had read a number of romantic novels, of course, and she had long come to suspect that, lurid descriptions to the contrary, real kissing couldn't possibly transport either party to the gates of ecstasy and back. Still, she found herself hoping, even through the soft click of Mrs. Leeds's knitting needles. Norbert's lips softly brushed hers

—and then he pulled away. "Thank you, darling. Let me know what the solicitor says, would you?"

The horse and carriage delivered Alice and Click to the offices of Stoneworthy, Marvins, and Lott, a tastefully small brownstone with an equally small sign hanging near the door. As Alice alighted, a flicker of motion caught the tail of her eye, and she glanced upward. On the roof one building over from the law office was a familiar figure. It wore a long brown coat, and a white skull mask covered the upper half of its face. The figure grinned its wide, dreadful grin and waved at Alice. A cold finger slid down Alice's spine. She cast about, but no one else on the street seemed to notice the figure, and no policemen were in sight. Before Alice could react further, the figure threw a small package into the air over the street. Alice shouted a warning, but it was lost in a loud boom as the package exploded. Horses reared in harnesses. People screamed and covered their ears or ran for cover. Alice ducked into the doorway of the law office with Click hiding beneath her skirts as a shower of little papers fell like snowflakes. She caught one.

Written on one side was a musical staff with a single interval: a C and an F-sharp. On the back were the words I REMEMBER.

Alice gasped and looked up at the rooftop, but the figure was gone. Heart pounding, Alice hurried into the law office, where a clerk who seemed oblivious to the goings-on outside immediately showed her and Click into Mr. Stoneworthy's private sanctuary, an office laid with carpet and lined with books. The desk was piled so high with papers that Alice could barely see the round figure of Mr. Stoneworthy on the other side.

"So good of you to come so quickly, Miss Michaels," he said in a surprisingly flutelike voice. Someone so rotund and white-haired should have a deep voice. "Are you quite all right? I heard some sort of commotion outdoors."

"I'll be fine," she said. "It was nothing." But she couldn't help wondering what the figure—the clockworker who had controlled the zombies—meant by *I remember*. A warning? A simple greeting? If he had wanted to harm her, he had every opportunity while she was walking obliviously past. And how had he known where she would be? Perhaps he had been following her or spying on her in some other way. The thought turned her stomach.

"You're looking positively peaked, Miss Michaels," said Mr. Stoneworthy. "Would you like some refreshment?"

"I've just come off lunch, but thank you," Alice said, pushing thoughts of the clockworker away, which only allowed the reason for her visit to catch up with her. A call for an emergency visit to Aunt Edwina's solicitor could only mean dreadful news, and although Alice hadn't seen Aunt Edwina in more than a dozen years, she still felt a certain fondness for the woman, strange and estranged though she was. Nausea gave way to dread. Click sat next to her chair, his tail curled nonchalantly about his legs.

"Then I won't keep you in suspense," Mr. Stoneworthy said. He coughed into a handkerchief, belying the promise he had just made. "Pardon. I'm afraid it is my duty to inform you that you are the sole heir to the estate of your aunt Edwina."

The chair rocked beneath Alice's body, and she gripped the arms tightly. Tears welled in her eyes, and her throat thickened. Surprised at the strength of her reaction, she could only murmur, "Good heavens."

Mr. Stoneworthy looked supremely uncomfortable. "Yes. Perhaps you would like some brandy?" Without waiting for an answer, he raised his voice. "Dickerson! Some brandy for Miss Michaels!"

A glass was pushed into her hand, and Alice drank without thinking. The brandy, her first, burned all the way down and pushed away the tears. She felt more able to speak. "How did she . . . pass away? And when? And why wasn't my father notified?"

"She hasn't died, exactly," Mr. Stoneworthy said. "She's missing."

"Missing? I don't understand."

Mr. Stoneworthy coughed into his handkerchief again, and this time Alice caught him peeking at the contents. She hoped he didn't have consumption, or worse, the clockwork plague. "You're probably aware that your aunt was a bit . . . eccentric, yes?"

"She has her ways," Alice said, feeling suddenly defensive.

"One of those *ways* was to send a letter to this office every month. I was instructed that if the letter should fail to arrive for twelve consecutive months, I was to execute her will. It names you as the sole heir to her estate."

"So she's definitely not dead?" Alice demanded. Click made a mechanical mew at her feet.

"I frankly don't know," Mr. Stoneworthy replied blandly. "I'm merely following her instructions."

"But I'm . . . I can't inherit her estate!"

He put on a pair of reading glasses that made him look like Father Christmas and examined a long piece of paper. "You are Miss Alice Michaels, daughter of Arthur, Baron Michaels, of London?"

"Yes."

"You have reached the age of majority?"

Was that his way of asking if she were a spinster? Slightly affronted, she said, "Yes."

"And you are unmarried."

"Now see here—"

"Meaning," Mr. Stoneworthy said, "you have no husband who would take over the property in your place?"

Her thoughts went to Norbert, but he wasn't her husband yet. "That's right. But my father—"

"Is specifically banned from having any part of this," Mr. Stoneworthy finished for her with another cough into the handkerchief. "That part took some legal work, but it's all arranged. The house and grounds are yours. Unfortunately, there is no monetary portion to the estate, but once the final legal hurdles are cleared, you could sell."

"How long will that take?" Alice asked faintly.

"Four or five months, if no one contests the will, but you can take possession now, if you like. Here are the keys and a card with the address. Have you ever visited the house?"

"No, I'm afraid not. Do I need to sign anything?"

"Indeed. Dickerson!"

Alice signed a number of papers she didn't quite understand, though she did read them to make sure she wasn't accidentally signing over her firstborn child, and later found herself outside the law offices with a ring of keys in her handbag. Norbert's carriage was nowhere in sight—apparently it had some sort of command that called it home—so she hailed a cab and let Click jump in ahead of her.

With a nervous glance up and down the street for the grinning figure, Alice handed the address card to the driver and sat back to think. In the space of a few hours, she had received a marriage proposal (of sorts), intercepted a strange message from a rogue clockworker, learned that her aunt Edwina had been missing for months and had managed to declare herself dead, and inherited a large house she had never actually visited. It was all a bit much. And oh yes—she had discovered that Click could talk, after a fashion.

"When did you visit Mr. Stoneworthy's office so he could give you that message?" she demanded of the clockwork cat. "I quite forgot to ask him. And how long have you been able to reproduce a human voice?"

Click looked out the cab window with phosphorescent nonchalance. Alice made an exasperated sound as the cab rolled over the stony streets. Exasperation was easier to deal with than fear, uncertainty, or sadness. Aunt Edwina was dead. Actually, she was merely missing. Actually, she had failed to alert Mr. Stoneworthy's office in a prescribed way for one year. Perhaps she wasn't dead or truly missing at all. Perhaps she had forgotten or grown tired of the arrangement.

After twelve months? she thought. *Unlikely.*

The ride took more than an hour, and it was nearing dusk by the time the cab arrived at a high stone wall well outside of town, in a place where houses and factories gave way to trees and meadows. The wall ran nearly a hundred yards down the road before curving away and out of sight. Presumably it surrounded Aunt Edwina's house, of which only the top half was visible. Alice couldn't see much of it except the roof, or roofs. Several of them poked upward in odd places and directions. A large gate of wrought iron guarded a long driveway, and a smaller entry gate stood beside it. Coming up the road toward them was a barefoot girl of twelve leading a pony. The driver halted near the gate and helped Alice down from the cab with Click jumping down beside her. It occurred to Alice that she had no way of getting home.

"Can you please wait, driver?" she asked, paying him from her meager supply of coins. "I had no idea it would take so long to get here."

"Not unless you'll only be a moment, mum," he said. "I have to put the 'orse up for the night."

Flummoxed, Alice stared at the set of gates. She would have to go back right now. A long ride for nothing.

"Mum?" The girl leading the pony had approached. "There's a train station, mum. Less than half a mile up the road. Trains run at night, too."

"Why, thank you." Alice gave the girl a farthing from her handbag. "What's your name?"

"Gwendolyn, mum. My dad calls me Gwenny."

"Do you live nearby, Gwenny?" Alice asked.

The girl remembered herself and curtsied. "All my life, mum."

"What do you know about this house, then?"

"I'll just be going, then, mum," said the driver, who had climbed back onto the hack.

"Yes, thank you," Alice said. "If you could just—"

At that moment, beautiful violin music floated by. It pushed the air ahead of itself, floated and rippled, shivered and sighed. All three people listened, entranced. The tune was even lovelier than the music Alice had heard in the mists of Hyde Park. After a moment, Alice realized her heart was beating quickly and her mouth was dry. Click touched noses with the pony, which whickered.

"Where is that wonderful song coming from?" Alice asked.

"The house, mum," said Gwenny. "Strange lights used to flash in the windows, and we heard odd noises when I was little, but those stopped a year gone. The music is new, something like two weeks old. I don't like it. It's ghosts."

"Don't be silly," Alice said. "It's a person. Or an automaton."

"The house is empty, mum. No one lives there."

The music continued, soft and insistent. The driver clicked at the horse and the hack jerked into motion, temporarily ruining the violin. Alice was seized with a desire to slap the man for interrupting the instrument's perfection.

"What about the lady Edwina?" Alice said. "The woman who lived here?"

"The strange lady, mum? I only heard about her. She never kept no servants, and we always stayed away."

"Hm. Would you consider coming inside with me? I might have a coin or two for you."

"Me, mum?" The girl backed away. "I'm sorry, mum, but I couldn't. Not ever." And she fled, taking the pony with her and leaving Alice alone on the road.

The sweet strings continued to play. Alice couldn't think where she'd heard anything more perfect for a spring evening in the country, odd and unexplained though it was. If no people were in the house, it must be an automaton or perhaps a reproduction. Click had come from this house, and he had recently shown an ability to reproduce a human voice. It stood to reason that whoever had created him could do the same with music.

Alice drew the key ring from her handbag and sorted through the cold bits of iron until she found one that would open the little entry gate next to the large main one. When she tried to use the key, however, she discovered the entry gate's lock twisted and broken, the gate itself slightly ajar. Mystified and a little nervous, she pushed through with Click at her heels and followed the crunching gravel driveway toward the manor.

The house was a rambling affair, clearly put together and added to over at least a hundred years. A stone building squatted in the center with wooden additions piled all about it. Several outbuildings dotted the overgrown gardens, and an attached tower rose up behind. The cool evening air smelled of damp grass intermingled with decaying flowers. The violin music continued, but Alice couldn't pin-point the source. She climbed the uneven front steps to the main doors and found them ajar as well. What on earth? Hesitantly, she pushed them open and entered the darkness beyond.

The moment she crossed the threshold, lights blazed to life, revealing a huge room three stories tall. It was filled with machinery that swooped to life with a great, grinding hum. Giant gears whirled; pendulums swung; huge pistons dipped and soared. Spidery automatons far more complex than the ones Alice had at home skittered everywhere on mysterious errands. In the corner, a giant arm swung back and forth with a loud, steady ticking sound. It was like standing inside a three-story clock. Alice glanced down at Click, who was watching the intricate metal dance with twitching tail and glowing eyes. Only one sort of person could have built all this.

"Aunt Edwina *was* a clockworker," Alice breathed. "But how?"

That was when she saw the pool of blood.

Chapter Six

Alice supposed she should scream or faint or flee, but really, what was the point? Blood couldn't hurt her, unless she slipped in it and fell. Besides, it was long since dry. Red-brown smears of it smudged the floorboards nearby.

"Good heavens, Click," she said. "What happened?"

She stepped forward to get a better look, but Click abruptly threw himself in front of her shins, nearly tripping her. "Click! What in the world are you—"

The door slammed shut behind her, and a pair of pistons leapt out of opposite walls. Their blunt ends smashed together at head height directly in front of Alice, right over the blood pool. The crash nearly knocked Alice off her feet, and she dropped her handbag. The pistons sucked themselves back into the walls again, leaving behind nothing but a waft of stale air.

"Oh," Alice murmured. "Oh."

That explained the blood. Now that she knew what to look for, she could make out the faint outline of a square cut into the floor directly in front of her—a section that was no doubt sensitive to pressure. Click looked up at her reproachfully.

"Yes," Alice said. "I do need to be more careful. Thank you, Click."

Satisfied, Click sat down while Alice studied the room and the noisy clockwork machinery. Did the blood belong to Aunt Edwina? Somehow she doubted it. Aunt Edwina had built the trap, and while it was possible she had been caught in it herself, it seemed unlikely. Of course, that left open the question of whose blood it was and what had happened to the body.

She tried the door. Locked, and from a drop bar on the other side, if she were any judge. Nothing she could open with the materials in her handbag. And all the windows were high off the floor. In any case, fleeing the house would leave many mysteries unsolved, including what had happened to Aunt Edwina, why she had left her house to Alice under such odd circumstances, and who was playing that amazing violin. No doubt everything was intertwined.

Alice retrieved her handbag and continued to study the room. Clockworkers were known for their paranoia, and where there was one trap, there would be others. The trouble was, such traps could be small or large, obvious or subtle. It might appear impossible that any one person could build so much, but clockworkers had two advantages over normal humans. One was that they needed little sleep. The plague that focused their minds also served to keep them awake, which, some theorized, contributed to their instability. The other advantage came in the form of progressive automatons. A clockworker might build an automaton, which might then tirelessly assist with the building of another automaton, and then another and another, each one exponentially adding to the amount of work that the clockworker could accomplish until the clockworker finally burnt out. Alice was looking at several years' worth of work.

This brought up another question—Aunt Edwina's continued survival. No clockworker Alice had ever heard of lived very long. Charles Babbage, the most famous clockworker in history, caught the clockwork plague in 1837 and died only two years later, just after he created the analytic engines that made modern automatons possible. The great composer Wolfgang Mozart, one of the first recorded clock-workers, wrote stunning operas and piano concertos in the final year of his life before the clockwork plague claimed him in 1791, only six months after he caught it. Many wondered what both men might have created had the plague allowed them to live longer. Aunt Edwina, on the other hand, had sent Alice her first automaton for her sixteenth birthday—five years ago. Could Aunt Edwina have been infected with clockwork plague all this time? It would certainly explain the interior of the house, though it wouldn't explain how she had survived the plague for so long.

Alice continued to think. If Aunt Edwina had wanted Alice to have the house, she wouldn't have created it in such a way that Alice wouldn't be able take possession of it. There had to be a way to circumvent the traps, or shut them down. On the other hand, clockworkers didn't think the way normal people did, and what made sense to one of them appeared mad to everyone else. A clockworker might think it perfectly sensible to help someone by killing him.

Machinery parts large and small continued to swing, drop, turn, and clank in the clockwork mansion, but the violin music filtered through the noise. Alice was finally able to pinpoint a direction—the back of the building. Very well, then, that was where she would go.

A pair of automatons rushed past her, creating a slight breeze with the speed of their passing. Three spiders clicked forward, paused, clicked forward, paused. A man-sized gear rolled along its track while pistons popped up and down out of the floor behind it. Alice pursed her lips and studied the system carefully. Even assuming there were no more traps laid—and she wasn't ready to assume that—the clockwork machinery took up quite a lot of the floor space, and it was always moving. Any bit of it could easily crush her. But the more she studied the place, the more she began to see a regularity, a pattern. A series of deep grooves was cut into the floor, and the automatons moved through the grooves in specific ways. Even the ones that flew followed the floor grooves. And the fact that the automatons moved throughout the room without harm told her she could, too.

When another automaton passed close by, a slower one, Alice leapt over the pressure square and, grateful she had chosen a simple dress for her luncheon with Norbert, landed behind the machine so she could follow it exactly. Her heart beat fast with fear and excitement. Another leap and step brought her behind the trio of spidery automatons skittering in another direction. She paused when they did, ducked beneath a swinging pendulum that would have brained her, twirled on her toes, and made a fast turn to stay behind the spidery trio. A few more steps brought her to the bottom of a staircase that circled the back wall, where she paused to catch her breath. No more traps triggered so far.

After a moment's thoughtful stare at the staircase, she put the wooden handle of her handbag in her mouth, flung herself astride the banister, and hauled herself hand over hand up its length. The process looked ridiculous and immodest, she was sure, but no one was around to see, so what did it matter? Better that than to risk an unhappy surprise on the stairs.

A certain amount of exertion got her to the top, breathless and panting around the handbag handle. Click was waiting for her on the final stair.

"How did you get up here?" she demanded.

Click didn't answer. Grumbling to herself, Alice clambered down from the banister. She was standing on a balcony that encircled the great room. A quarter of the way round, a set of double doors stood partly ajar. Below her, the automatons, pendulums, and ticking machinery continued in their strange, intricate dance on the grooved floor. The pattern hovered at the edge of recognition, but the longer Alice stared at it, the more her head began to hurt. Instead, she closed her eyes and listened carefully. The sweet violin music she had heard earlier seemed to be coming from beyond the double doors farther along the balcony.

Alice started carefully across the wood floor. One of the boards shifted beneath her foot, and she leapt back. Nothing further happened. Alice drew her skirts back and tapped at the flooring with a quick foot. Still nothing. She prodded harder. This time an entire section of the floor tilted and flipped over on a pivot. Alice barely had time to yank her foot back and catch a glimpse of the yawning space beneath the boards before they smashed back into place.

"Hm," she said. "Who were you expecting to break in here, Aunt Edwina?" Then she glanced down at the faraway smear of dried blood on the floor near the front door. "And did they manage it?"

The crack left by the pivot trap was now visible, and there was just enough room at the side, near the wall, for a careful person to edge around it. Thanking heaven her bustle was small, Alice pressed her back and hindquarters close to the wall and scooted around the deadly trap. The automatons below continued to ignore her. Alice cleared the dangerous section of flooring, which lay just before the double doors, and checked carefully for trip wires or anything else that might cause a messy death. She found nothing, so she stepped through and found herself on another balcony, this one overlooking a cobblestoned courtyard large enough to play rugby on. To one side, attached to a wall, rose the tower she had seen outside, from the front of the house. A narrow window toward the top glowed, and Alice heard the violin play. To her astonishment, she recognized the song as the one from Hyde Park. The wistful tune created an intense longing inside her, a desire for something she couldn't name, a feeling that she was in the wrong place or the wrong time, but that the right place and the right time were just a step around the corner.

A touch on her ankle gave her a start. Click looked up at

THE DOOMSDAY VAULT 109

her quizzically, and she realized she'd been staring at the tower, mesmerized.

"That can't be the same player I heard in the mist, can it?" she asked him.

Click cocked his head, then put out a steel-wool tongue and washed a paw with little scratching sounds.

Alice sighed and started down a set of stone stairs that led to the courtyard lit by a half-moon. A high wall ran all the way around the yard, and small gargoyles glared from the top. The ground was immaculate—no cracks in the mortar, no weeds or ivy sprouting anywhere.

Gingerly, Alice made her way across the courtyard. Click walked ahead of her, segmented tail straight up, claws clicking on the stones. As she came closer to the tower, she realized that the dozen-odd gargoyles staring down from the top of the wall were made of metal, not stone. Their iron glare made her uneasy, and her mouth went dry. The musician played on, his melancholy music the perfect accompaniment to the eerie night.

Click reached the base of the tower and flopped down on his side with a *clank*. Alice looked up. A shadow hovered in the window high above her. Her heart beat staccato, and feelings she couldn't name shifted inside her.

"Hello?" she called.

The music squawked and stopped. The shadow in the window shifted, and out leaned a young man, not yet twenty. Alice couldn't tell more than that in the moonlight.

"Hi!" the young man called back. "Are you here to rescue me?"

That made Alice blink. "Er . . . do you need rescuing?"

"Yes, please. I've been in this tower for . . . well, I don't know how long. At least two weeks, I think. I can't get out. I've been playing like crazy, hoping someone would hear me and come."

"Are you an American?" Alice asked, and immediately wished she hadn't. It was such an inane thing to say.

"Boston. Are you English?"

"Of course." The entire situation made Alice feel oddly sideways. "I don't normally speak to strange men when I first meet them, you know, however extraordinary the circumstances may be."

"Sorry! I'm Gavin Ennock. I'd shake your hand, but I can't quite reach."

Alice stifled an unladylike snort of a laugh. "I understand, Mr. Ennock. My name is Alice Michaels. This is Click, my cat."

"He's very nice. I don't think I've ever seen a clockwork cat before. Can he help get me out?"

"That depends. Er . . . who put you up there?"

"No idea. Two men knocked me out, and when I came to, I was here. The door's locked, and little automatons bring me food."

"Were you playing in Hyde Park two weeks ago?" Alice blurted out. "In the mist?"

Gavin drew back, wary. "Why?"

Because you played like an angel, and I can't imagine a world so cruel as to lock such a wonder away. "Because I think I heard you."

"That was probably me. I'm the only busker stupid enough to play Hyde Park on foggy days. Can you get me out? I've tried everything."

"I'll do my best." Alice realized her heart was pounding and her hands were shaking. That bothered her. Was she surprised at finding an inhabitant in the tower? Not particularly. She knew *someone* was up there playing music—the most wonderful, soul-melting music she had ever heard. And it was played by the same musician she had heard in Hyde Park. The idea that she now had the chance to meet this fine fiddler sent shivers over her entire body, which bothered her again.

Was it a coincidence that this particular young man had

been imprisoned in Aunt Edwina's house? Or was something else going on here? The questions nagged at Alice, but she had maddeningly little information and a mind that was distracted by a young musician she hadn't even met. Firmly she ordered herself to get a grip and look at the problem. Where was the tower entrance? She hoped it wasn't inside the mansion.

It wasn't. She found it halfway round the tower, just out of sight. It was made of tired-looking wood and locked, of course. Alice rummaged around in her handbag and came up with a small set of tools rolled in black velvet. Embroidered into the soft cloth were the words *Love, Aunt Edwina*. Alice extracted two bits of metal.

"Click," she said, "light, please."

There was a *pop*, and two bright phosphorescent beams lit the lock. It was shaped like a clock. If the hands were set to a particular time, Alice could doubtless unlock it without a key, rather like knowing the combination to a safe. It was ingenious—and fiendishly difficult to pick. Peering into the keyhole, she could also make out two little needles on springs. No doubt they were coated with some dreadful poison. Alice stood up and stared at the door, hands on hips.

"Well, really," she said, and kicked it with all her might. The tired old wood smashed inward. *Hmph.* Clockworkers might be wonder geniuses, but sometimes they focused so tightly on the details, they forgot the bigger picture.

"Are you all right?" Gavin called from above in his odd American accent. "I heard a noise."

"Everything's fine, Mr. Ennock," Alice replied as Click shone his glowing eye beams inside. "I've found a way in."

The interior of the tower was hollow, with a single wooden staircase winding a spiral around the inside wall. The edge of the stairs had a foot-high rim at the base instead of a handrail, which Alice found strange. It wouldn't keep anyone from toppling over the side. At the top, Alice made out a landing and another door. She didn't trust the stairs for a moment, but she didn't see any other alternative.

"Click," she said, "would you run up there and see what happens?"

The clockwork cat bounded up the steps and made the first turn. A moment later, there was a wooden clatter, and the stairs all flattened into a spiral slide. With an indignant yowl, Click skidded past Alice and clanked to a halt a few feet from the door. His eye beams went out as Alice bent over him.

"Are you hurt?"

Click straightened, one limb at a time, and shook himself. Then he deliberately turned his back on Alice and sat down.

"Oh, Click, dear, I'm so sorry," Alice said. "Can you forgive me?"

Click's tail twitched a dismissal.

"I'll give you a piece of steel wool when we get home; how's that?"

No reaction.

Alice sighed. "Very well. You may play with my magnets first thing tomorrow morning."

Click turned his head but didn't look at her.

"*And* the steel wool."

Click stalked to the bottom of the slide, sniffed at the bottom, then sank all eighteen brass claws into the wood and clattered his way upward like a careful feline spider. In moments, he had climbed out of view.

"That's very clever," Alice called after him, "but it doesn't get *me* up there. Do you see a lever or a button or a—"

Clank. With another clatter, the slide re-formed itself back into steps. Alice clutched at her handbag. "Is it safe to come up, then?"

She heard a mechanical meow from the darkness above.

"Was that a yes or a no?"

She heard another meow.

With a sigh, Alice climbed the steps, taking her time and testing each one. It was exhausting work, but she refused to take chances. About halfway up, she found Click on a landing near a lever. It was pushed upward and pointed toward a sign that read OFF. Other choices included ON, EXPEL, and DEATH. Alice wondered what the original setting had been.

"You're a very clever cat," she said.

They continued to the top of the stairs and the door Alice had seen earlier. She knocked politely. "Mr. Ennock?"

He knocked back. "I'm still here." His voice was muffled. "Can you open the door from that side?"

She threw the bar, but the door itself was still locked, and no convenient key hung from any nearby hook. A quick examination of the lock showed it to be another poisoned time lock, but this door looked distressingly solid.

"I'm afraid it won't budge," Alice said. "Just a moment. Click, give me your left forepaw, please."

Click held up the appendage indicated, and it clattered to the floor. Alice took it up, depressed a hidden switch, and all six claws extended with a little *shwing* noise. She inserted a claw into the lock.

"Are you trying to pick it?" Gavin asked from the other side.

"No." Alice heard a *sproing* and a *clink*. She withdrew the paw to peer into the lock, where she found to her satisfaction that both needles had deployed against the hard brass of Click's claw and paw, harmlessly discharging the poison and bending the needles into ruin to boot. "Much better." She handed the paw back to Click, who reattached it, and checked with the lock again.

"Light, if you please, Click."

With another *pop*, Click illuminated the door. Alice unrolled her tools again and this time set to work for real. Her own automatons came with little locks meant to hold them shut, and Alice had assembled dozens of locking mechanisms over the years.

"*You are trespassing on my property*," boomed a woman's voice. "*You have one minute to vacate my tower, or face the consequences.*"

Alice was so startled, she dropped the lockpicks. It was Aunt Edwina's voice, though Alice only vaguely remembered it from her childhood. She glanced around for the source but saw nothing.

"What was that?" Gavin asked through the door.

"A minor problem," Alice replied. "I suggest you gather any possessions you want to bring, Mr. Ennock. Our exit is likely to be hasty."

She set back to work on the lock. A always led to B always led to C. She could do this.

"*You are trespassing on my property. You have thirty seconds to vacate my tower, or face the consequences.*"

Sweat trickled down Alice's neck and into her corset, but she ignored it and selected another tool. Click held the light steady, though she had to force her fingers not to shake.

"*You are trespassing on my property*," boomed Aunt Edwina. "*You have fifteen seconds to vacate my tower, or face the consequences.*"

The lock gave. Alice stuffed her tools into her handbag and shoved the door open. Gavin was waiting on the other side, hands empty and violin case strapped to his back. He had striking white-blond hair—no hat—eyes the color of a summer sky, and a startlingly handsome face. He also looked slightly younger than Alice had originally thought—seventeen or eighteen.

"I'm ready," he said. "And you're amazing."

"Oh!" Alice said. "Thank—"

"*You are trespassing on my property*," boomed Aunt Edwina. "*You have five seconds to vacate my tower, or face the consequences.*"

"Run!" Alice grabbed Gavin's hand and fled down the stairs. Click followed.

"What do you think will happen?" Gavin asked as they made the first turn.

A crash vibrated the steps and made them both glance over their shoulders. A vat that was painted to look like part of the wall at the top of the stairs tipped over, spilling an evil-looking liquid that gushed down the steps toward them at a dreadful speed. Even as Alice watched, it began to dissolve the wood it passed over. The low rim that ran around the edge of the stairs kept the liquid—acid?—from dripping over.

"I had to ask," Gavin shouted.

"Hurry!" Alice shrieked. She flung her handbag over the side, grabbed her skirts in both hands, and bolted as fast as she dared. Gavin and Click kept pace with her, though the acid was gaining on them like a hungry sea creature.

"We'll never make it!" Gavin yelled.

"Just run!" Alice yelled back.

They made the second turn, and the third. The acid gushed around the curves, losing a little speed, but it was plain it would sweep over them long before they reached the bottom. It filled the entire stairwell behind them in an area too large to consider jumping over, and there was no space on the stairs to let it go by. The smell was sickening. Alice's lungs burned and her shins ached. Gavin's face became grim.

"I'm sorry I brought you into this!" he shouted as they made the fourth turn, the one with the lever on it. "If I had known—"

Alice shoved the lever to EXPEL. Instantly, the stairs flattened into the giant slide. "Go!" Alice ordered.

Gavin didn't hesitate. He flung himself headfirst onto the smooth wood like a boy on a sled hill. Alice snatched up Click and followed just as acid flooded the landing. They rushed around the turns, much faster now and gain-

ing speed. Alice's stomach lurched, she lost her hat, and
her hair came loose. Gavin reached the bottom and slid
across the stone floor. He regained his feet with incredible
dexterity, and the moment Alice reached the bottom herself, he swept her up and moved her aside. The acid river
gushed past them and swept through the door Alice had
broken down. Panting, Gavin carefully set Alice on her
feet.

"That was . . . was . . ." He swallowed. "Do all your first
meetings with strange men go like that?"

Hoping nothing was broken, Alice retrieved her handbag from the spot where it had hit the ground, then looked
about in vain for her hat. "No, thank heavens. I think our
next step should be to—"

A terrible shuddering noise and creaking of wood made
Alice look up. Her face blanched. The damaged staircase—
slide—was coming away from the tower walls. Even as she
watched, a beam snapped and plunged toward them.

"Move!"

She wasn't entirely sure who had spoken—she herself
or Gavin. Both of them leapt for the broken doorway. They
touched down briefly in the thin film of acid left on the
stones just outside the tower, then flung themselves sideways to safer ground, where they landed in an ignominious
heap. They lay there a moment, trying to catch their breaths.
Click strolled over and nosed at Alice, who began to realize
she was huddled against Gavin in an extremely inappropriate manner. She rolled away, tangling her skirts, and scrambled to her feet. When she managed to get her breath, she
found Gavin opening his violin case, a worried look on his
face.

"Has something important happened?" she demanded,
feeling a bit put out that he hadn't offered her a hand up.

"Checking for damage," Gavin explained, removing the
instrument. "It belonged to my grandfather. So far it's sur-

vived smacking a man on the chin, playing Hyde Park in the mist, and, apparently, sliding down a madwoman's tower staircase. It's a miracle it isn't broken." He skimmed the bow across the strings.

"I'm sure I'll want to hear all the details," Alice said, surprised at how much she meant it, "but for now, I think we need to find our way back out."

He stopped playing. "Don't you know how to get out?"

"The way in was rather sticky, in more ways than one."

"Why exactly *are* you here? Do you know why *I'm* here?"

"Oh!" Alice put a hand to her mouth. "In all the excitement, I didn't have a chance to say, did I?" She gave a quick explanation about the strange conditions of Aunt Edwina's will, Alice's own meeting with the solicitor, and of how she'd tracked Gavin through the house.

"I wonder if your aunt Edwina is the woman who got me captured, the Red Velvet Lady," Gavin said when she finished. He ran his bow over the strings again in a merry lilt. "I saw her when I was brought here. Not that it matters much if we're leaving. And have you noticed that the gargoyles seem to like my playing?"

The knee-high metal gargoyles that crouched on the wall surrounding the courtyard were staring at Gavin, and their eyes glowed red.

"Why are they doing that?" Alice breathed.

"I don't know. They didn't do it when I was in the tower."

He stopped playing. The gargoyles continued to stare. Gavin took several steps toward the house, and the gargoyles' heads rotated to follow. "How did you get into the courtyard?" he asked.

"That way." Alice pointed to the double doors at the top of the balcony. "But the room beyond is filled with traps." She turned to look at the rest of the courtyard, fists on hips. Several other doors led into the main house, and a gateway had once provided a larger exit. Unfortunately, the gateway had been bricked over, and all the doors to the main house but the one Alice herself had used seemed to have iron gratings welded over them. Alice pursed her lips.

"I don't like being herded," she said. "And certainly not by a dead relative."

"Did you bring anything to cut bars or climb walls with?"

"No."

"Then we'll have to put up with being herded." He strode toward the stairs leading up to the balcony. "Are you coming?"

"Mr. Ennock!" She hurried to catch up. "We haven't properly assessed all the—"

"Look," he said without breaking his stride, "we can stand in the courtyard debating the obvious all night, or we can do something about it. I've been sitting in that tower for days, so I'm ready to act. You can act stupid and stay, if you want."

She caught his elbow. "That's no way to talk to a lady."

"I wouldn't know," Gavin said. "We've assessed there's no other way out, so let's go. Would you like my arm?"

Alice noticed she still had his elbow. "Please!" she said huffily.

"Though I sort of wonder," he added thoughtfully, "if *they* object to our leaving."

The dozen-odd gargoyles were clambering down the wall and knuckling toward them like grotesque apes. Iron fingers and feet clattered on the cobblestones.

"No more assessment," Alice said. "Quick!"

All three of them ran up the stairs. The gargoyles gained speed. They swarmed up the steps and climbed the balcony wall itself, their fingers and toes punching holds into the mortar. Gavin slammed the double doors, and Alice shot the bolt. A heavy weight slammed the other side. The door shuddered, and the bolt started to give.

"Do exactly as I do!" Alice ordered. She pressed herself

to the wall and retraced her original steps to get around the pivoting trapdoor. Gavin didn't question her, but he imitated her. Click followed more sedately as the doors cracked. Alice cleared the pivot near the top of the stairs that led down to the main room, where the automatons rushed about the grooved floor. Pendulums swung, pistons clanked, and pipes jetted steam for a purpose Alice couldn't begin to imagine, and all of it between them and the exit. Gavin stared down at it all, entranced. The double doors shook again.

"What is it?" he asked in wonderment.

"I don't know," Alice said. "But it's laced with deadly traps, and I barely got up here alive. *And* the front door is locked. Even if we got through it, we couldn't get out."

"So why did we even come in here?"

"*You* were the one who said we were done assessing," she said. There was another blow to the balcony doors. Dust trickled down from the ceiling.

Gavin didn't seem to hear her. His eyes grew vacant as he studied the noisy chaos below. "There's something I can't quite see," he said. "If I can just figure it out . . ."

The door smashed inward, and the gargoyles swarmed through, their grim faces and glaring eyes filled with metal anger, or so it seemed to Alice. Uncertain, she glanced at Gavin, who clearly wasn't registering his surroundings. The gargoyles knuckled toward them, straight over the pivot trap, which didn't budge.

Of course not, Alice thought grimly. She waited until the closest gargoyles were only a few steps away, then set her foot on the trapdoor and pressed down. Instantly, it pivoted. With a simian screech of metal across wood, most of the gargoyles plunged into the pit beneath, scrabbling ineffectively as they went. One took a swipe at Alice's dress, but she yanked herself free. The trapdoor flipped over, and they were gone. The remaining four gargoyles eyed Alice warily from the other side of the balcony.

"Come on, then, if you've a mind to," she said with more bravado than she felt. "I can probably kick your . . . assessments quite handily. Mr. Ennock, what *are* you doing?"

"Grooves in the floor with four spaces between," he muttered, "and automatons that roll across them. What's going on?"

One of the gargoyles pointed at the narrow path near the wall, the way Alice and Gavin had bypassed the trapdoor. They moved toward it, joints creaking. Click arched his back and hissed at them.

"Mr. Ennock," Alice warned, "I could use some—"

"I've got it!" Gavin said. "It's a song!"

"And how will that help us?" Alice demanded.

"The grooves in the floor are staff lines. The pendulums beat time. The automatons are the notes. They move the music forward like a player piano. So, what happens if I play it?"

The gargoyles edged along the wall, nearly halfway to them. "Try it!" Alice said. "Do it now!"

"No assessment?"

"Gavin!"

He looked over the edge, violin in hand, then raised instrument and bow and began to play. The melody was fast and complicated, in a minor key, and it made Alice think of demons dancing in a volcano. How was Gavin managing to sight-read that? The song sent shivers down her spine.

The gargoyles continued edging toward Alice. She stepped back, toward Gavin, but a few bars into the song, the gargoyles froze. Their heads, then their bodies, swiveled toward him. Each one took a step toward him like a sleepwalker caught in a lovely dream. Alice waited for the right moment, then stepped on the trapdoor again and snatched her foot back. The door pivoted, and the gargoyles vanished.

"They're gone," she said. "You can stop now."

But Gavin ignored her. The song gushed from his violin, flowing like magma down the staircase to fill the room. His handsome face remained absolutely fixed in concentration, and the tendons on his hands stood out like wires. Alice swore she felt heat radiating off him. It lapped at her skin and slid down her body. Below, the automatons sped up, but Gavin kept pace, his fingers flying across the neck. Steam gushed from the pipes, and the pistons blurred so fast, Alice couldn't tell they were moving. Toward the back of the enormous room, a hammer the size of a carthorse drew back on a spring. Now that she was aware of it, Alice could see that every movement of every automaton had become geared toward winding the spring that pulled that hammer back. The heat and speed intensified, and a trickle of blood ran down Gavin's left hand. Still he played, caught by the fiendish melody. The hammer cranked back to its full potential. Gavin played one long, long note. Alice tensed. Then Gavin stopped. He stood panting at the balcony rail, his hair mussed and his eyes wide. The automatons were frozen in place.

Alice found she was breathing hard herself, and she felt unaccountably excited.

"Why did you stop?" she whispered.

"That's it," he whispered back. "The song's over."

"But what was it *for*? Why did we go through all that—Duck!"

The hammer fell. Alice and Gavin dropped behind the balcony wall with their hands over their ears as the poll struck. The bell thundered doomsday through Alice's bones. Every window in the big room shattered, the glass falling like broken feathers to the stone floor. Gavin curled around his fiddle. Click shut his ears and pressed his nose into Alice's skirts. Alice's entire body vibrated. Her world became that one dreadful note.

And then it was over. Silence fell over the room. Alice peeped over the edge of the balcony. A few shards of glass tinkled to the floor. The motionless automatons lay scattered everywhere, and the machinery stood stock-still.

"You did it," she said. "Holy God, you did it. You were absolutely amazing."

"Was I?" Gavin uncurled and stood up. "Thanks, Alice."

She blinked, affronted. "Miss Michaels, if you please."

"You called *me* Gavin a moment ago."

"Did I?"

"Absolutely."

"I must have forgotten myself in the heat of the moment. I beg your pardon." Alice brushed her dress down and wished desperately for her hat. At least she still had her handbag. "Is it safe to go down there, do you think?"

"Nothing's moving, so probably. You could toss Click over the side and see what happens."

Alice didn't dignify that with a response, though her cheeks were still burning from her faux pas with Gavin's name. As a test, Alice nudged the pivot trapdoor. It didn't move. She stepped on it, then jumped on it. It still didn't move. "Well, this trap is frozen. That's a good sign."

They carefully descended the stairs into the main room and got no reaction from the automatons or anything else. Alice made her way back over to the bloodstain and, keeping low, prodded the floor space. The crushing pistons failed to appear. She stood and dusted her hands.

"I'm willing to say we're safe," she declared.

"If you say so." Gavin put his violin back into its case and strapped it to his back. "Are we going to explore this place or get out?"

"Since the traps are deactivated, I intend to explore," Alice said. "Aunt Edwina left me this house for a reason, and I want to find out what it is. You may do as you wish, of course."

"I don't have anything else to do," Gavin replied. "And I want to know why she kidnapped me. So, if it's all the same to you, I'll stick by. There has to be another door in here somewhere."

"Where should we begin, then?" Alice asked, glad for the company, and inexplicably glad that the company was

Gavin. His presence made her feel more alert, more alive, and she found herself moving with an energy she hadn't experienced before.

They looked about the room. In addition to the scattered automatons, broken glass, and motionless machinery, there were several closed doors. Alice hadn't taken much notice of them earlier—Gavin's violin music had come from the balcony, and she had ignored other exits as irrelevant. Gavin gingerly opened one.

"I'm guessing this goes to the kitchen," he said. "And that one leads upstairs."

Alice peered inside the latter. "Nothing of interest up there."

"How do you know?"

"The steps are dusty. No one—or thing—has trod them for months, or even years."

"Ah."

Alice opened another door and found a worn set of stone stairs heading downward. She caught a whiff of damp air and chemicals. "This looks promising."

Gavin sniffed the air as well. "Laboratory?"

"That's my assessment."

"Let's have a look."

"Click," Alice called, "light, please."

Another *pop*, and Click was ready to light the way.

"You do realize," Gavin said, "that we're about to descend into the hidden laboratory of a mad scientist who kidnapped me and tried to kill both of us."

"Perhaps madness runs in my family."

"That's not very encouraging."

With Click going ahead to provide light, they headed down the stairs.

Chapter Seven

Gavin Ennock touched the mechanical nightingale in his pocket for luck as he followed Alice and her clockwork cat to the bottom of the stone staircase. After days of captivity on the *Juniper* and two weeks in the tower, he found it a blessing to talk to another human being, and especially to a woman as remarkable as this one. He supposed he should be going first down the steps, but it was technically Alice's house, and she had taken the lead before he could say anything. His fingers were sore and a little bloody from the frantic playing earlier, and he felt tired, let down from the fear and excitement.

"Good heavens," Alice said at the bottom. Her voice echoed in a large space, but Click and his eye beams were too far ahead for Gavin to make out what she was looking at.

"What is it?" Gavin asked. "I can't see anything."

"I think there's an electric light here," she said.

Alice turned a switch just as Gavin arrived at the bottom. Lights blazed up, revealing an enormous room with ragged stone columns. Sprawled across the space lay a maze of worktables, equipment, glassware, bookshelves, and machinery.

And it had all been smashed.

The glassware lay in shards. Books were scattered across the floor. Flasks of chemicals had been shattered. Machines had been pulled apart. A wall safe had been broken open, the door left hanging by one hinge. Alice put a hand to her breast.

"This is awful," she murmured.

"You don't hear me arguing." Gavin stepped carefully around a pile of broken glass.

"It makes me want to weep, Mr. Ennock," Alice said. "I've always scraped along with secondhand tools in a tiny bedroom. Now look at this waste and wreckage. And I still don't know what's happened to my aunt."

Gavin wanted to put an arm around her in comfort. She had lost her hat somewhere, and her honey brown hair was coming loose from a French twist, making her look forlorn. Her wide brown eyes complemented her triangular face and small nose. Despite being disheveled, she was beautiful, and strong, and fascinating. This woman knew what needed doing, and she seemed determined to do it. Hell, she had navigated that nightmare room of automatons before he had played them into silence and had faced down marauding mechanical gargoyles. He wasn't sure he would have had the nerve.

"I know what you mean," Gavin said. "Losing something important is hard."

"Yes." Alice slipped a handkerchief from her sleeve and dabbed at her eyes. "Well. Do you suppose whoever smashed all this also kidnapped or killed Aunt Edwina?"

"It's possible," Gavin said, "but the timing is a bit off. You said she stopped contacting her—what was the word? Solicitor?—several months ago, except I've been here for only a couple weeks. If your aunt Edwina is the Red Velvet Lady, that would mean she had those men grab me *after* she disappeared."

"After she stopped contacting her solicitor, you mean,"

she replied. "But yes, you're correct. And we don't know when this damage was done. Today? Last week? Last year? And is any of it related to that bloodstain near the front door? So many questions I don't have the answers for. It's maddening."

"Let's keep looking around," Gavin said. "Though I don't know what I'm looking *for*. I'm more of a musician than an engineer or mechanic."

"You're a very fine musician, too," Alice said.

"Oh." The compliment brought a warm feeling to Gavin's chest, and he flashed Alice a smile. "Thanks."

Alice seemed embarrassed, and she quickly turned to examine a pile of machinery. "That's an unusual arrangement for a violin case, I have to say," she said. "Don't most players carry theirs by the handle?"

"Not on an airship," he said. "You want both hands free."

"You mentioned a ship," Alice said. "I assumed you were a sailor. But you're an airman."

"Was," he said. "Flying is the most wonderful profession in the whole damned world, pardon my language. You glide above the clouds and everything is fresh and fine and pure. You can see the whole world, and music carries a hundred miles."

"How did you come to London, then?"

He told her while they poked through the wreckage of the laboratory, though he deliberately left out the part about Madoc Blue and his harsh hands. Blue still nipped and tore at Gavin's clothes at night, and behind Blue stood the first mate with his heavy whip, and Gavin often woke up soaked in terror sweat. Even talking around it made his heart jerk. It was difficult enough to tell Alice about the deaths of Tom and Captain Naismith and the loss of the *Juniper*. As he spoke, his hand began to ache, and he realized his fist was clenched around the nightingale in his pocket, though the longer he spoke, the more he began to relax. It felt strangely good to tell someone else about it.

"I'm so sorry, Mr. Ennock," she said when he finished. "Perhaps when we're done here, we can find a way to get you back to Boston."

Hope touched Gavin. After the pirates and clerk at Boston Shipping and Mail and the kidnappers, the idea that someone was willing to help him brought an unexpected lump to his throat.

Click meowed and batted at a pile of metal in a side niche. It was the shell of another automaton, painted black and white, as if it were wearing a butler's coat. Two light-bulbs formed eyes, and a metal grate gave it a sort of mouth on an otherwise blank brass face. On a table beside it lay a jumble of parts—gears, pistons, wheels, and other bits Gavin didn't understand. Click meowed again.

Alice came over to investigate. "What is it?"

The cat swiped at the automaton with metal claws.

"What's that on its side?" Gavin said. "Looks like writing."

They both leaned in. Inscribed on the torso in graceful script were the words *Love, Aunt Edwina.* Alice went pale.

"What is it?" Gavin asked, afraid she was going to faint.

"She wrote that on every one of the automatons she sent me. And look—there's a diagram on the inside of his front panel."

"What do we do?"

"Aunt Edwina meant me to find him. She assumed that her attackers wouldn't notice him or wouldn't know how he goes together. Clearly Aunt Edwina wanted me to assemble him so he could tell me more."

"This is the same woman," Gavin reminded her, "who imprisoned me in a tower and set deadly traps."

"Yes," Alice said. She picked up a wrench from a scattering of tools on the floor. "And I'm assuming she had reasons for all of that. The traps, for example, may have been set to keep out whoever destroyed this place."

"They didn't work."

"Not everything goes as planned, Mr. Ennock. Hand me that spanner, would you?"

He did. "Let's work out what happened so far, then. First, your aunt comes down with the clockwork plague, but instead of dying, she becomes a clockworker."

"And she lives as a clockworker longer than any clockworker I've ever heard of." Alice examined a gear, discarded it, picked up another.

"She vanishes—or seems to," Gavin went on. "Which triggers a provision in her will that leaves you her estate. Does that make you a wealthy woman?"

"No." Alice opened the back of the automaton's head and peered inside. "The memory wheels seem to be intact. That's helpful. The house isn't inhabitable, as you can see, and it will take months, perhaps years, to sell the land. And since I'm not technically nobility yet, I will have to pay exorbitant taxes on the sale. Now that I think about it, I may have to pay taxes on it now."

"You're not technically nobility? What does that mean?"

"My father is a baron, but I won't be a baroness until I inherit his title. And before you interrupt with the question you Americans always seem to ask, Mr. Ennock, there *are* no men in my family to inherit the title. In such a case, the daughter inherits. But until that happens, I'm *not* nobility, and I must pay taxes."

Gavin stared. Alice was the daughter of a baron? "Incredible," he whispered.

"What all of this means," Alice continued, "is that I may have to pay an enormous inheritance tax on this estate, and Aunt Edwina's solicitor was extremely lax in failing to mention it."

"Uh, sorry I brought it up," Gavin said, still impressed. "Anyway, your aunt disappears, leaving you an estate full of traps. Which brings us to the first question—why would she leave you a house that tried to kill you?"

"I said before that I don't think she was trying to kill me,"

Alice said. "I think she was trying to keep someone else out. It worked, but only for a while—someone got down here. The traps *didn't* keep me out, either, but they weren't intended to. Aunt Edwina knew I would outsmart them."

"She must have a lot of confidence in you," Gavin said.

"Presumably."

"In the meantime, she also had me kidnapped and put in that tower. Why?"

Alice unwound a coil of copper wire and snipped off a length. "I think she wanted me to let you out so you could help defeat the traps and help me take the house. It's certainly what happened."

"But *why*?"

"That I don't know. Clockworkers do go mad. Now, where did I put that piston lubricant?"

Gavin watched her work, her movements confident and quick. She looked a little older than he was—somewhere in her early twenties—and he wanted to ask her exact age, but that would have been really rude, and he didn't want to offend her. Hell, more than anything he wanted to impress her, but what would impress this woman?

"Uh . . . Miss Michaels?"

Alice had stuck her head into the automaton's chest cavity. She withdrew and blinked at him. A bit of grease smudged her cheek. "Yes?"

"Er . . ." His entire face felt hot, and he realized he was blushing. Cursing himself for an idiot, he plunged ahead anyway. "Would you like some music while you work?"

She blinked at him again, and he looked away, scuffing the stone floor with one foot. What kind of fool would—

"I would love some music, Mr. Ennock. Do you know any Mozart? I find his music focuses my mind on mathematics."

"Uh . . ."

"Something from *The Marriage of Figaro,* perhaps." She hummed a few bars of a familiar tune.

"Oh, yeah—I know those songs. I didn't know Mozart

was the composer." He set bow to strings and played. Despite the pain in his fingers, every note came out sweet and quick, like flavored ice on a summer day. Maybe it was the time he had spent in the tower with nothing to do but practice, but his playing seemed to have improved lately. He didn't think he could have played that hellish song the automatons had laid out before he'd been captured.

Alice went back to work, and she seemed to be going even more quickly now. Gavin slipped from one song to the next, always keeping with Mozart, the famous clockworker composer, while Click watched. Their work melded, music and science melting together with every twist of Alice's wrenches and every slide of Gavin's bow. In what felt like very little time, Alice was tightening a final bolt on the automaton's chest plate. She straightened, and Gavin heard her back pop even over "Open Your Eyes." He stopped playing.

"Finished," Alice said unnecessarily. "His Babbage engine is fully functional; his power sources are wound and charged. And your playing helped, Mr. Ennock. Really, you should play professionally."

He thought about his time in Hyde Park. "I guess I have, in a way." Then he realized she was praising him and that he had just possibly impressed her, and that made him flush again.

"Now we just switch him on." Alice inserted a tool into the automaton's left ear and twisted. The automaton twitched. Its eyes flickered, went out, then glowed steadily. Gavin felt an insane desire to shout, "Live!"

The automaton turned its head with a creak, apparently taking in its surroundings. It looked at Alice and said in a quiet, reedy voice, "Good evening, miss. My name is Kemp. What service do you require?"

"It works!" Gavin exclaimed.

"Of course it works," Alice said. "Hello, Kemp. Do you know where you are?"

"I appear to be in Madam's laboratory. And it is a frightful mess."

"What is your function in this house?" Alice asked.

"I am Madam's valet."

"Isn't a valet a manservant?"

"Madam has her own ideas about the way the world should run, miss. Might I ask who you are?"

"My name is Alice Michaels, daughter of Arthur, Baron Michaels. I am your mistress's niece."

"I see," Kemp said. "There is extensive information about you in my memory wheels. But why are you here? Where is Madam?"

"What's the last thing you remember, Kemp?" Alice asked.

Kemp's eyes flickered. "Madam called me down to the laboratory. She ordered me to remain still. Then you were standing before me."

"How long ago was this?"

"What is the date, miss?"

"May twenty-fourth," she said, then added, "1857."

Kemp's eyes flickered again. "Oh my. I have been inactive for more than a year!"

"I'm sorry, Kemp," Alice said. "Aunt Edwina vanished sometime ago. She left me this house and its contents in her will. This is Gavin Ennock. Did Aunt Edwina say anything about him before she deactivated you?"

"Code forty-seven delta," Kemp said. "Code forty-seven delta. Active. Active."

"What?" Gavin said.

Kemp swiveled his head left and right several times, then refocused on Alice. "According to the terms of Madam Edwina's last will and testament and code forty-seven delta, everything in the house belongs to you, which means I am now your valet, Madam."

"Oh!" Alice put a hand to her mouth. "Well. I suppose you are."

"*Love, Aunt Edwina,*" Gavin put in.

"Tell me, then," Alice said, "did Aunt Edwina say anything about capturing Mr. Ennock here or about her upcoming disappearance?"

"That information is not in my memory wheels, Madam. I am sorry."

"Do you know who might have broken in here and destroyed the laboratory?"

"That information is not in my memory wheels, Madam. I am sorry. Would Madam care for something to eat or drink?"

Gavin's stomach growled at that moment. "I would. What time is it?"

"After three in the morning," Alice said, checking a watch in her handbag. "Good heavens, no wonder I'm so hungry. I didn't even have supper."

"Madam!" Kemp said. "You mustn't neglect yourself so. I will return in moments."

"I don't know what you'll find in the kitchen after a year, Kemp," Alice said doubtfully as Kemp headed toward the stairs with stiff steps.

"Tins keep." Kemp put his foot on the bottom step. "I regret that it won't be the best meal, but I daresay it will—code one seventeen omega. Code one seventeen omega."

"What was that one for?" Gavin demanded.

"*Sixty seconds,*" boomed Edwina's voice. "*Fifty-nine. Fifty-eight.*"

"Oh dear," Kemp said. "My attempt to leave the laboratory appears to have activated a destruction code."

Gavin gave Alice a wild look. "I thought the traps in the house were all deactivated."

"This one must have been separated from the rest. I don't know *everything.*"

"Madam," Kemp said, "we must leave immediately." Before either Gavin or Alice could respond, Kemp flung Alice over his shoulder and skittered up the stairs. Gavin hurried to follow with Click on his heels. At the last moment, he snatched up his fiddle and Alice's handbag.

"Put me down, you brass idiot!" Alice shrieked. "I can walk myself."

"Forty-one. Forty." Kemp was moving faster than a mechanical man should have been able. "I cannot obey, Madam. My program is quite clear."

"Twenty-two. Twenty-one."

They were at the cellar door. The house creaked. Beams groaned like an airship in a gale, and bits of plaster fell to the floor. Terror tightened Gavin's stomach, and his heart pounded at the back of his throat. It wasn't enough time to get out. Something snapped with a report louder than a hundred guns, and a section of ceiling crashed to the floor.

The ground rumbled beneath Gavin's boots as they reached the front door. Kemp smashed it open with a metal fist. Ears back and all his claws out, Click bolted through the opening, the metal making scrabbling noises on the stones.

"Twelve seconds. Eleven. Ten."

Outdoors, they ran for it, though Kemp refused to pause long enough to put Alice on her feet. She stopped yelling, but her expression said there'd be hell to pay later. Edwina's voice chased after them like a banshee.

"Four. Three."

Kemp deposited Alice behind a low stone wall. Gavin dived behind it with Click, skinning his palms on dirt and gravel. They huddled there, plastered against hard rock.

"Zero."

Gavin expected an explosion. Instead, there was a strange quiet. It rushed over them in a silent wave. This silence went beyond a simple lack of noise. This silence devoured all other sound and left behind an odd purity, as if Gavin's soul had been scoured with sand and rinsed clean. Air rushed past him, blasting his hair. Gavin and Alice peeked over the wall just in time to see the manor house crumple inward and compress into a wrinkled mass like a schoolboy's spitball. In less than a second it sucked into it-self and vanished, all without the slightest sound.

Gavin clapped his hands and snapped his fingers, but heard no sound. He shouted at Alice, felt the tension in his throat, but heard no sound. Her mouth moved, but he heard nothing. She pointed at one ear and shook her head. For a horrible moment, Gavin was afraid he'd gone deaf. Kemp remained impassive. Then a bird called, and another, and another. A damp breeze rustled leaves in nearby trees. Kemp's joints creaked. Gavin sighed with relief and heard the sound in his own ears. He offered Alice a hand up.

"What *was* that?" Gavin asked, never so relieved to hear the sound of his own voice.

But Alice was staring over the wall at the house, or the space it had occupied. The entire building, including the tower, was gone. In its place, a perfect half sphere had been carved into the ground, revealing layers of earth and stone. Gavin edged up to it and peered over the side. The bottom looked to be four or five stories down. It could have swallowed the *Juniper* with ease.

"Shit," he whispered.

"Indeed, Mr. Ennock," Alice said. Her face was pale. "I would rather not remain here. One of the locals mentioned a train station. Shall we go look for it?"

They arrived at the station more than an hour later, grubby, tired, and hungry. Gavin was used to being all three, and the two automatons weren't bothered by physical needs, but Gavin worried about Alice. Her face grew more and more pale with every passing moment, but she refused both Gavin's and Kemp's repeated offers of assistance.

The train station was brightly lit to ward off plague zombies, and the schedule informed them that the next train to London would arrive in only a few minutes. Gavin and Alice sank gratefully to a bench to wait. It was nearly four in the morning, and a fair number of other people, ones with jobs in the city, were also waiting for the train so they could get to work. Kemp vanished and reappeared with their tickets and four bread rolls.

"I am sorry breakfast is so poor, Madam," he said. "It was the best available."

Alice handed two of the rolls to Gavin, who wolfed them down without hesitation. "Where did you get the money, Kemp?" she asked.

"Madam—previous Madam—has an account for tickets. I hope Madam will trust me about the rolls."

Alice's expression said that Madam didn't, but Gavin touched her wrist, and she said nothing. The train's arrival ended further conversation.

Gavin automatically moved toward one of the open-air boxes that made up third class, but Alice called out to him, "Mr. Ennock! Our car is over here!"

Trying to keep the awe off his face, Gavin followed Alice, Kemp, and Click into the first-class car. No other passengers were in evidence, and the two of them took up plush chairs facing each other across a carpeted floor. Gavin sank into the seat, feeling like a grubby imposter next to Alice's cool grace.

The train jerked forward, and a bit later Kemp reappeared with a food seller wheeling a cart. Kemp folded tables down in front of Gavin and Alice, whisked a selection of bread, meat, and fruit from the cart, and set them on the tables while the dark city rushed past the windows. Alice ate immediately, but Gavin just looked down at his plate, his mouth watering at the smells of fresh bread, sausage, and boiled eggs.

"What's wrong, Mr. Ennock?" Alice asked. "I can't imagine you're not hungry."

"I've got no money," he said, feeling his face flush.

"The meal is part of your ticket, sir," Kemp put in.

So Gavin ate gratefully. It must be wonderful to be rich and the daughter of a baron. When he finished, he leaned back in the comfortable chair to close his eyes for just a moment, and then Alice was shaking him awake. The sun had just risen outside, and the train was stopped at a station.

"We're in the city, Mr. Ennock."

"Oh." He yawned and got to his feet. "Uh . . . thanks. For rescuing me and for the food, I mean. I suppose I should be going."

"Do you have a destination in mind?"

He shrugged. "Hyde Park, I guess. It looks like a fine day for busking."

"What if someone tries to kidnap you again?"

"I have to play somewhere. That and flying are all I know, and no one will let me fly."

Alice seemed to be warring with herself. At last, she said, "Come to my house, Mr. Ennock. You could meet my father."

Gavin considered refusing. He was a street busker in dirty clothes, not someone who should meet a baron. On the other hand, the baron might reward the young man who had saved his daughter's life. Besides, the idea of not seeing Alice again caused him a strange amount of pain. Every time he saw her disheveled hair, he wanted to reach out and stroke it back into place. Every time he saw her move, he wanted to follow after her. Every time he heard her voice, he wanted to sing along with it.

"That would be wonderful," he said.

Alice hired a cab, and sometime later, they were pulling up to a shabby-looking row house. Kemp, who had been clinging to the back of the cab, hopped down.

"Is this Madam's home?" he asked.

"It is," Alice responded with overmuch cheer in her voice and a bit of color in her cheeks. Gavin caught on quickly. Either she'd been lying about the baron thing or they were poor regardless of the title, and Alice was embarrassed. He felt bad for her, but not too bad—it was a mansion compared to his family's grimy flat in Boston, and a palace compared to the cellar he'd slept in until just lately.

Remembering his manners at the last moment, Gavin jumped down from the cab and held out a hand to help her out, then stood uncomfortably by while Alice paid the driver.

"If Madam will give me her key." Kemp held out a hand for it, then hurried up the short steps to open the front door. Click swiped at Alice's bedraggled skirts with a plaintive meow, and Alice picked him up. Just as she was bustling toward the short steps to the front door, two men emerged. Kemp stood back to the let them by. Both men were middleaged and wore simple brown business suits and hats.

"Hello," Alice said. "Who are you, please?"

"Are you the Baron's daughter?" one of the men asked.

"I'm Alice Michaels, yes."

"Ah. We just had a . . . business meeting with your father. It's nothing you need concern yourself with, miss."

"Is this about his"—she glanced at Gavin and lowered her voice, but Gavin still heard her—"debts?"

"It's talk for men, miss," said the second man.

"You're from the debtors' prison, aren't you?" she said, her voice still low. "I've seen you sniffing round other people's houses. You can't imprison a baron for debts."

"True, miss, true. But we can imprison a baron for a crime."

"Crime?" Alice looked alarmed. "What kind of crime?"

"We're in a public place, miss," the first man said, "and this isn't the sort of talk for a young lady to—"

Alice took a step toward him, a terrible look on her face, and the man actually backed up. "Tell me."

"Er, theft and embezzlement, miss. He took money that didn't belong to him and failed to return it, which, by a certain measure, is theft. We're all aware that in the end the charges will probably not go anywhere, but Baron Michaels will have to spend the duration of the trial—many weeks—in prison, unless he can raise money for bail. And he will have to find money to pay a barrister." The first man recovered himself and tipped his hat. "But all this is nothing you need worry your pretty little head over. Go on in and feed your cat, or wind it up or whatever you do. Is that cab available?"

Without further discussion, both men jumped into the hack and ordered the driver away. Alice, still holding Click, pursed her lips.

"Well. Father must be worried sick." She hurried toward the steps, and Gavin followed uncertainly. "Last he knew, I was having luncheon with my fiancé yesterday afternoon."

It felt like a boot slammed into Gavin's stomach. The entire world stopped, and he could feel every particle of air striking his skin like a barrage of tiny arrows. "Fiancé?" he echoed.

"Yes." Alice crossed the threshold while Kemp held the door. "Norbert Williamson asked me to marry him this afternoon. Yesterday afternoon. I'm still in shock."

"I can understand that." Gavin entered the little house, feeling stupid and a fool.

Don't be an idiot, he told himself. *You've just met her. And she's the daughter of a baron. Why do you care if she's engaged to someone who can probably pay her cab fare and buy her a castle with the change?*

"Father?" Alice called, dumping Click on the floor. "Are you up?"

An affirmative response came from a back room, and an old man emerged, pushing the wheels of his chair with frantic, gnarled hands. He blinked at the roomful of people and automatons.

"Alice!" he said. He voice was tremulous with worry, and he sounded close to tears. "Thank God! I thought you had been attacked by zombies or worse. What happened to you? Who are—?"

"I'm so sorry, Father." Alice knelt by his chair and took his arm. "I didn't mean to worry you. I didn't know things would turn out this way, or I would have sent a message."

He put a shaking hand to his mouth in a gesture that

Gavin had seen Alice use. "I didn't get a wink of sleep. This is not what a proper daughter does to her father."

Alice looked down, clearly ashamed. "No. I'm very sorry. I can't explain or excuse it. I should have come straight home after meeting with Norbert. Can you forgive me?"

"Your aunt Edwina acted like this," he continued, still distraught. "Even before the Ad Hoc ladies. And look what happened to her."

Alice's face tightened. "I'm sorry, Father."

"Well." He patted her shoulder. "I'm glad you're all right."

"May I introduce Mr. Gavin Ennock?" she said in a different tone. "He quite saved my life. Mr. Ennock, this is my father, Arthur, Baron Michaels."

Gavin didn't know if he should bow or shake the man's hand or grovel on the floor. He waited to see what Arthur would do, and when he held out his hand, Gavin took it. He wondered why Arthur was in a wheelchair. Old age? Lost limb hidden by the blankets? Disease? The last thought made him wonder about the safety of shaking hands, but it was too late. Arthur's grip was devoid of strength, and Gavin was careful not to press the frail fingers.

"Nice to meet you, sir," he said.

"And you," Arthur said a little faintly. "What happened, exactly? And where did this automaton come from?"

"It's quite a story," Alice said.

"Perhaps," Kemp said, "Madam could tell it after a wash and a change of clothing? You must look after yourself."

"That's a fine idea, Kemp. Thank you. Gav—Mr. Ennock could use a wash as well, and I think some of Father's old clothes might fit him until we can launder the ones he's wearing. And perhaps you could also arrange for Father's breakfast? He usually has tea and toast."

"Immediately, Madam."

The washtub hung in an alcove just off the kitchen. A bath and new clothes made Gavin feel much better, though he was yawning to split his head. He returned to the front room where Alice, who had cleaned up in her own room, was just finishing the story of their long night.

"Good Lord," Arthur said at the end. "And you say there's nothing left of the house at all?"

"Just Kemp," Alice replied. "And Mr. Ennock, here. He has nowhere to go, Father, and considering that he saved my life, I thought you could offer him a place to stay for a while."

"Er . . ."

The hesitation was obvious. Gavin kept a pleasant expression on his face, but was mentally heading for the door: So much for a reward, or a return to Boston. Or the chance to see Alice again. He felt like a bird covered in lead feathers. "I couldn't impose, sir," he said.

"I'm not sure about the proprieties," Arthur said. "As a newly engaged woman, Alice, you can't invite a young man to—"

"I won't invite him, Father," Alice interrupted. "You will."

"Ah. Quite. In that case . . ."

"I'm afraid the only room available has no window, Mr. Ennock," Alice apologized. "It's across the hall from mine."

Some of the lead lightened, and Gavin managed a wider smile. "It's better than a basement." He covered another yawn, which made Alice yawn.

"You're falling over from exhaustion, Madam," Kemp said. "I must insist on a lie-down while I fix a place for Mr. Ennock."

Moments later, Gavin was lying on a pallet in a warm, windowless room. He touched both his fiddle case and the nightingale for reassurance and thought there was no way he would actually be able to sleep after everything that had happened. Then he fell asleep.

Chapter Eight

Alice stared at the ceiling. By all rights she should be asleep, but the events of the previous day replayed in her mind. It was the night of the zombie attack all over again. She should have found it all horrifying and frightening, but here, in the honesty of her own bed, she was forced to admit she had found every moment fascinating and invigorating. Even multiple brushes with death hadn't so much filled her with dread as thrilled her with excitation, as if being close to the grave had made her find more sweetness in life. Perhaps that was why she couldn't sleep—she felt she was wasting breath.

Her mind also kept returning to Gavin. He was handsome, with a smile that made her think of sunshine and musical skill that made her soul soar. But he was the wrong social class, and Alice was *engaged*. It wasn't proper for any woman in her position to be interested in him, and certainly not for a woman from a traditional family.

But she couldn't have turned him out into the street after he had saved her life—twice. That wouldn't have been proper, either.

Alice sat up and moved to her worktable, where she fiddled idly with a driveshaft and a pair of gears. Perhaps

Norbert would consent to hire Gavin as a footman in his country home, where Alice could hear him anytime she wished. Then she scoffed to herself. Now she was just being foolish. She looked down at her hands and realized she had set the gears down and was toying with Glenda Teasdale's calling card, the one Louisa had commented on earlier.

If you find you need a change in your life, write to me, all right?

Alice didn't need a change in her life. For once, everything was going where it should. But the entire affair with Aunt Edwina continued to puzzle her. Where had Aunt Edwina gone? Who had broken into her house and destroyed her laboratory? Why had she kidnapped Gavin? How had she survived the clockwork plague for so long? And why was that clockworker in the skull mask spying on her?

The Third Ward clearly dealt with questions of this sort. And so, although Alice Michaels definitely didn't need a change in her life—most certainly did not—she scribbled a quick letter, folded it expertly into an envelope, and turned back to the calling card. Glenda hadn't written an address on it. After a moment's thought, Alice wrote *Miss Glenda Teasdale, The Third Ward, √2.*

"Kemp!" she called.

The door opened. "Madam?"

She handed him the letter. "Post this for me right away, please."

"Of course, Madam."

Alice climbed back into bed and surprised herself by instantly falling asleep.

Alice awoke, thinking only an hour or two had passed, but Kemp informed her she had slept through the entire day and the following night. So had Gavin.

"Baron Michaels wished to wake you earlier, but I wouldn't hear of it," Kemp said as Alice's little automatons brought her a dress. "I have seen to his needs."

"Thank you, Kemp." Alice almost ordered Kemp out of the room while she dressed, but although Kemp was shaped like a man, he was only a machine. Still, she ordered him to turn his back.

"Madam, I must ask," Kemp continued. "Why do you and Lord Michaels live in such frightful conditions? The Michaels family lineage is long and proud."

"It's what we can afford." Alice slipped into the dress and waited while two little automatons fastened the buttons behind her. "Titles and wealth don't always go together."

Kemp gave a mechanical sniff. "Yes, Madam. I have taken the liberty of doing the shopping. Previous Madam still had a bit of petty cash money on account at a local bank, and I restocked the larder with something better than day-old bread and dried cheese. I think fresh fruit will do Lord Michaels some good."

"That's a relief, Kemp. Thank you."

"And when you are finished with your toilette," he said, "I will inform your callers that you are ready to receive them."

Alice paused, a hairbrush in her hand. "Callers?"

"A Miss Glenda Teasdale and a Mr. Simon d'Arco arrived something over an hour ago. It's the reason Lord Michaels wished to wake you." Another sniff. "Mr. d'Arco appears to be of Italian extraction."

But Alice wasn't listening. She stuffed her hair into a serviceable bun and rushed down the stairs to the front room, where she found Gavin seated with Glenda Teasdale and Simon d'Arco. Simon, his dark eyes sparkling, was engaged in lively conversation with Gavin while Glenda, dressed in skirts and a puffy-sleeved blouse instead of trousers, sipped at a teacup.

Father was nowhere to be seen. The men rose when they caught sight of Alice. Gavin looked very fine; well-rested and dressed and combed. His white-blond hair shone in the gaslight. He caught her eye and smiled. She started to smile back, then caught herself.

"So good to see you, love," Glenda said, taking Alice's hand with Ad Hoc familiarity. "I was hoping you would contact us. We clearly have a great deal to discuss."

Alice hesitated. Yesterday—or the day before—contacting the Third Ward had seemed a good idea. Now, with Glenda and Simon in her drawing room, it seemed less so.

"I prefer Miss Michaels," she said carefully, "and I'm glad you came. My aunt—"

"Sorry to interrupt," Simon said, doing so, "but this whole affair is a bit delicate, and we should probably talk about it at headquarters, where it's safer."

"Definitely." Glenda, who hadn't released Alice's hand, was already towing Alice toward the stairs. "Shall we?"

"I can't leave my father alone again," Alice said. "It's not right."

"Your automaton can see to him," Glenda breezed. "He's only napping."

It would be so easy to go with her. Then Alice thought of her father again, and of her new fiancé. She crossed her arms. "No. I can't."

Simon looked uncomfortable. "Please don't put us in a difficult position, Miss Michaels. We speak with authority granted by the Crown, which gave us legal jurisdiction over anything to do with clockworkers, and this isn't a secure place for a discussion. By authority of the Queen, we must insist. If you please, Miss Michaels."

His tone was polite, but Alice heard the iron beneath it. She set her mouth and nodded once. "Fine."

"Coming, Mr. Ennock?" Glenda asked.

Before Alice quite knew what was happening, the four of them were clattering up the steps to the second floor, Gavin with his fiddle case strapped to his back.

"Why are we going up here?" Alice asked.

"It's how we came in, of course," Glenda replied. She pushed open the half door at the end of the hall and stooped to crawl through, barely slowing down. Gavin shrugged and followed. Alice almost refused, but Simon d'Arco was standing right behind her, obviously expecting her to go, so she went. The little door led to a dusty airing cupboard that Alice hadn't entered in years. A trapdoor opened onto the roof. Gavin turned to give her a hand out, and Simon came behind. A damp breeze teased at her hair, and a dizzying drop fell away to the street below. People bustled past on the narrow byway, looking tiny and unimportant. Even the noises they made were small. Alice prayed no one would look up and see her. But even as the thought crossed her mind, a boy pointed, and several people paused to stare upward. Alice turned her back. If word got back to Father that Alice was climbing about on the roof . . .

"Don't worry. We're not staying up here," Glenda explained.

"We're going in that?" Like the boy, Gavin pointed upward, his face shining with excitement.

Above them hovered a small dirigible, perhaps the size of a cottage. The dirigible's gondola hung suspended by silken ropes, and the entire thing was tethered to one of the chimneys. Alice had been concentrating so hard on the people below that she hadn't even noticed its presence. A wooden ladder extended itself toward them as she watched in startled amazement. Dirigibles she had seen, but never one hovering over her own house.

"There's no space to land it on the street, which is why we're on the roof. Up we go," Simon said. "Does it make you nervous, Miss Michaels?"

It did, but the thought of appearing nervous in front of these people spurred Alice forward. "Not at all. Eyes down, Mr. Ennock. You, too, Mr. d'Arco." She swarmed up the ladder. At the top, a thin, balding man with elaborate muttonchop whiskers gave her a hand into the gondola, then helped Glenda, Gavin, and Simon aboard. Simon folded up the ladder.

"You're Pilot?" Gavin asked.

The thin man nodded and wordlessly turned to a small wheel Alice remembered was called a helm. Gavin expertly flicked the tether free, and the little propeller engines on the sides of the gondola whirred to life.

"Have you ever flown before, Miss Michaels?" Gavin asked.

"No," Alice said as the city slid away below. Bitter-smelling coal smoke rose from a thousand chimneys, and a thousand people, horses, and automatons filled the streets. From up here, she could even see into the alleyways, where plague zombies shambled through the shadows, looking for garbage. A trio of well-dressed women in emerald dresses strolled the cobblestones, carrying signs that read DON'T THROW YOUR VOTE AWAY and THE AD HOC NEEDS YOU, unaware that only a few paces away a zombie lurked in the shadows, forced to hide from painful sunlight. Alleys emerged into side streets and joined larger streets, like tributaries joining rivers.

"It's fascinating," she breathed.

"It's the most wonderful place to be," Gavin told her, and she noticed how closely they were forced to stand in the confines of the tiny gondola. He looked happy, even thrilled, and that started a warm bit of happiness glowing inside Alice. She almost took his hand. He leaned over the side, and for a moment she thought he might leap over the edge and soar away.

"How do you know where to go?" Alice said. "Don't you get lost?"

"It's the same as on a ship, ma'am," Pilot said. "We can use a chart with coordinates. We're coming up on Buckingham Palace, for example, and that's at fifty-one degrees, thirty minutes north, zero degrees, and eight minutes west. Of course, over London, it's easier just to look down. You learn your way."

"Does this ship go any higher?" Gavin asked of Pilot.

"Not with all these people in it," the man grumbled.

Simon clapped Gavin on the back. "Lots of chances for flying in the Third Ward, Gav—Mr. Ennock."

"You can call me Gavin," he said. "I don't mind."

"I'm Simon. We're very informal around the Ward, you see. It sets us apart from . . . everyone else."

"What exactly is the Third Ward?"

"It'll be easier to show you than tell you," Glenda said.

As Pilot predicted, they passed almost directly over Buckingham Palace, official residence of Queen Victoria for twenty years now. Alice felt her own excitement and almost jumped up and down like a little girl at the sight. The Queen had ascended the throne when Alice was a baby, and like many English, Alice couldn't remember or imagine a time without Queen Victoria and Prince Albert ruling the Empire. Alice looked down at the square, stately building surrounded by green gardens and wondered if the Queen were at this moment signing a proclamation or receiving an important dignitary or perhaps just sipping tea from a porcelain cup in a lavishly decorated hall. How wonderful and strange to glide above her.

Another section of the city passed beneath them, and then the airship passed over a stone wall surrounding another generous section of greenery, in the center of which lay a white mansion surrounded by outbuildings. The airship drifted gently downward to land with a soft bump on the lawn in front of the great house, and a pair of workmen dashed over to secure the ship. Everyone scrambled to disembark, and Glenda led them up the steps into the house.

The interior bustled with activity. Men dressed in business attire, servant livery, and ordinary workaday clothing hurried about on mysterious errands. There were even a number of women, though that shouldn't have surprised Alice by now. Glenda guided them down a series of corridors, past rooms large and small. Alice and Gavin caught sight of several laboratories and workrooms. An enormous half-constructed automaton stood in one of them, while two men attached sheets of metal to it. Another laboratory sported bubbling beakers and winding copper tubes. A cage in the corner held half a dozen plague zombies who watched Alice with empty eyes as she passed. Yet another room was coated in fog, and a male figure appeared to be frozen in a block of ice. Alice couldn't keep from staring.

"You're very busy here," she said breathlessly.

"They keep us occupied," Simon replied with a smile.

"Where are we going?" Gavin asked.

"Here." Glenda knocked once on a closed door, then ushered Gavin and Alice into an office, or perhaps it was a library. Floor-to-ceiling shelves held books, maps, scrolls, and strange instruments Alice couldn't identify. Tall windows looked out over the grounds, and thick Persian rugs covered the floors. The center of the room was dominated by a large desk piled with neat stacks of papers. An odd combination telegraph machine and typewriter occupied one corner. Behind the desk sat a tall woman with black hair pulled into a French twist. She wore a man's military uniform, crisp and blue, with gold epaulets. It was specially cut to expose her left arm, which was entirely mechanical. Alice noted with a start that it had six fingers. An elaborate brass-rimmed monocle covered the woman's left eye, and a small sign on her desk read LIEUTENANT SUSAN PHIPPS.

"The ones from our report, Lieutenant," Glenda said. "Alice Michaels, daughter of Arthur, Baron Michaels, and Gavin Ennock from Boston."

"Thank you, Glenda," said Lieutenant Phipps. Her voice was quick and sharp as a pair of scissors. "Excellent work, both of you. Simon, please meet us down in the sound laboratory in ten minutes."

Glenda and Simon withdrew. Phipps pointed to a pair of wooden chairs across from her desk. "Sit. Please."

Alice and Gavin sat. Gavin looked solemn but at ease, and Alice supposed that as an airman, he was used to a military chain of command. For her own part, Alice found Lieutenant Phipps more than a little intimidating, and she forced herself to sit with her hands in her lap, though she wanted to twist at her skirt as she had as a child. She tried not to stare at Phipps, this woman who dressed and spoke like a man, and broke so many traditional rules. But of course, she was part of this Third Ward, and the Ward clearly welcomed Ad Hoc women.

Phipps set a packet of papers aside and pulled the telegraph-typewriting machine toward them on its rolling stand. The machine had a recording horn on it. Phipps spun a crank on the side and fed a long scroll of paper into the typewriter's platen. "I'm sure you're wondering what's going on and why you're here, so I'll come straight to the point. First, I need to hear from you everything that happened at that country house. Don't leave anything out. Mr. Ennock, you start. I understand you used to play fiddle in Hyde Park."

Gavin told his story. As he spoke, the machine sprang to life. The typewriter clacked, and Gavin's words skittered across the scroll. Gavin paused in surprise. Alice leaned forward. Her fingers itched to take the side panels off the machine so she could examine how the insides worked, discover how many memory wheels it took to translate sound into written words. Phipps pressed a switch on the machine and it stopped.

"Ignore the transcription, Mr. Ennock," she said. "It's for our records. Continue."

He did. When he finished, Phipps had Alice tell her story as well. The machine wrote it all down. Phipps tore the scroll off, rolled it up, and put it in a drawer.

"Is that all?" Alice asked. "Are we free to go?"

"One more point." Phipps steepled her fingers, brass and steel on flesh. "I need you both to listen carefully. The Third Ward is a busy and chronically understaffed organization, and we're crying for talent. Based on what I've learned about the two of you over the last several days, I'm prepared to offer you positions as agents with us. The salary starts at five hundred pounds per annum, and room and board at cost, if you desire it."

Alice gaped. It was the last thing she'd been expecting to hear. She exchanged a quick glance with Gavin and understood that he felt the same way. "I don't understand," she said slowly. "What exactly does the Third Ward—"

"Did you say five hundred pounds?" Gavin interrupted.

"I did," answered Phipps. "And before you answer, let me show you what it means to be an agent of the Third Ward."

She strode for the door without looking behind. Alice and Gavin rushed to catch her up. Phipps marched ahead of them, her bearing straight as a tin soldier's.

"You've probably guessed that I've already looked into your backgrounds," she said. "Both of you are quick, intelligent thinkers, and you have talents we need. And"—she lifted a metal finger before either of them could interrupt— "I'm going to explain what we do as we walk, so listen and look."

They passed a gymnasium where groups of men and women sparred with fists and feet. "The Third Ward was established during the reign of King George the Fourth by the Duke of Wellington," Phipps began.

"The Iron Duke," Alice said.

"Yes, and if you interrupt again, this will take longer," Phipps admonished. "Wellington defeated Napoleon at Waterloo, but only just. The French had access to horrifying machines of war created by three clockworkers Napoleon had . . . persuaded to work for him. Wellington decided then and there that the best thing he could do for England was to gather up these madmen and -women and keep their inventions under control before one of them managed to destroy the country—or the world. He established the Third Ward to do that."

"His Majesty George the Fourth was amenable to this?"

Alice said. "I'm sorry to interrupt, but that doesn't sound like him. King George wasn't known for—well, he was more of . . ."

"An insular sybarite? A man who found the contents of his bedchamber more important than the contents of his country? Yes. That was why Wellington kept the Ward a secret. He diverted Crown funds for it and kept it hidden from His Majesty until William the Fourth took the throne in 1830."

"William was Victoria's uncle, right?" Gavin said.

Phipps gave him a curt nod. "By then, the tradition of secrecy was well established, so even though the Crown supports the Ward, we don't officially exist. Too many people would be unhappy if they were aware of what we were doing right under their noses."

"What *are* we—you—doing?" Alice asked.

"I told you—we gather clockworkers. We give them a supervised place to work, and we harvest their inventions to serve the Empire. Why do you think England rules most of the known world?"

"And what about China?" Alice couldn't help asking. Phipps's snappy tone set her a bit on edge.

"They have their own system for dealing with clockworkers," Phipps acknowledged. "And it's why they've managed to hold their own against us."

"The revolt over the Treaty of Nanking," Gavin said. "And Lord Elgin's fight with Emperor Xianfeng."

Phipps looked at him. "Yes. How does a cabin boy from a shipping dirigible know about that?"

"I'm young, but I'm not stupid," Gavin said airily, and Alice suppressed a smile.

"Quite." Phipps took them into a small, square room and pulled shut an iron gate. "Other countries look at clockworkers and see a threat. They think of plague zombies carrying disease, and never mind that clockworkers don't communicate the clockwork plague. And they see terrifying technology, of course. So they shun clockworkers or kill them."

She turned a crank and flipped a switch on the wall of the room. The floor gave a sharp jerk, and the entire chamber descended. Alice squeaked and grabbed Gavin's elbow.

"It's called a lift," Phipps said. "It's perfectly safe. One of our clockworkers modified the original design from America. It runs on electricity."

"Oh," Alice said. "I'd like to examine it sometime."

"If you come work for us." Two floors passed by them, followed by a thick layer of stone.

"Why do clockworker inventions remain so rare?" Gavin asked. "I mean, we saw that giant automaton upstairs, and you mentioned the war machines at Waterloo. Why doesn't the Crown build more and more of them?"

"We can't," Phipps told him. "A few inventions can be re-created, certainly. Babbage engines. Electric lights. Hardened glass. Designs for dirigibles. But the vast majority of clockworker inventions, especially the ones with any sort of power source, are so complicated, so complex, that no one can re-create them. Not even if the clockworker manages to draw extended diagrams."

"As my aunt has done?" Alice asked.

"Exactly as your aunt has done. That's one of the reasons why we're interested in you, Miss Michaels. As far as we know, you're the only person able to follow a clockworker's thinking well enough to assemble a clockworker's inventions. Your cat Click, for example, and that automated valet."

"But I don't *understand* them," Alice said. "I just assemble them."

"That's a singular ability, Miss Michaels. With few exceptions, only a clockworker can create the pieces of advanced technology we need to keep the Empire running, and once something has been created, only a clockworker can maintain or re-create it. Perhaps you can assemble these inventions because your family has been touched by the clockwork plague so often. Or perhaps you're some sort of clockworker yourself. A demi-clockworker, if you will."

All the strength drained out of Alice's body, and the blood left her face. Her voice dropped to a whisper. "I hadn't considered that."

"Don't go all fussy," Phipps growled. "If you were going to die of clockwork plague or infect someone else, you would have done it long ago. I don't put up with the idea that women are the weaker sex or that females are particularly prone to hysterics, so if you're going to prove me wrong, do it elsewhere."

The words stung like a slap, and Alice came to herself. "You may have researched my background, Lieutenant," she snapped, "but you know nothing of *me*, so you may keep your comments to yourself, thank you."

Phipps gave her a curt nod, and Alice wondered if that had been some sort of test. "At any rate, America is starting to see the value of clockworkers, but it remains too deeply divided over slavery and economic issues to make proper use of them. India treats clockworkers as untouchables, of course, and the Africans and Muslims stone them to death. Ever since we've colonized these places, the Ward has been able to snatch clockworkers away for our—the Crown's—use. China, as I said, has its own clockworkers, and we seem to be locked in a constant struggle to stay abreast of them."

"We invent something; they invent something a bit better; we have to invent something a bit better than that," Alice said.

"Exactly. Just recently, a Chinese clockworker bred an entire new species of silkworm. It produced thread that could be woven into a lightweight cloth that blends into nearly any surrounding, much like a chameleon. The military implications were staggering."

"Not to mention what a smuggler could use it for," Gavin pointed out.

"An airman would think of that," Phipps said. "Fortunately for us, one of our own clockworkers created a special lens that converts heat—he calls it infrared energy—into visible light. He created several, in fact, and we handed them out to the army, which rendered the chameleon cloth much less useful." She tapped her own monocle. "They're also quite nice for seeing in the dark."

The lift came to a stop, and Phipps slid the iron gate open. A chilly stone corridor greeted them. Electric lights provided a steady glow, though the place smelled of damp.

"What's this place?" Alice asked.

"The high-powered floor."

Phipps took them out of the lift, and Alice abruptly realized she was still holding Gavin's elbow. Her face grew hot and she let go. Gavin didn't seem to notice, or pretended not to.

"This is where we keep the most powerful clockworkers and their technology," Phipps said. "This is what our agents live to find—and protect. It's what holds the British Empire together."

Alice was expecting even more wonders than she'd seen upstairs, but they only passed a series of side corridors and heavy, closed doors. Behind one of them, however, she heard a muffled explosion and what might have been a scream.

"What's that?" Gavin asked. He was pointing down a short corridor that ended in a round steel door that looked to be ten or twelve feet in diameter. Flanking it were four guards armed with wicked-looking rifles Alice couldn't begin to identify. They certainly didn't fire bullets.

"That's the Doomsday Vault," Phipps said. "Sometimes a clockworker will create something so terrifying or dangerous that using it would be unthinkable, even in dire need. We lock all such inventions in the Vault, where no one can touch them. There's enough power beyond that door to demolish the world a dozen times over."

"Why not simply destroy such devices?" Alice asked, aghast.

"Believe me, Miss Michaels, we've had many discussions about that over the decades. Some devices are too dangerous to destroy. Other devices might turn out to be useful later. Another clockworker might invent a safeguard, for example, that makes the original device highly useful. In the end, Her Majesty decreed that we keep everything, just in case."

"How do they create these inventions, Lieutenant?" Alice asked. "And how far can they go?"

"That's the question that gives me nightmares, Miss Michaels. We used to think that clockworkers were bound by the laws of physics, and they could do something only if it were physically possible and they had enough money and the right equipment. But now the clockworkers are discovering that the boundaries of these physical laws are . . . porous. I hear them use phrases such as *gravity sinkhole* and *extra-temporal commutation*. I think that last term has something to do with traveling in time. I've had two—*two*—clockworkers tell me that matter and energy are the same thing, and another one said he could see entire universes that occupy the same space as this one. I thought he had reached the complete lunatic point in his illness, but then he turned up with three parallel versions of himself, and it was only with great difficulty that we persuaded him to send them back. The world is very lucky that they need extensive and expensive equipment to create their most powerful inventions, or Earth would have been destroyed long ago. They create with great glee and don't think about the repercussions, which is why the Third Ward has to search them out and bring them here, where we can keep their work in check."

She took them to a particular door, selected a strange-looking key from a ring on her belt, and tapped it near the lock. The key rang—it was actually a tuning fork.

"C-sharp," Gavin said.

"I wouldn't know," Phipps said. The lock clicked, and she pushed the door open. "This is the sound laboratory, and we need you here, Mr. Ennock."

"Gavin!" Simon d'Arco rose from a marble worktable. "Glad you arrived. And nice to see you again, Miss Michaels."

"It's been only a few minutes, Mr. d'Arco," Alice said.

"'Simon,' please. I said we're very informal in the Ward."

"Do you call the lieutenant 'Susan'?" Alice asked, genuinely curious.

"No," Phipps said.

"And this"—Simon gestured to another man—"is Gabriel Stark, but he prefers to be known as Doctor Clef."

A shortish, balding man in coveralls, goggles, and a stained white coat looked up from the strange object he was working on. The object appeared to be a wire framework, but it twisted Alice's eye. The lines of the cube came together . . . wrong. The more she looked at it, the more the front of the lattice seemed to fade into the back, or maybe the back was coming into the front. The man pushed his goggles onto his high forehead, revealing watery blue eyes set into a round face. "Good day," he said in the broad, loopy tones of a north German.

"What is that thing?" Alice asked.

"Do you like it?" Dr. Clef said. "It is a cube, and it is quite impossible. Watch this." He reached for a machine mounted on his desk. A wire led from the machine to the Impossible Cube, and when Dr. Clef spun a crank on the machine, the wires in the cube sparked and glowed blue. As Alice watched, the cube trembled, then rose a good inch above the table.

"It can *fly*!" Gavin gasped.

"Good heavens!" Alice said. "Is it a magician's trick?"

"No, no." Dr. Clef stopped cranking, and the cube dropped back to the table. "It is an alloy of my own design. When the electricity goes through the metal, it ignores gravity a little. It allows the Impossible Cube to do what it must do."

"And what is that?" Alice asked.

Dr. Clef blinked at her. "How can I know? It is not yet finished."

"It can fly," Gavin muttered. "Fly!"

"Doctor Clef is one of our more prolific clockworkers," Simon told them. "His work is currently at a delicate stage, and he didn't want to stop, so—"

"Go on, go on." Dr. Clef made shooing motions with his screwdriver. "Do not mind me. I make no sound."

"So come in," Simon said. "The laboratory awaits."

The sound laboratory was a brightly lit stone room filled with equipment Alice didn't recognize, some of it small, some of it large, and Alice's fingers itched to take every piece apart and examine them from the inside. One wall was taken up by a variety of musical instruments—harp, drum, piano, violin, cello, flute, bugle, trumpet, and more. Another wall was filled with bookcases and books. Simon led Gavin to the instrument wall.

"Do you know why we're excited to have you, Gavin?" he asked.

Gavin shook his head. He was still staring at the Impossible Cube.

"We suspect you have a musical talent of a type that appears perhaps once a generation," Simon explained. "Or even less often."

"How did you know he *has* such a musical talent?" Alice interrupted.

"Our agents heard him play in Hyde Park, and we suspected," Phipps said. "But before we could move to find out more, he inexplicably vanished. We couldn't find him any-where. You can imagine our reaction when Agent Teasdale got your letter and he turned up at your home, Miss Michaels, especially since we've been investigating your aunt."

"*Have* you?" Alice said in a chilly tone.

"Of course. She falls under our jurisdiction. We learned of your aunt's condition several weeks ago and sent agents to investigate. When our people arrived, they found her house in a difficult state. A trap near her front door instantly killed one of my people. His name was Franklin Mayweather, and he had a wife and two children."

Alice remembered the puddle of dried blood on the floor. Guilt stabbed her stomach, even though she'd had nothing to do with the trap or Franklin Mayweather's death.

"My people tried to capture the woman Edwina," Phipps continued, "but she eluded them and vanished. Her house was heavily trapped, and after some investigation, they decided the place was too dangerous for further exploration, so they left."

"Then who demolished her laboratory?" Alice asked.

"I couldn't say. However, apprehending Edwina is still a high priority. She has already killed Franklin Mayweather, and we need to stop her before someone else pays the same price. In addition, the clockworker who controlled those plague zombies and wreaked havoc the night of the Green-fellow ball is still at large, and we have a number of cases on the Continent we're overseeing. In other words, we need all the agents we can lay hands on."

"And musical talents such as Gavin's are useful in the extreme." Simon sat at the piano and played a single key. "What note is this?"

"B," Gavin said, tearing his gaze away from Dr. Clef's cube. "I have perfect pitch. You don't need to test that."

"Indulge me." Simon played several notes, all of which

Gavin named perfectly. Then he played chords, and Gavin named those as well. Occasionally he played one chord with one hand and another chord with the other, which Gavin helpfully pointed out. "Good, good."

"This young man is pleasing to me," Dr. Clef called from his worktable. "How well do you remember the music?"

"I learn fast," Gavin said, taking out his fiddle and tuning it quickly. Alice leaned forward on her stool.

"How fast?" Dr. Clef asked.

"I'm running the tests, Doctor Clef," Simon said. "I thought you had work to do."

"Yes, yes, yes." Dr. Clef bent studiously over his cube, though Alice could see him peering at Gavin, despite his goggles.

"Play something," Gavin said.

Simon played in a minor key. Gavin listened through one verse and one chorus. Simon stopped playing, and Gavin played it through perfectly. Simon joined back in again, and Gavin played harmony. They played other songs back and forth, songs Alice couldn't identify. Gavin's fiddle swooped and spun, though every note echoed off hard stone. Dr. Clef gave up all pretense of working and listened. Alice heard a quiet longing in the music, a wish for every note to fly free, and it brought a quiet tear to one eye.

"That was perfect," Simon breathed. "Can you sing, Gavin?"

"Yes."

"Sing something for me, then. Your favorite song."

"'The Wraggle Taggle Gypsies,'" Gavin said. He raised his fiddle for accompaniment and sang.

> *There were three gypsies a-come to my door,*
> *And downstairs ran this a-lady, O!*
> *One sang high and another sang low*
> *And the other sang bonny, bonny Biscay, O!*

Alice stared. She had never heard Gavin sing. His light, clear voice arrested her. His white-blond hair shone in the bright electric light, and his lithe body moved with the fiddle. He played and sang with his entire soul, and Alice wanted to get up and dance.

> *Then she pulled off her silk finished gown*
> *And put on hose of leather, O!*
> *The ragged, ragged rags about our door*
> *She's gone with the wraggle taggle gypsies, O!*

Gavin's voice and fiddle tugged at Alice. They sang of adventure, of new places, of casting off rules and conventions. In that moment, she would have followed Gavin anywhere. Dr. Clef had abandoned his work and was now sitting at Gavin's feet like a small child. Gavin's blue eyes met Alice's brown ones, and she couldn't look away. She didn't want to.

> *What care I for my house and my land?*
> *What care I for my money, O?*
> *What care I for my new wedded lord?*
> *I'm off with the wraggle taggle gypsies, O!*

The song ended. Dr. Clef jerked as if he had been slapped awake. Simon applauded. Phipps stood nearby with her arms crossed, expression unreadable. Alice spun sideways on the stool, face flushed.

"Marvelous!" Simon said. "Worthy of a concert hall."

"Not the first time someone has told me that, actually," Gavin said with a wry smile. He tried to catch Alice's eye, but she didn't dare meet that gaze. "You still haven't explained why this is worth something to you."

Dr. Clef crept back to his table and set back to work, one eye still on Gavin.

"One last question before I answer." Simon turned back to the piano. "What kind of interval is this?"

He played it, and Dr. Clef yelled. Alice twisted on her stool in alarm. The clockworker clapped both hands over his ears and yelled and yelled. Lieutenant Phipps was instantly by his side. She touched his cheek with her mechanical hand, and he calmed.

"I'm sorry, Doctor Clef," Simon said. "I forgot you were in the room."

"What was that all about?" Alice demanded. She was still half-ready to run for the door.

Gavin grimaced. "I don't know the name of the interval, but no song I know uses it."

"A tritone," Alice put in. "The Devil's Interval. The one you asked me to play during the zombie attack."

"Exactly." Simon closed the piano lid. "And it all comes back to clockworkers. They love music. They can even be entranced or hypnotized by an exceedingly well-played song, the more complicated the better, as Doctor Clef demonstrated. So you can see why someone who can sing and play like you do, Gavin, would be a tremendous asset to a group that collects clockworkers."

"Why tritones?" Alice asked. "We used one during the zombie attack, but no one would explain why it worked."

"They are horrible," Dr. Clef muttered. *"Ungeheurlich."*

"Most clockworkers experience actual pain when they hear a tritone," Simon explained. "The instrument you repaired during the zombie attack was designed to play music especially loudly, and you saw the impact a loud tritone had on that clockworker."

"In addition," Phipps added, "it's important to understand that all musical intervals can be expressed as numbers, determined by the frequency ratio."

"Frequency ratio?" Gavin said.

"In simple terms," Simon said, "when an object such as a

string of a certain length vibrates at a certain speed to create a certain sound, it produces a certain number of cycles—a measurement of sonic energy. If you compare that string with another string vibrating at a different speed, you get a ratio. Perhaps one string produces three cycles each time the other produces two cycles, giving us a ratio of three to two. That particular ratio, incidentally, makes the sound of a perfect fifth. Two strings vibrating at a ratio of two to one will give us an octave."

"I don't understand what this has to do with clockworkers finding tritones painful," Alice said.

"The frequency ratio of a perfect tritone does not exist," Simon said. "In mathematical terms, the ratio of a tritone is one to the square root of two." Dr. Clef shuddered at his table.

"The square root of two?" Alice repeated. "But that can't exist."

"That's what I just said. The square root of two is an irrational number. On the one hand, it must exist—we can see it in a right triangle. We can hear it in the frequency ratio of a tritone. But on the other hand, no two identical rational numbers will multiply together to make two. The square root of two can't exist, and yet it does. Irrational. We think this is why tritones bother clockworkers so much. They sense aspects of the universe that normal people can't, and the paradox created by that irrational frequency ratio causes them distress."

"And that's why the symbol of the Third Ward is the square root of two," Phipps said. "We shouldn't exist, but we do. Which brings me to our next point. Gavin Ennock, you have a musical talent that would be very useful to the Third Ward. I would like to officially offer you a position as an agent. Will you accept?"

"Yes," Gavin said instantly.

Phipps nodded, though her expression didn't change.

"And Alice Michaels, you have a talent for assembling and using clockworker technology, one never before seen. This would also be extremely useful to the Third Ward. Will you accept a position as an agent?"

Alice looked at Gavin's expectant face, then at Phipps's impassive one.

"No," she said.

"No?" Gavin said. "Al—Miss Michaels! Why not?"

"I don't wish to discuss it, Mr. Ennock," Alice replied primly. "But I do wish to leave. Now."

Phipps's expression remained neutral. "If you like. But first I have to perform a quick procedure."

She drew a strange-looking pistol, and Alice pulled back with a hiss. "What on earth?"

"This is not a weapon, Miss Michaels." Phipps unwound a cable from the stock and plugged it into a receptacle in her own forearm. A high-pitched whine grated in Alice's ears just as Phipps pulled the trigger, and Alice was half-blinded by a dazzling pattern of color. She rubbed at her eyes, trying to regain her vision.

"What was that?" she demanded.

"Another clockworker invention," Phipps said. "As I understand it, the light patterns disrupt the connections between the portion of your brain that stores recent memory and the portion that controls speech. In other words, you won't be able to talk about anything that has happened in the last two hours, more or less. It's standard practice for all those who see our installation but aren't part of the Third Ward. Simon will see you out. Gavin will, of course, stay here to begin his training immediately."

And she turned her back on Alice to talk to Gavin. Alice left the room, leaving Simon to scramble after her. She kept an icy silence all the way up the elevator, out the main doors, and to the main gates, where Simon hailed a cab for her.

"Can you tell me why, Miss Michaels?" he asked, dark eyes almost pleading.

"I'm late for luncheon with my fiancé, Mr. d'Arco," Alice said. "Good day."

And she was gone.

Chapter Nine

Dear Gramps:

You must have got my telegram, so you
know I'm all right. Now I can write a
longer letter and tell you more than
ESCAPED PIRATES. AM FINE.

Some friends told me that the
Juniper's capture made the papers in
Boston. You must have been worried sick.
I'm all right. Really. The pirates
boarded us and we fought, including me.
I'm sorry, Gramps, but Tom was killed.
So was Captain Naismith. Both of them
fought, and they were brave. Tell Ma,
but do it gentle, all right?

And how is Ma? And Jenny and Harry
and Violet and Patrick? Did Jenny get
married? Was Ma able to send Patrick to
school? He's smarter than any of us, so
I hope so.

Anyway, I escaped the pirates in
London, but Boston Shipping and Mail

wouldn't put me on another ship. Now I
have a job at ███████████, and it
pays a lot better than cabin boy or
airman.

I guess I should explain some more.
At ███████████ my job is ███████, so
I can't say much about it. Don't worry!
It's not illegal or bad or anything. I'm
helping people. I'm a sort of policeman.
They want me because I can ███████.

Oh, come on! Does that have to be—
hey! Don't write that part down! Or
that! Don't you have a button for when
I'm editing or something?

Gramps, you can already tell I'm not
writing this letter. It's called a
transcription, and it's supposed to be
my thoughts as they come out of me, like
a song I make up as I go. I'm speaking,
and my words are being written on a kind
of printing machine for me by ███
███████████—fine, by someone else. The
████████ blocks out what I'm not
supposed to talk about, and ███ corrects
my grammar, too.

My new boss is ███████████ and—oh
gosh. All right, I'll call her P. Does
that work? Good. So P. paired me up to
work with—uh, I can see a black mark
coming—with Mr. D. and Dr. C. for my
training. Mr. D. is a good man. He seems
to like me quite a bit, and don't
worry—he makes sure I eat. In fact, he
eats almost every meal with me. He said
that I should write a long letter to

you, and ███████████ would pay for
the airmail postage, so that's what I'm
doing. He also said that I should talk a
lot about everything that's going on in
order to sort out how I feel about it
all because it'll help. What he means by
that, I don't know.

So on the first day here, I was
brought in with a very pretty woman
named ████████████, who— Hey, come on!
She didn't even join ████████. Why do
you have to blank her name out?

████. Hey, look—the machine blanks
out profanity, too. ████████████████
it all to ████! And █████ your auntie
while you're at it. Huh. So much for the
saying, "He curses like an airman."

Right, so ████—I guess I'll call her
Miss A.—is very pretty, and I like her a
lot, Gramps. I wish you were here,
because I could really use some advice
about her. She's older than I am—twenty-
one or twenty-two—but that's not the
problem. Or I thought it wasn't. She got
█████████ off and left when P. offered
her a job at ████████████. I haven't
had a chance to talk to her about it,
and, well, it makes me sad that she
isn't here. We kind of went through a
lot together. ████████████████████████
████████████████, ████████████████
████████, ████████████████
████████. ████████████████████—and
I just noticed that you're not able to
read any of this. What's the point of my

talking about this if none of it
actually gets down on paper, you stupid
██████████?

That wasn't a curse word, Gramps.

Anyway, she left, and I was upset
about it. I didn't know what to do. You
don't have the chance to talk to a lot
of women on an airship, and I have no
idea what to do. Should I run after her
or write to her or just leave her alone?
If you can write back and tell me, man
to man, it would help.

Next, Mr. D. took me upstairs to show
me the dormitory where I'd be staying. I
have a room to myself! I have a bed, not
a hammock, with a mattress, and fresh
sheets every week, and a wool blanket.
There's a bookshelf for my things, when
I get some, and a desk where I can read.
It even has a radiator, and I can make
the room as warm as I want just by
twisting a knob. You'd like this place.
I wish you could see it.

Mr. D. gave me a tour. This place is
huge, Gramps, and always busy. People
are running up and down the halls all
the time, and going in and out of
██████████████ and puzzling out
clockworker inventions. The place has
huge kitchens to feed everyone and a
research library and a conservatory and
a lot of other stuff you'd find in a
school or college.

After that, Mr. D. took me to a shop
because I didn't have any clothes. He

said ██████████████ would pay for it at
first and then I could pay them back. We
went to his tailor, who owns a big shop
and does a lot of work for ███████████.
This tall, thin man with a white fringe
of hair came out from behind a counter,
smiling and nodding like I was royalty,
and measured me up, down, and sideways.
I almost socked him when he measured one
part that Mr. D. said was just my
inseam. He—I—ordered shirts, jackets,
and trousers. It felt strange. I've
never owned so many clothes before. We
ordered different kinds of clothes, too—
workman's clothes and farmer's clothes
and servant's clothes. They're for when
I ██████████████████, which I
apparently can't talk about, either.
They also had leather outfits like the
ones I used to wear on the ship, but
they were all black instead of white.
Some of the stuff, including the
leathers, happened to fit or they were
tailored on the spot and I could take
them back with me. Actually, Mr. D. told
them to deliver it all, and I felt
strange about that, too—no one's ever
fetched or carried for me before. Mr. D.
said I look really good in black, and I
couldn't tell if he was kidding or not—
all the men at ██████████████ wear
black. Mr. D. gives me a lot of
compliments, and I guess I'm not used to
that.

   Mr. D. had me put on one set of my

new clothes—they itched a little—and we got into a cab. I thought we were going back to the . . . back to where I work now. But we went a different way.

London is like Boston in some ways, Gramps. They're both busy all the time. The streets are crowded with people and horses and wagons and carriages. The smells change every few feet—bread or manure or cloth or flowers or just people. Voices shout and yell. Vendors sell anything you need, and there are lots of ███████████ offering up— Oh, come on! Gramps lived in the █████ part of Boston his whole life! He knows what a ██████ is.

Fine. Anyway, half the city is being built up to the sky, and the other half is being dug down under the ground. Everything is dust or rain or mud. It's depressing. And the fog! You can slice it up and eat it for dinner.

Something happier to talk about: They gave me a piece of my salary, but I don't need much because I live at work, so I'm sending you some. You can buy medicine. And get Ma a new dress, all right? Or maybe you can send Patrick to school with some of it. Tell him his big brother is still watching over him.

Anyway, I was saying that Mr. D. had the cabbie drive us to his men's club for lunch.

I've never been in a club. I tried to act as if I knew everything, but to tell the truth, I was scared I'd make a

mistake and they'd throw me out. The
club looks like an ordinary brownstone
house, except on the door hangs a brass
plaque that reads THE E CONSTANT CLUB. Mr.
D. says the name is a joke, but I don't
get it.

We went inside. It was red wallpaper
and rugs with designs and heavy
furniture and bookshelves and big rooms
with men smoking everywhere. Mr. D.
introduced me around, then took me to
the dining room. The tables were set
with crystal and china and silver. I was
really nervous now. I'd never eaten in
such a fine place. Mr. D. ordered food
for both of us, and then a little
trolley walked up to our table with a
champagne bottle in a silver ice bucket
on it. Two mechanical arms from the
trolley popped the bottle and poured us
each a glass.

"We have to celebrate," Mr. D. said.

I thought he meant we had to
celebrate me joining ███████████, and
I felt kind of excited—I'd never had
champagne before, or anything worth
drinking champagne about—but instead,
Mr. D. raised his glass and said, "May
you live a hundred years, Gavin, with
one extra year to repent!"

And then I remembered it was my
eighteenth birthday. I'd completely
forgotten. I would have made airman
today. The entire crew would have made a
double line on deck beneath the envelope,
and I would have run down the middle

while they swatted me with wooden
paddles. Captain Naismith and Pilot would
have greeted me at the end of the line,
pulled off my cabin boy leathers and
boots, and thrown them overboard. Then I
would have had to climb the netting,
barefoot and in my underwear, to the
highest part of the envelope, where the
newest airman—that would have been Tom—
would be waiting with my new boots and
leathers, the ones with wings on the
lapel. Once I put them on, I would have
climbed back down to the rest of the
crew, who would cheer and feed me bread,
salt, and beer. "Go up a boy; come down a
man." Then there would be a party.

Instead, I was sitting in a strange
club with a man I'd met only a few hours
before, holding a glass of champagne,
and seeing my shock reflected in a cold
bucket made of silver. I wondered if
they had champagne in heaven for Tom and
Captain Naismith. It wouldn't be fair if
I had it and they didn't.

Mr. D. must have seen my face,
because he put his glass down. "I'm
sorry. I didn't mean to upset you. Is
your birthday a bad thing?"

"No," I hurried to say. "I'm sorry.
Thank you." I raised my glass to him and
sipped. It was like drinking sour air.
"It'd just slipped away from me, with
all that's happened. I'm fine."

"We'll get some food in you and
you'll be right as rain, eh?" Mr. D.
said cheerfully. He didn't want to see

me upset, and I didn't want to look
upset. So I nodded.

Our lunch arrived. It was some kind
of chopped chicken with vegetables over
mashed potatoes, but done up fancy. For
dessert, the waiter brought ice cream
and a small chocolate cake. I liked that
and thanked Mr. D., and he looked happy.

"Once you're more established, we'll
have to sponsor you for membership
here," he said.

"Do you think Miss A. has a club?" I
blurted out.

"I wouldn't know." He lit a cigar and
offered me one, but I thought about
Captain Naismith and turned it down.
"You have your eye on her, do you?"

"Um . . ." was all I could say.

He muttered something that sounded
like "██████" around his cigar. "We can't
force her to join us, you know."

"I know. I was just surprised she
didn't." I glanced at the grandfather
clock in the corner. "I think I have
training soon. Should we go?"

"Of course, of course." Mr. D. signed
the check and we left. A few minutes
later, we were back at headquarters, and
I was in combat class, learning how to
fight and trying not to think about
Miss A.

P. teaches the combat class herself.
I guess she used to teach a lot of
classes, but now that she's a
██████████, she only has time for
combat.

I have to tell you, Gramps, P. may be
a woman, but she scares the ████ out of
me. She has only one ████, and she wears
a special ███████ on her ████, and she
has this way of looking at you as if you
had no skin.

There were six of us in the class—
four men and two women. We were all
wearing something like black swim
outfits. The women's had skirts attached.
P wore a plain version of her uniform—no
medals or epaulets to grab. I was the
newest student, but I'd be fine—I knew
how to fight. ████, I'd survived an
attack by ████ing pirates.

The class took place in an echoing
gymnasium with mattresses on the floor.
Everyone stood in a circle, and P.
called me into the middle to face her.

"Show me what you can do, Gavin," P.
said.

I eyed her right arm, the ██████████
one.

"Don't worry about that," she said.
"I won't cheat. Though eventually you'll
have to learn how to fight me—or someone
like me."

"Are we fighting fair or are we
fighting to win?" I asked.

"Good question," she said with
approval. "In ██████████████, we fight to
win. In this class, though, we don't
want anyone to get hurt. Even our
doctors can only do so much."

"Got it. Then let's—" I faked a swing
at her face, then punched her stomach.

Or tried to. She blocked me, and then I was flat on a mattress with her fist an inch from my nose.

"Good," she said, and hauled me to my feet with easy strength. The other students were grinning. "Nice attempt at distraction, decent reflexes. Try again."

"How did you do that?" I asked instead. "Show me."

"Try again, Gavin."

"Sorry." I punched; she swept my hand aside. I tried again and again and again, but I couldn't touch her. Soon I was panting and sweaty, but she was unruffled.

"Not bad," she said. "You fight like a pirate and have some bad habits, but we can work on that. What weapons can you use?"

"Uh . . . cutlass, belaying pin, flechette pistol."

"Handy. Rifle?"

I shook my head. "You don't use anything that sparks on an airship unless you're deadly stupid."

"Right. Bernard, I want you to take Gavin through some basics of self-defense, better than what a pirate learns. Everyone else, pair off for sparring."

Bernard, a brown-haired man about ten years older than me, came forward, but I turned back to P. "Ma'am," I said. She raised an eyebrow at me. "I'm not a pirate. I'm an airman. There's a difference."

She gave me a long look, then said, "Noted. Now learn, Gavin."

And I did. I thought I knew something about fighting, but it turns out I didn't know anything. ███████████████ uses boxing techniques from China, and they're nothing like anything you learn on an airship. It was an entirely different way to move. A different way to think. And you have to shout every time you do something. It's strange, but it works.

After that, I changed clothes and met Mr. D. and Dr. C. down in Dr. C.'s laboratory. He's a ███████████, and he has a special alloy that can ████ if you pump ██████████ through it. He also discovered that sound travels in waves like ripples across a pond. He's even figured out how to measure sound waves— and change them. So he's supposed to train me in music.

At first, I didn't think there'd be much he could teach me, but after that fight class, I wasn't so sure. Turned out I was right. I know a lot about "practical application," as Dr. Clef calls it, but I don't know much about music theory, and that's what he's teaching me. A lot of it is giving names and numbers to what I know by instinct. Dr. C. says we're taming my music.

But I really miss flying, Gramps. It's been weeks, but I jerk awake mornings, and my back aches and I can hear the sky

calling like a song I can only half
hear, and it hurts. On those mornings,
gravity pulls down every note I play,
and I swear they shatter on the floor.
Dr. C. throws up his hands. "Ach!" he
shouts. "You have the hands of a brick!
Go away before you break my ears!"

This letter is getting long. Tell
everyone I love them. I don't know when
I'll be able to visit again, but
remember that I'm safe and I'm doing
fine.

Love to all,

Gavin

PART
II

Chapter Ten

The music box clinked through another uniform round of music. Alice put down her teacup and smiled across the breakfast tray at Norbert, who was skimming the *Times*, freshly ironed by one of the automaton maids. "Anything interesting?" she asked.

"The uprising in India has finally been put down," he said. "Maybe now Lord Elgin will get enough men to put the coolies in their place. Some are wondering if this will be another war over opium."

"One can hardly blame the Chinese for their anger," Alice said as Kemp refilled her cup. "As I recall, the Treaty of Nanking forced them to pay enormous sums of money to England and make a number of trade concessions while England gave virtually nothing in return."

"It only means one thing." Norbert set the paper aside and picked up his own cup. "More demand for weapons. I might expand the factory in that direction. Good news for us, eh?"

They were sitting in the morning room in Norbert's enormous house in London eleven months after their engagement. The windows were shut against a dreary April sky, but a shared breakfast tray on a small table between them sent up smells of fresh bread, butter, sausage, tea, and chocolate. Norbert sipped the latter. The breakfast menu always remained the same. The one day when Alice had suggested they have something besides bread and sausage, Norbert's face had turned bright red and his hands had shaken. Alice quickly retracted her suggestion, and he returned to normal.

In the last several months, Alice had learned that all of Norbert's habits were exact and regular. Every morning when she arrived at his house for their customary breakfast together, she found him bathed and fully dressed in the same cut of business suit. He greeted her with the same "Good morning, my darling," gave her the same kiss on the cheek, and seated her at the same chair at the same table in the morning room. The music box she had pretended to admire on the day he had more or less proposed to her played the same songs quietly through the meal. He read the front page and business sections of the *London Times* while they ate, commented on one or two stories, and was ready for the day at 7:20. He would return by eight o'clock, when supper was to be served.

On Tuesdays and Saturdays, Norbert brought flowers, chocolates, or some other gift for her. After supper, he gave her the same cheek kiss and bid her the same good-bye. If she hadn't seen Norbert accidentally cut himself with a fish knife once, she would have suspected he was some kind of extremely advanced automaton.

As for Alice herself, Norbert had moved her to a much nicer flat within walking distance of Norbert's house. Since he owned the flats, Alice could stay rent-free. Alice also noticed her father's creditors had stopped calling. A secret look through the ledgers told her that Norbert had paid the worst of Father's debts, but he still owed more than ten times the annual salary Alice had been offered by the Third Ward. This problem, of course, would evaporate the moment Alice said, "I do."

Alice passed the majority of her days in Norbert's house, ostensibly to take care of her father, and she did spend a fair amount of time doing just that, of course. After Norbert had announced their engagement in the *Times*, he had offered to move Arthur out of that run-down residence and into Norbert's own home, where he would be warm and the resident automatons could see to his needs with tireless attention to detail, since Alice couldn't provide round-the-clock care even in her own flat, and a hospital was out of the question. Alice, naturally, could not fully move in with Norbert. That would be far from proper. However, her father provided a built-in chaperone, which meant she could visit at any time, even if Father spent the entire visit shut up in his room with the heat on. As long as the proprieties were observed, society would approve.

This is what you wanted, she told herself. *Father's debts are paid, he's happy you're "taken care of," he spends his remaining days in a suite of his own, and you . . . you have a wealthy, traditional husband—or you will very soon. Thousands of women would tread hot coals to trade places with you. You've won.*

So why did it feel so much like losing?

Norbert swallowed the last of his chocolate, set his cup on the saucer with a *clink*, and checked his watch. "Nearly time," he said. "Have you finished going through the household accounts?"

Alice nodded. One of her duties as Norbert's wife would be to keep track of domestic finances. The staggering sums she was to oversee had come as a bit of a shock. "I think I can keep the house's books without trouble."

"You're very quick," Norbert said, clearly pleased. "This evening, then, I'll show you the other task I'll need you to take on after we're married. It's hard to believe the wedding's less than three months away."

"What task is that?" Alice asked.

"No time to explain it now," he said, rising. "I'll be late.

You're beautiful." He kissed her on the cheek and left exactly on time.

"Louisa Creek to see you, Madam," said Kemp.

Alice all but leapt to her feet. "Don't keep her standing in the hall, Kemp. Show her in!"

Louisa didn't wait for the black-and-white automaton's permission. She bustled into the enormous drawing room and flung her arms around Alice. "I shall never forgive you," she cried. "Never in my life!"

"It's nice to see you, too," Alice said, hugging her back. "What did I do now?"

"It's what you haven't done." The older woman held Alice at arm's length and looked her up and down. "Wonderful dress. Blue silk suits you, darling, and I've never liked crinolines, either. Maybe between the two of us we can start a revolution. Hairstyle from Paris, of course—good choice. Smashing necklace. I'll be borrowing that later. Shame about the shoes, but we'll work on those."

"What's wrong with my shoes? And what are you never going to forgive me for?" Alice was trying not to laugh. "Really, Louisa, I haven't seen you for two months, and you're acting as if it's only been a day."

"Best way to handle absences," Louisa declared stoutly. "And I'm never forgiving you because you *still* haven't called on me. Not once, even after you get back from having your wedding dress made in Paris! You got back two *weeks* ago, darling."

"I have no excuse. I'm a terrible person, and I throw myself on your mercy."

"Noted," Louisa sniffed. "I won't even *mention* that you didn't even send me a postcard and that I learned about your arrival by reading the *Times.*"

"I've been planning!" Alice protested.

"Is that what you call it? Show the dress. Now."

"I can't. It's being shipped, and I do promise to let you know the moment it arrives so you can see it."

"So you say." Louisa plumped herself into a chair. "Tell me *everything*. How was Paris?"

"Wonderful! I'd love to go back for our wedding trip, but Norbert wants to visit Spain and Italy." Alice took a seat of her own. "I'll have to leave Kemp behind again—the Papists shun automatons that act human. He almost popped his gears when I told him."

"My position is to ensure Madam's physical comfort, regardless of human spiritual concerns," Kemp sniffed. "It is difficult to do so from across the Channel. Shall I bring the tea?"

"Yes, Kemp," Alice said, and he stalked out. "Anyway, the dressmaker sews everything by machine, so she could make the dress almost overnight. It's incredible the times we live in, Louisa."

"Yes, yes, very interesting." Louisa leaned forward. "Norbert went along, didn't he?"

Alice colored. "Well, yes. But in a different train and he stayed in a different hotel, and I hired a maid who was with me every moment we—"

"So is he a good man, then?"

"Oh. Well, yes. So far. He doesn't shout or order me around or—"

"I *meant*," Louisa interrupted, "is he any good where it counts, darling? In the bedroom."

"Louisa!" Alice put a hand to her mouth. "Honestly!"

"Don't come over all shocked with me, darling. I practically fed him to you at that ghastly Greenfellow ball, and then you offer yourself up to him like a tabby to a tom and don't even drop me a *card*. After all that, you can certainly tell me if Norbie measures up after two months in Paris."

"Louisa!" Alice flushed and tried to regain control of herself. "We haven't . . . All he's done is kiss me. On the cheek."

"How English of him. Do you want some advice? There are a number of ways to stoke a man's furnace, if you—"

"No, no. I'm . . . I've read quite a lot, thank you. And planning has kept me busy, in any case. I think Father's on pins and needles."

Louisa paused, and her tone became more tender. "How is your father?"

"As well as can be expected," Alice said, feeling on safer ground.

"Don't *do* that," Louisa admonished. "Everyone needs someone to talk to. It's why the Papists invented confession. How is he *really*?"

The safer ground had shifted. "Not well." A bubble of anxiety rose up even as Alice said the words. "I was hoping that moving him here, with good food and warm rooms, would improve his health, but he's only gotten worse. It's as if he's decided to let himself go, now that I'm engaged. Oh, Louisa, I don't know what I'll do when he . . . when he . . ."

Louisa looked misty herself, and Alice wondered why— she had met Father only the one time. She reached over and patted Alice's hand. "It happens to us all," Louisa said. "When the end comes, you have Norbert and me to help you through it."

Kemp entered with the tea cart, the sound of the wheels muffled by the thick Persian rugs. He had already drawn back the drapes from the two-story windows to let in early-spring sunshine, which spilled across perfectly matched red velvet furniture, meticulously placed end tables, a perfect settee, and a fainting couch pulled just close enough to a square marble fireplace. And it was just one of dozens of what Norbert called "cozy little rooms." Just one could have swallowed up the cold-water flat she had shared with her father, a fact that followed her every evening when Kemp accompanied her home to the new flat.

At first, Alice had spent these little walks glancing nervously over her shoulder for the grinning clockworker, but he hadn't appeared; after a few weeks, she had finally stopped looking. Alice had spent a large part of one day fruitlessly checking back issues of the *Times* for any mention of him. Now she was wondering if he had gone completely mad and died, as every clockworker inevitably did.

With that off her mind, however, she found herself a bit timid about exploring Norbert's house, as if she were an interloper. No, that wasn't quite it. The place intimidated her. The lack of human servants made the place echo like an empty cavern, and machines moved just out of her line of vision. It unnerved her. She knew it was silly—soon she'd be the lady of the place—but she'd put off exploring, even after all these months. It wasn't as if she had to do much. The automatons took care of the daily chores with no need for Alice to oversee them. Every evening, a spider brought her a punch card with menu choices for the next day's supper on it, and she poked out the ones she wanted. At her own flat, Kemp helped her dress, and he helped with her hair, and he brought her a tea tray. In fact, Kemp refused to allow any other automaton to wait on Alice at all. Even now Kemp fussed with the pillow on her chair while Alice poured for Louisa and herself.

"Is the room of a comfortable temperature, Madam?" he asked. "My thermometer indicates it may be chilly."

"It's fine, Kemp. Thank you." Alice added pointedly, "I'll ring if we need anything."

"Yes, Madam." Kemp withdrew with stiff formality.

Louisa dropped a sugar cube into her tea. "Is he listening outside the door?"

"Kemp, are you listening at the door?"

"Yes, Madam."

"Please stop. Go check on Father."

"Yes, Madam."

Louisa sipped, then reached for a cake. "Rumor has it you had some mysterious visitors right around the time you became engaged."

"Really?" Alice said in a neutral tone.

"An airship hovered over your father's row house for a considerable period just after an entire house disappeared at an estate outside London. And I seem to remember a certain calling card in your room. I have to wonder if these events are connected. Did you write that Teasdale woman?"

"Honestly, Louisa—how do you remember her name after all this time?"

"I remember everything about everyone, darling. That's what makes me so much fun at parties. So you *did* write her. Was she the one in the airship? Where did they take you?"

Alice opened her mouth to explain, to tell Louisa about the Third Ward, but what came out were the words, "I can't talk about it." And then her mouth clamped shut. She remembered Lieutenant Phipps and her strange pistol full of flashing lights.

"What? I'm your closest friend. I told you about that incident with the undergardener when I was fourteen. Surely you can tell me about this."

Alice tried again. "I can't talk about it." She grimaced. "Louisa, I'm just ... not allowed, all right? Please don't press. Help me explore the house instead. I haven't done it properly, and I don't want to do it on my own."

"Oh, very well." Louisa finished her cake and rose. "I can give you decorating advice."

The first room they came across was a library. Books of all sizes and thicknesses lined enormous shelves and filled the air with the smell of leather and paper. A pigeonhole section contained scrolls. Alice skimmed the titles. Predictably, most of the books dealt with physics, automatics, chemistry, and other sciences. Alice pulled several volumes on automatics and set them on a table. Each one held a punch card in it like a bookmark.

"What are the cards for?" Louisa asked.

"Spiders can't read," Alice said. "The punch card tells them what the book is and where it should be shelved."

"I've never been one for reading," Louisa said. "Except the *Times* and bombastic fiction, which are much the same thing."

"You," Alice said to a spider that was industriously running a feather duster over a set of atlases. The spider paused and turned to face her. "Leave these here, please. I want to read them later." The spider squeaked once and set back to work.

"You know," Louisa said as they exited, "everyone who's anyone is wondering when you're going to hold some sort of event in this mausoleum. A large tea for the right ladies, a small dinner for forty, perhaps even a dance. You do have a ballroom, don't you?"

"I think it's down that way," Alice said. "And you're right, of course—it's what everyone expects." She thought of issuing invitations, hiring musicians, arranging food, and coordinating service, and more, more, more. Alice grimaced.

"It's overwhelming," she said. "I know what to do in theory, but I didn't grow up watching my mother organize large events and order servants about."

"I'll be right here to help, darling—as long as you do something outrageous."

"Oh, Louisa, I don't know if that's me. I'm not Ad Hoc, you know, and I have no plans to become so."

"I didn't say *scandalous*. I said *outrageous*. We need to get everyone talking about you."

"You mean they aren't already?"

Louisa made a noncommittal noise. "We'll start small with the tea I mentioned. They're appropriate for a fiancée, since Norbie has no other female in his life to handle such things for him. After the wedding, we'll work through the dinners up to a major ball next season. I think your dinners will have to be exciting in some way, to make sure everyone wants to come."

Alice gave Louisa's arm an impulsive squeeze. "What would I do without you, Louisa?"

"Wither and die like the rest of London. What else do we have down here?"

They found a second drawing room, a parlor, a sun-porch, a formal dining hall, the aforementioned ballroom, and several exits to the courtyard out back. They also found the kitchen, which was quiet at the moment. A large black stove dominated the back wall. Pots, pans, spoons, skewers, and other implements hung from ceiling hooks. A set of sinks took up most of one corner. Everything was perfectly clean, partly due to the efforts of a large spider, which was currently scrubbing the floor. Several human-shaped automatons in uniforms stood silently by, their blank eyes staring at nothing. One wore a tall chef's hat.

"You could cook and serve an entire feast with them," Louisa said. "I have to wonder why your dear fiancé employs no human servants. They'd come at less than a tenth the cost."

"I have no idea," Alice admitted. "While we were courting, I didn't bring it up because it felt like prying, and now that we're . . . that is, *he's* home, I haven't had a chance to bring it up."

Kemp appeared at the kitchen door. He carried a salver with a calling card on it. "Madam, a Mr. Richard Caraway to see you. Actually, he asked for Mr. Williamson. And your father is fine. I brought him another book and a cup of milk with brandy."

"Thank you," Alice said. "Tell Mr. Caraway that Mr. Williamson is not at home."

"He claims to have an appointment with Mr. Williamson, and he says it is quite urgent."

Alice blinked. "Then tell him—never mind. I'll go."

"Richard Caraway, Richard Caraway," Louisa muttered.

"Oh yes. Young rake. Father owns tin mines in Wales and recently put Richard in charge of half of them to see how he does."

"Do you have the entire social register memorized?"

"I told you I like bombastic fiction. Shall I wait here?"

"If you don't mind. I won't be long. Kemp, you needn't come." Alice started to scurry off, then forced herself to slow to a ladylike pace.

Richard Caraway, a thin, ash-blond man in a dark business suit, all but bolted to his feet as Alice entered the front room. His hat perched on a rack in the corner. He looked both nervous and familiar, but Alice couldn't place him, and she wished for Louisa's gift with names and faces.

"I'm sorry you came all this way, Mr. Caraway," Alice said after introductions and handshakes, "but my fiancé isn't at home, and my father isn't seeing visitors."

He blinked pale eyes. "I had an appointment. Wednesday, four o'clock."

"Oh! There's the confusion, then. Today is Tuesday, Mr. Caraway."

He blinked again. "I see. Of course. Sorry to have bothered you."

"What was the nature of your business with him?" Alice asked, genuinely curious. "I would think most people would go down to the factory or to his office."

"It was . . ." He swallowed, staring at her, and Alice felt a little uncomfortable. "I'm sorry, Miss Michaels, but I don't know how much your fiancé involves you in his daily business, and I don't feel quite right about—"

"Quite, quite," Alice said, mystified. Did it have something to do with munitions? Or some other secret project? But if that were the case, why would this man come here rather than go to Norbert's factory? She wanted to ask further, but manners didn't allow. "I could offer you some tea. We have some lovely—"

"I should go." The hat rack handed him his hat as he approached the door. "Please tell your fiancé I was here. So sorry."

The moment he turned his back to walk out, Alice remembered him. He was one of the men who had left this very house on the day Norbert had proposed to her. It piqued her curiosity.

"Excuse me," Alice called, hurrying after him, "Mr. Caraway, I remember seeing you here before, with another gentleman. Don't you run a mining concern in Wales?"

He stopped and turned. His face was pale. "Why do you ask?"

"It's rather unusual for someone of your stature to stop by a private home during business hours, and I was truly wondering—"

"I do have to go," he said shortly. "Good day, Miss Michaels." And he fled the house.

"What was that all about?" Louisa was sitting at a kitchen table with another cup of tea at her elbow. Kemp stood nearby holding a plate of biscuits. The spider paused in its work to eye the biscuit plate for falling crumbs, then went back to scrubbing.

"I honestly don't know," Alice replied.

"Biscuit, Madam?"

"No thank you, Kemp. So odd." She related the details of the conversation. "It's a complete mystery."

"So many of them in your life," Louisa said.

A bubble of emotion Alice hadn't been aware she was carrying suddenly burst, and Alice slapped her hand on a worktable. "And I'm tired of it!" she cried. "It's been nearly a year, and I don't know what happened to my aunt, and I don't know what happened to that grinning clockworker, and I don't know what happened to Gavin, and I don't know what's happening in this house, and I'm bloody tired of it!"

"Gavin?" Louisa said. "Who's Gavin?"

Alice paused in her tirade. "Did I say Gavin?"

"You did," said Louisa, zooming in for the kill. "Who is he?"

"A young man I . . . assisted."

"How exciting! And romantic! Do you like him? Is he handsome?"

The hell with it. "Very handsome," Alice snapped with an angry toss of her head. "Stunningly handsome. Gorgeous. Blond and blue-eyed and quick and strong, with a voice like an angel and hands that create music to make heaven weep."

"Did you kiss him?"

This was rather fun. Alice leaned forward with pointed wickedness. "I didn't, but I wanted to, and more, even though I had just given my hand to Norbert only hours before. I still think about him all the time. When I fall asleep, I see his face in the dark, and when I wake up, his memory is in my dreams. How do you like *that*?"

"I think it's marvelous!" Louisa's eyes were sparkling. "Is he rich?"

"Dirt poor. He's a street musician."

"Lowest of the low. Shocking! How old?"

"Eighteen when I met him. He must be nineteen by now."

"Cradle robbing already. Darling! I'm so proud!"

The remark, however, yanked Alice back to reality. The daring anger drained away and she deflated. "It is, isn't it? Good heavens. Even if I weren't engaged to Norbert, I couldn't pursue Gavin. Not in a hundred years."

Louisa blinked. "Why on earth not?"

"You just said why not. He's nineteen years old, and I turn twenty-three next month. I'm a cradle robber."

"Oh, please!" Louisa took up a biscuit and angrily bit off a chunk. "These are modern times. How old is Norbert?"

"Thirty. Why?"

"But you're twenty-three? No one bats an eye when a man marries a woman seven years younger, but if a woman looks at a man four years her junior, everyone gets in a tizzy." She crumbled the rest of the biscuit onto the platter. "If your ages were reversed, would you see a problem?"

Alice thought about that. Louisa had a point. No one would think twice about a relationship if Alice were nineteen and Gavin were twenty-three—or even older. Why should it be any different when it was the other way round? It wasn't as if Gavin acted anything other than like a man. He was smart and resourceful and witty and—

"All this is hypothetical," Alice said stiffly. "I'm marrying Norbert. Gavin is—was—a passing fancy."

"I don't think so," Louisa replied. "Gavin stirs up strong feelings, even after a year. I can see it in your face. Why not walk out on Norbert and pursue him?"

"I *can't.* I even had a chance to work with"—the Third Ward's machine froze her tongue again—"with him. At a salary. And I turned it down."

"What? Why, for heaven's sake?"

"Because Father owes more than I could hope to pay off on my own. Because Norbert has moved Father in here and is providing for his care. Because the banns have been published, and if I back out of the marriage now, Norbert would have the legal right to sue me for the title I had promised his firstborn child. Logic dictated I turn the offer down."

"You're a woman, Alice, not an automaton."

"I don't want to discuss it anymore."

"There's more to this than mere logic," Louisa said shrewdly. "I can tell."

There was, but Alice refused to think about it. "I said I don't want to discuss it anymore."

"You have a lot of things you don't want to discuss," Louisa replied. "Well, what do you propose we do?"

"I want to clear up some of the mysteries in my life," Alice said. "I want to know at least one thing that's going on round here. I want to take apart one of these blasted automatons and find out why Norbert is so fascinated by these things."

"*You're* fascinated by them."

"Not in the same way. Kemp, bring me my tools. And if you see Click, tell him to—oh. Here he is. How did you know I wanted your help?"

Click, who had jumped up to the kitchen worktable, didn't respond. In a few minutes, Kemp returned, wheeling a walnut cabinet the size of two steamer trunks. Brass fittings gleamed, and every surface was carved to show gears, pistons, rotors, and other bits of machinery. One of the rubber wheels left a small mark on the floor, and the spider rushed over to work on it with frantic movements of the scrub brush. Alice twisted the cabinet's handles, and the doors sprang open, revealing rotating shelves of tools and dozens of tiny drawers for spare parts.

"Well!" Louisa said. "This is a step up from your garret."

"An engagement present from Norbert," Alice said. "It's a definite improvement."

"If you like ostentation, Madam," Kemp put in with disapproval.

"Madam didn't ask your opinion." Alice crooked a finger at one of the motionless footmen standing against the kitchen wall. "You! Are you awake?"

"Yes, ma'am." The automaton's voice was flat.

"Come."

The automaton obeyed. It had a female shape, and it swayed when it walked. Its black-and-white uniform clung to a curvy brass body, and its skirt swished with every step. Somehow it seemed more naked than Kemp, whose clothes were only painted on.

"What is your function in this house?" Alice asked.

"I serve whatever function is required of me," the servant said.

"Helpful," Louisa observed. "You don't suppose . . ."

"What?"

"I've heard about automatons that serve a certain purpose. *You* know the one I mean."

"Oh, Louisa." But the protest was halfhearted. "Such . . . congress between men and machines is strictly illegal. Besides, Norbert wouldn't."

"Really? I know this is a little harsh, but how well do you know him? Until you came along, he lived alone in this huge house. He had no social life to speak of. What do you *think* he was doing in here?"

Alice was going to protest again, then decided against it. What was the point when she was thinking the same thing? A sick feeling roiled in her stomach, and she wanted to flee the room. But no—she had asked for answers, and she was going to have them. "Let's get this over with. Help me get her—its—dress off, Louisa."

They did. The automaton stood for it without protesting, and Click batted at one of the sleeves. The last layer of undergarments was shed, revealing brass skin broken only by regular patterns of rivets. It looked less human this way, like a mannequin or dressmaker's dummy. Alice quickly examined it and found only unsuspicious, smooth metal.

"Well," she said, straightening. "This is a bit embarrassing."

Louisa was holding Click. "Perhaps other methods were employed?"

"Hm. Just how suspicious am I allowed to be?"

The spider, which was the size of a hatbox, finished removing the scuff mark and was turning to scuttle away when Click abruptly leapt from Louisa's arms and pounced on it. The spider squeaked, and its scrub brush skittered across the floor. The two of them rolled about, Click's eyes reflecting phosphorescent glee.

"Click!" Alice scolded. "Stop it! Leave it alone!"

Click abruptly snapped free and strolled away, tail in the air. The discombobulated spider lay on its nose, its backside in the air.

"That cat," Alice said, leaning down to right the spider. "I don't know what I'll—"

She halted and stared.

"You'll what?" Louisa said.

Alice didn't answer. Instead, she lifted the hatbox spider onto the table, spun it around, and used a screwdriver to lever open a small door mounted on the rear.

"What are you doing?" Louisa asked.

"This spider has two panels to access the inside instead of one," Alice said. "Unusual. Hold still, you."

The door popped open. Alice and Louisa both leaned forward to look inside. There was a moment of silence. Then Alice reached inside and pulled out a device, the shape of which made its function quite clear.

"I don't suppose," Louisa said, "that this object has some machine-related function not so obvious to a layman."

"I'm afraid not." Alice shut the spider down. Her hands were shaking, and she felt about to throw up. She remembered Mr. Caraway and the other man she had seen leaving the house during business hours, and she remembered that Norbert had been home. "Kemp, please bring every inhuman automaton in the house to the formal dining room. And don't let Father know."

"Yes, Madam."

"What are you going to do?" asked Louisa.

"I'm going to see how many of these things are equipped like this one. Then I'm going to talk to my fiancé."

"You look upset."

"I am."

Kemp hastily threw a drop cloth over the dining room table, allowing Alice to make a lineup of automatons on it. It turned out most of the spiders and walkboxes were equipped the same as the first.

"Do you drink?" Louisa asked from one of the high-backed chairs. "If you don't, now might be a good time to start."

"Hm," Alice said again.

"You could install some spikes. As a little surprise."

Alice had to laugh at that. "Thank you for that thought. But I think talking to Norbert will do." She glanced at the grandfather clock ticking in the corner. "And he'll be home in an hour."

"Then I'd better scamper away." She rose and kissed Alice on the cheek. "Whatever you decide to do, darling, remember I'm on your side. Though I have to say that your Gavin is sounding more attractive by the moment."

When Norbert arrived home an hour later with a bouquet of roses, he found on the table, instead of dinner, a number of spidery automatons with their covers off. Tools and parts lay scattered up and down the drop cloth. Alice stood among them, feeling like a black widow in a wiry web.

"Really, Norbert," Alice said icily. "How long did you think it would take me to find out?"

Norbert looked at her for a moment, then set the roses down and pulled off his gloves. "I did say at breakfast that there was another task I needed you to take on."

"What do you mean by that?"

"I received a telegram from Fred Caraway at my office today. It said he'd stopped by on the wrong day for his appointment. He always was a little scatterbrained."

"What does that have to do with these . . . things?" Alice tried to keep her voice neutral, but anger and humiliation burned two red spots into her cheeks.

"A remarkably imprecise description coming from someone of your caliber." He yanked the corner bellpull, and Kemp immediately stepped into the room. "Gin and tonic. And where's supper?"

"On a cart in the kitchen," Alice said. "I'm tired of waiting for explanations, Norbert, though I've already figured out quite a bit."

"What have you figured out, then?" Norbert seemed perfectly at ease, which served only to infuriate Alice.

She took a deep breath to get herself under control. "These machines ... entertain your friends, or business contacts, or whatever they are. In return, your contacts provide you good business deals. Mr. Caraway, for example, ensures low tin prices. You don't keep human servants because human servants talk, and word would eventually reach the authorities. The only part I don't understand is why none of them are interested in the more human-seeming automatons."

Kemp held out a glass of gin and tonic on a tray, and Norbert accepted it. "You'd be surprised at how many men are too shy even to pay for female companionship, and how many others are put off by human-shaped automatons." He gulped from his drink. "There are men who find the idea of a small machine that doesn't talk or even appear human quite appealing. And the man who owns the machines becomes popular."

"What has this to do with me?" Alice demanded.

"I didn't build these automatons. My uncle did. He died before I met you, leaving me with no way to repair them."

"And that's where I come in? A female?"

"Why not? The sex of the mechanic is unimportant. I had small-business dealings with your father, and through him I learned about you and your talent with automatons. I helped wrangle you an invitation to the Greenfellow ball so I could look you over. The fact that you repaired Lady Greenfellow's cellist on the spot sealed it, as far as I was concerned."

"In other words, you only proposed to me so I could keep your . . . toys in good working order?" Fury overwrote every word.

"Good Lord, no!" Norbert came over and took her hand. "Alice, you're also heir to a title. Over time we may grow to love each other, or we may not. But this"—he swept a gesture over the motionless automatons—"this is business."

The question popped out before she could stop it. "Have *you* used them?"

"No," he said simply, and sat back down. "At any rate, you've already discovered that several of them are broken. I want them repaired. We'll set up a workroom so you needn't clutter up the dining room, and I'll give you the name of a shop that can be trusted if you need parts."

"Why don't you have your factory make them?"

Norbert shook his head. "My factory turns out materials in large quantities, far more than my little machines might need. Besides, the parts have to be custom-fitted. Don't worry—I pay the metalsmith well to keep silent. And it'll be easier now that I don't have to worry about scheduling appointments for days when you don't visit." He drained his glass. "The beauty of it all, my dear, is that everything appears perfectly normal. Your father will continue to get proper care, and when we're married, his debts will be paid. My first son will be a peer. You may work on whatever other projects you like, as long as my machines stay in good repair. Everyone comes out ahead."

"I see." Alice sank into a chair of her own, barely noticing the soft velvet cushioning. She felt suddenly tired, as if she had worked a full day on her knees scrubbing floors. Norbert was right, of course. Father would be cared for. His debts would be paid. Most importantly, everything would be for the best because it would all appear *normal*. She would be—or seem to be—a normal, traditional woman with a normal, traditional husband, living a normal, traditional life. As long as no one knew that anything odd was happening, everything would be all right. Everything would be under control. That was the rule. Here, at least, she was on familiar ground.

"Very well," she said.

The days passed into weeks, and Alice worked out a new routine. Breakfasts still belonged to Norbert, but mornings found Alice in the new workshop. She couldn't think of it as her workshop yet, even though Norbert made it clear it was as much her domain as the kitchen was to most wives.

The workshop lay behind an anonymous locked door at the end of an unlit hallway on the second floor. It looked perfectly normal and respectable from the outside. Inside was a place clean, spacious, and well lit by electricity, where Alice spent secret time hunched over a worktable, refitting rubber rings and lubricating little pistons. She stayed strictly away from the rooms where Norbert entertained his business contacts.

Alice didn't bury herself entirely in the workshop. There were wedding arrangements, but not many, since theirs was going to be so tiny. Her wedding dress arrived, and she modeled it halfheartedly for Louisa. And now that she had explored the house and taken over the household accounts, Alice took on Louisa's help and put on afternoon teas for ladies who were fascinated with the houseful of automaton servants. The events were always highly attended, especially after she fitted one of the footmen to spout tea, milk, and hot water from his fingertips (though she told everyone she'd had it done for her). Alice remained bright and merry on the outside, but underneath she felt lost and frightened. The idea of ferreting out more secrets had lost its appeal, and although she felt flickers of curiosity about the fates of Gavin and Aunt Edwina and the grinning clockworker, she no longer felt a burning need to uncover more ugly truth and take the emotional bruises that came with it.

"I don't know why I did this, Father," she whispered at his bedside one morning. "I'm wearing a shell, and it gets heavier every day."

Arthur Michaels shifted slightly on the silken sheets. His eyes were sunken; his white hair brittle. His hands had shrunk to sticks, and he weighed so little that Alice could lift him with ease. He slept almost all the time now and ate nearly nothing.

Alice held his hand for a while, then pursed her lips and left the room. The automaton stationed near the bed would alert her to any change. Right now she had errands to run. Specifically, she needed to visit the special shop Norbert had mentioned. Three of Norbert's automatons were malfunctioning beyond her ability to repair at home, and she needed to commission parts. She put on her hat, skewered it with pins, and went downstairs.

Although Norbert preferred his mechanical carriage, Alice had persuaded him to buy for her use a more conventional vehicle, a small, boxy carriage pulled by a pair of well-matched horses. A vehicle like Norbert's attracted a great deal of attention, and there were times when Alice didn't want all eyes on her. Kemp drove in a cloak and hat to disguise his own identity, and when they arrived, he carried two muslin-wrapped automatons into the shop while Alice took the third.

The shop was crowded from floor to ceiling with shelves and bins, all of them filled with a jumble up of tools and parts—cogs, wheels, levers, pistons, drill bits, spools of wire, steel sheets, rivets, bolts, screws, nuts, and more. At the back of the shop behind a counter, a wizened little man perched on a stool with his hands tucked into the pockets of his leather apron. An enormous pencil was stuck behind one ear, nearly lost in the wrinkles that covered his bald head. His name was Mr. Smeet, and he had once been a smith himself, but now his son and grandsons ran the forge out back while he ran the business out front. Nothing in the shop itself was ordered in any way that made sense to Alice, but experience had taught her that Mr. Smeet could lay his hands on anything from the shelves in seconds.

"Ah, the young miss and her automatons," Mr. Smeet said in a piping voice that matched his tiny body. "What do you need today?"

Alice made herself march up to the counter and set the bundle down. She had gone through this many times, and she still hated it. Nausea oozed through her stomach, and her skin itched, as if dozens of accusing eyes were watching her. She had to continually remind herself that she was protected. The machines were hidden under muslin, and their true function was also hidden behind an access panel.

"I need parts to repair these three," she said briskly as Kemp set the other two beside the first.

Mr. Smeet reached for one of the bundles. "Let's have a look."

Alice helped him unwrap the three automatons. Two were spiders, and the third was shaped like a large vase, though the opening at the top was not used for flowers. All three had been deactivated. Mr. Smeet put on a jeweler's loupe, got out a large sheet of foolscap, and spun the automatons toward himself with little *tsk* noises.

"These've been abused," he muttered.

"Yes," Alice said. "I'll need—"

A dreadful wrenching noise tore the very air, and a section of the roof came off the shop, taking a large portion of the front wall with it. Alice screamed, flung herself sideways, and went down, hampered by her skirts. Shouts and screams filtered into the shop from outside, and a hail of wood and metal pelted over Alice. In an enormous hole where the front of the shop used to be stood a two-story machine. It had a squat, round build, with heavy legs, long arms, and gleaming brass skin. A glass bubble enclosed the top, and a young man with ash-blond hair pulled levers and spun wheels inside it. He wore a high collar and an evening coat that fit him badly. Alice stared up from the floor of the shop, trying to take everything in. The man, who pulled up a speaking tube from between his ankles, somehow struck Alice as familiar, though she couldn't say how.

"Wonderful!" His voice crackled thin and tinny. "Don't fight me, and I'll remember it as a kindness when I'm ruling London. Blow me a kiss, and I'll make you my queen."

The machine clanked into the shop, and its front opened like a drawbridge. It leaned down, long arms reaching. Alice scooted back, her eyes wide. She was panting in fear. Kemp lay trapped under a wooden beam, one of his eyes smashed, and Mr. Smeet had fled out a back door.

The machine scooped up handfuls of machine parts from the bins and shelves and dropped them into the opening, like a child stuffing his pockets with boiled sweets. "Memory wheels!" The young man laughed. "I'll build myself an army! Blow me a kiss, and you'll be my queen."

He sang a little song as he worked.

> *Bring a bowl and plate and soup tureen*
> *And shirt and collar of velveteen.*
> *If you clean and oil my brass machine*
> *And blow me a kiss, you'll be my queen.*

More parts went into the compartment. Outrage overcame some of Alice's fear. He was a thief! A common thief! She scrambled to her feet as the machine shoved more parts into its chest cavity. But then to her horror, the machine plucked Norbert's little automatons from Mr. Smeet's counter and held them up so the driver could examine them through the glass bubble.

"Premade automatons," he cried. "Yours, my queen? I'll be grateful. May I have the honor of a dance?"

And then Alice knew him. He was the ash-blond man in a bad coat who had asked Louisa to dance at Lady Greenfellow's ball. He was the second son who had seen Louisa home—and stayed for breakfast. He was even wearing the same badly cut coat.

"Patrick Barton!" she gasped, then clapped her hand over her mouth.

Patrick's machine leaned down for a closer look. His eyes were wide and wild. Clockwork madness. Alice wondered if he'd been infected with the clockwork plague before or after the ball and prayed it was after, for Louisa's sake.

"Alice Michaels!" he said. "Well! I'll be glad to make you my London queen, my luscious Boadicea, my warrior angel. Especially if you made these automatons. I'll make you famous."

A shot cracked through the air and ricocheted off the glass. It was quickly followed by another. Alice heard shouts and clattering hooves.

"Police always come in legions," Patrick groaned. He stuffed the three automatons into his machine's chest cavity, and it clanked shut. "I'll come back for you, my Boadicea, my spider. Give my best to Louisa."

With that, he turned and stomped away, leaving Alice in the shambles of the shop.

Chapter Eleven

Gavin leapt from his horse and pushed through the crowd of people that surrounded the ruined shop. Smashed wood and twisted metal lay everywhere like random notes flung from a staff, and the discordant smell of fear hung in the air, though it did nothing to dispel the crowd, most of whom were waiting for the chance to make off with something. Everything he hated about London was in evidence—dirt, chaos, evil-minded people hovering about. Still, it was pure luck that he and Simon had been only a few blocks away when the report came over the wireless. "Move aside, please! Police!" he called. "Police! Let me through!"

The word *police* always did it. The crowd rippled aside to reveal the demolished shop front. Gavin hurriedly picked his way inside, his black leather jacket protecting him from snags and jabs. He didn't bother to remove his simple workman's cap. Clearly, the machine had come and gone, but it might have left clues—or victims—behind. His practiced eye automatically picked out several four-pronged claw marks in the walls and deep circular gouges in the floor that marked out huge footprints. Gavin noted their size and did some mental math. The machine had been between twenty and twenty-five feet tall, the same size as the mechanicals used during the Napoleonic Wars, and that made Gavin nervous. If the pattern he had become all too familiar with held true, the mechanical would be armed with a number of dangerous weapons. He sniffed the air. Paraffin oil. Some clockworkers had begun experimenting with new, more efficient fuels for their machines. This was clearly one of them. Several shop shelves, what remained of them, had been swept clean, indicating theft as a motive.

A figure popped up from behind the counter at the back of the shop, and Gavin reflexively went into a fighting stance. The figure, a woman, brandished a crowbar. Her hat was askew and she had a wild look in her eyes, but Gavin recognized her instantly. His heart did a little jump, and happy surprise thrilled through him. He swallowed a small lump in his throat and dashed across the shop, where he reached out to embrace her, then stopped himself at the last moment.

"Alice!" he gasped, and snatched off his cap. "Alice Michaels! What are you doing here? Are you all right?"

Alice dropped the crowbar and grabbed Gavin's jacket lapels with both fists. He smelled her perfume, a sweet, roselike fragrance at odds with the frantic look on her face. "We have to get them back!" she barked. "Now!"

"Get what back?"

"The machines! He took the machines! We have to get them back before he figures out what they're for and tells everyone when he comes back to make me his queen!"

For a terrible moment, Gavin was afraid Alice was the clockworker who had destroyed the shop. She was babbling like Dr. Clef on one of his bad days, and her expression said she wasn't quite all there. Then he realized she was just upset, a victim.

"It'll be all right," he soothed. "Just tell me what happened."

"There isn't *time* for that, you idiot. Let's move!"

"Is someone going to help me up?" groaned a reedy

voice from near Gavin's feet. "Or am I to lie here until the scavengers strip my rivets?"

What Gavin had taken for a pile of debris on the floor in front of the counter turned out to be an automaton trapped under a beam. "Kemp?" Gavin asked. "Holy cow! Can you get up on your own?"

"Do you really expect me to answer that, sir? I believe Madam dropped a crowbar on the counter."

"Quite a crowd out there." Simon d'Arco stepped into the shattered shop. He wore a black coat and cap like Gavin's and a large pack with indicator lights and dials on it. A crank stuck out one side. "Good heavens! I didn't expect to see you again, Miss Michaels—or soon-to-be Mrs. Williamson. Are you enjoying your betrothal?"

"Oh dear Lord," Alice groaned. "Mr. d'Arco, we *must* catch that clockworker immediately. We can use my carriage."

"If you mean the one out front"—Simon cocked a thumb over his shoulder—"I think the mechanical stepped on it. There's an awful wreck out there, and the horses are gone."

"Damn it!" Alice shouted, and Gavin stepped back, shocked at hearing such language from a woman. "You brought horses of your own, didn't you?"

Gavin asked, "Why are the machines so important, Miss Michaels? Tell us, and we'll do our best." He flashed what he hoped was a confident grin. "The Third Ward's best will amaze even you."

"I doubt that, Mr. Ennock," she snapped. "Those machines belong to my fiancé. They are extremely . . . valuable, and he'll be very upset if they're lost. We *must* recover them."

Gavin found himself nodding. It had been a year since they'd parted, but she was just as he remembered her— furious, beautiful, and crackling with more energy than a Mozart symphony. He straightened the lapels on his black leather jacket. "We'll get them back. I promise."

Just then, several colored lights on Simon's pack lit up.

Gavin, adept at reading the codes they indicated, gave the crank a whirl and plucked a large round microphone from the side of the pack.

"Emergency message from headquarters," he said to Alice as Simon twisted his head in an attempt to see what was going on.

From the floor, Kemp said, "Isn't anyone going to—"

"Is that a wireless communication device?" Alice asked, interested despite herself.

"Yep. Agent Ennock here," Gavin said importantly into the microphone. "What have we got? Over."

Static hissed and crackled, and a ringing feedback noise played a note two cents above F-sharp. Gavin winced. Perfect pitch wasn't always an advantage.

"*This is Lieutenant Phipps, Ennock,*" said the radio. "*Put d'Arco on. Over.*"

With a sideways glance at Alice, Gavin deepened his voice a little and said, "I can handle the problem, Lieutenant."

"*Put d'Arco on. Now. Over.*"

Flushing slightly, he handed the microphone to Simon, who pressed the button. "D'Arco here. Over."

"*Remember that grinning idiot of a clockworker you and Teasdale had it out with last year? He's resurfaced. At this very moment he is rampaging on Fleet Street with another zombie horde, even though it is broad daylight.*"

Alice stiffened.

"*Since you have met him before,*" Phipps continued, "*I want you to get down there and capture him immediately. Acknowledge. Over.*"

"What about the clockworker that smashed the metalsmith shop?" Simon asked. "The longer we wait, the farther away he'll get. Over."

"*You mean you didn't capture him? Over.*"

"He had already left the scene by the time we arrived. Over."

There was a brief pause. "*I need you on Fleet Street,*"

d'Arco, but I don't want Ennock going after that clock-worker by himself. If—"

Alice snatched the microphone. "This is Alice Michaels, Lieutenant. I'll go with Mr. Ennock."

"Miss Michaels? What the hell are you doing on this frequency?"

"I said I'll go with him. There's no time to argue, and you can't stop me, anyway."

"I most certainly can. I can order Agent Ennock to kick you in the head."

"No sense wasting time. We're off." She tossed the microphone back to a startled Simon d'Arco and turned to Gavin. "With that settled, we need to find transportation."

"Uh . . ." was all Gavin could say. For months he had dreamed of something exactly like this. He'd constructed elaborate fantasies about swooping into Alice's life with some grand gesture that would make her fall into his arms, betrothed or not. Now here she was, disheveled and upset after a clockworker attack that *he* was supposed to remedy, and she was taking charge of the situation.

"D'Arco! Agent d'Arco! Are you there? Over!"

"I'm here. What should I do?"

"I told you to meet Teasdale at Fleet Street! Now! And tell Agent Ennock to get moving. Over."

Simon shot Gavin a look, and his dark eyes were filled with concern. "Lieutenant, Agent Ennock has never operated solo before. I'm not sure that—"

"It's an order, Agent d'Arco. Over."

"I can do it, Simon," Gavin said hurriedly.

"What about Miss Michaels?" Simon asked the radio. "Over."

"If she wants to get herself killed chasing clockworkers, that's her own lookout. Over and out."

The lights on Simon's pack winked out. He slowly lowered the microphone. Gavin wanted to leap into the air for joy, but he kept his feet on the ground.

"Well!" Alice said, straightening her hat. "You heard the woman. Mr. d'Arco, you should be off."

"Give me the pack, Simon," Gavin said. "And take the extra horse with you before someone steals it."

"Listen." Simon slid out of the pack and set it down. "This won't be like chasing L'Arbre Magnifique through the Forest of Fontainebleau, or the time we fought those floating freaks at Furnival's Inn. You'll be operating on your own. I don't want you hurt."

"Right," Gavin said.

"So. Good luck." Simon abruptly caught Gavin in a rough and uncharacteristic hug.

Gavin's ribs creaked. "Um . . . sure. Thanks!"

Simon seemed to realize what he'd done, and he let go with a cough. "Miss Michaels. Fine seeing you, as always. Good day." And he fled.

"I know I am only an automaton and barely worth bothering about," Kemp moaned, "but if *someone* gets a spare moment . . ."

"Was he that sarcastic before?" Gavin pulled a wand on a wire from the pack.

"No. Something was probably jostled in the accident." Alice used the crowbar to lever off a chunk of debris, and Kemp sat up. "Can you walk?"

"I believe so." Kemp got to his feet and staggered in a small circle. In addition to his having a shattered eye, his body was scratched and dented, and his left foot was turned. "I'm half-blind. I work and slave all day, and this is the thanks I get."

"Go home," Alice told him. "Tell Mr. Williamson what happened, and I'll fix you when I get back."

"I'll be stripped to my oil pan, and see if I'm not," Kemp muttered as he limped away. "Not that anyone would miss me. 'Where's Kemp?' they'll say. 'No one's ironed the paper today. Oh well. What's for tea?' "

"Thank you, Kemp," Gavin called after him.

Alice turned to him. "How are we going to follow the clockworker?"

"The thing is two stories tall. Someone's probably seen it."

"And it has a big head start. It could be halfway to Islington by now."

"That was a joke. You Brits have a hard time with American humor." Gavin waved the wand about in a business-like manner. "Give the handle on that pack a few turns, would you? I need more power."

Alice obliged, and several lights on the pack flickered weakly. "What does that object do?"

"It's an extremely sensitive artificial nose. I smelled paraffin oil when I first got here, so I think I can pick up the mechanical's exhaust and—aha!" An orange light on the pack gave off a steady glow. "Flip that switch there and help me get this on."

Gavin winced as the pack's immense weight landed on his back and shoulder muscles. The beating had been more than a year ago, but his back, crisscrossed with white scars, remained sensitive to sudden jolts. Simon said it was all in his head, but that didn't make it less painful. He could see the orange light out of the corner of his eye as they picked their way out of the ruined shop, and the glow remained steady, telling him he was on the right trail. A thick layer of clouds covered the sky, but fortunately it wasn't threatening to rain and wipe out the trail.

"How are we going to catch up with him?" Alice asked. "Run?"

"Better. That switch you flipped sent out a wireless signal. Our transport should be here any moment."

Heavy footsteps thudded beyond the shop wall and came to a halt amid cries of astonishment from the gathered crowd. Gavin and Alice went outside, where Alice's eyes widened. Waiting for them was an oak tree as tall as five men, a strange bit of green beauty walking amid the city squalor. Its bottom half was split into a pair of legs that ended in a tangle of roots. Fine vines of copper and brass ran up and down the trunk and wound around the branches. In the sturdier lower branches, seats and benches were carved into the wood. The crowd outside the shop had fled like ghosts fleeing a crucifix.

"What on earth?" Alice gasped.

"It used to belong to L'Arbre Magnifique," Gavin said, pleased she was impressed. "A clockworker Simon and I captured in France. It's partly intelligent, which is why it didn't step on anyone when it followed the signal."

"I see." Alice paused. "How do we get up there?"

Gavin put his cap back on and whistled. The tree leaned down, bringing its lowest branches within reach of the ground and allowing Gavin and Alice to climb aboard. Handholds carved into the bark made it easy, and Gavin helped Alice settle into one of the carved wooden seats before choosing his own seat, one near a control panel and in the center of a series of levers, pedals, and ropes. He strapped himself in. The tree straightened with a stomach-dropping swoop that always made Gavin think of a glissando.

"GAVIN . . . GO . . . NOW . . . ?" the tree said.

Alice jumped. "It speaks?"

"A little."

"Where? I don't see a mouth."

"Yeah, we haven't been able to figure that out, either. Tree, this is Alice. She's a friend."

"ALISSSSS . . . LEAFY . . ." The voice creaked and hissed, like wind rushing through treetops on a summer night.

"Leafy?" Alice wrinkled her forehead. "What does that mean?"

Gavin started to blush. Then he straightened. What the hell was he doing? He had fought pirates, watched his best friend die, survived a brutal beating, and faced down a number of mad geniuses who had all tried to kill him. Compared to any of those, a beautiful woman was no threat.

Time to stop acting like a stammering boy. He put his hand in his pocket and touched the mechanical nightingale. He had kept it with him all these months, and never once had it been damaged or even scratched. It had become a talisman that kept death away.

"It means he thinks you're pretty," he explained, then added, greatly daring, "He's right."

"Oh. Well," Alice said, clearly flustered, and Gavin wondered whether Tree's remark or his were the actual source of her embarrassment. "Thank you, Tree."

"LEAFY."

"We're off!" Gavin said. He worked pedals and pulled levers. Tree, responding to signals sent through the metal vines, stomped away amid a swish of leaves. Houses and shops rushed past them nearly as fast as a train. People pointed and gawked. Lips parted, Alice clung to her seat, her gaze darting in a dozen directions, and Gavin felt a little thrill at her excitement, as if he had invented Tree just for her. Through it all, he kept an eye on the orange light just over his left shoulder. When it flickered or dimmed, he pulled Tree around to change direction until the light glowed more strongly.

"Does your instrument tell you how far ahead Mr. Barton has gotten?" Alice asked.

"No," Gavin said. "It only tells direction. And how did you know his name?"

Alice muttered a curse, the second one Gavin had heard from her that day. "We met briefly at a ball in the spring, before he'd contracted the clockwork plague. His full name is Patrick Barton."

"OIL . . . MAN . . . FAR," said Tree.

"You can tell how far away he is, Tree?" Gavin asked.

"YESSSS. BAD . . . SSSMELL."

"How far, then?"

"MANY . . . SSSSTEPSSS. SUN . . . KISSESSSSS . . ."

"Sun kisses?" Alice said. "What does that mean?"

Gavin hauled on a rope and pressed a pedal. In some

ways, it was similar to piloting an airship. He could feel Tree's movements as vibrations through his own hands and feet, and the creaking of Tree's joints reminded him of the sounds an airship made as it coasted through the air, but there was also a definite jolt each time one of Tree's feet came down, and the overall movement had an up-and-down swing to it instead of the steadier glide of the airship. Tree's speed and his ability to step over and around traffic let them make excellent time.

"He means we'll catch up at sunset," Gavin said. "When the sun kisses the horizon."

"That's very poetic, Tree." Alice reached out and stroked a branch. Gavin felt a bit of envy.

"YESSSS."

They were already leaving London proper, and the houses were thinning out, fading into farmland and wooded country estates. Herds of sheep grazing near the road in their paddocks fled at Tree's approach, and a cool breeze cleared the clouds away to reveal a heavy sun. The air smelled cleaner, more like grass and forest. Gavin inhaled appreciatively. He hated being trapped in London, with its grime and demon smoke and stony streets, its square buildings that hemmed him in and ground him down. Clean air stripped away the demonic ashes.

Just as the sun touched the horizon, Gavin and Alice saw a stone tower rise up ahead of them. It was surrounded by a ruined stone wall, and from his vantage point in Tree's foliage, Gavin could make out the remains of several other foundations lying around it. Rose vines grew over many of the stones and climbed all the way up the tower, and a river drew a silver ribbon along one side.

Perfect place for a clockworker to hide, Gavin mused.

Even as the thought crossed his mind, the mechanical unfolded itself from atop the tower like a metal blossom, and the glass bubble gleamed in the setting sun. The figure of Patrick Barton was barely visible inside.

"What do we do?" Alice said.

"First we try to talk to him," Gavin replied. "He might come peacefully."

Light flashed from one of the mechanical's arms. A moment later, the ground near Tree's right leg erupted in a small explosion that showered all three of them with bits of sod.

"Or he might be hostile from the outset," Alice said. "I hope you've prepared for this eventuality."

"You're awfully calm," Gavin observed.

"Panic never solved anything, Mr. Ennock."

Another flash of light. Gavin hauled on the lines and swung Tree around toward the river just as another explosion hit the ground where they'd been standing.

"ROCKY," Tree said.

"That means he doesn't like it," Gavin explained before Alice could ask.

"*Run, little mice!*" boomed Patrick Barton.

"What is he shooting at us?" Alice asked.

"Simple gunpowder bombs, I think. He's good at timing the fuses, but not so good at launching them."

"I'm not complaining, Mr. Ennock."

"ROCKY."

Gavin pulled a speaking tube down to his mouth and whistled a hard G into it. The note sang out clear and loud, meaning Tree's amplification system was working. Tree was now a few steps from the river.

"*Mr. Barton!*" Gavin shouted at him. "*We don't want to hurt you. If you come with us, we'll give you a fully equipped workshop and let you work on anything you want.*"

"*Can you give me a moving target to practice on?*" Barton shot back. "*The moon is too far away.*" Another bomb whistled toward them. Gavin eyed it, then yanked a line. Tree swatted the object aside, and it exploded harmlessly above the river beside them.

"Bombs bursting in air," he muttered.

"Well-done, Mr. Ennock!" Alice called.

"LEAFY."

"Now let's shut him off." He took two tuning forks from his jacket pocket, one tuned for C and one for F-sharp. He struck them against Tree's bark and held them up to the speaking tube. A tritone, strong and ugly, rang out across the clearing. It dragged like a fingernail across Gavin's eardrums, and he felt a twinge of actual nausea.

Barton's mechanical put metal hands to the sides of the glass bubble. *"La la la la! I can't hear you!"*

"Damn," Gavin muttered.

"What happened?" Alice said from her own chair.

"He built sound baffle into his bubble," Gavin told her.

"Then how can he hear you shouting at him?"

"We'll ask after we've captured him."

Barton, meanwhile, began to sing. "'Hi, diddle diddle, the cat and fiddle, the cow jumped over the moon'!" Part of the vine-covered tower wall ground aside to reveal an enormous cannon, but with glassy fixtures on it. Power whined, and sparks snapped from the gaping mouth. Gavin made a small sound, and his mouth went dry.

"He's lost it completely." Alice was gripping the sides of her chair with white knuckles as the cannon clacked around, aiming straight at them. Tree's branches creaked with tension. Gavin moved Tree left, then right, but the cannon tracked the movements with terrifying precision.

"We'll be all right," Gavin said, hoping he wasn't lying. Tree reached the river fewer than thirty paces from the tower and stepped into the water. "Alice! Can you pump those bellows by your feet?"

"It's Miss Michaels, if you please, and yes, I can." She did, and there was a deep sucking sound. Tree sighed heavily.

"THIRSTY."

A high-pitched whine shrilled through the air as the cannon powered up. Gavin swung Tree around and smacked a switch. Water jetted from a hollow branch and struck

Barton's cannon. The lights along the barrel shattered, and the cannon trembled. Its whine became a scream, and Gavin had to fight not to clap his hands over his ears.

"Keep pumping!" he shouted to Alice.

"'The little dog laughed to see such sport'!" Barton barked from the tower. Water continued to crash over the cannon. And then it exploded.

The entire top of the tower went up in a spectacular firework of light and stone. Heat washed over them and blasted Tree's leaves. An enormous boulder splashed into the water next to them. Tree stumbled backward into the river, every branch swaying, and Gavin clung to his chair for dear life. Alice looked seasick—or perhaps treesick. After a moment, Tree recovered his roots. Gavin took a deep breath.

"Is everyone all right?" he asked.

"LEAFY."

"I am, Mr. Ennock," Alice called. "You were incredible!"

"We need to track down Barton," Gavin said evenly, though he was sure he had died and gone to heaven. "I don't think the explosion would have destroyed that mechanical of his."

"I agree. Perhaps we should—"

A boulder slammed into Tree, knocking him backward. Gavin experienced a sharp jerk, a moment of weightlessness, and a cold shock. River water exploded in all directions as Tree went down. More water filled Gavin's mouth and nose, and he strained against the straps that held him in his chair and the pack that held him down. Desperately, he tried to undo them all, but the buckles were stubborn. He hadn't grabbed a good breath before he'd gone under, and his lungs were already crying for air. He could see the surface that cruelly was less than two feet above him. Panic tightened his muscles, and he tried to force himself to work methodically at the buckles, but the water made the leather treacherous and difficult. Black spots swam in his vision. His lungs begged for a spoonful of air.

He felt a sharp tug, and the straps fell away. An arm hauled at him, and, with his last strength, he kicked free of the chair and pack. A second later he broke the surface and inhaled sweet, clear air. His feet stood on the river bottom, and Alice stood next to him, brandishing a knife. Tree lay beside them, half-submerged and unmoving.

"Are you all right?" Alice asked. Water streamed from her long brown hair, and her face, shining with beauty and concern, was less than a foot from his. He became aware that her other arm was around his body. Rose petals floated all around them.

"I think so," he panted. His jacket, soaked through, pulled heavily at him, and his cap had vanished. "Where did you get a knife?"

"I never go anywhere without the tools my aunt gave me."

Another boulder exploded into the water only a few feet away, and they dived away from it, making for the shore. Standing near the ruined tower was Patrick Barton's mechanical, a little worse for wear, but evidently still functional. He was already reaching for another boulder.

Alice glanced over her shoulder at the river. "He hurt Tree. The . . . the cad! The *puppy*!"

"We should get under cover until we can figure out what to do," Gavin said.

"I know what to do, Mr. Ennock," she said, and stormed straight toward Barton over a path of ruined roses. She had lost her hat, and water poured from her dress in a river of its own. Gavin irrationally thought of the stories of King Arthur and the Lady of the Lake. Then he realized what she was doing and dashed forward.

"Miss Michaels! Alice! What—" The boulder smacked into the ground just ahead of him. Heart pounding, Gavin dodged behind a rock pile and peered over the top. Alice was still walking straight toward Barton in his mechanical. The mechanical picked up yet another rock and hefted it like a boy ready to bring down a bird with a broken wing.

Alice, her wet dress clinging to her body, stopped a few paces in front of him. Rose petals from the river dotted her hair.

"Mr. Barton!" Alice shouted. "Your Boadicea has arrived. May I blow you a kiss?"

She's gone completely crazy, Gavin thought. *She's gone crazy and he's going to kill her.*

But Barton paused. From inside the glass bubble, he peered down at her, and Gavin thought he saw a grin slide across his face.

"*My queen!*" he said. "*Why are you wet?*"

"I have crossed the wide ocean to be with you, my king," Alice said. "And now that we're together, nothing will stop us from ruling the world!"

Gavin stared. What the hell?

"Open your bubble and receive my blessing, O my king," she continued. "Prove your love to me!"

"*You're trying to trick me,*" Barton said. "*You're a queen of spades.*" He raised the boulder again, and Gavin's heart lurched.

"You refuse your queen?" Alice's voice rose to a shriek. "Then watch my blood spill across the ground, for I cannot live without you!" She raised the knife and held it over her breast. Gavin gathered himself to lunge for her.

"*Wait!*" Barton set the boulder aside. "*I love you, my queen. I can't bear to see you in pain.*" The bubble hissed and slid back, though Barton made no move to come down. "*Climb up and receive my love.*"

"With pleasure, my king." From her sleeve Alice pulled a pair of tuning forks and brandished them like a pair of swords. Gavin slapped his own jacket pockets and discovered them empty. As the startled Barton watched, Alice clanged the forks together. From Gavin's vantage point, the tritone was thin and weak, but Barton was only a few feet away from it. He clapped his hands over his ears and howled. The tone died down, but Alice struck the forks again to keep it going. Gavin didn't wait. He burst out of hiding and swarmed up the mechanical to the seat where Barton screamed. One practiced punch put the man out. Gavin shook his stinging fist and looked down at Alice.

"Boadicea?"

"I'll explain later." Alice sighed. "We should check on Tree."

Tree, it turned out, was already struggling to an upright position in the river. Water rushed from his branches and bedraggled foliage, and a chunk of the brass vines had been torn away.

"SLEEP," he said, and went still.

Gavin sloshed into the water and climbed into the branches, where he retrieved the machine pack. Alice had slashed the straps with her knife, and water had shorted out all the machinery. Still, he sloshed back ashore with it.

"Wireless is dead," he said. "No way to contact London for a pickup. We'll have to make camp here tonight."

"What about Mr. Barton?" Alice gestured at the man in question, who now lay sprawled on the ground near his mechanical.

Gavin produced a small bottle from a drawer on the pack. "Laudanum. It'll keep him quiet until we can get back. Let's check the tower and see if it's livable for the night."

The first floor of the tower contained a single room with a stove and a small bed. The upper floor, destroyed in the explosion, had apparently been the laboratory. "At least he didn't set traps and machines down here," Gavin said. "I'm too tired to hunt them down. Let's get Barton in here before he wakes up."

"Oh!" Alice put a hand to her mouth. "In all the excitement—how could I have forgotten?"

She rushed outside. Gavin hurried after her. The late-evening air was damp and chilly, and night birds called. Tree formed a tall shadow at the edge of the river. Already Alice was climbing into the mechanical.

"What are you doing?" he demanded. "Miss Michaels!"

She dropped into the seat, her wet skirts sticking to her legs, and examined the machinery in the rapidly fading light. "Nothing's labeled," she muttered. "So how does it work?"

She pulled a lever, and the mechanical's right arms swung down and around. Gavin ducked beneath it just in time. "Oh dear! Sorry, Mr. Ennock!"

"What in—?"

"If that's right, then this one is left." The mechanical's left arm swung, but this time nowhere near Gavin. "And these are the feet." The mechanical stomped in place. "This must be the bubb—" The glass dome snapped shut. Gavin retreated to a safe distance, watching Alice fiddle with the switches and levers inside the mechanical, until at last the front popped open and machine parts spilled out onto the grass. Of course! The machines Alice had been so hot to find. The bubble opened and Alice scrambled down to the ground, where she sorted frantically through the materials until she came up with three hatbox-sized automatons. These she stacked like firewood and struggled to pick up.

"Let me help with that," Gavin volunteered.

"I'll do it, Mr. Ennock," she snapped. "Please leave them alone."

He stepped back and let her haul them into the tower. She set them on the stone floor while he built a fire in the stove. His wet clothes were starting to chill him, and it would only get worse as the night wore on.

"Check that wardrobe over there, would you?" Gavin asked as he tried to coax larger flames. "See if Barton has any spare clothes."

Barton did. Though a little large for Gavin, they would do for the moment. Alice obligingly turned her back while Gavin scrambled out of his wet things and into some of Barton's dry ones. In the process, he found the silver nightingale still in his pocket, and he hoped it hadn't been damaged. The dry clothes felt immensely better, in any case, though he was forced to remain barefoot. He held out a set of trousers and a shirt to Alice.

"You should put these on," he said. "They aren't women's things, but you'll catch your death in those wet skirts."

"I couldn't," Alice said.

"You have to. I don't want you catching a chill or pneumonia."

"You don't understand, Mr. Ennock," Alice said. Her face flushed red in the firelight. "This dress requires assistance. I can't reach the buttons and laces."

"Really? Oh. Um . . . I guess I could . . ."

"No," she said evenly, "you definitely could not."

"I don't mean anything . . . you know." He gestured helplessly. "I could just undo the buttons and turn away while you handle the rest."

"Including the unmentionables?"

Now Gavin flushed. "Oh. Right. But you can't stay wet all night. You'll get sick."

She sighed. "Hand me that knife, please, and turn your back."

He obeyed, though he had to admit that the intriguing sounds of ripping cloth were a little exciting, and he forced himself to stare at a single block of stone, memorize its contours, and not think about the fact that the woman he had dreamed about for more than a year was standing half-naked—maybe even completely naked—only a yard behind him. His heart pounded faster than it had when Tree had fallen into the river.

"You may turn around now," Alice said.

Gavin did. Alice looked strange in trousers, though she wore Barton's shirt untucked, like a tunic, to create the illusion of a short dress. She had twisted her hair back up, and the firelight playing over her face and neck lent her warm brown eyes a glow that set Gavin's heart racing again. She held a handful of tattered red blossoms.

"Great," he said. "You look great. Where did the roses come from?"

"They were caught in among my things."

"Even something damp and bedraggled can be pretty," he said without thinking.

There was a pause, and Gavin flushed.

"I feel strange," Alice said. Her dress lay in rags at her feet. "And immodest. Like an Ad Hoc lady."

"Everything's covered up," he replied. "No one will know but me, and I'll never tell, Miss Michaels."

"I believe you." She sighed, and a certain amount of tension seemed to leave her. "Thank you."

Gavin recovered himself. "Let's see if we can find any food. I'm starved."

Barton had a stash of canned fruit and beans. While they were eating, the man started to come around, and Gavin forced some laudanum-laced water down his throat. He quieted quickly.

"Are you sure he's not contagious?" Alice asked anxiously. They were sitting at a rough set of table and chairs pulled near the stove for warmth. The damp roses lay scattered on the table between them, scenting the air.

"Very sure," Gavin said. "Clockworkers do something to the clockwork plague, or the clockwork plague does something to clockworkers. We don't know how it works or why, but clockworkers don't spread the disease. If they did, I'd be dead by now."

"How many clockworkers have you encountered since you joined . . . them?"

"The Third Ward?"

"I can't talk about it directly. Your . . . superior saw to that."

"Right. Standard procedure." Gavin moved beans around in the tin with his spoon. "I've encountered three or four, not counting the ones we keep at headquarters. And I work with Doctor Clef all the time."

"What's it like?" Alice leaned forward slightly, as if hungry for something other than beans and peaches.

He flashed a wide grin at her. "It's scary as hell—sorry—but it's also the greatest job I've ever had. I fly to new places and see new people all the time, and the inventions are incredible. Tree is the just the beginning."

"Tell me about the inventions," Alice said.

"Well, Professor K. is working on a way to grow a copy of a living creature from a bit of its flesh or blood. He's done mice and sheep, but Lieutenant Phipps says if he manages humans, she'll put his research into the Doomsday Vault. Master Prakash, a clockworker from India, is working on a camera that creates photographs instantly. His lab tends to explode at least once a week, so we have to be careful. And Doctor Clef is still working on his Impossible Cube. I also had him cook up more of that alloy that floats when you pump a current through it."

"It sounds incredible." Alice sighed. "I envy you, Mr. Ennock."

"Then why did you say no when Phipps asked you to join?" Gavin blurted out. "We could even have been partners."

For a moment, Gavin thought she might refuse to answer. Then she sighed again. "I couldn't."

"You worry a lot about *couldn't*, Miss Michaels," Gavin said.

"My father was tens of thousands of pounds in debt, Mr. Ennock, and after a lot of work, I managed to catch the eye of a wealthy man who was willing to marry me, despite my advanced age and lack of means. I was also afraid . . ." She trailed off, flushing a little.

"Of what?"

"Er . . . that I wasn't suited to the job," she finished lamely.

There was clearly more to it than that, but Gavin didn't press the issue. In the spirit of being straightforward, he said, "Well, I wish you had joined. You'd be a hell—sorry—heck of a field agent. Besides," he hurried to add before he could lose courage, "I miss you."

She smiled tightly and patted his hand across the table. "Thank you, Mr. Ennock."

The air went out of him. "You're welcome," he mumbled. So much for straightforward. Well, what had he expected? A sudden declaration of undying love? She was engaged, for God's sake.

The fire crackled in the stove, putting out a welcome warmth. Gavin took the nightingale out of his pocket and set it on the table near the roses.

"What is that?" Alice asked.

"A sort of friend gave it to me." He touched the bird's head, and the nightingale sang its sweet little song.

"Hm. It lacks soul." She paused. "Mr. Ennock, would you . . . sing for me?"

He blinked. "Sing?"

"I remember your singing voice," she said. "I'd very much like to hear it again."

"Sure." He glanced out one of the tower's narrow windows and saw the moon rising through Tree's branches. The silvery light slanted across the floor and played across Alice's face. "How about a lullaby?"

"Whatever you prefer."

Gavin sang.

> *I see the moon; the moon sees me.*
> *It turns all the forest soft and silvery.*
> *The moon picked you from all the rest*
> *For I loved you best.*

As the final line left his mouth, he realized what he had just sung. He flashed back to the moment he had sung "The Wraggle Taggle Gypsy" at Third Ward headquarters, when he had carefully chosen a song in which a woman left a man she didn't love for a man—a musician—she did. Now he had just done the same thing, but by accident—he was thinking of the moon in the trees and had forgotten about the final line. He hurried on.

> *I once had a heart as good as new.*
> *But now it's gone from me to you.*
> *The moon picked you from all the rest*
> *For I loved you best.*

That only made it worse. The hell with it. If he was trapped in the song, he might as well sing with every bit of power he had. He closed his eyes and put his heart into every word.

> *I have a ship; my ship must flee.*
> *Sailing o'er the clouds and on the silver sea.*
> *The moon picked you from all the rest*
> *For I loved you best.*

That made him think of the *Juniper*, forever lost among the clouds. Abruptly, he forgot Alice, forgot the Third Ward, forgot everything. He longed to soar again, go back to his true home, and he found tears gathering at the backs of his eyes.

> *I picked a rose; the rose picked me,*
> *Underneath the branches of the forest tree.*
> *The moon picked you from all the rest*
> *For I loved you best.*

He opened his eyes. A single rose from the bunch on the table was lying near his arm on the table. Had it been there before? He couldn't remember. He looked at Alice, but her face was impassive.

"Thank you, Mr. Ennock," she said.

"You're welcome, Miss Michaels."

"I think after everything we've been through we can use our Christian names. Please call me Alice."

"If you'll call me Gavin."

"I shall, Gavin." She pulled a damp handkerchief from her sleeve and dabbed at one eye. "Pollen." She sniffed delicately. "We should think of the sleeping arrangements."

"You can have Barton's cot over there." Gavin gestured. "I'll take the floor near Barton himself in case he wakes up. I think we could find a way to string a curtain or something for you, if—"

"Not necessary," she said with a small smile. "Good night."

Gavin checked his own clothes—they were drying nicely near the stove—and rolled himself up in a spare blanket from the wardrobe. There was only one, and he decided Barton would just have to suffer, though the laudanum would probably give him a better night's sleep than Gavin would get. The stone floor was hard and chilly, but eventually he fell asleep.

Sometime later, a sound jerked him awake. He tensed, though his training kept him from leaping to his feet.

The moon slanted through the narrow windows, providing just enough light for Gavin to make out Alice moving about in her baggy shirt and trousers. Barton snored on in his drug-induced slumber. Gavin watched through slitted eyes as she wedged a bit of wood underneath the door to keep it from swinging shut. Then she picked up the first of her husband's little machines and carried it outside. A moment later, she returned for the second and the third. Once Alice had left the final time, Gavin counted to thirty and stole to the door, where he peered outside into the bright moonlight.

Alice had moved the machines some distance from the tower. As he watched, she flipped the machines over and, with a tool from her pocket, popped each one open and yanked various parts out of them. Before Gavin could make out what they were, she took the parts down to the river and threw them in with a splash. Tree, still asleep in the water, didn't move.

Several things clicked at once in Gavin's head. Alice hadn't cared so much about getting the machines back as she had about making sure no one saw what the machines were for, either because their function was illegal or socially unacceptable. She had been especially frantic because Patrick Barton knew her, and he might babble about the machines' origins to someone else, or worse, improve their design and show them off. Furthermore, Alice had said the machines actually belonged to her fiancé and he would be upset if they were lost. Gavin now took that to mean Mr. Williamson would be upset if their secret got out. The robbery had revealed the existence of the machines to several people—Gavin, Simon, Barton, and anyone who read the report that Gavin would eventually write—so Alice had apparently decided to destroy the illegal or unacceptable parts, leaving "clean" machines behind. She could even blame the damage on Barton.

So, what were the machines for? The obvious answers—theft, smuggling—didn't bother Gavin so much as the idea that Alice was being forced to cover up for her soon-to-be husband. What kind of man engaged in illegal activity and then dragged his fiancée into it? He clenched a fist.

Alice hurried back toward the tower, and Gavin rushed back to his place near the stove. He feigned sleep as Alice crept back into bed. After some time, her breathing deepened and steadied, while sleep eluded Gavin entirely. Finally, he got up and slipped over to the table, where the roses still lay scattered across the wood. With a glance at Alice, he picked up the rose closest to his chair, kissed it once, and crept over to the bed to lay it gently beside her pillow. She inhaled deeply, and he froze, but she only smiled in slumber. Gavin returned to his hard stone floor and lay awake for a long, long time.

Chapter Twelve

Alice awoke with a groan. Her muscles screamed when she rolled over to sit up on the lumpy camp bed, and she prayed she would never go through anything like yesterday again.

No, that was a lie. Yesterday had been the greatest thrill she'd had since . . . well, since she had rescued Gavin from Aunt Edwina's tower. She stretched and grimaced at the soreness. It felt strange to be wearing trousers. By all rights, she should be embarrassed wearing them in front of Gavin, but it didn't bother her. Perhaps it was because Gavin didn't care about rules.

The fire in the stove had died out, and Gavin lay before it, wrapped in his blanket. Morning sunshine sliced through the narrow arrow slits and cut strips across the stones near him. His white-blond hair, tousled with sleep, seemed to glow pale in the soft light. She swallowed. Yesterday, when he strode into the ruined shop dressed in black leathers, her heart had nearly stopped. Every moment they had shared came rushing back. His beautiful playing. His hypnotic singing. His bright smile. His optimistic, we-can-do-it attitude. The months fell away, and she was standing next to him while he played the devil's own music to destroy the traps in Aunt Edwina's house. He grinned with undisguised joy in the Third Ward's little airship. He sang to her in Dr. Clef's laboratory and touched her soul.

That day had been the most dreadful in her life. The Third Ward, with its fascinating inventions, its daring female agents, its promise of adventure, called to her. It wanted her, would accept her. The Ward didn't care that she was a woman or a lady. She could explore the world, dissect dozens of gadgets, and the Ward would pay her for it.

All of which had made it hard to turn Phipps down. Even the Ward's stunning salary wouldn't come close to clearing Father's debts. But that wasn't the main reason. The main reason, the one she had refused to think about despite Louisa's prodding, lay asleep in front of her. Gavin. She was already half in love with him, and worse, she was sure he knew it. Alice simply didn't think she had the willpower to stay faithful to Norbert if she worked in close proximity to Gavin. Consequently, when Phipps had offered her a position with the Third Ward, she had forced herself to refuse.

Alice creaked to her feet and found a tattered rose on the floor. Her feet carried her over the floor to the stove. Patrick Barton snored in drugged sleep a few feet away from Gavin. Her heart beat quickly at the sight of him. Gavin had grown in the past few months. His shoulders had broadened, and his movements had become more confident. He had always been handsome, but now he was breathtaking. His black leathers contrasted sharply with his pale eyes and hair, his features had sharpened, and he showed a strength she hadn't noticed before. Last night, she hadn't been able to resist asking him to sing for her. The lullaby's beauty nearly made her weep, and when he closed his eyes, her treacherous hands flipped one of the roses to the table in front of him. She had half hoped he would confront her about it, but he'd kept quiet.

What would it be like to touch him? He wouldn't

know—he was asleep. Even as the thought formed, that same treacherous hand reached down to caress his cheek. She could almost feel its raspy warmth beneath her fingers.

She snatched her hand back. That was quite enough. Alice set her mouth and turned to check on Barton. He was still unconscious. She didn't want him to wake, but she didn't know anything about dosing a man with laudanum, either, so she decided to let him be and get breakfast.

At the last moment, Alice stole back to the bed and slipped the battered rose into her pocket.

The sounds she made rattling through the tins woke Gavin with a start. He came to his feet before he fully woke, apparently ready to fight.

"Good morning," Alice called over a tin of pears. "I hope you like fruit."

Breakfast had nothing to do with hot chocolate. There was neither sausage nor newspaper. But a madman slumbered on the floor. When he showed signs of stirring, Gavin forced more laudanum down his throat.

"Won't that hurt him?" Alice asked.

"It might eventually," Gavin admitted, "but we have to keep him quiet until I can get him back to headquarters. Simon and I kept L'Arbre Magnifique asleep for almost a week, and he was fine."

"He's a clockworker. How would you know?"

After breakfast, Gavin changed back into his own clothes, which had dried overnight, and went outside to examine his backpack. He fiddled with the switches and gave the crank a few turns. No response.

"I think it died," he said. "I was hoping to radio London before we left, but—"

"I can have a look." Although she could now afford another set, Alice still kept the portable tools from Aunt Edwina in her handbag. She had used them last night to disassemble Norbert's machines and throw the incriminating parts into the river.

The backpack came apart in short order, and Alice peered inside with delight. It was refreshing to examine something that wasn't designed for . . . that had another purpose than the one she had become accustomed to. Almost instantly she saw the trouble. Water had shorted out several connections and circuits.

"How can you repair that?" Gavin said.

"Easily, Mr. Enn—Gavin." She gestured at the mechanical. "Mr. Barton stole a large number of spare parts. Why don't you check on Tree while I handle this?"

Tree, it turned out, had almost entirely recovered overnight. Gavin was even able to refasten the brass pieces that Barton's barrage had knocked loose yesterday.

Alice, meanwhile, finished her own repairs and switched the backpack's wireless on. Feedback whined and screeched.

"You did it!" Gavin said. "You're fantastic!"

"Thank you," Alice replied, glowing at the praise even as she realized she shouldn't. "Can you raise London?"

Gavin tried, and got nothing but static. "We're out of range. We can try again when we get closer."

"Speaking of which," Alice put in, "how are we going to handle the travel and explanations?"

Gavin looked puzzled. "I don't understand."

"Gavin," she said gently, "as a traditional woman, I can drive about London with a man who isn't my husband or father as long as we're in public. But I can't go away overnight with him. Even an Ad Hoc lady couldn't do that. I'm not even coming back in my own clothes."

"Oh. Right. It's always something stupid." He scratched his cheek, which was growing raspy. "Look, I don't think anyone saw you leave London with me. Tree scared away the crowd outside the shop, and you can't really see who's riding him. And if we give you Barton's hat for the ride back, you'll look like a boy. If anyone *does* know you left town overnight, we'll tell him Barton captured you. I, an agent of the Crown, rescued you in a daring raid at dawn, and now I'm seeing you home. Your dress was badly torn in the rescue, so you bravely donned a spare set of man's clothing. How's that?"

"Why am *I* the one who gets captured?"

"You're the traditional lady."

Alice let that pass. "And what do we tell my fiancé? *He* certainly knows I was gone."

"Tell him whatever you want. If you trust him," Gavin said, his tone carefully neutral, "tell the truth. If you don't, give him the lie. Simon and Lieutenant Phipps will back you up."

Alice thought about that. On the one hand, she had rushed off only to ensure Norbert's filthy machines remained a secret, so he had little right to be angry. On the other hand, she had spent the night in a tower with another man, begged him to sing for her, and more or less handed him a rose, which would give any fiancé the right to be upset. Perhaps there was a third option—if no one but Gavin and the Third Ward knew the truth, Alice could give Norbert an edited version of what had happened, a version that left Gavin out of it. She had tracked Barton to his lair, cracked him over the head, disguised herself with his clothes, and brought him back to the authorities in his own mechanical. That might work.

Spinning lies and donning disguises felt suddenly stupid and frustrating. Gavin was a good friend, and nothing more, but the rules of traditional society made it clear that men and women could only be lovers, especially if they went away overnight together. For a moment, she considered casting it all aside. So what if someone recognized her and gossiped? What was the worst that could happen?

Norbert might become angry. Some of the people he did business with might lose respect for him and take their business elsewhere. Her children, when she had them, could end up with the social stigma of an unfaithful mother. A heavy sigh escaped her.

"I think your solution will do," she said. "I'll drive the

mechanical. You take Barton in Tree, though we'll have to find his hat first."

The trip back to London went quickly, and Alice thoroughly enjoyed driving the mechanical. The metal shell gave her a sense of height, strength, and power quite new to her. Earth thudded beneath the mechanical's feet, and the landscape sped by or slowed at her command. She had become a giant, a great warrior from mythology. The damp English air rushed over her, teased at her hair, pulled at her clothes. The feeling of speed and freedom exhilarated her in ways she had never thought possible. No one could stop her or stand in her way. Beside her, Gavin was just visible through Tree's branches with Barton chained nearby, and Alice couldn't decide which was stranger—driving a great mechanical beast or walking beside an ambulatory tree.

"Race?" she called.

"First one to the crossroads wins!" Gavin yelled, and Tree said, "WINDY." They thundered up a hill and down the other side, frightening a herd of cattle on the other side of a hedgerow. Alice shouted like a little girl and ran. She was one with the mechanical now. Its legs were her legs; its arms her arms. Power thrummed through her, and she ran and ran and ran. Beside her, Tree rustled and thumped, scattering leaves and bits of bark. Gavin lost his hat. They reached the crossroads at exactly the same moment and came to a stop.

"A tie!" Alice shouted. "Well-done!"

"It was!" Gavin called back. Then he jumped and abruptly twisted in his seat so he could turn the crank on the backpack. The backpack squealed, spat static, and spoke, though Alice couldn't make out the words.

"What is it?" she asked.

"That was Lieutenant Phipps. Simon and Glenda weren't able to capture the clockworker they went after yesterday."

Alice started. She had forgotten all about the grinning clockworker's reappearance. "And?"

"He vanished, but now he's resurfaced with more plague zombies in the City. We might be able to catch up with him if we cut over to City Road. We'll pass right by St. Luke's Hospital and into the center of London."

"Isn't the Third Ward already there?"

"Two bombs exploded not far from headquarters. No one was hurt, but they dropped rubble across streets and clogged traffic in a dozen directions. And the dirigibles are out of the country. Our people can't get to the location. The clockwork must have planned it that way."

"What is he doing?"

Gavin said, "He's trying to storm the Bank of England."

They left the little road, stepping over hedges and ancient stone walls. The earlier exhilaration that came with the speed left Alice, replaced with a grim urgency. Not only had the grinning clockworker returned; he was endangering lives. By forcing a group of plague zombies into a crowded, daylight street, he was potentially infecting dozens, even hundreds of people with the clockwork plague. Every thought of propriety left Alice's head. She didn't care what happened to her or her reputation—no other families would suffer from the clockwork plague as hers had; not if she could stop it.

They reached the wider, cobblestoned City Road. Horse, carriage, and foot traffic moved along its length, but they wove around or through it all, leaving startled horses in their wake. Drovers shouted and shook their fists, but Alice didn't respond. When they reached London proper, the City Road became brick, and Alice heard the screams. Gavin did, too, and they steered their respective mounts toward the sound. City Road became Moorgate and Prince's Street, with their staid, respectable buildings. Alice and Gavin angled east, and chaos greeted them. People milled everywhere. Half of them were trying to get away, and half were trying to get a better view of the happenings. Panicky horses pulled carriages and wagons into a hopeless snarl.

Glass from shattered windows crunched under hundreds of feet, and a broken gaslight had erupted into yellow flame. Over it all, Alice heard eerie music. Memories from a year ago sent a chill down her spine. For a moment, she was wearing The Dress and facing a horde of zombies at three in the morning.

People scattered when they saw Tree and the mechanical, though it was still tricky to maneuver around the snarled vehicles. Ahead of them, Prince's Street met Threadneedle and four others at odd angles to make an intersection the size of a marching field. Looming over it was the Bank of England, a white structure begrimed with decades of coal smoke. The building covered multiple acres and was built around an irregular network of courtyards, ramps, staircases, and pillared halls. At the moment, it was being attacked by a crowd of zombies. Alice stared. Gold bouillon, no doubt what the clockworker was after, lay buried in vaults deep underground. The zombies, nearly a hundred in all, were attacking what amounted to a tiny corner of the bank, and they had no hope of getting to anything worthwhile, but that didn't seem to stop them. Zombies created a sea of bodies three and four deep around one small part of the building. They flung themselves at the heavily barred, arched doors, attacking with stones pried up from the street or with their bare fists. A bell on the bank roof rang and rang in a call for help, but Alice knew the police wouldn't want to get involved directly—they stood the same risk of infection as anyone else. Fear twisted in her own chest at the thought of a zombie's touch, but she remained determined to help.

In the center of the zombie crowd stood the grinning clockworker. His brown coat nearly reached the ground, and his ragged top hat, out of place so early in the day, poked up like a smokestack. The white mask covered the upper half of his face, and his lower face kept that impossibly wide grin. He was playing the strange instrument Alice remembered from their first encounter. Clearly he had repaired it, and perhaps had even made some improvements. It still looked like a bagpipe with strange little machines attached to it, though the clockworker didn't blow into it. The dreadful music poured ceaselessly from the instrument, and it seemed to be driving the zombies into a frenzy. The sickly men, women, and children, gaunt and ragged, pounded at the building, moaning and crying with inhuman ferocity.

Tree and the mechanical worked their way to the intersection. A trio of policemen waved their arms, trying in vain to restore order, and a fourth officer on horseback wrestled with his mount to keep it under control, though none of the officers approached the zombies or the clockworker. People screamed and pointed or simply fled. A carthorse lay on its side, its eye fixed upward in death. Gavin halted Tree within running distance of the bank, opened a cupboard door concealed by Tree's bark, and extracted a violin case.

"Can you play tritones on that?" she shouted across to him, her voice barely audible over the clockworker's music and groan of the zombies.

"Not effectively." He was already climbing down, leaving the sleeping Barton chained to one of Tree's branches. "But I have a different idea."

He sprinted toward the zombies—and the clockworker in their midst. Alice, unused to trousers, fumbled through her pockets. "Gavin! Wait! I have the tuning forks!"

But he was already too far away to hear. He reached the edge of the zombie crowd, put bow to strings, and played. His fiddle blended with the clockworker's otherworldly song. The grinning clockworker spun, flaring the tails of his long coat. He stared at Gavin, but didn't pause in his own playing. His fingers continued to skitter over the controls of his instrument, and the terrible music rippled from it in endless waves. Gavin stared back, and something passed between them. The clockworker nodded once, and Alice held her breath. Her hands went cold on the controls of the mechanical.

Gavin set his shoulders and played louder. His fingers flew up and down the fiddle's neck. His melody wound around the clockworker's, combined with it, and created a new one. The zombies paused in their rampage. They turned, entranced by the duet.

The clockworker changed the tune, and the zombies screamed with one voice. Alice clapped her hands over her ears to shut out the horrible noise. It was like listening to the dead. They went back to attacking the doors.

"ROCKY," Tree said beside her. "LOOK."

A man poked a rifle through the bars of an upper window of the bank. Alice instantly came to herself. She didn't like the clockworker and she feared the plague zombies, but the man with the gun might hit Gavin. Without thinking, she reached down with her mechanical hands, tore two chunks of brick and mortar from the street, and hurled a piece at the man. The chunk was only the size of cat, but it clanged hard against the window bars. Startled, the man dropped the rifle and jerked himself back inside.

"LEAFY," Tree said.

Gavin switched his song to match the clockworker's again as Alice stomped toward the zombie crowd and stopped there. Tree, bereft of a driver and with Barton chained in his branches, stayed behind. The zombies paused a second time. They and the clockworker turned to stare, this time at Alice. The clockworker's song continued, though the grin fell off his face. Alice felt tall and powerful as she glared down at the clockworker who had frightened her, threatened her, disrupted her city. Her fist clenched, nearly shattering the second piece of brick and mortar.

"Stop that music!" she yelled into the mechanical's speaking tube. At her feet, Gavin halted. "Not you!" she amended hastily. "You!"

Gavin started up again, but the clockworker ignored Alice's order. The zombies made a thick wall between the mechanical and the clockworker, and Alice couldn't quite reach him. She didn't want to stomp through the crowd, either. It would be horrible and messy, and as much as she hated and feared the clockwork plague, she couldn't bring herself to crush the skulls of its victims. Alice fumbled through her pockets, yanked out the tuning forks, and clanged them together. The tritone rang out, but it drowned in the duct below. Disgusted, Alice shoved the forks back into her pockets and grabbed the mechanical's controls again, but she couldn't do anything with the zombies in the way. The clockworker's grin returned. They were at an impasse.

"You'll have to stop playing sometime," Alice called.

The clockworker ignored her and changed his song again. The zombies abruptly turned their collective gaze on Gavin, who was without defenses. They were only a few paces away. With the rigid precision of mechanicals under control, they reached for him.

"Run, Gavin!" By reflex, Alice hurled the piece of brick and mortar at the clockworker. The clockworker leapt backward with a yelp and bumbled into a zombie. The chunk crashed into the ground where the clockworker had been standing. The song stopped.

Silence fell over the square. Then the zombies cringed and flung up their arms to shield their eyes from the sunlight. They scattered, fleeing the terrible light. Gavin shinnied up the mechanical, fearful of being touched and infected, and dropped into the padded bench seat beside her without even a how-do-you-do. It made for a tight squeeze, and she was acutely aware of the way his hard muscles pressed against her body.

"The tuning forks," he panted. "Quick!"

But Alice was busy with the controls. She tried to slip the mechanical through the thinning crowd of zombies toward the clockworker, who had already scrambled to his feet.

"Drat!" she muttered. "He's getting out that instrument of his again. Get ready to play."

"I don't know if I *can* play squashed in here. Where are the damned forks?"

"In my pockets."

Gavin slid his hands down Alice's outer thighs. Even under the circumstances, she felt a thrill at his touch, and her breath caught. He found the forks and pulled them out. Alice, meanwhile, moved the mechanical a step ahead despite the scattering zombies. The clockworker fished in his coat with one hand and produced a set of padded metal cups connected by a length of polished wood. These he popped over his ears.

"Fantastic," Gavin muttered, tossing the forks to the floor of the mechanical with a discordant clatter.

Mouth set, Alice leaned the mechanical forward and reached down with its arms, but she wasn't quite close enough to touch the clockworker. The zombies lurched around, looking for shadows but not finding any. This side of the bank faced south, and there weren't any alleys nearby. This caused the zombies to mill about in painful confusion. They mewed and squealed almost like children. Alice tried not to look too closely, but she couldn't help seeing their pain and misery. This one used to be a young woman, and her ragged dress was soaked through with patches of blood where her skin had sloughed off, and her hair had come out in clumps. An old man limped painfully on the stump of one foot. A little girl clutched a filthy stuffed dog and cried tears of blood as she tried to escape the all-powerful sunlight.

The clockworker, for his part, pumped the bellows on his instrument and blasted out two powerful notes, paused, and rumbled out a third, one so deep it throbbed through Alice's bones.

"What the hell?" Gavin said.

The clockworker repeated the set—one, two, pause, and three. Alice reached again, but he dodged out of the way. The instrument deflated with a ghostly wail that set Alice's teeth on edge, and the clockworker skittered between the mechanical's legs with the agility of a spider. He scuttled off. Swearing, Alice turned the mechanical in time to see him reach the corner at Prince's Street.

"Get him!" Gavin shouted needlessly, for Alice was already in pursuit. She dodged an overturned carriage and stomped around the corner just in time to see the clockworker standing motionless in the center of the street. He snapped a salute to Alice, took one step sideways, and dropped out of sight.

Chapter Thirteen

"No!" Alice tromped over to the spot and found nothing but the open sewer hole. The smell of rotted waste oozed upward. "Do we dare?" she said.

Gavin, still clutching his fiddle, jumped down to peer into the hole. "We'd have a fifty-fifty chance of going in the wrong direction," he said. "And I don't have a light."

"I had the same thought. I'm not sure if I'm unhappy or relieved, to tell you the truth. Slogging through the sewer is hardly my idea of fun."

"I've done it," Gavin said. "It's even worse than you're thinking."

"What now, then?"

"We need to get out of here before reporters show up and start asking questions. The Ward doesn't like publicity. And we need to get Tree and Barton and his mechanical back to headquarters. Can you still drive it?"

"Reporters?" Alice twisted around in the seat as if one might leap out of a window at her. "Are any here now?"

"Might be." Gavin shrugged. "They run toward disasters instead of away from them."

Alice slumped down. "I can't be recognized."

"You won't be. You still look like a boy in that hat and those trousers. But let's get out of here, just in case."

The zombies had dispersed, finding their way back into alleys and side streets. Gavin clambered into the mechanical, and Alice hurried it toward Tree. Once again, Gavin's body pressed unavoidably against Alice's. She tried to ignore the feelings this aroused in her but found it a losing battle. He smelled like leather and sweat, unlike Norbert's scent of cologne and linen. His muscles were hard and powerful, unlike Norbert's softer frame. His—

"Lamppost!" Gavin yelled.

"Sorry." She skirted the object and reached Tree. Already, people and traffic were returning to the intersection. One of the policemen they'd seen earlier hurried up to them as Gavin was climbing down. He looked nervous but determined.

"I need to ask you some questions, sir," he said, then glanced up at Alice. "And you, lad."

"Crown business." From somewhere in the recesses of his clothing, Gavin produced a metal badge. "I have to get my prisoner to headquarters."

Before the bobby could protest further, Gavin whistled and Tree bent down so he could hoist himself upward. Barton continued to snooze among the branches. The policeman retreated uncertainly. "Now look—," he began.

"Ask for Lieutenant Phipps through Scotland Yard," Gavin called down. "She'll tell you it's taken care of. Follow me, Allen."

It took Alice a moment to realize he meant her. She touched the brim of her borrowed hat at the policeman and turned the mechanical to follow Gavin. They reached the spot where Fleet Street and its noisy press shops and smelly factories joined the wide thoroughfare of the Strand, which followed the river Thames down to Westminster and, ultimately, Third Ward headquarters. Guarding the spot was the Temple Bar, a two-story stone archway that blocked the street between the three- and four-story buildings. The top half was solid stone, adorned with bas relief statues of the Queen and the Prince of Wales. The lower half was an archway barely tall enough for a beer truck, and only wide enough for two carts to pass in opposite directions. Pedestrians were shunted through a pair of side doors on either side of the Bar, but cart traffic was forced in like sand through an hourglass. When Alice was little, she had happened to be walking nearby with Father when the Queen in her grand carriage had come up the Strand, intending to enter the City from Westminster. The gates of Temple Bar were slammed shut to bar the way—hence the name—and John Humphrey, Lord Mayor of London, strode out to meet the young Victoria, who was in her fourth year of reign. This was before Father's illness, and he was easily strong enough to lift Alice so she could see over the heads of the crowd. The men had all removed their hats. The Queen ascended from her carriage, looking young and beautiful in a silken gown of deep blue. Jewels gleamed at her throat and on her fingers. She approached Humphrey and, in a voice that rang clearly, asked for the Lord Mayor's loyalty. Humphrey presented her with a pearl-encrusted sword, and they exchanged other formal pleasantries as traffic piled up on both sides of the Bar. Eventually, the Queen ascended back into her carriage, the Bar reopened, and the royal carriage drove through, allowing traffic to move.

"I got to see the Queen!" Alice said breathlessly. "The Queen!"

"You did indeed." Father set her on the sidewalk. "Something to remember forever, eh?"

"What was all that for?" she asked.

"Old tradition, dating back to Queen Elizabeth. The Lord Mayor is technically the sovereign of the City, so the Queen asks for his loyalty. He gives her one of the five City swords to show she indeed has it, and he orders the gates open. Some say she's asking permission to enter the City as well, but that's rubbish."

"What happens to the sword?" Alice asked. "Does the Queen give it back for next time? Does she get a new one every time she comes into the City?"

Father scratched his head. "You know, I never thought about that. You'll have to ask the Queen the next time you see her."

"I will," Alice said. "May I have an ice?"

Back then, Alice had thought Temple Bar awe-inspiring and the ceremony fascinating. Now, however, she saw only congested traffic where the crowded street narrowed from four lanes to two. They slowed, joining the line of carts and carriages. Alice fidgeted. People stared at Tree and the mechanical as they passed, though traffic didn't halt. Machines and other strange objects weren't uncommon in London, as long as they behaved themselves. Still, Alice was nervous about being recognized, and she kept her hat pulled low. The line of traffic at the Temple Bar stalled, edged slowly forward, stalled again.

And then she saw Norbert. He emerged from the pedestrian gate on the south side of the Temple Bar and strolled straight toward them. The fine material of his conservatively cut suit and waistcoat stood out from the crowd of rougher men, as did his confident air. Alice's heart jerked. Whether she told Norbert the full-blown lie or the edited truth wouldn't matter in the slightest if he caught her red-handed with Gavin. She put a hand over her mouth as if scratching her nose, turned her head away from him, and prayed he would walk on by.

"You, lad!"

His familiar voice filtered through the street noise. Alice flicked a glance downward. Norbert was standing at the mechanical's feet, arms folded.

"Yes, you, lad!" he called. "Tell me who built this machine. I can't imagine it was you."

All the breath left Alice's breast. Panic constricted her chest with iron bands and her bowels turned to liquid. She couldn't think. If she spoke, or even lowered her hands, he would recognize her. What could she—

"Oi! Don't talk to 'im!" Gavin said from Tree. His American accent had been replaced with something one might hear from Seven Dials. "He's just an apprentice, and anyway 'e lost 'is voice in an accident. Inhaled the wrong fumes."

Norbert turned. Traffic edged forward again, but he was easily able to keep pace with Tree and the mechanical. "Are you his master? You look young for—"

"No, guv'nor. That's our master." Gavin pointed to Barton. "What do you wants to know?"

Alice sat motionless in the mechanical. Relief that Norbert was no longer looking in her direction eased some of the panic, but the danger was still imminent.

"I run a machinery concern," Norbert said to Gavin. "If your master builds mechanicals and needs a source of machine parts, I would like to speak with him."

"Yeah, all right. I'll tell 'im when he's finished sleepin' it off. You got a card, guv?"

Norbert handed one up, and Gavin thanked him. He turned to go, then paused and came back to the mechanical. He squinted up at Alice, and she started to panic again. He knew.

He tossed a coin upward. It landed on the seat beside her. "Go see a doctor about your voice, lad." And he was gone.

Alice deflated on the padded bench. The relief was so complete, she lost all strength to stir a limb until the drover behind the mechanical shouted at her to move forward. She complied.

"Are you all right?" Gavin called.

"You were wonderful." Gratitude overfilled her like water in a tiny glass. "A real hero. A true—" Then she remembered she was supposed to be a boy and stopped herself.

"That was your . . . I mean . . . you knew him, didn't you?"

"Yes. Thank you."

And they said no more.

Getting through the Temple Bar was tricky. Tree had to turn around, stoop, and go backward so the low arch wouldn't rip at his branches. Alice had to put the tall mechanical in a crouch and make it take baby steps. Both processes took considerable time and did nothing to endear them to the people behind. Once they were through, the Strand widened considerably and traffic flowed much more quickly, allowing them to move with speed.

"That stupid Bar thing stops everything dead right at the busiest point in London," Gavin complained. "And it's ugly to boot. They should just tear it out."

"Temple Bar?" Alice said, aghast. "It may be ugly, but it's been there for hundreds of years. The Queen stops there every time she enters the City. It's a long-standing tradition. They'll never take that down, not in a millennium."

Gavin grimaced. "I suppose. But now we really need to hurry. Barton's waking up, and I'm out of laudanum."

The Strand sped past them. Alice caught occasional glimpses of the Thames, crowded with boats and small ships. Many of them were powered by coal-fired steam engines. But mostly she saw tall buildings, all square and no-nonsense and covered with coal soot. Her earlier exhilaration had left her, and now she wanted only to deliver Barton and the mechanical to the Third Ward so she could go home to a bath, a good meal, and a nap. Driving the mechanical, with its constant pedals and pulleys, was beginning to tire her.

At last they cleared the more crowded part of London and entered the greener parks and squares of Westminster. A fog rolled in off the Thames, sending a chilly gray blanket after them. It was already growing hard to see by the time they reached the gates of the estate Alice barely remembered from a year ago. In the center of the wrought iron was the numeral 2 surmounted by a square root symbol. They opened as Tree and the mechanical approached. Moments later, Alice and Gavin were both climbing down from their mounts. A crew led the restless Barton away and, at Alice's direction, stowed Norbert's little machines in a crate. Since there was no incriminating evidence on them, Alice didn't much care what happened to them at this point, though she didn't relish the thought of refitting them.

The fog chased Gavin and Alice inside the great brick house, where Alice was escorted to a dressing room. She was allowed a quick bath and was given a simple green dress and straw hat. Feeling immeasurably more normal and secure in skirts, she was fastening the last button when the door opened and the woman who gave her the clothes poked her head in.

"If you're done," she said, "Lieutenant Phipps wants to see you in her office."

"Of course she does," muttered Alice, who wanted nothing more than to go home.

The door to Phipps's office was shut, but Alice could hear the woman's voice inside. She was giving someone a firm dressing-down, and her displeasure sounded clear, even through two inches of solid wood. Alice knocked and Phipps's voice stopped.

"Come!" she called.

Alice entered the book-lined office. The odd transcription machine stood at the ready beside the desk. Gray fog pressed against the windows as if it were trying to get in, turning afternoon into evening. Gavin, newly bathed and shaven and so damned handsome, came to his feet when Alice cleared the threshold. Susan Phipps, behind the desk, kept her seat. Her metal arm and brass eyepiece gleamed in the lamplight. Obviously, Gavin was the victim of the dressing-down, and she wondered what had gone wrong.

"As I was discussing with Agent Ennock, Miss Michaels, I'm torn," Phipps said when Alice sat down. "On the one hand, I'm upset that you created such a spectacle in the City streets and called attention to our organization in a way that cost me enormous amounts of money to keep out of the newspapers. We don't do things that way in the Third Ward, and Agent Ennock here knows better than that."

"Oh," said Alice, nonplused. "I'm terribly sorry. I didn't realize."

"Granted. Unlike Mr. Ennock here, you didn't go through Ward training. But that brings me to my other point. I do find myself impressed with you. No training, no plan, no support, and you still managed to bring in a clockworker on your first outing for the Ward."

"I don't work for the Ward," Alice replied primly.

"Not yet," Phipps shot back. "And I do want to hear your version of what happened. You can speak freely. Your fiancé and everyone else outside these walls will never read the report, and as I already pointed out, I've arranged for the newspapers to remain silent."

Alice glanced at Gavin, who nodded, and told the story, though she left out the true function of Norbert's machines. The transcription device clattered and thumped, and every word appeared on the paper scroll.

"Very well," Phipps said when she finished. "Now I need to show you something downstairs. It won't take a moment."

Before Alice could protest, Phipps swept her and Gavin out of the office and into the lift they had used last time. The cage sank into the stony fortress beneath the mansion, and Alice shifted her weight from one foot to the other, partly interested and partly wanting to get home. Norbert was no doubt worried, or furious, or both, and her first duty was to him.

"While you were freshening up, we brought Patrick Barton down to the clockworker level." Phipps exited the lift with Alice and Gavin close behind. The chilly corridors stretched out in several labyrinthine directions. Clanks and thumps and shouts echoed against the stones. "Miss Michaels, you reported encountering Barton at a ball approximately one year ago."

"That's right."

"And he exhibited no strange behavior?"

"Not unless you count coming to the Greenfellow ball in a badly cut coat."

They passed the Doomsday Vault, and the four armed guards came to attention.

"Did you notice any markedly increased intelligence, heightened reflexes, an increased interest in music, or sensitivity to poorly played or off-key music?"

"No, but I barely noticed him at all. He asked Louisa to dance, not me. Why are you asking all this again?"

"Because." Phipps stopped at a particularly heavy door and extended her metal hand toward it. The first two of her six fingers extended with a sharp sound and created a key, which she inserted into the lock. "The laudanum has fully worn off, and this is the result."

The door opened into a small cell with stained mattresses lining the walls and floor. Patrick Barton sat on the floor. He wore a dingy straitjacket. His hair stuck out in a dozen directions, his eyes were wild, and his straitjacket was chained to the rear wall. When the three of them entered, he shoved himself backward.

"My Boadicea has fallen," he whimpered. "Money and machines, cash and mechanics. You sold your soul for coins, and now you walk with an angel who fell from the sky. Are you here to pull me into a velvet pit or fling me into unforgiving air?"

"He's insane," Alice whispered.

"The earth travels through the sky and the sky pulls the earth." Spittle ran down Barton's chin, and words flowed in a waterfall. "The earth thinks it moves in a straight line, but the eye of God warps space, so the earth travels in a circle, a spiral that grows a little smaller each time, moves us closer to hell, even though we think we're moving toward heaven."

"He's in the final stage," Gavin breathed. "How?"

"We don't know," Phipps replied.

"Final stage? What's going on?" Alice demanded.

Barton screamed and threw himself at them. Alice leapt back with a cry. Barton didn't get very far. The straitjacket hobbled him, and the chain brought him up short. He growled and snarled like a dog on a leash.

"Out!" Phipps ordered.

Alice fled with the others right behind her. They slammed the door just as Barton began to howl. The heavy door cut the sound off. The trio stood in the hallway a moment, silent. Alice's knees were weak.

"I don't want to do that again," she whispered at last. "I can't."

"How long before he dies?" Gavin asked.

"Three days, perhaps a week," Phipps said. "And that's puzzling. I don't know how much you know about clockworkers and the clockwork plague, Miss Michaels."

"Not much," Alice admitted uncomfortably. "They don't teach about it at finishing school, and clockworkers are ... well, you know."

"Insane, yes," Phipps said. "And people fear and dislike them, often with good reason, so they don't discuss them in polite company. All right, listen—the Third Ward has made an extensive study of clockworkers and their pathology. Every case is different, but most follow a general pattern. When someone who is going to be a clockworker first catches the clockwork plague, their symptoms are very different. Most plague victims come down with fever and muscle tremors in the early stages. Those that survive are often scarred."

Alice clenched her jaw. She remembered with absolute clarity when her father and mother and older brother came down with the fever and muscle tremors that heralded the clockwork plague, and she remembered the helpless terror she felt as her mother and brother worsened and died. Father had worsened as well, and then recovered, more or less. He never walked again, would never lift Alice above his head so she could see the Queen.

"The ones who don't die right away or survive with scarring almost have it worse," Phipps continued heartlessly. "Their symptoms intensify until they include delirium, loss of muscle tone, thinning of the skin, pustules, and sensitivity to light, which result in what the public likes to call plague zombies. Eventually they die as well."

"I know how that aspect of the clockwork plague works," Alice said icily.

"Your family is well acquainted with it," Phipps acknowledged. "But clockworkers are different. People who will, through a mechanism we do not yet understand, become clockworkers, begin with different symptoms. The plague seems to work *with* their brains instead of against, at least for a time. In the first phase, which lasts three or four months, they show increased intelligence, insomnia, an interest in good music, and a strong dislike for bad music. They are not contagious, and we still don't know why. In the second phase, their intelligence increases vastly, often within one or two specialties, such as biology or art. Their sensitivity to bad music leaps to include a sensitivity to tritones. They sleep very little, and they gain heightened physical endurance, as if their bodies were burning up future resources all at once. This allows them to work tirelessly on their strange machines and abstract mathematics. They also begin to think differently from normal people, which lets them commit acts of great brilliance or stunning cruelty. This stage can last anywhere from fourteen months to three years. The longest time on record that a clockworker in this phase lived was three years, two months, and four days."

"Until your aunt Edwina came along," Gavin added. "We're still looking for her."

"The third and final phase," Phipps said, "is the one you just observed. The disease seems to devour the clockworker's brain all at once. He loses all touch with reality."

"What does this have to do with—oh!" Alice exclaimed. "I see! If Patrick Barton was healthy at the Greenfellow ball just a year ago, he hasn't had time to go through the entire plague yet. That's what worries you."

"Correct. We'll interview his family and friends, of course, but even if he was somehow exposed to the plague at the ball—and it seems likely he was infected rather later—he should still be within the first or second phase. Why was the plague so advanced in him?"

"Was that a rhetorical question?" Alice countered. "Because I have no way of knowing the answer."

"I can't answer it, either," Gavin pointed out.

"A great many odd questions seem to come up where you're concerned, Miss Michaels." Phipps straightened her uniform jacket. "As Agent Ennock pointed out, we still don't know the true fate of your aunt Edwina. The clockworker who plays to zombies also seems to have an attachment to you, and you just happened to be in that shop when Mr. Barton robbed it. It's very curious."

"Are you insinuating something?" Alice asked hotly. "Because I resent the implication."

"I'm insinuating nothing. I want you to *work* for me and bring all this clockworker strangeness with you." She handed Alice a piece of paper from her pocket. "Look at this."

Alice unfolded the letter and froze. Graceful script flowed across the page, and at the bottom was a seal in scarlet wax of a woman in a flowing dress mounted on a horse. The paper suddenly felt both heavy and delicate. "This is from the Queen. The Queen wrote to *you*."

"In her own hand," Phipps agreed. "She's polite—she's never anything else—but she still regrets to inform me that if I can't capture the maniac who's been stirring up plague zombies and wreaking havoc in London, she'll find someone who can."

Alice's mouth was dry. She could imagine Victoria sitting at a desk with a gold pen and inkpot, her brow furrowed in thought. Her hands had caressed this bit of paper, and now Alice held the same bit. The connection felt almost too powerful to bear. "The Queen," she murmured again.

"We need to find this grinning clockworker," Phipps said, "and I think you can help. Please, Miss Michaels. Come work for us."

"No." The word popped out by reflex.

"Is it because of your position?" Phipps pressed. "A traditional lady doesn't labor for money, I know, but actual *work* doesn't seem to bother you. You could work for free, you know, or donate your salary to charity."

"No."

"You think your fiancé would object? We might be able to persuade him. The Prime Minister doesn't know we exist, but a few high-level officials do, and I'm sure one of them would be willing to discuss the matter with him and—"

"No."

Alice couldn't help flicking a glance at Gavin. His eyes, blue as an April sky, caught her earth brown ones and held them. At that moment, a powerful rush of emotion made her knees tremble beneath her borrowed dress. This man had saved her life, and she had saved his. He was handsome, and thrilling, and made the angels weep for envy of his music. If she joined the Third Ward and worked with this man, she would either give in to base temptation or weep every night for what she couldn't have during the day.

Alice cleared her throat and spoke, though every word was a stone that crushed her down. "It's simply impossible. But it's nice to be wanted."

Gavin's face fell. He looked unhappier than Phipps, and Alice nearly recanted then and there.

"Lieutenant Phipps," Alice said suddenly, "are you an Ad Hoc woman?"

A look of surprise crossed Phipps's face. "Of course."

"So you vote," Alice pressed. "And your husband . . . ?"

"Doesn't object in the slightest," Phipps said. "He died of the clockwork plague years ago."

"How do you cope?" Alice asked in abrupt desperation. "How do you deal with the death and hell you see in London every day?"

"Work, Miss Michaels. It keeps the body busy and gives the mind time to heal. Pick a cause and work for it. You'd be surprised at what can be accomplished by one person. Or by a small committee."

Alice stared at her. Phipps stared back. "I've heard rumors," Alice said slowly, "of an anonymous benefactor who helped the Hats-On Committee retain power by providing funds and connections. Someone who moves outside the normal social circles and has access to incredible resources. You wouldn't know anything about such a person, would you, Lieutenant?"

"My offer of a position still stands, Miss Michaels," Phipps said.

Alice felt Gavin's eyes on her. Before she could give in to weakness, she shook her head and marched woodenly back to the lift.

Just as she was shutting the gate, Gavin darted between the closing bars. "Hold the lift, please," he said with a weak smile.

The gates clanged shut, and Alice wordlessly pulled the lever to start their ascension. She didn't want to be in the lift with Gavin, not now. But it would have been rude to slam the gate shut on him. The lift rumbled as it climbed the shaft.

"Listen," he said, "I don't know why you keep pushing me—us—away, but—"

"Did Phipps send you after me?" Alice interrupted.

"No!" He touched her elbow, then quickly withdrew his hand. "I . . . I like you, Alice. I missed seeing you all those weeks and months, when I was training and then in the field."

She folded her arms, partly to conceal that her hands were shaking. "That's not a proper thing to say to an engaged woman, Mr. Ennock."

"What happened to Gavin?" He shifted uncomfortably, and his leather jacket creaked. "Alice, I'm not trying to be a . . . a cad. But we can be friends. Why do you believe everyone is so suspicious all the time?"

The words spilled out of her with unexpected vehemence that filled the lift with hot oil. "Because everyone *is* suspicious, Gavin. Everyone is waiting to think the worst. I watched it happen to my family after the clockwork plague took my brother and mother and crippled my father. Rather than try to help us, our former friends shunned us because they blamed us. They don't trust me. I don't trust me."

"What do you mean?"

"Mr. Ennock, if I work with you, I won't be able to . . . to keep my distance. You know why."

"Do I?" His voice was thick.

"You do." A lump formed in Alice's throat. "And when my control breaks—as I know damned well it will, Gavin— the harpies will be waiting to pounce. They'll tear me to shreds with their nasty claws and spread my heart and lungs to dry in the sun. I won't let that happen, Mr. Ennock. I won't. Too much is at stake."

He looked her up and down with those damnable blue eyes, and she knew he was seeing through her. "That isn't all of it," he said.

"It is."

"No." Gavin yanked a lever, and the lift halted with a

clank. Somewhere, a faint alarm bell rang, but he ignored it. "In the end, it has nothing to do with me. Tell me the rest."

She looked around in desperation, wanting to flee, but there was only the cage. "I've as much as told you how much I— There isn't any more."

"No." His face was stony, but his jaw trembled. "Your face changed when you were talking about blame. Tell me about that, Alice. We have lots of time now."

"I—I don't—"

"Alice, when the pirates took my ship and killed my captain and my best friend and flogged my back and . . . tried to do other things, I blamed myself. I thought it was my fault for a long time. I hate the pirates, Alice. I hate the horrible things they did to me, and I hate this dirty city they dropped me in. But now—just this moment, just now—I realized that if they hadn't done those things, I would never have met *you.* I would be so unhappy and not even know it." He took a deep, shuddering breath. "Bad things happen sometimes. That's just the way the world works. But sometimes bad things send us in a good direction. None of it was my fault. None of it was your fault. It wasn't."

"You don't even know what it was," Alice choked.

He touched her face with the back of one finger as the alarm continued to shrill in the distance. "Then tell me."

"They did blame me, and it *was* my fault."

"What was?"

Words spilled out of her. "When I was little, I managed to slip away from my governess and got outside the walls of our garden. It was so much fun! I found a group of street children, and they let me play with them in exchange for the ribbons in my hair. My parents were frantic, as you can probably imagine. My mother thought a child-snatcher had taken me for ransom or to steal my clothes. Near sunset, Lady Greenfellow, of all people, happened to be riding by in her carriage and saw me with those children. It was bad enough that a baron's daughter was playing with street urchins, but, worse still, a plague zombie was rummaging around in a dustheap not far from where we were playing. We didn't even notice. Lady Greenfellow snatched me away and delivered me home. Everyone was horrified, and I was spanked. Only a few days later, fever struck my brother and both my parents. My mother and brother . . ." Tears choked her voice, but the words continued to flow. It was the first time she had ever told this story to anyone, and once she started, she found she couldn't stop.

"They died," she finished. "My father survived, but he was crippled. When the news came out, people whispered. Lady Greenfellow had seen a plague zombie only a few yards away from me, so everyone knew."

"Knew what?" Gavin's eyes were filled with sympathy, and Alice couldn't bear to meet them.

"That it was my fault!" she exploded. "The zombie had brushed against me, or I had touched something it had contaminated, and I brought the plague into my family's house. And later, Father arranged for me to marry Frederick, the son of an earl, but then *he* took sick and died of the plague, and that was my fault, too. It was all my fault." Tears were dripping off her chin. She fumbled in her dress pocket and belatedly realized she had no handkerchief. Gavin pressed one into her hand. She thanked him and turned her back to wipe her face in an attempt to get herself back under control. The faint alarm bell continued its shrill, unhappy cry.

Two strong arms encircled her from behind, engulfing her with strength and the smell of leather. "It's all right," Gavin murmured. "It wasn't your fault."

"It was," she whispered. "Oh God, it was. And now I've finally earned my way back into society's good graces. I'm engaged to a proper man, and I'll live in a proper house, and I've finally begun to pay back my father for bringing the plague into his house and killing my family and making everyone say dreadful things. I won't give them a chance to say those things again, Gavin. I won't. That's why I can't ever be with . . . why I can't join the Third Ward."

He said, "I understand."

His arms were still wrapped around her. For a moment, Alice let herself relax against his male strength, let herself imagine that this moment would go on forever. She felt safe here. Then she straightened and stepped from him. He let his arms drop.

"I need to go." She handed him back his handkerchief. "Start the lift before someone panics."

He did. They emerged at the main floor and found a small crowd of people looking anxiously at them.

"We're all right," Gavin said. "Small malfunction, I guess."

"I guess," said Simon d'Arco. He looked between Alice and Gavin as the crowd dispersed. "Miss Michaels looks a bit upset."

"I'll be all right." Alice forced a smile. "Agent Ennock offered to summon a cab for me."

Outside, the chilly fog surrounded them like a damp fist. Alice could barely make out the street from the gate and heard only the clopping of hooves and rattle of wheels on the stones, both of them slow and cautious. It was perfect plague zombie weather, which meant everyone who could stayed indoors, but two English institutions—the Royal Mail and London carriage drivers—were famous for ignoring the plague zombie threat and making their services available at all times. A hack was waiting just outside the gate, in fact, and whether it had been there all along or whether someone had summoned it for her, Alice didn't much care.

Gavin offered her a hand into the cab, and she felt as if she were leaving home instead of heading toward it. He shut the door and suddenly leaned through the open side window. The driver checked the horses.

"Listen," Gavin said. "The first thing I bought for myself when I got my salary was a pair of standing tickets to the symphony at the Theatre Royal in Drury Lane. The orchestra plays twice a month, and the next performance is tomorrow. Come with me. As my friend."

"I can't, Gavin." She didn't think her heart could stand being torn so often and still keep beating. "Please don't ask again. It hurts too much."

He reached for her hand, then pulled back when she shied away. The damp invaded the cab and clung to her skirts. "You're right," he said. "I'm sorry."

"I need to go," Alice whispered. "Norbert is worried."

Gavin's eyes were bright. "He is. I know he is." He stepped back from the hack, and the driver clicked to the horses. Alice had to turn and watch him as the cab pulled away. In seconds, the fog devoured Gavin in whiteness, and he was gone.

Norbert was waiting for her when she got home. His brown eyes were worried but reserved. "So," he said, "what happened?"

Alice handed her borrowed straw hat to the footman, who managed to take it with disdain despite its painted features. "I was delayed."

"Overnight?" His voice rose a little on the last syllable.

"It wasn't planned. Get me a cup of tea and I'll explain."

Over a hot drink in the parlor, she gave him the half lie, that she had gone after the stolen machines on her own and gotten them back from Barton by herself, thereby protecting Norbert's reputation. She left Gavin out of it entirely, and since Phipps had arranged for the newspapers to remain silent, there was no way for Norbert to gainsay her.

Norbert had narrowed his eyes just a little as she finished her story, and she was sure he didn't believe her. For a moment, she thought he was going to call her out. But then he nodded. Everything remained smooth and tidy as a newly swept rug. Norbert drained his whiskey glass and set it down hard.

"I'm glad you're all right," he said. "Let's elope."

Alice's hand jerked, and she slopped tea into her saucer. "What?"

"Let's elope," Norbert repeated. "We're not planning a big wedding, anyway. You've often called for simplicity, and nothing is simpler than eloping. Besides, your little adventure showed me how easily I could . . . lose you. How about the end of the week?"

Alice felt as if she'd been whacked on the back of the head with a board. The room remained silent except for the faint hissing of the radiators and the soft crackle of the fire in the grate. The heavy velvet curtains were drawn against damp evening fog, and it felt as if they would eat any answer she gave. What could she say to this? She couldn't help comparing dry, stolid Norbert and the squalid secrets he kept in a square, mechanical house to bright, merry Gavin and the golden music he made in a rose-strewn tower. The comparison made her want to fling her cup down and flee.

"Tongues have been wagging at the amount of time you spend here," Norbert said into the silence, "even if nothing untoward is happening. People know your father is an invalid and not much of a chaperone. I'd hate to move him out at this stage just for the sake of propriety."

Alice froze at the implied threat. "Of course not," she said faintly.

"And I forgot to mention—some bill collectors came round while you were gone. I put them off, but they said they'd be back. Something about criminal charges again. Rubbish, of course, and a good legal man would put a quick stop to it. I have an excellent barrister and a team of solicitors on staff, so you needn't worry that your father will be dragged to jail. As long as I'm on your side."

"Oh," Alice said. Her social reflexes took over, and her

mouth moved of its own accord. "Thank you. That's . . . You're very kind."

"Nothing's too good for my fiancée." Norbert sipped his drink again and looked at her hard. "It would be much easier to handle these problems if we were married. I can't pay the debts of a young woman I'm not married to. People would say it was—well, you know what they would say. And people *do* say."

"Right," she said. Norbert's arguments were hot pokers drilling through an armor Alice had only recently managed to build. Norbert was right. More importantly, Norbert was *safe*. Alice didn't know what Gavin wanted from her, not really, but Norbert had never been anything but forthright about his expectations. With Norbert, her future might be dull, but it was absolutely certain. Gavin offered excitement, but with it came chaos, for both her and her father. It wasn't fair to punish Father for her choices.

"At any rate," Norbert said, sipping again, "to the matter at hand. Time's running out. Shall we elope?"

He didn't say the word *or*, but it hung in the air nonetheless, harsher for all its silence. Alice forced a smile over her cup.

"Of course, darling," she said. "What other answer could I give?"

Louisa snipped the head off a rose and dropped it into the water bowl, where it floated like a drop of blood. "I want the truth. Rumor has it you're eloping."

Alice jumped and nearly dropped the daisies in her hand. She and Louisa were standing at a table in the sunroom, arranging flowers because the automatons were no good at it. Outdoors it was cloudy, but the sunroom's tall windows were still thrown open to let in the mild summer breeze and interesting traffic noises. Lately, Alice had taken to letting her little automatons loose about the house—no sense in keeping them cooped up in her workshop in a houseful of larger automatons—and a pair of them flittered about the room like whirligig bats. Click, draped lazily over the fireplace mantel, watched them with slitted green eyes. Kemp, newly repaired after his unfortunate encounter with Patrick Barton in the metalsmith shop, stood in the corner.

"Where did you hear that?" Alice demanded. "We only decided yesterday evening and haven't said a word to anyone."

"So it's true, then." Louisa toyed with a clockwork button on the front of her green satin dress. "By *we*, do you mean you and Norbert, or you and Gavin Ennock?"

"Louisa! It's Norbert, of course!" The whirligigs squeaked and rushed out an open window, as if startled by Alice's outburst. Click jumped down and bolted after them. "We're getting married in three days, in fact. But you still didn't say how you heard about it."

"Please, darling!" Louisa snipped off more rose heads and let them fall into the bowl. "I know all and tell nothing. I just don't understand why you're sticking with Norbie after learning about his ... odder habits. I was *there*, darling, so you can't lie about it."

"I don't want to go into it again, Louisa. I've already had it out with Gav—Mr. Ennock on this topic. Can't we just drop it?"

"No."

Alice blinked at the sharpness in Louisa's tone. "No?"

"No. It's clear to me that you're unhappy with Norbert and that you're only marrying him for his money."

"And he's only marrying me for my title. It happens all the time, Louisa."

"That doesn't make it right or desirable."

Alice jammed the daisies into a vase and stuffed in some baby's breath. "Why the sudden change of tone? You've always supported whatever decision I've made so far. Now you're gainsaying me."

"There's no time left, darling. Not with your freedom ticking away like a dying automaton. Why so sudden?"

"We saw no reason to delay further," Alice said, resolving to stay firm.

"Ah. Norbert suspects there's something going on between you and Gavin, and he wants you married quickly."

Heat rose in Alice's chest. "Nothing is going on between us!"

"The color in your face says otherwise," Louisa replied. "However, we can talk about something else. Such as the young man who's about to burst into the room with fascinating news."

"Young—what?" The abrupt shift derailed Alice's train of thought. "Who are you—? What—?"

"You're a landed fish, darling. Ah, here he is."

Hat still on his dark head, Simon d'Arco rushed into the room, brown eyes wide and wild. One of the automatic footmen trailed him. Its face had been dented, apparently in an unsuccessful attempt to bar Simon's way. Kemp also stepped forward.

"Miss Michaels!" Simon panted. "Quick! You have to come!"

"Zzzzzir!" buzzed the footman. "Zzzzzzir, you muzzzzzt leavvvvve at—"

"It's all right, Charles," Alice told it. "You may go. Stand down, Kemp. Mr. d'Arco, what do you mean by bursting in like this?"

"Saw his horse through the window," Louisa said. "I feel rather like a detective."

"We need you, Miss Michaels," Simon said. "At once!"

"Whatever for, Mr. d'Arco?" Alice replied. She kept her face calm, but underneath, her heart beat fast and she leaned forward with a growing excitement she could barely contain. "You have a number of people at your disposal."

He glanced at Louisa, remembered himself, and snatched the hat off his head, revealing mussed black curls. "We," he said, avoiding mention of the Third Ward, "captured a powerful war automaton in Germany, and we're transporting it to headquarters via dirigible. The automaton is too powerful to leave running about, and we've deactivated it so we can put it into the Doo—" He shot another glance at Louisa. "Into permanent storage. The ship carrying it will reach London airspace any moment."

"What has this to do with me?" Alice asked.

"If that war machine falls into the wrong hands, thousands of lives could be lost," Simon continued. "But we've received word from an anonymous source that a clockworker intends to steal it en route. We can't allow a lunatic to control such a machine, Miss Michaels."

"I agree, Mr. d'Arco," Alice said with a nod. "But I repeat: What has this to do—"

"Our information says the clockworker intends to use *your* automatons to capture the device."

"What?" Alice leapt to her feet. "That's impossible!"

"Where's Click?" Louisa asked.

A frantic search turned up no sign of Click or of any of Alice's little automatons, though all Norbert's automatons seemed to be present. Alice remembered her whirligigs fleeing out the window with Click on their heels, but she hadn't thought anything of it at the time.

"Hurry!" Simon towed Alice's toward the door before she could even snatch up her hat. "The W—our associates are meeting us halfway."

"I'll just let myself out, darling," Louisa called. "Have fun!"

Chapter Fourteen

In moments, Alice found herself on a horse behind Simon, clutching his waist as they galloped through the streets of London. She nearly let loose with a little whoop. Perhaps this was how Queen Boadicea felt, though the ancient warrior queen probably hadn't ridden sidesaddle on the back of someone else's mount. Still, it was much more fun than drinking tea in a parlor.

Alice had no idea how Simon managed to negotiate traffic, but in very little time they arrived at the park. Hovering above it was the same little airship that had brought Alice and Gavin to Ward headquarters all those months ago. A short climb up a rope ladder brought her and Simon to the tiny bridge. Alice wasn't surprised in the least to find Gavin at the helm. Her heart did a little skip at seeing him there, his strong hands on the wheel and his black leathers contrasting sharply with his white-blond hair. His blue eyes held hers for a moment.

"Miss Michaels," he said.

"Mr. Ennock." *No*, she told herself firmly. She was eloping with Norbert, and that was that.

"I'm here, too," Glenda spoke up. Alice hadn't even noticed her. "Simon, cast off. We're out of time."

The propellers whirred madly, and the airship swung round to the east. Below, people went about their business. Airships over London were nothing special. Alice did wonder what was going to happen to Simon's horse.

"I don't understand any of this," Alice said aloud. "All my windup automatons ran off, including Click, and now you tell me that you received a . . . a 'tip' about it?"

"An anonymous telegram." Glenda opened a hatchway and started pulling equipment from the little hold below. She handed bits to Simon, who assembled the pieces. "We decided to act as if the information were good. So far, it has been. The telegram mentioned the war machine—that's been a secret until now—and it mentioned your automatons getting involved."

"How is that possible?"

Glenda shook her head. She was wearing trousers that clashed terribly with her woman's white blouse. "We don't know yet."

The blocky city slid past below them, and the dirty gray scales of the Thames twisted across the landscape. Gavin was following its course. Up here, the air smelled cleaner, with no hint of coal smoke or manure. A flock of ravens tore through the air under the ship with their harsh caws and croaks. Perhaps two miles ahead glided a much larger dirigible, gray and slow as a pregnant whale.

"That's our transport," Glenda said, pointing. "They're only lightly armed—weapons draw attention, and this was supposed to be a secret mission. We're right over Greenwich, so if our informant has it right, the attack will come at any minute."

"Why are we the only ones out here?" Alice demanded. "Where's the rest of the Ward?"

"More agents are on the way," Simon said, "but it takes a while to get from London to Greenwich on horseback, and this was the only dirigible available. Gavin, can't this ship go any faster?"

"We're too heavy," he said. "I've been working on a ship design of my own, but—"

"Yes, yes, yes." Glenda lifted a harness with folded bat-like wings attached to it. "You'll need to put this on, Alice."

"Miss Michaels, please." She eyed it dubiously. "What is it?"

"A glider." Glenda spun Alice around and started buckling. The harness was heavy, but the weight was distributed well, so it also felt strangely light. "Think of a giant kite. When you lean left, you'll turn left. Lean right to turn right. Raise your torso to climb. Lean forward to dive. Watch out for downdrafts. The bottle of compressed air on your back provides thrust. When the light on your control bar turns red, you're nearly out, so come back immediately or you'll be dependent on whatever the wind decides to do with you. It won't be hard for someone of your intelligence to master it all."

"But what am I supposed to do?" Alice nearly wailed.

"You know your windup machines better than anyone else." Simon was shrugging into a glider harness of his own. "Stop them, defeat them, destroy them. Don't you have a special code or switch to shut them down?"

"Each one has a switch, yes," Alice said. "But they're all custom-made, and each machine's switch is in a different place, so—"

"Exactly why we need you," Simon said.

"How many machines have you?" Glenda was now buckling Simon in.

"Twenty," she said instantly. "Twenty-one, counting Click. But I can't imagine Click would disobey me."

"Of course not." Glenda turned. "Simon, buckle me in. Miss Michaels, use those clips to fasten your skirts round your ankles and preserve your modesty while you're in the air. Next time, I suggest trousers. And you'll want these goggles to protect your eyes."

Alice drew on the proffered eyewear. "Next time?"

The big ship was already looming large, perhaps two hundred yards away.

"Off we go, Simon." Glenda caught up a fat pistol and leapt over the side. Alice gasped in automatic fear for her, but there was a hiss as the bottle on Glenda's back came to life and the batlike wings snapped fully open with a *whump*. She caught the wind and glided away. Simon snatched a large pistol of his own and jumped after her to glide toward the larger ship, leaving Alice alone with Gavin on the tiny deck.

"Aren't you coming, G—Mr. Ennock?" Alice asked.

Gavin's mouth was set, and his fingers tightened on the helm. "I don't fly that way. Pirates do. Come back if you need an air refill."

She nodded in understanding. "Wish me luck, then."

"Good luck, miss," he said stonily.

His stiffness slapped her hard. "Are you angry at me, Mr. Ennock?"

"Nope. You'd better fly."

"You *are* angry at me."

"You made your choice. I'm happy for you. Marry him. Be well."

Alice's mouth fell open. "Does everyone know about that?"

"Anonymous telegram from someone named 'L.'"

"I'll murder her," Alice muttered. "Listen, Mr. Ennock, I—"

"You'd better go," Gavin said. "Look!"

A glittering line of tiny brass machines rushed toward the ship. Even at this distance, Alice recognized them as her own little automatons. Her jaw tightened in anger. These little ones belonged to her, and someone had stolen them. Yet she also wanted to talk to Gavin. He was correct in that she had made her choice, but she didn't feel right in leaving him like this.

"I'll be back," she promised. She peered over the side at

the dizzying drop to the Thames and the buildings lining it far below. What if the harness didn't work? Then she saw the line of brass machines—her machines. Determination won out over fear, and she jumped.

There was a terrifying, sickening drop, and then the harness wings snapped open. Alice swooped upward. The bottle hissed on her back. She was flying! The sensation quite took her breath away. She leaned left and right, working out hand and foot motions that made her turn and dip just as Glenda said. It was easier than she'd thought. Bright air flowed all around her body, and even though she was supported by the harness and a bar, she felt like part of the sky. Her hair came free and streamed behind her. Queen Boadicea had nothing on this! It was freedom. It was independence. It was *life*. She whooped aloud, not caring who might hear, and sped toward the larger ship.

More than half her machines were whirligigs that could fly, and they were carrying spiders that couldn't. On the deck of the large ship, the crewmen were watching, but were unable to do anything; their weapons weren't accurate enough to hit such small targets. Simon and Glenda chased the whirligigs, but even laden with spiders, the little machines were far more agile than the gliders; the Ward agents had no more hope of catching them than hawks had of catching hummingbirds. Alice hung back, observing, trying to understand what the machines were attempting. Where was Click?

One of the whirligigs dashed up to the dirigible. Like most airships, it consisted of an enormous cigar-shaped envelope of hydrogen gas. The ship part was suspended from a rope rigging beneath it. The whirligig dropped a spider onto part of the rigging between the envelope and the main ship, and the spider extruded a blade. The rope snapped with a discordant *twang*. Then the spider leapt to another rope and cut that one. Another whirligig deposited its spider on another rope. *Twang!* The rope parted. Alice's skin went cold as she realized what was going on. They would drop the ship and crack it open, freeing the war machine inside.

Crewmen clad in airman white were already swarming into the ropes, climbing agile as monkeys up to the attacking machines. One of them reached a spider, but a whirligig dived in and crashed into his face. He lost his grip and fell screaming into the Thames far below. More spiders attacked the ropes.

Alice set her mouth and dived toward them. She knew every one of the machines like another woman might know her lapdogs. A whirligig popped up in front of her, but she grabbed it, twisted its arm upward, and depressed the switch underneath it. The switch released all the tension in the winding spring at once, and the whirligig went limp. With regret, Alice let it go—she had no way to carry it— and the little automaton dropped into the river. By now, she was within arm's reach of the large ship's rigging, and she managed to pluck a spider from its work as she passed by and deactivate it. This one she tossed down to the deck.

There was a *crack*. Below and to Alice's left, Glenda fired her pistol at a whirligig. A small bolt of lightning hit it dead-on. The whirligig popped and crackled and fell like a stone. Simon had circled around to the other side of the ship, out of sight, but there were still half a dozen spiders in the rigging now, all snipping at the ropes. Fully a third of them had already snapped, and the bow was dipping downward. Shouts and cries rose from the deck. The ship was losing altitude, and Alice didn't know whether she was crashing or just trying to land. Alice swooped upward, snatched at a spider, and missed. Another rope twanged, and the parting strands slashed across her arm, opening up a biting cut. Alice gritted her teeth and leaned away, trying to decide what to do. Glenda fired at another whirligig, but the shot went wide and vanished into the distance. Another whirligig was converging on her. More ropes snapped on the airship.

Alice's mouth was dry. What was going on? Her automatons weren't very intelligent. They could obey fairly simple commands and maintain themselves within limits, but they had no imagination or drive. The idea that they could adapt to new conditions—like the Third Ward showing up in gliders—was laughable. Someone was giving them fresh orders. But who? And where was the person hiding? On the ship itself? That didn't seem likely. Not when the whole point was to make it crash. The ground? No. Too difficult to see. So where? The answer had to be here somewhere, but her inability to see it itched at her.

Alice swooped past the rigging again and grabbed for another spider, but a whirligig popped up to interfere. Alice snatched it, deactivated it, dropped it. Then Simon popped up from nowhere, nearly hitting Alice's left wing, and grabbed the spider she had missed. He pried it from the ropes and flung it away, but a whirligig swooped down to rescue it. There were only four spiders left in the rigging now. The humans might be able to win this and let the ship limp to home field. Alice's heart pounded at the thought of victory. They could solve the mystery later if they just got the ship safely home. She guided her glider toward another snipping spider.

"Help!" Glenda's thin cry came across the open air. She was struggling with two whirligigs that had landed on her pistol arm. Alice instantly brought her hissing harness around and dived toward the other woman, but even as Alice watched, the two whirligigs managed to pull Glenda's arm round with aching slowness. Alice tried to speed up, but she was still too far off. Glenda fought the whirligigs, sweat beading on her face, but her treacherous hand was forced to aim the fat pistol at the ship, and a whirligig wrapped its strong metallic fingers around hers.

"No!" Alice screamed. She reached out, even though she was still several yards away.

The pistol fired. A lightning bolt cracked from the barrel and struck the hydrogen envelope full in the center.

The explosion started in the middle and worked outward, like a demon unfurling its wings. It consumed the envelope in fire, and the internal skeleton glowed red. A series of concussions thudded against Alice's bones, and wave after wave of hot air shoved and tossed her glider about. She fought with fists and feet to keep it steady. Black ash and debris blew in all directions. The last of the airship's ropes snapped, and the main ship, three stories tall, dropped two hundred feet straight down. It crashed into a warehouse on the Thames and demolished it. Alice grimly fought to keep her glider aloft and was vaguely aware that both Simon and Glenda were in the same predicament. The two whirligigs, their terrible job done, had abandoned Glenda. Below, the dust and ash and bits of flame rose from the wreckage, and fire continued to rain down from above as the remains of the envelope burned away and died. From her position above, Alice got an all-too-excellent view of the wreckage. The ship had cracked open from bow to stern, revealing a glimpse of the giant brass mechanical everyone was so worried about. Alice also caught sight of some of the crewmen's bodies, their white leathers awash in scarlet. They would never fly again, or kiss their wives or embrace their children, and her machines had done this to them. Black guilt washed over her. Her gorge rose, and she vomited up the remains of her afternoon tea.

"Damn it!" Simon shouted. He was gliding beside her. *"Gesù e Maria!"*

Glenda, her face pale, swooped over to join them, and they circled tightly over the wreckage like ravens over a battlefield.

"This must have been the thief's plan from the beginning," Glenda said. "Destroy the ship so he could get to the war machine. We have to land and guard it before the clockworker can get to it."

"It'll be hard." Simon pointed downward. Ash continued to rain from the sky. "Crowds are gathering, and police. The clockworker could be any one of them."

"No," Alice said. "Something's off. How could he know exactly where the ship would crash-land? What if it had landed in the Thames and he lost the mechanical? And that machine is enormous. What is it—three stories tall? How would he manage to spirit it away without being seen?"

"Clockworkers are insane," Glenda said. A wind was rising, and they were nearly shouting now.

"This was too carefully planned for someone who's lost touch," Alice said. "Look, there's no way for your anonymous clockworker to actually steal the machine. Not with this plan."

"So you're saying the thief doesn't want the machine at all," Simon shouted over the wind. "Why do all this, then?"

"A distraction," Glenda hazarded.

Realization slammed Alice like a rock hammer. "Where's Gavin?"

She turned back for the little airship without waiting for an answer. Her heart lurched as she scanned the sky. Already the smaller airship had turned away and was flying steadily off, and just visible on the deck were two figures, not one, and the taller figure wore a familiar top hat. Alice's hands went cold. No, no, no, no. What did the grinning clockworker want with Gavin? Revenge for foiling his attack on the bank? Or something entirely more sinister? She clenched her teeth. The time to ask would be when she had her hands around the lunatic's throat. But even as the thought crossed her mind, a red indicator light on her left wing's control bar flashed. Her air bottle was running out. With the airship now so far away, Alice had no hope of catching up. Her heart sank, and she felt sick. She was losing Gavin again, both metaphorically and physically. She would never—

No. Damn it, *no*. Not this time. Alice turned and dived for the ground.

"What are you doing?" yelled Glenda behind and above her. "Alice!"

But Alice ignored her. The glider shot downward with stomach-dropping speed toward the wreckage. The flames had gone out—hydrogen fires always ended quickly—but the crowd around the massive ruin remained uncertain, giving the area a wide berth. Alice brought the glider lower and, averting her eyes from a gory mess on the splintered deck, managed her first landing without losing her feet. She smelled burned wood and flesh. With shaking hands, she unbuckled the harness, flung the wings aside, and ran toward the gaping fissure that rent the deck from bow to stern. Simon landed a little ways from her.

"What are you doing?" he demanded.

"No time." Alice dropped into the dim hold and landed on the chest of the brass war machine, her shoes scrabbling on the metal. It was a mechanical, somewhat similar to the one Patrick Barton had used, but much larger and more human-shaped. It had a head instead of a bubble, with vestigial eyes and even a mouth, but the top was clear glass, with a place for the controller to sit and direct it. Alice's skilled, practiced eye ran over it, gathering instant details. In seconds, she found the switch that popped the dome open, and she lowered herself into the seat therein. Because the giant was lying on its back, Alice was consequently lying on her own back. She pulled the dome shut and looked around at the switches, dials, and pulleys. There was always a logic to this sort of thing, and her talent, the one that allowed her to understand and assemble clockworker inventions, let her see exactly how it all fit together. She pulled a lever and spun a dial. Steam hissed, and somewhere deep inside the machine's chest, a boiler roared to life. Power boomed through the pistons, and Alice made the machine sit up. It cranked upright, shouldering aside debris with easy power.

Alice was panting with fear and worry. Every moment it took to work this out meant the clockworker was getting farther and farther away with Gavin. Under Alice's direction, the mechanical got to its feet. Bitter-smelling coal smoke leaked from the joints, and she found herself three stories above the wreckage. Below, Simon looked up at her from the ruined deck in openmouthed surprise. Glenda swooped in for a landing of her own. Alice didn't stop for explanations. The little airship was already dwindling in the distance, following the Thames. Alice moved her feet, and the metal giant walked. The crowd screamed and scattered. Treading carefully, Alice stepped clear of the ruins and onto the thoroughfare that went alongside the river. Then, her mouth a grim line, she started to run.

Power stormed through her, and she exulted in it. The war machine was hers now, and she would use it to set things right, to restore order. People saw her coming and scattered long before she arrived, leaving an empty street. Her feet left deep gouges in the cobblestones and gravel, and buildings rumbled in her path. In moments, she caught up to the little airship, which, being slightly above her head, obscured her vision of the deck. Alice reached upward with a hand to grab at it, but her control wasn't perfect, and she missed. The ship bobbled in the air and tried to gain altitude, but Alice grabbed at it again. This time her fingers caught the keel. It crunched a little, and she eased off, then pulled the ship down like a child taking a model down from a shelf. If the mechanical had been human-sized, the ship would have been the size of a pair of hatboxes, and it was easy to hold. The envelope bobbed up and down like a balloon on a string.

Alice brought the deck down to eye level. Near the stern stood Gavin, his face pale and angry. He was chained by one wrist to the stern railing, and on his right shoulder was

Click. The brass cat's left claws pricked Gavin's jugular. Click could slash deeper than any knife, and Gavin was being careful not to move. Nearby waited the grinning clockworker in his ragged coat and tall top hat. Alice's stomach churned with fear for Gavin's safety and hatred for the clockworker who was endangering him.

"You!" Alice said, and her voice came out through the mechanical's mouth. "Let him go!"

The clockworker shook his head and gestured for Alice to back away.

"I won't let you have him," Alice said.

The clockworker drew a finger across his throat, a deadly gesture enhanced by the skull mask that covered the upper half of his face. Alice's chest tightened.

"You won't kill him," Alice said. "You went through too much trouble to get him, though I have no idea . . . no idea why."

But even as she finished the sentence, Alice did know. The certainty stole over her with the clarity of a puzzle that locked together at last.

"Aunt Edwina," she said. "You're Aunt Edwina."

Gavin went pale. "The Red Velvet Lady."

The clockworker cocked his—her—head. It all made perfect sense. Only Aunt Edwina, who had built Alice's automatons, would have a way to take control of them. Only Aunt Edwina had the apparent obsession with Gavin. Only Aunt Edwina was a clockworker who had dropped out of sight at the same time the clockworker in a skull mask had popped up in London. Now that Alice had the chance to look closely, in daylight, when the clockworker wasn't jumping and moving around, she could see that he—she—was a tall, thin woman rather than a short, slender man. The male clothing, hat, and mask were a simple but effective disguise. People saw a man's outfit and assumed the wearer was male. Alice herself had benefited from this on the trip back from capturing Patrick Barton. The world spun, and Alice clutched the mechanical's controls. There would be time for hysterics later. Right now, she had other issues to deal with.

She had intended to tell Edwina to let Gavin go again, but instead she blurted out, "Why, Aunt Edwina? Why kidnap Gavin and fake your death and destroy your house and start these rampages over London? What are you *doing*?"

The clockworker made a gesture, and Click's claws moved. Gavin made a noise, and a thin trickle of blood oozed down his neck.

"Stop!" Alice cried. She had forgotten that, aunt or no aunt, clockworkers were still insane. "Aunt Edwina, don't! I'll let the ship go. Just don't hurt Gavin."

"No!" Gavin croaked. "I won't be a prisoner again."

"It'll be all right, Gavin. But first—Click, give me your left forepaw, please."

There was a moment, and then Click's left forepaw dropped away, just as it had when Alice had given the same command in Edwina's tower. Gavin reacted. He ripped Click off his shoulder and threw him at the clockworker. Caught off guard, Edwina took the brass cat full in the midriff. She stumbled backward, then dived over the gunwale. Gavin yelled. Alice shrieked, her voice amplified by the mechanical. Then the clockworker rose up, supported by four madly spinning whirligigs, so tiny against their giant brother. She snapped her fingers, and three of the whirligigs sang a note, the same notes Alice remembered the clockworker playing at the Bank of England. Edwina snapped her fingers again, and the notes played a second time. Then she touched the brim of her hat and the whirligigs sped her away.

"Why the notes?" Alice said.

"Who cares?" Gavin snarled. "Why does she keep kidnapping me? Is it the way I dress? Do I smell good?"

She needed to keep moving. Whatever happened, she needed to keep moving. If she stopped, the hysterics would take over. Alice extended the mechanical's free arm to the deck and checked the controls. Certain the mechanical would stay frozen in place and hold the airship steady, she released herself from the chair and made her way carefully along the arm until she was able to swing herself onto the deck. Click limped over to greet her, freed of whatever influence Edwina had put on him. Alice patted his head, took up his missing paw, and popped the claws out. One of them had a lockpick on it. She used it to work at the cuff chaining Gavin's wrist to the rail without meeting his eye, though she felt his body heat and smelled sweat and leather. He didn't comment, either, but his breath came in her ear. At last the lock came free. He rubbed his wrist as Alice replaced Click's paw.

"Thanks," he said. "I think we're gathering a crowd down below."

She straightened, Click at her feet. "No doubt."

"So." Gavin shifted his weight. "Your aunt Edwina."

"Yes."

They stood in silence, looking at each other high above the ground. A sudden exhilaration swept Alice. It came to her that she had defeated a genius, a clockworker, and more than once. Up here, with Gavin and the Third Ward, all that mattered was what she could do, not who she was. Up here, she was free.

And then Gavin was kissing her. His strong arms were around her, and he was kissing her. Her heart took up her entire chest and her breath fled and he was kissing her.

"I'm sorry I was angry at you," he murmured against her lips.

"My heart stopped when I saw you leaving," she murmured back. "I don't want to go through that again."

Movement caught her eye, and they broke apart. Glenda and Simon, with fresh bottles powering their gliders, dropped to the little deck. Explanations came fast and furious, though Alice never strayed far from Gavin's side.

"I'm only unhappy that I didn't figure out who she was

earlier," Alice said. "I think the little automatons have been reporting back to Aunt Edwina about me since I was a girl. She must have left some bit of program within their memory wheels that let her take control of them for spying and now for this. It was how she knew I was attending the Greenfellow ball."

"Ah," Glenda said. "She was able to extrapolate the most likely route you would take home and time the zombie attack so you would run straight into it."

"Yes. She also 'happened' to be present at the solicitor's office with that paper bomb because she knew I'd be there to discuss an inheritance she herself left me. She even knew I would hear Gavin play in Hyde Park because Click or the other automatons told her Norbert and I took drives there."

"I've never seen this kind of careful planning in a clockworker before," Simon said. "They're usually fantastic with the inventions but not so grand with long-range plans. This woman is a new breed, and I don't mind telling you, she scares the heavens out of me. We *have* to find her, and quickly—before she kills someone else."

"No chance of that today," Gavin muttered, staring off into the sky.

"A recovery team will be here soon to handle the mechanical," Glenda said, "unless you want to walk it back to headquarters, Miss Michaels."

"Oh, I don't imagine she'll want that." Simon grinned. "What if her Norbert hears of it?"

At the mention of Norbert's name, Alice's exhilaration faded. "Norbert," she said. "Yes. I need to talk to him."

Gavin caught her hand. "What are you going to say?"

"Oh, Gavin." She closed her eyes. "I don't know. I need to think. I'm all mixed-up. In one day, I lost my automatons, watched an airship explode, stole a giant war machine, and learned my long-lost aunt is actually still alive and controlling zombies in London."

"What do you think of all that?" Gavin countered.

Alice paused. "I loved it," she burst out. "Damn it all, I *loved* it!"

Gavin laughed. So did Glenda. Simon grimaced slightly, and Alice wondered why.

"Unbelievable! Simply unbelievable!" Norbert plucked his cup of chocolate from the breakfast tray and sipped as he read the *Times*. It was the morning after Alice had returned from her adventure with Gavin and the giant mechanical. "The East India Company gives the Punjabis gainful employment, and they repay the Empire by rising up against it."

Alice nibbled at a piece of toast. The newspaper's front page headline screamed MAD MECHANICAL MANGLES GREENWICH, with a smaller headline that announced DIRIGIBLE DETONATES and DOZENS FEARED DEAD, but Norbert was pointedly, carefully, and scrupulously ignoring all that for international news, and Alice had to scramble to keep up.

"Cartridge papers are soaked in pork and beef tallow," she replied. "The cow is sacred to Indians, and Muslims say pigs are unclean. Is it any wonder Punjabi soldiers refused to tear them open with their teeth? The natives over there were already restless, and their commander only made it worse when he sentenced all those soldiers to hard labor over a foolish technicality—one that he could have avoided by allowing them to use fingers instead of teeth."

"Military discipline must be maintained. Now they have to pay the consequences, and that's the end of it." Norbert set the paper down and drained his little cup. His voice was a bit too loud, his gestures a bit too expansive. "But this and the fighting in China have made me especially anxious to open that new munitions factory. Need to provide for my new wife after this week."

Alice gave a small smile. "Of course, darling, of course."

"The papers are ready, and I'll come home early on Friday so we can sneak down to the church." He rubbed his hands together with overly precise movements. "So exciting!"

"Indeed."

"And then we'll have to get back to the appointments," Norbert continued, his excitement over. "It'll be so convenient with you not having to go back to that silly flat every evening."

Alice said, "Absolutely." Good God, he was dull. Compared to the deadly machinations of Aunt Edwina, Norbert's mechanicals seemed insignificant and banal. How had she ever found him shocking? Her own little automatons were far more dangerous than anything Norbert could dream up.

"Are the machines in good working order?"

For a moment, Alice thought he meant her little automatons. Most of them had come slinking back a few minutes after Alice herself had arrived at Norbert's house with Click. As a precaution, Alice had deactivated all of them, including Kemp and Click. It had hurt more than she had anticipated.

"Yes," she said aloud. "Your friends should be . . . entertained."

"Perfect." Norbert rubbed his hands together again with the same precise movements. It was the same excitement he had shown about their upcoming nuptials. She wondered what he would be like in the bedroom and gave an inward shudder. "I'll be late. You're beautiful." He kissed her on the cheek, and departed.

Alice left the breakfast tray for the mechanical maid to clean up and went down the hall to her father's room. The automaton assigned to his needs stood in the corner, its eyes never leaving Father's chest as it rose and fell, paused, then rose and fell. He'd been sleeping since she returned. His hair was gone, and his face was shrunken and shriveled. His body barely made a dent in the soft mattress. A heavy, stale smell hung in the overly warm air. His curtains were pushed back, revealing another day crushed by yellow mist.

Alice touched his cold hand, but it remained motionless. Father's breath paused, then resumed.

In the many hours since she had returned with the memory of Gavin's touch on her body, she had nearly left a number of times. Each time, this particular chain had pulled her back. She imagined men coming into the house and throwing her father into the street. Two men—Norbert and Gavin—had different sets of hooks in her, and they pulled her in two different directions.

"I thought I had decided," she whispered. "And then it all went topsy-turvy again. What should I do, Father?" But he didn't answer. She sighed. He didn't need to. This man, the third one with hooks in her, had sacrificed everything to give her a proper future, and she knew what she needed to do. It was why she hadn't said anything to Norbert about canceling their elopement—she had long known what the right decision was. Continued to be. A tear slid down her cheek as she held her father's hand and mentally said goodbye to Gavin and the Third Ward.

After a while, she left the room to wander the house's empty halls. Spiders and other automatons continued their work with little input from Alice. She had asked, even begged, Norbert to hire some human servants so the house would feel less empty, but he had remained adamant.

A door shut behind her, and she realized she had automatically entered her workroom. The long table with its array of tools stretched across the back wall. Kemp stood frozen near the table, and Click lay on his side amid the debris. She expected the cat to turn his phosphorescent eyes on her when she walked in, but he didn't move because she had shut him down last night. Suddenly the thought was horrendous, as if she had shut down a part of herself.

"Oh, Click." She opened a small panel on the back of his neck and extracted a brass winding key. His brass skin felt chilly and rigid, as if he had died. "How could I do this to you?"

She wound the key, but Click was no child's toy. It took considerable winding to undo the loss, and her wrists became sore with the effort. To pass the time, she hummed a soft melody under her breath.

> *I see the moon, the moon sees me,*
> *It turns all the forest soft and silvery.*
> *The moon picked you from all the rest*
> *For I loved you—*

She bit her lip and stopped singing. At last, Click was finished. Alice replaced the key and pressed a switch. For a moment nothing happened. Then Click shuddered hard, and his eyes cranked open. He gave a metallic mew, trembled again, and gave Alice a reproachful look.

"I'm sorry, Click." She gathered him into her arms, where he made a cool, heavy weight. "So very sorry. I promise it'll never happen again."

Click remained miffed awhile longer, then pressed his chilly nose into the crook of her elbow. Alice stroked him for a moment. Her eye fell on the storage box into which she had set the automatons that had survived yesterday's adventure. With her free hand, she opened it. The little automatons lay in a jumbled pile of wings and segmented legs, dead as dried spiders. She ran a finger over several, remembering every plane and contour. One of them jerked slightly, using up a tiny vestige of windup energy, and went still again. Alice felt heavy.

Fog still hung its damp curtain against the windows. It seemed to hem her in, closing around the house just as her dress closed around her body. Outside, everything looked smooth and perfect. But it was only a shell, a soft illusion.

She wanted to fly. She wanted to learn. She wanted to fix machines that did something interesting, machines that would change the world. And she wanted to do it with Gavin.

Click looked up at her, his joints creaking softly, his eyes green and steady. She could almost hear him speak. *Then what,* he asked, *are you waiting for?*

Alice looked at her dead automatons and then at the fog. Fog might hem her in, but it couldn't push her back. Not unless she let it.

Suddenly, the idea of spending one more hour in the house became utterly intolerable. With Click in her arms, she fled from the room. She fled down the hall. And then, before she could stop herself, she fled toward the stairs. She was doing it. She was leaving.

Her heart pounded with both fear and excitement. She would do it. She would do it today. Now. This minute. She would join the Third Ward, and she would see Gavin every day, and maybe something bad would come of it, but oh! Wasn't it equally possible that something good would happen?

She needed nothing, wanted nothing from Norbert's house. She would leave right now and never come back. With a laugh that made her giddy, she clattered down the hall and made it halfway down the grand staircase near the front door when she abruptly remembered: Father. She couldn't leave him.

But her momentum was too great. The avalanche that had been building inside her propelled her on, and speed lent clarity. She hadn't been worried about Father—not really. She had only been foolish and afraid, and had used Father as an excuse. His health was no obstacle! She could join the Third Ward on the condition that they move Father to their headquarters. If they wanted to take his care out of her salary, so be it. Why hadn't she thought of that before? And the debts? They couldn't imprison a baroness for debts, and that was what she would become, all too soon. Everything she wanted was within her grasp. She had just been too afraid to take it.

Heartened, she ran farther down the stairs and halted

again. What about Kemp and her little automatons? If she left now, she'd never get them back, and she couldn't leave Kemp to rust and tarnish, or—this thought brought a shudder—allow Norbert to melt him down in a fit of pique.

At the bottom of the stairs, Alice changed course. Scurrying past the soulless eyes of the footman, she entered the library and took out ink and writing paper. Click sat in her lap at the writing desk and watched as, with shaking hands, she wrote a quick paragraph. After a moment's hesitation, she recklessly added another sentence and signed it. There were still four deliveries left before the Royal Mail halted for the night, meaning Phipps would have plenty of time to respond to the letter by tomorrow, perhaps even by this evening. Meanwhile, Alice would finish repairing Kemp and prepare Father to be moved.

The weight left her, and she felt as if she could jump off the top floor and fly. Why on earth—no, why the *hell*—had she waited so long? Folding the paper into an envelope, she scribbled *Lt. Susan Phipps, The Third Ward, $\sqrt{2}$* on the front and rushed to the front door, where she dashed out into the clearing fog without pausing for a wrap, or even a hat.

"Would the lady like me to arrange for a cab?" the footman called after her.

Alice ignored it. The Royal Mail had an office only a few hundred yards down the street, and she ran toward it, skirts bunched in her hands. People on the sidewalk turned to stare at her, a hatless woman rushing in an unladylike sprint up the sidewalk, but Alice found she didn't care in the least.

Chapter Fifteen

"**A**gent Ennock! Could you come in here for a moment?" Gavin paused as he passed the office of Lieutenant Phipps, an uneaten apple in his hand. His first thought was that he was in trouble again, but Phipps didn't look any more severe than usual.

"Lieutenant?" Gavin asked.

"I received this from Alice Michaels a few moments ago." She pushed a handwritten letter across the desk toward him, and Gavin picked it up.

To Lieutenant Phipps:

After a great deal of consideration, I have decided to accept your offer of a position with the Third Ward, pending the Ward's ability to care for my sick father. If this is acceptable to you, please let me know by post or in person. I remain at your disposal.

Also, please tell ~~Agent Ennock~~ Gavin that I have changed my mind and would very much enjoy the chance to accompany him to the symphony.

Very sincerely yrs,
(Miss) Alice Michaels

Gavin's heart did a little jump, and he scanned the letter a second time to make sure he hadn't misread. "Is this . . . Is she really . . . ?"

"It would seem so," Phipps said, and she actually gave a tiny smile. Gavin didn't know whether to be more amazed by that or by the letter.

"Is it . . . Can the Ward . . ." He was stammering like an idiot, and he coughed hard to get himself under control. "Is the Ward willing to care for her father?"

Phipps steepled her fingers, metal piling up against flesh. "I think we can manage the care of one old man. There's time to send her a reply by evening post, but I think Alice might appreciate a more personal touch."

Gavin was moving toward the door before Phipps had even properly dismissed him. Down at the stables, he found a groom waiting with a horse, and, moments later, he was riding as fast as he dared through the chilly evening mist. Traffic on the streets was light, and voices were hushed. Buildings loomed over him, always hemming him in and holding him back. Gavin hated the chains London threw over him. There was no beauty here, no softness; nothing but greed and poverty and disease.

As if in answer to these thoughts, bare feet slapped brick, and a ragged woman, accompanied by a young child, dragged out of an alley, reaching toward Gavin's horse. Plague sores wept yellow fluid. In a mixture of fear and pity, Gavin tossed the apple from his pocket toward them. The child caught it, and Gavin urged his horse to greater speed.

He rounded the corner and let his horse drop into a trot as he entered the square that faced Norbert Williamson's too-large house. He had never visited this place, but he knew exactly where it was. It took up one entire side of the square and was part of the dull, blocky architecture that made up so much of London. The mist was thickening again, a ghost trying to keep him out of the square. Heart beating fast, Gavin tied the horse to a hitching post out front, then dashed up a set of marble stairs to the double doors. He yanked the bellpull, and the door immediately opened.

"Sir?" said the mechanical footman.

Gavin handed it his card. "Tell Miss—tell your mistress that Agent Gavin Ennock of the Third Ward is here to see her."

"Please come in, sir. I will see if the lady is receiving visitors."

Gavin waited in the echoing foyer while the footman stalked away. He supposed someone of higher birth or position would have been shown to a seat and offered something to drink, but as a tradesman, he was forced to stand by the door, shifting from one foot to the other.

A woman came down the big main staircase ahead of him. For a delightful moment, he thought it was Alice, but he quickly realized this woman was much older and more curvaceous. She wore a dress of black bombazine and a rough straw hat, also black.

"Mr. Ennock?" she said as she descended. "Forgive the rudeness of the abrupt introduction. My name is Louisa Creek. I'm a good friend of Alice's."

"L.," Gavin said.

"Yes."

"Is Alice all right?" Gavin asked. "What's going on? I got—that is, we got—a letter—"

"Yes," Louisa interrupted. Her expression was grim. "But things have changed. Her father passed away moments after she posted it. She sent a servant with word to me, and I came right over. She's not in any condition to receive visitors right now."

"Oh." Disappointment dashed cold water over him. Then he took a breath and said, "I'm sorry, but I have to ask—did she say anything about the Third Ward?"

"She did." Louisa took a deep breath, as if she had to

summon courage. "She asked me to tell you that she can't take advantage of your offer now. There's the funeral to arrange—very expensive, since he's a baron—and she said she couldn't possibly leave her dear, wealthy fiancé now, though at least the idiotic elopement has been postponed. I may have embellished that a bit."

"Right." Gavin found he was twirling his cap around and around in his hands and made himself stop. He imagined Alice collapsed by her father's bed, weeping while his corpse cooled in the sheets, and the image made him want to rush up the stone stairs to comfort her. "I suppose that means I should go."

"I'm afraid so, Mr. Ennock, much as I would like you to stay." Louisa reached out and ran a hand over Gavin's shoulder. "Though perhaps I could offer you a ride home?"

"Uh . . . I don't . . . I live at—"

"I didn't mean to *your* home," Louisa said.

Gavin felt his face turn hot and his feet seemed to grow overly large. "No, thanks. Just tell Alice—Miss Michaels— that I was here and she has my condolences."

He fled the house before Louisa could respond. The fog drew its curtain across the mansion behind him as he climbed on the horse and rode sadly away.

The magnificent music lifted Gavin, transported him away. He leapt from cloud to cloud, chased lightning bolts, and spiraled upward across bright and brilliant air, then tiptoed and glided over stairs of delicate glass. For a moment, the music held him, hovering, then smashed into a storm, a whirling tornado that flung him up into an unbearable crescendo that held a long note and ended.

The conductor dropped his hands, and the audience burst into thunderous applause, snapping Gavin back to Earth. He almost felt the concert hall chair slap his back. On his left, Simon d'Arco clapped with enthusiasm, his hands muffled by white evening gloves. Gavin finally managed to applaud as well. The concert hall echoed with the noise. It swelled as the conductor turned and bowed twice, then faded as he left the stage and the houselights came up.

"Wonderful," Simon said. All around them, people rustled to their feet. "And that was just the first one."

. "Yes," Gavin said absently. "First."

"Are you all right? You look distracted."

Gavin shook his head to clear it. "The music. It was just so . . . fantastic. Mozart always is. The *Jupiter* Symphony, especially. Let's go up to the lobby and get something to drink."

"Of course."

They wandered up the aisle with the other concertgoers dressed in gowns and evening jackets. Gavin himself wore the black jacket and white tie Simon had insisted were required for anyone who held season tickets for the symphony. He had bought two tickets because no one ever bought just one and, besides, he wanted to be able to bring someone—all right, Alice—with him, but in her absence, a friend such as Simon would have to do.

"What's so special about the *Jupiter* Symphony?" Simon asked as they threaded their way toward the exit.

"It's hard to describe. The finale is the best movement. It's as if Mozart held back all the resources of his science, and all the power, too, science and power that no one else has, and he made the music a release for both."

Simon clapped Gavin on the shoulder and rubbed it, a familiar gesture he did often. "You're a poetic man, Gavin Ennock. Let me buy you a drink."

In the crowded lobby, Simon handed Gavin a glass of red wine. "I'm glad you decided to get out and about again, Gavin. Frankly, you've been moping around the Ward too much, and we're all worried about you."

"You are?" Gavin took a gulp from his glass.

"I know you have your cap set for Alice Michaels," Simon went on, his voice low, "but she gave her final answer two weeks ago when her father died, and it isn't healthy for you to keep on about her. There are a lot of other . . . people who could make you a happy man, you know."

Gavin stepped aside to let pass a group of women dressed in emerald. In their hats they wore small cards that read TRUE LADIES VOTE! Had he been that obvious? He was aware that Phipps knew about his feelings for Alice, but did the whole Ward know about them, too? He suddenly felt embarrassed and unhappy, and he missed Alice more than ever.

"Other people," he repeated dully. "Like who?"

Simon took a deep breath. "Well, people like m—"

"Alice!" Gavin interrupted.

"What?" Simon asked, clearly flustered. "No, I didn't mean her. I meant—"

"No, it's Alice," Gavin hissed. "Don't look. I mean, don't be obvious. I mean—shit." He turned his back and drained his glass. Across the lobby strolled Alice on the arm of her damned fiancé, Norbert Williamson. She was dressed in black from head to toe and her expression was neutral, even dull. Behind her came Kemp. His black and white paint had been freshly redone, and he fussed with the back of Alice's dress. Norbert snapped something at him, and he stopped.

"I suppose this means she's up to socializing again," Simon said. He sounded disappointed.

"No point in hiding how I feel if everyone knows, right?" Gavin said. His voice cracked, to his mortification. "It kills me, Simon. It kills me seeing her with him. It kills me to think he's with her every day and doesn't know what he has, while I'm alone, you know?"

Simon's expression set. "I do know. You see what you want every day, but can't have it."

"Yeah." Gavin's eyes never strayed from Alice, despite his earlier warning. "I'm a wreck."

"I know exactly how you feel." Simon took a deep

breath and abruptly grabbed the surprised Gavin in a rough embrace. His cheek scraped Gavin's, and he smelled the wine on Simon's breath as the other man whispered, "I'll give you this chance. Don't waste it."

He let go, and Gavin, slightly stunned, watched as Simon wove his way through the lobby crowd—

And deliberately spilled his wine all over Norbert's shirt-front.

Norbert leapt back with an oath, and Simon made effusive apologies. Alice put a hand to her mouth in a gesture Gavin recognized. Simon dabbed at the bloodred stain with a handkerchief, still apologizing, and hustled Norbert toward the bar to ask for seltzer water. Kemp, in a flutter, went with them, leaving Alice standing alone. Gavin, now understanding what Simon meant, recovered himself and hurried over.

"Miss Michaels," he said, "I didn't think I'd ever see you again."

His voice was shaking, and he wanted to hold her close, but he kept his hands at his side. Alice turned, and her eyes widened.

"Mr. Ennock." Was that a catch in her voice? "I shouldn't be surprised to see you here, so I won't act as if I am. Was that your friend who ruined Norbert's shirt?"

"Yes." Gavin glanced in their direction. Simon was towing a stormy-faced Norbert toward the men's room with Kemp bringing up the rear. "He made a sacrifice, and I need to use it."

"What in heaven's name are you talking about?"

Heedless of the crowd, he took Alice's elbow and walked her toward the main door. "Walk with me."

"I'm still engaged, Mr. Ennock, and I'm—"

"We're just talking, and we're in public. It's not unseemly. Come on." And then they were outside on the front steps of the theater. Concertgoers moved in and out, exchanging the stuffiness of the hall for the cool damp of the outdoors. Alice stood just inside a pool of light cast by a streetlamp, the golden light casting her mourning clothes into sharp relief, while Gavin stood in darkness, where his hair and shirt shone silver. Gavin rehearsed what he would say, formed every poetic word in his mind.

"What are we talking about, Mr. Ennock?" Alice asked, her voice soft as earth.

And all the words left Gavin, as if the darkness had chased them away. The silence stretched long and dank between them, and suddenly he said, "I've been studying music frequencies with Doctor Clef."

Alice stared at him. "*That's* what you wanted to talk to me about?"

"He's the one who discovered that every note has its own unique frequency based on the number of times the sound waves cycle per second." Gavin was babbling now, and he couldn't stop. "I have perfect pitch, so he's been training me to recognize different notes by their frequencies, even though pitch and frequency aren't exactly the same, since pitch is subjective and frequency is absolute, but Doctor Clef says perfect pitch is more correctly called *absolute* pitch, so maybe they're more closely related than anyone knows."

Alice drew back. "Gavin, what *are* you talking about?"

"Frequency. Weren't you listening? Every note can be expressed as a number, a frequency. Middle C is two hundred sixty-one point six three, and if you add those digits together, you get eighteen, and if you add those digits together, you get nine."

"Is that important?"

"I don't know," Gavin said helplessly. Stupid, unrelated words poured out of him, and still he couldn't stop. "Numbers are the key to everything, Alice, even to musical notes."

Alice stared at him. "Say that again."

"Numbers are the key to everything, even to musical notes."

"Musical notes. Why the musical notes?" Her face suddenly grew animated. "The key. The key to musical notes!" Now *she* was babbling. "Gavin, tell me—do you remember the notes Aunt Edwina played on that strange instrument just before she ran away from us at the bank? Didn't she also make my automatons play the same notes on the airship?"

"I remember everything," he said, and it was true. "And yes, they were the same notes both times."

"She was trying to tell us something with them. What were those notes?"

"G-sharp, B, a rest, and a D."

"And what frequency did each of those notes have?"

"The G had a frequency of fifty-one; the B had a frequency of thirty; the rest had a frequency of zero; and the D had a frequency of nine—so low you could barely hear it."

The excitement on her face became plainer. "Say those numbers again."

"Fifty-one and thirty, zero, and nine."

"Oh!" Alice put a hand to her mouth again. "Oh, Gavin! I know what's going on! I know where Aunt Edwina is hiding! I *know*, Gavin! Or, rather, I can find out!"

At last, the insane babble left him, and he seized her right hand in both of his. "Then come with me, Alice. Come with me to the Third Ward. They still want you. *I* still want you."

"I can't, Gavin." Her face was flushed in the yellow gaslight. "I can't just rush off with you, however much I might have wanted to. I thought I had learned what I needed to leave, but then my father passed away, and everything changed. If you hit an automaton just right, Gavin, its memory wheels reset, and it loses everything it learned. Father's passing hit me very hard."

"So we're back to appearances again." He swallowed. "Who are you preserving appearances for, Alice?"

"Everyone!" Alice protested. "Gavin, you have this idea

that anyone can just fly off and do whatever he wants. But I have a traditional title now and the traditional responsibilities that come with it. I have to have a legitimate child to pass the title down to, or the title will die. And Norbert paid off thousands of pounds of debt for me—"

"For your father," Gavin corrected.

"It's much the same. He paid for Father's funeral, too. And I have a responsibility to Norbert in return. We keep up appearances in order to fulfill those responsibilities to each other. You think that changing everything would be so simple, so easy, but it isn't, Gavin. People are complicated. Relationships are complicated, and you don't seem to understand that. We don't always get what we want."

"It doesn't stop us from trying to get it," Gavin countered. "And it doesn't mean we should give up." He shifted tactics. "What about your responsibility to the Crown? To the people of the British Empire? Your aunt killed dozens of men, and if you know where she's hiding, you have a responsibility to find her and save other lives."

"And this responsibility just happens to coincide with what you want."

"Is that wrong? For once can't the world work *for* us?"

"Oh, Gavin." Tears welled up in her brown eyes, but her hand remained within both of Gavin's. "You are so young."

"And you act so old. So what? Your whole life you've followed logic and reason, rules and regulations, but you're not an automaton. Close your eyes and jump. I'll catch you and we'll fly. I love you, Alice. It's always been you."

The electric lights over the theater doors flashed three times, indicating intermission was over. Most of the crowd had already drifted inside, leaving them nearly alone on the damp sidewalk. Norbert appeared in the doorway, a pinkish stain on his dress shirt. Behind him, Kemp tried to get through, but Norbert resolutely blocked his way.

"Alice?" he said. "What are you doing out here?"

Alice slipped her hand out of Gavin's and turned toward him. "Getting some air, darling. I'm on my way in."

"Come with me," Gavin whispered. "Tell me how to find your aunt."

She paused, caught between the two of them. She licked her lips. Gavin forced himself to remain still. Norbert glanced impatiently at a pocket watch.

"Alice," he said, "we won't be able to find our seats in the dark."

"Madam?" Kemp said. "What do you wish to do?"

Alice glanced at Gavin, and he knew her answer. An icy shell crushed his heart as she turned toward Norbert. Abruptly she spun back and said, "I'll send you a telegram about what I know." Then she was up the steps and through the doorway with her fiancé. Kemp gave Gavin a short glance with his expressionless eyes and shut the theater door.

Gavin sank to the bottom step, heedless of the damp and dirt. Every scar on his back ached, and they pulled him down like taut chains. He drew the little nightingale from his pocket and pressed the side of its head so it sang. The mechanical notes sounded dull as a pile of lead shot. Gavin silently swore he would never sing or play the fiddle again, not in a world where Alice would never hear him.

The theater doors banged open. Alice burst through them and rushed down to Gavin. He leapt to his feet just as she flung herself into his arms.

"I'm an idiot," she whispered in his ear. "To hell with Norbert. It's always been you, too."

And then she was kissing him. Gavin pulled her to him and tightened his arms around her. His aches vanished and his heart soared. They joined hands and fled through the dark.

Gavin didn't even remember how they got back to Ward headquarters or when Kemp caught up to them. He only knew he was running up the steps to the main doors of the house, and it felt as if his feet barely touched the ground. A breathless Alice ran beside him, her eyes bright. He stopped in the doorway to kiss her again. She kissed back, and he wanted to shout and laugh even while his body pressed hard against hers.

"Mr. Ennock!" she gasped when they parted. "One doesn't kiss a baroness like that!"

"One doesn't?" he said with a wide grin.

"Certainly not! One kisses a baroness like this." She moved closer and kissed him again. Gavin closed his eyes and breathed hard. He'd died. That was the only explanation.

"Madam," Kemp said uncertainly.

Alice ignored him. "Now it's your turn," she breathed against Gavin's teeth.

He stepped back, touched her face with one gloved hand, found he couldn't bear that, and flung the gloves aside. He let his bare fingers brush her face as lightly as wings, and he leaned down for another kiss, one that stopped time.

A gentle cough pulled them apart. Lieutenant Phipps stood a few feet away, her metal fingers drumming softly against her thigh. Alice covered her mouth, then put her hand down. Gavin, for his part, couldn't stop smiling.

"I'm glad you plan to join us, Your Ladyship," Phipps said.

Kemp regained his mental footing. "Since Madam has finally seen fit to take the advice of certain people and leave Sir, shall I arrange for the delivery of Madam's things?"

"The only things I need," Alice replied with a small toss of her head, "are Click and the box of little automatons from my workshop. My favorite tools are in my handbag"— she held it up—"and everything else came from my . . . from Mr. Williamson, and I don't want any of it."

Phipps gave a curt nod. "I'll send a pair of agents round for the automaton box."

"What about Click?" Alice said.

"Strange about Click." Phipps stepped aside, revealing the little clockwork cat, who was licking a paw. "He showed up about five minutes before you did."

"Click!" Alice scooped him up, and Gavin felt glad that she was so glad. "How did you know to come here?"

The cat only looked pleased with himself. A rusty purr emerged from his chest. Kemp sniffed.

"We'll also get you some clothes," Phipps added. "Grand gestures may be dramatic, but they're rarely practical. Welcome to the Ward, Baroness Michaels." Phipps held out her flesh-and-blood hand.

"Shouldn't it be just Alice?" she said, shaking hands around Click.

The corners of Phipps's mouth twitched. "Indeed. We'll start your training in the morning. Early." With that, she strode away.

Alice started to say something, but Gavin stopped her. "Don't."

"Don't what?"

"Tell her you have an idea about finding Edwina. Let's keep it to ourselves for now."

"Why, for heaven's sake?"

"Because the last two times she yelled at me," Gavin said.

"Two times?" Alice repeated.

"Once after the incident at the Bank of England, and once after your adventure with the giant mechanical. You didn't stick around for that one." Gavin rubbed his face. "If your idea doesn't pan out, I don't want her to yell at me again. I don't like being yelled at."

Alice looked doubtful, but finally nodded.

"So tell me what's going on."

"Do you have a map room in this place?"

A few minutes later, she was unrolling a large, detailed map of London across a table in a room illuminated with gas jets Kemp lit for her. Click lounged on the table and batted idly at the scroll weights Alice used to prevent the unwieldy parchment from rolling back up.

"Aunt Edwina kept playing that same chord," she said. "It was a message, one only someone with perfect pitch would understand."

Gavin scratched his head. "Well, it didn't work. I don't understand it."

"You did—you just didn't decode it. Look here. You said the G-sharp has a frequency of fifty-one; the B's frequency is thirty; the rest would be zero, of course; and the D is nine. Those four numbers were almost exactly the same as fifty-one, thirty, zero, and eight, the map coordinates Pilot gave for Buckingham Palace when he flew us on the airship from Father's house. I don't know much about map coordinates, but I reasoned the music numbers must give a spot for a place close by. And I was right. Look— fifty-one degrees, thirty minutes north and zero degrees nine minutes west."

"Holy cow!" Gavin's finger stabbed down onto the map. "Hyde Park!"

"Oh! We should have known from the beginning!" Alice exclaimed. "Everything comes back there. Norbert and I often went to Hyde Park, and you played in Hyde Park. I first heard you there, though I didn't know it at the time. If that's where Aunt Edwina's hiding, no doubt she heard you as well. It may be the reason she settled on kidnapping you—availability."

"It wouldn't explain why she came back for me," Gavin pointed out.

"What say we go ask her?" Alice asked.

"After you, Your Ladyship."

"Might I suggest a change of clothing first?" Kemp said. "Neither Madam nor Sir is quite attired for tramping through the verge."

"Oh! I hadn't thought. Can you find something more appropriate for me, Gavin?"

Kemp's eyes flickered and flashed. "I have already contacted the Third Ward's main Babbage engine and discovered both the location of Sir's room and the location of the main clothing stores. What color dress would Madam prefer?"

"Madam would prefer trousers, please," Alice said wickedly. "If Madam is going to break the rules, she may as well break them *badly*."

"If Madam and Sir will give me a moment."

"He's full of surprises, isn't he?" Gavin said as Kemp bustled away.

Her arms went around his neck. "We have more rules to break, Mr. Ennock."

When Kemp returned a few minutes later with more appropriate clothing, he found Alice and Gavin in a state of dishabille. He coughed, and they separated. Gavin flushed, but Alice only laughed. It was the first time he had ever heard that sound from her, and his heart gave a little leap.

"Thank you, Kemp." She planted another kiss on Gavin's mouth and scuttled behind a tall fire screen to let Kemp help finish removing her dress while Gavin changed out of the remainder of his evening clothes. His groin ached, and he was glad that Alice couldn't see his present state. Click cocked his head across the map table.

"What are you looking at, cat?" Gavin muttered.

Click licked a metal paw.

Alice emerged from behind the screen wearing brown trousers, a white blouse, a riding jacket, and a boy's cloth cap. Gavin barely recognized her, but she was still beautiful. The trousers and jacket outlined her shape and made her femininity even more apparent. Gavin longed to snatch her up and flee to a remote mountaintop, where the air was clear and the clouds washed the world clean and where they could be alone together for an eternity of moments.

Kemp said, "I took the liberty of ordering a pair of riding

horses from the stable. I will stay behind to ensure proper quarters are prepared for Madam's return."

They were heading out the door when Alice stopped and dashed back to Kemp. She spoke to him briefly, then rejoined Gavin.

"What was that about?" he asked.

"I'll want tea and a hot bath when I get back," she explained, "and Click will need winding, since he's staying behind. Life is in the details, Gavin."

"At least you're not calling me Mr. Ennock."

They didn't go the stables, though. Instead, Gavin led Alice to a staircase that took them down to the first basement level and a heavy door with several keyholes on it. Gavin spun a combination lock several times, depressed a number of keys on a large adding machine set into the door itself, and produced a key, which he slid into the third keyhole from the right. The door clanked and groaned, then creaked slowly inward.

"What is this?" Alice asked.

"The weapons vault. We're not going unarmed."

The large, *large* room beyond was filled with racks and shelves and drawers. Gun barrels made of metal, glass, and other substances gleamed in the overhead electric lights. Pistols in a variety of shapes waited to be loaded and used. Many were connected by long, heavy cords to power packs meant to be strapped to the wielder's back. Other racks sported explosives—bombs, dynamite, barrels of gunpowder. One section was lined with syringes, ampules, and rows of brown medicine bottles.

"Goodness," Alice said. "You're well equipped."

"We try." Gavin felt unaccountably pleased at the remark, as if he had something to do with the Ward's weaponry. "Most of them are singular pieces invented by the clockworkers we find. The worst ones go into the Doomsday Vault, of course, but these are for us agents to use as we see fit."

Alice picked up a small ball of red porcelain. "What's this?"

"It's filled with pollen from a plant developed by L'Arbre Magnifique. Don't drop it! It'll put you to sleep for several minutes unless you drink absinthe first."

"Absinthe?" Alice shuddered. "Why absinthe?"

"Ask L'Arbre Magnifique."

She set the ball down and hefted a bulky rifle. "What's this one do?"

"Good choice. It shoots a balled-up net that springs open to engulf the target. Not much accuracy over long distances, but good at close range." Gavin selected several syringes with corks on the end. "Opiates. Clockworkers don't sleep much, and it takes a lot to keep them out, as you saw with Patrick Barton."

"Why didn't we take any of this with us when we went after him?"

"No time, remember? He was running, and we had to track him before the trail faded. Besides, Tree came armed. Here, take this one, too." He handed her a pistol and holstered one for himself. "*Now* we can get those horses."

Chapter Sixteen

Alice, Baroness Michaels, swung down from her horse with the net rifle heavy on her back. Everything felt odd. It felt odd to ride astride. It felt odd to wear trousers. It felt odd to think of herself as Baroness Michaels. It felt odd to think she had left her fiancé.

One thing that *didn't* feel odd was having Gavin beside her. That felt perfectly right. She was theoretically about to walk into the den of a notorious clockworker who was also her own aunt; yet right now she felt happier and more secure than she had since before her mother died.

Gavin dismounted from his own horse with a creak of leather, and the animal snorted hard. His pale hair shone almost like a halo from under the simple cloth cap he favored. They were in the middle of Hyde Park, some distance north of the Serpentine. Trees and bushes and lawn stretched out around them, and a misty drizzle made the moon a fuzzy disk. Yellow gaslights shone here and there, but the park itself was deserted. Alice glanced around, wondering exactly where to start looking.

"This is more or less where the map coordinates would put us," Gavin said. "It may take several hours of searching before—"

"Here it is!" Alice called out. She was examining a small gardener's shack that stood beneath a spreading beech tree. It appeared completely normal, except for the overly complicated lock on the door. Gavin trotted over and shone a large electric torch on it. Brass gleamed, and Alice saw scratches above the lock.

"Too much for a simple gardener," Gavin agreed.

Alice's heart rate climbed, and her lips were parted with excitement. "How do we get in?"

"These scratches." His fingers dragged across them. "It's musical notation, but old-fashioned—medieval. Doctor Clef showed me some stuff like it."

"What happens if you sing it?"

Gavin sang, a short, quick melody that trilled like a nightingale. Alice found it pretty, but she glanced nervously around. Staying in one place after dark was a good way to encounter a plague zombie, especially in a place like Hyde Park, where the lights were scattered and far apart. Even as the thought crossed her mind, a shadow moved to their right. Two plague zombies lurched out of a clump of bushes. Both were women in tattered dresses. One carried a battered parasol. To their left came a trio—three teenaged boys, barefoot and in rags.

"Gavin!" Alice hissed.

He caught sight of the zombies, and the melody stopped with a startled choke. A red light flashed above the lock.

"Let's get out of here," Alice said. "The Ward can find this place again."

"Agreed."

But more zombies oozed out of the damp darkness, a crowd of pale men, women, and children, all groaning their misery. There was no way through them. Alice shrank back against the shack, her excitement forgotten.

"Where did they all come from?" she asked desperately. "Why are they coming for *us*?"

Gavin turned back to the door and started the song

again, but his voice shook, and he got only a few notes in before the red light flashed. He started a third time. Alice drew her pistol. There didn't seem to be much point in using the net rifle against a whole crowd, though the single pistol in her hand didn't seem a great defense, either. Could she kill a plague zombie? They had once been—perhaps still were—human beings. The closest ones were only a few paces away now, and she could smell the rotten meat, even see the maggots that crawled around their open sores. Gavin continued to sing. Alice drew back the pistol's hammer and aimed with a shaky hand.

The lock clunked and the bolts drew back. Gavin's torch revealed a staircase heading down.

"Go!" Gavin shoved her inside without waiting for a response, then dived after her and slammed the door shut. Alice leaned against the shack wall, breathing heavily. Her knees quaked inside the unfamiliar trousers.

"Are you all right?" Gavin put an arm around her shoulders. "Did they touch you?"

"Yes. I mean, no. I'm fine. They didn't touch me."

Fists thudded slowly on the door and walls. Alice shied away from them. "I don't know why I'm so nervous about them. I faced down a small army of them at the bank."

"You were sitting atop a mechanical at the time. Drink this." He handed her a flask, and she sipped something that burned all the way down. "Brandy. For the jitters."

It did help. What helped even more was the way Gavin took her hand as they stood at the top of the stairs.

"Since we don't have much choice," he said, "let's see who's home."

They descended the creaky staircase and came to a wide tunnel lined with brick. A deep trench ran down the center. Water dripped, and rats scuttled away from the light of Gavin's torch.

"This looks like part of the sewer," Alice said. "Though it smells rather fresher."

"How would a baroness know what the London sewers are like?" Gavin flicked a foot at a passing rat, and it squeaked angrily at him.

"I do read. Let's go."

They followed the tunnel cautiously, weapons drawn. Alice's world narrowed to quiet footsteps, dripping water, and the scrabbling of rat claws behind Gavin's strip of light. Gavin halted, and Alice nearly ran into him.

"What is it?" she whispered.

"That." He pointed the light at the floor. A wire glimmered at ankle level above the bricks. Alice took the torch from Gavin and followed the wire along its length. It led to an enormous round weight suspended on a heavy pole at the opposite side of the tunnel. Tripping the wire would cause it to swing across the tunnel and crush whoever might be standing there.

"It's almost halfhearted," Alice said critically. "It wouldn't fool a child."

"Maybe it's a distraction from the *real* trap," Gavin offered. "Simon and I once went after a clockworker in Germany who cooked up—I swear I'm not making this up—a variation of Limburger cheese that exuded deadly gas. Except it turned out the Limburger was to cover up what he was really making."

"What was that?"

"Exploding crackers."

She smacked him on the shoulder. "You did make that up."

"Ask Simon! Anyway, maybe something else is going on."

They searched for several minutes but turned up nothing. Alice grew cold, and her earlier excitement deflated entirely now that she was on her hands and knees in a chilly, damp tunnel inhabited by rats.

"If there's nothing, there's nothing," Alice said at last. "Let's keep going."

Alice had to admit to a certain amount of trepidation as they both stepped over the trip wire. Still, nothing happened. They continued on their way and rounded a corner. The tunnel went on a little farther and ended in a simple door limned with light. They each pressed an ear to the wood. Nothing. Gavin set his shoulder against it and mouthed, *Ready?* Alice drew the net rifle and nodded.

The door yanked itself open, and Gavin stumbled with a yelp into the space beyond. Painful light blinded Alice, and she fired the net rifle. It jerked in her hands with a muffled *phoot.* Gavin yelled again, and she heard a scuffling noise. Alice's eyes adjusted and she could see. The space was a large underground laboratory filled with esoteric equipment. Lying on the floor in front of her wrapped in a net was Gavin. Standing over him was the strange clockworker in the long coat, top hat, and grinning skull half mask.

"Halt, Edwina!" Alice fired the net rifle again. A pellet the size of a rugby ball burst from the business end and rushed toward the clockworker, but she twisted out of the way. The pellet exploded into a full-sized net that wrapped itself around a support pillar. The clockworker thrust a hand into one pocket.

"Don't move!" Alice barked. "I will fire, Edwina. You know I will."

The clockworker froze.

"I could use some help down here," Gavin said from inside the net.

Alice didn't move. "I want answers, Edwina. You're not getting away, and you're going to tell me *why.* Why would you send plague zombies to attack your own niece? Why would you leave me a house filled with death traps? *And why didn't you help me when I really needed you?*"

Aunt Edwina just stared at her, the skull mask hiding all expression. Gavin was trying to untangle himself from the net without much success. Words poured out of Alice in a geyser of acid.

"Did you think that sending me a bunch of stupid automatons would make up for leaving me alone to take care of a sick old man all my life? You could have slipped me money, or visited in secret, but you didn't. Was I that horrible? Was I that ugly and stupid? How terrible I must have been for you to abandon me when I needed you the most, and only your ticking clockwork automatons to comfort me."

"I'm sorry, darling," Edwina said. "Truly I am. And I'm afraid it'll get worse before it gets better."

Alice froze. The voice. The tone. It couldn't be. "Louisa?"

"Please, darling. Call me Aunt Edwina." The clockworker swept off the mask and hat to reveal the face of Louisa Creek.

Alice was struck speechless. All she could do was stare while Gavin continued to struggle within the net on the floor.

Louisa—Edwina—clapped her hands in glee. "I know I've put you through a lot, darling, but look at you now! You're wearing trousers! A true Ad Hoc lady. And you've trussed up that delicious young musician for yourself. How can the night get any better?"

"What the bloody *fucking* hell is going on?" Alice shrieked.

The room went silent. Gavin stopped moving within the net. Even Louisa/Aunt Edwina seemed at a loss for words.

"Well?" Alice asked dangerously. "I want an explanation, Louisa or Aunt Edwina or whoever you are, and it had better not involve transplanting a human brain."

"Of course, darling," she agreed. "But why don't we help your young man out of that net first? Unless you want to leave him all tied up and helpless."

"He's not my—oh, never mind. Just stand over there and don't move."

She looked hurt. "You don't trust me."

"Should I?" Alice knelt down. "Hold still, Gavin. Squirming only makes it worse." She twitched him free, and he rolled away. He'd lost his hat and torch, but his pistol was in his hand.

Edwina wrung her hands. "Don't be too put out, darling. I put the kettle on the moment you entered the park and sent my helpers up to ensure you came down here instead of haring off to the Third Ward. I have eyes all over, you know."

"You know about the Ward," Gavin said.

"Obviously. Oh, Alice, may I give you a kiss? It's been so long. Well, it hasn't really, but you thought I was Louisa Creek."

"Don't come close," Gavin warned. He still had the pistol trained on her, and in his other hand he held a syringe. He flicked the cork away with his thumb.

"I'm confused." The angry geyser had ended, leaving Alice feeling empty and uncertain. "I don't know who's who or what's what."

"You already figured out that I'm your aunt Edwina," the woman said. "I adopted the guise of a wealthy Ad Hoc lady and arranged for your invitation to the Greenfellow ball so I could become your friend. I had no idea that idiot Norbert Williamson would make a serious run for you. He set me back *months*."

"Father and Norbert arranged for that invitation," Alice said weakly.

"No, darling. The old dear was a stiff-necked traditionalist to the end, wasn't he? His business contacts were long dried up, and your former fiancé is a perfect liar. *I* arranged for the invitation. I was sure you wouldn't recognize me. It's been almost fourteen years, and Louisa wears padded dresses, a wig, and an excess of cosmetics."

"But *why*?" Alice cried again.

"Could we discuss this sitting down?" Edwina asked. "I have tea. You can still shoot me whenever you like, Mr. Ennock."

Gavin thought about it, then gestured with the pistol. Only now did Alice notice how tight his face was, how stiff his movements. He was angry, too. But of course—Aunt

Edwina was the Red Velvet Lady who had drugged him, tested him, and locked him in a lonely tower. Seeing Gavin in distress brought her a twist of pain, and Alice wanted to comfort him, to put her arms around his shoulders, but this wasn't a good time.

Edwina led them around the edge of the laboratory. It was equipped with glassware and the newfangled Bunsen burners. Three microscopes stood on a table surrounded by notes and glass-topped dishes. The strange musical instrument she had used to control the plague zombies hung on one wall.

"None of this is about automatics," Alice observed.

"No," Edwina said. "I've moved on to other fields. Come, sit."

A long laboratory table held tea things, including a tray of cakes. Aunt Edwina poured tea into three cups, then took hers and a cake to the far end of the table, where she sat down, still wearing her long brown coat. Alice sat opposite her. Gavin, in an understandable display of bad manners, half sat on the table itself, his pistol trained in Edwina's direction. Neither he nor Alice touched the tea or cakes, though Alice was glad of the chance to sit down.

"Much better." Edwina sipped her tea, and Alice saw her friend Louisa in her movements. Strange grief touched Alice's heart. In a way, Louisa had died. "All right. You know I suffer from the clockwork plague."

"You're a clockworker," Gavin said flatly.

"I don't care for that word, or for the term *zombie*," Edwina said. "These people are infected with a deadly disease, and they deserve compassion, not fear or scorn."

"How did you survive it for so long?" Gavin asked.

"Through a great deal of research and hard work, Mr. Ennock. You might say the clockwork plague has allowed me to survive the clockwork plague."

Alice stiffened. "Your work with zombies. All this medical equipment. You're working on a cure."

"More than that, darling. I've found one."

The words hung in the air for a long moment. Finally, Edwina took a bite of cake and washed it down with tea. The gesture seemed so prosaic. After a pronouncement like that, the earth should move or thunder should roll. Instead, there was only the click of china. Finally, the last bits of strength drained out of Alice, and she slumped again. "I think you need to start at the beginning, Aunt Edwina."

"Which one, darling? Genesis has two accounts of the creation, which—"

"Not *that* beginning," Alice interrupted. "Are you . . . ?" She trailed off.

"Mad?" Edwina flicked a crumb away. "Of course, though some days are worse than others. That was a small joke to break the tension."

"We like tension," Gavin said in a flat voice. "Just explain."

"No one appreciates me," Edwina complained. "All right. Eight or nine years ago, not long after your dear mother died, Alice, I came to myself in the middle of my own house. The place was a wreck. Clockwork devices were everywhere, including a new valet who told me his name was Kemp. I had built them all in a mad fugue. I realized the disease that plagues our family had turned me into a rare genius, and I was enjoying a rare moment of lucidity after a prolonged period of madness. I managed to turn my newfound intelligence toward two areas—keeping my finances in good order so I could continue to build whatever I wanted, and finding a damned cure."

"And succeeded at both," Gavin said.

Edwina nodded. "It didn't happen all at once, of course. I learned that the plague is caused by a type of bacterium, to use the word coined by Doctor Ehrenberg. It's an organism so small, only a microscope can see it. It's actually a kind of plant, and very pretty, with tiny—"

"Aunt Edwina," Alice interrupted. "The cure?"

"Right." Edwina rubbed her forehead. "I fear I'm heading for another bad spell. I still get them. After a lot of work, I gained some control over the plague. I could speed its course, or slow it down. The latter meant I wouldn't die, but it was only a treatment, and it was difficult and time-consuming to make. I was spending nearly all my time just keeping myself alive. But then I made a breakthrough. An actual cure. And that's why I'm on the run, darling."

"I don't understand," Alice said, but that was a lie. Terrible understanding was growing like a mushroom inside her, pushing out everything else she'd been feeling and filling her with airy decay.

"At this point, the Third Ward broke into my home. They came looking for me, and I had to flee." Edwina produced a handkerchief and wiped delicately at her eyes. "I had only a few moments' warning, just enough time to nip out. The cure was locked in my laboratory safe."

"But the Third Ward found it," Gavin said, and Alice remembered the wall safe that had been ripped open in Aunt Edwina's basement workroom.

"They did"—she gave her eyes another delicate wipe—"and they destroyed my laboratory so I couldn't continue my work."

"So Phipps lied," Alice said. "She said the Ward left after your first trap killed one of its agents, and she said the Ward didn't know who demolished your laboratory. Why did she lie?"

"You know the answer to that, darling," Edwina said.

"Because," Alice said slowly, "Phipps didn't want me to know the cure existed."

"Or because you're lying now, Edwina," Gavin pointed out.

"Why would I lie now, dear boy?" She sipped her tea again and made a face. "Cold." She reached over to a nearby table, pulled a Bunsen burner over, lit it like a pet dragon, and held her cup over it. "The Ward left me little to work with—a few drugs, some rudimentary equipment, and the early stages of my research. I built a second laboratory down here and lived as Louisa Creek up there."

"I want to know why you grabbed me off the street," Gavin growled. "What did I ever do to you?"

"A perfect segue, Mr. Ennock," Edwina said. "This is exactly the point where you came in. My plan to create and disperse a cure wasn't working quite right, so I had to expand it. I needed Alice."

"That's not an explanation about me." Gavin's face was hard with a hatred Alice had never seen before, and it chilled her.

"I'm trying to stay chronological, Mr. Ennock, as Alice requested. We're arriving at you." She shut off the hissing burner and added a sugar lump to her tea. "I needed a way to get my cure back from the Third Ward. But Ward headquarters are tightly guarded, and the Ward knows how plague geniuses think. My only hope of getting at it was to draw out my dear niece, Alice."

"Draw me out?" Alice came upright again. "What on earth are you talking about?"

"You were so timid after the clockwork plague struck the family down, darling." Edwina got up to pace, and Gavin tensed. "No, that's not the right word. I think the Americans call it hidebound. You wouldn't budge outside the safety of traditional society. All that talent gone to waste. My dear, stubborn brother wouldn't let me see you because he thought—quite rightly—that I'd try to corrupt you into Ad Hoc society, but he decided a few presents couldn't hurt, and he let my little automatons through. I had already been working on you for your own good, hoping those little machines would stimulate you enough that you would start to chafe and finally break free of your father. I didn't send you help of the monetary sort because then you would have had no need to break free. My hope was to starve you into the open. By sheer luck, the groundwork for furthering my plan was already there. I just needed to act on it."

"What does this have to do with kidnapping me?" Gavin demanded. He had gotten to his feet as well, tense as a lion.

"Patience, Mr. Ennock. You waited in my tower for weeks. You can wait a few minutes more. The problem was, you stayed stubbornly with your father, Alice, and refused to try anything on your own. So I involved myself more directly."

"You disguised yourself and became my friend and mentor," Alice said dully.

"Exactly! What better way for me to mold your thinking than to become your best friend? After I met you, I took Patrick Barton home with me from the Greenfellow ball and drugged him senseless so I could—"

"You drugged Patrick Barton?" Alice interrupted. "What for?"

"I had to. I did tell you I would leave the ball with him."

"Oh my God," Gavin whispered. He sank back to his perch on the table, and his revolver shook. "You infected him with the clockwork plague. That was why he showed no signs of the disease before the ball, and that was why he became a clockworker so quickly afterward."

"I injected him with my own accelerated recipe, yes. Mr. Barton did everything I'd hoped."

"And that was?" Alice asked, feeling more than a little sick. For a moment, she had been lulled into seeing Aunt Edwina as merely odd, someone who dressed up in strange clothes and played an elaborate prank. But the incident with poor Patrick Barton slapped her back into sensibility. Aunt Edwina was completely mad.

"I'm getting ahead of myself." Edwina sipped at her cup, realized it was empty, and tossed it over her shoulder. It shattered on the stone floor behind her. "After the ball, I arranged that little plague victim riot so you would get some exposure to the Third Ward, Alice. I didn't have high hopes that you would come out of your shell right then, so I continued with my plan—until that idiot Norbert Williamson whisked you away into betrothal, anyway. I tried to talk you out of it, but I was handicapped by having to be subtle. It was infuriating. So I had to bring in Mr. Ennock."

"I don't follow this." Gavin was clearly expending a lot of energy holding on to his temper, and Alice was afraid he was going to leap across the table. "Tell me why you kidnapped me and held me. Why you killed those airmen just to grab me again."

Edwina nibbled a cake. "Frankly, you enchanted me, Mr. Ennock. Your fiddle and your voice and your natural charm—irresistible! In addition, you're young and strong and have no children. Perfect material for the Third Ward, if only they noticed you. I suspected Alice would find you as attractive as I do, and I was fortunate to learn that she took all those rides in Hyde Park. I dressed in red velvet so you would notice me, and I paid you plenty to ensure you would play there often. And when the time was right, I hired a pair of men with a rope and a sack. Then it was just a matter of time before Alice rescued you."

Alice's mouth fell open. "You locked Gavin in that tower because you wanted to *introduce* us?"

"Well, obviously! Good God, girl, I practically threw the two of you together!"

"I don't believe it," Alice said faintly. "It all comes down to a maiden aunt who plays matchmaker—clockwork style."

"Why did you leave the traps running?" Gavin said. "They almost killed us."

Edwina stared at him. "I couldn't deactivate the traps. The wrong person might get in."

"Indisputable logic," Alice muttered.

"Mr. Ennock is worth a few traps, don't you think? He's much better looking and far more talented than dull, drab Norbie."

Anger thundered through Alice. "How *dare* you manipulate us this way."

"I see." Edwina looked genuinely hurt. "Your father arranges a marriage that makes you unhappy, and that's all right, but I match you with someone you actually love, and that's wrong?"

Alice felt ready to explode, and Gavin's gentle hand landed on her shoulder. "It's all right," he soothed. "You don't want to throw the teapot. Let's hear the rest."

Was she holding the teapot? She was. Alice set it down with careful control.

"Thank you," Edwina said. "At any rate, you rescued Mr. Ennock but refused to contact the Ward, so I talked to you as Louisa and 'accidentally' found the card with the agent's name on it. And then there was the incident with the paper bomb outside the solicitor's office. I was hoping you'd notify the Ward then, too. It was a relief when you and Mr. Ennock went off in that dirigible, and I was very upset when you agreed to marry little Norbie anyway and moved Arthur into his house. I had to come up with a whole new plan to break you free. Once young Mr. Barton was ready, I distracted the rest of the Ward and turned him loose so it would be just the two of you going after him. So romantic!"

"How could you possibly have known you'd need Patrick Barton?" Alice said, surprised at how level her voice was. She felt more and more as if she were attending a tea party in a lunatic asylum. "It was a year between the time you met him at the ball and the time he attacked the smithy."

"Well, I wasn't *sure* I'd need him. I was only planning ahead, just in case. It takes time for the plague to develop, especially for someone who's going to become a genius, and I was sure my new version of it would develop Mr. Barton into one."

"What if I had joined the Ward right away?" Alice said.

"Then Mr. Barton would have had a wonderful time inventing any number of things before the plague took him off. Really, darling, I don't know why you're so upset. You didn't even know him. And he wasn't very good in the bedroom. Though now that I think of it, that may have been the drugs."

"Your version of the plague burns clockworkers out even faster than normal," Gavin said. His voice was tight. "I watched him die. It was horrible."

"I was afraid of that. Fortunately, he served his purpose first. You two did become closer. But then my automaton spies gave me the news that Alice was planning to elope, so I had to act fast. I'm sorry the plan was so crude—short notice and all. Still, your adventure with the war machine *did* make it clear how much you need Mr. Ennock, Alice. My dear brother's death was a minor complication, but in the end you made the right decision. If it makes you feel any better, darling, you're going to get notice tomorrow that all your debts have been paid off by an anonymous benefactor. You don't owe Norbert a thing."

Oddly—or perhaps understandably—the news didn't make Alice didn't feel any better. "Edwina," she said in a dangerous voice, "I need you to tell us what the point is. Why did you want Gavin and me to . . . to fall in love and join the Ward?"

She held up a finger. "You haven't asked why I attacked the Bank of England."

"You needed money?" Gavin said.

Edwina laughed like a society woman who had heard a small joke. "I have pots of money, Mr. Ennock."

"Then why did you do it?" Alice sighed.

"Partly to bring you two lovebirds closer together, and partly so I could play those notes for you, the ones that gave you the map coordinates for this little den of mine. I knew you and your perfect pitch would eventually figure it out, Mr. Ennock."

"Alice figured it out," Gavin told her coldly. "I just gave her the frequency numbers."

Edwina waved this away. "It still worked. You're here."

"Aunt Edwina, I'm quite confused. Why did you lead us here?"

She stared at Alice. "So we could have this little chat, of course."

"We have a wonderful telegraph system," Alice nearly shouted. "And the Royal Mail. You didn't need to attack the National Bank to get our attention."

"Paper communiqués can be intercepted. Your sharp mind and Mr. Ennock's perfect pitch gave me the means to send the perfect coded message. It was the only way to be safe."

"Safe?" Alice echoed. "Attacking the bank with an army of zombies was *safe*? Blowing up a dirigible and killing dozens of men was *safe*?"

"Safer than sending a letter or telegram." Edwina finished her cake.

"You sent *me* a telegram," Gavin pointed out.

"That was from Louisa, not me. And I signed it 'L.' Could have been anyone."

Gavin groaned.

"Getting back to the cure," Alice said. "What do Gavin and I have to do with it?"

"The cure. Yes." Edwina leaned forward. A red light, one among many, flashed on the wall not far from Edwina's chair. It went out, and another one flashed. "We don't have much time. The first cure I discovered was only partially effective. I had . . . *manufactured* another microorganism that attacks the clockwork plague bacterium. It's smaller than bacteria and structured quite differently. I suspect similar agents already exist in nature. I call it a 'virion.' Do you like the term? I think it might catch on."

"I thought we didn't have much time," Gavin said.

"Right, right. My first virion, the one the Ward stole, is very delicate and can only survive inside a living host. It must be injected directly into the bloodstream. Very disappointing, if one wants the cure to spread throughout the world. I put it in my safe, and then the Ward chased me away and stole it. I had to start again down here."

"Did you do it?" Alice leaned across the table. "Did you succeed this time?"

"Of course." Edwina dabbed at her cheek with a napkin. The lights were all flashing red now. "The second virion is much hardier. Once a person is infected with this second virion, he becomes a carrier, and his saliva and mucus will spread it to other people, who become carriers in their own right. Once released, it will spread throughout the world and destroy the plague entirely. The only problem"—and here she sighed—"is that it doesn't cure plague geniuses. Their bodies change the plague somehow and make it immune to the cure. I tried an early version on poor Mr. Barton and a few others I've come across, and it didn't help any of them."

"But even so!" Alice breathed. "Edwina! We have to release it right now!"

Edwina held up a hand. "It's not that simple, darling. I can't finish incubating the second virion down here, with these limited facilities. It's going to take some—"

"Wait," Gavin interrupted. "You're lying."

"Oh?" Edwina's tone was light, but with an edge.

"You said the Third Ward stole your first cure months ago," Gavin said. "So why haven't they—we—used it?"

"Ah." Edwina steepled her fingers and stole a glance at the lights. They all went out. "I'm afraid I won't be able to explain that quite yet. You need to play má què with the Queen."

"I—what?" Gavin said.

"Play má què with the Queen. Play má què with the Queen."

"What are you talking about?" Gavin demanded. "What's—?"

The main door burst open, and a dozen agents flooded the room.

Chapter Seventeen

In an instant, Edwina was surrounded by pistols, rifles, and other weapons Gavin hadn't yet learned to identify. Gavin himself stared down the barrel of a very strange gun with copper wiring that twisted all along it. He smelled ozone, and his heart beat at the back of his throat. Then he saw who was wielding it.

"Damn it, Simon," he snapped, "it's me."

"Play má què with the Queen," Edwina said.

Simon d'Arco didn't move, and for a moment Gavin wondered if the man intended to shoot him. His thoughts flashed back to the moment at the symphony a few hours ago. Gavin hadn't had any time to think about what had happened or what any of it had meant, but now he wondered if Simon was angry. Then Simon lowered the weapon.

"Jesus, Gavin," he said. "I nearly blasted you to Sussex. Are you drinking *tea*?"

"I would prefer," Alice said in a small voice, "if you didn't point that at me."

"Alice?" Glenda holstered her weapon. "Good God, you look a fright. Are you all right? When did you start wearing trousers?"

There was a clatter of shackles as a set was closed over Edwina's wrists. She did not protest or struggle. A look of sadness came over Alice's face. Gavin wanted to hold her tight and let her head rest on his shoulder, let her cry if she needed to. He also knew she would be angry if he touched her in front of all these people. In the end, both of them just stood and watched Edwina be led toward the door in her long brown coat. One of the agents put the battered top hat on her head.

"Play má què with the Queen, darlings," Edwina called as she was towed out the door. "Má què!"

"Poor bugger," one of the remaining agents muttered. "Gone completely round the bend already."

Lieutenant Phipps stood to one side. Her arms were folded, flesh on brass. Gavin hadn't heard her arrive, and he wondered how much trouble he was in. "It's three o'clock, ladies and gentlemen," she said. "Smith, Peters—get the clockworker back to headquarters before morning traffic. The rest of you, dismantle this place immediately."

A "yes, ma'am" chorus echoed around the room. Phipps dropped into Edwina's chair. Alice and Gavin were on their feet.

"How did you know to come here, Lieutenant?" Gavin asked.

Phipps nodded at Alice. "Her automaton told us."

"Kemp?" Gavin blinked. "He wasn't supposed to—"

"I told him to tell them if we didn't return within two hours," Alice said quietly. "I'm sorry, Gavin. I didn't think it was a good idea to go off alone."

His mouth hung open. "You lied about the hot bath and the tea."

"Yes." She looked unhappy. "But it was a good thing, in the end."

"We'll talk about it later," Gavin said.

"Once again," Phipps put in, "I'm torn between praising

you and shooting you. This *is* the clockworker who's been terrorizing London with the zombies and who tried to steal the war mechanical, correct?"

"Yeah," Gavin said. "She was also Alice's aunt Edwina in disguise, so we got two for one."

Phipps bolted to her feet. "*That* was Edwina?"

"It was," Alice replied.

"You're both in for a bonus and a holiday," Phipps said. "See me back at headquarters for your report." And she was gone.

"That was strange," Gavin said. "She never gives bonuses, let alone holidays."

"It's not strange at all. The Queen's letter said her job was in danger if Edwina wasn't captured, remember? And Edwina can make the cure for the clockwork plague."

"Which the Ward already has, if we can believe her," Gavin said. "Alice, I hate to say it, but I think your aunt is entering the final stage. She said she has bad spells, and she was losing her mind there toward the end. All that business about má què with the Queen. All that stuff about a cure may have been rambling."

Alice shook her head. "I don't think so. It was all too careful, too reasoned."

Meanwhile, agents were rushing about the laboratory. They had already brought down crates and boxes and were packing up Edwina's materials with swift movements that bespoke long practice. Simon was dismantling some equipment while Glenda took notes on how it went together. Glass clinked and metal clanged. Within three or four hours, all traces of the laboratory would be gone. Alice was swaying on her feet, her face drawn with exhaustion, and Gavin remembered how long they'd been awake. Their encounter at the symphony had happened this evening, but it felt like days ago. When had he last slept? He couldn't remember, though he didn't feel particularly tired—not with everything that had happened.

"We should get you back to headquarters," he said to Alice. "You look half-dead."

"If that's the sort of compliment you're going to give from here on out," Alice said, yawning, "perhaps I should have stayed with Norbert."

They left the other agents and went topside, where they found their snorting horses amid a crowd of Ward carts and carriages. The ride back was chilly, partly due to the early-morning mist, and partly due to the fatigue that drained the heat from Gavin's bones. When they reached Ward headquarters, Kemp met them at the door with two cups of hot tea on a tray.

"Madam and Sir should have taken a hackney cab and let someone else bring the horses," he fussed. "Shall I bring a warmed wrap for Madam?"

"Thank you, no, Kemp."

Gavin drank hot tea and felt better as it warmed his insides. "You should go to bed, Alice."

"I agree, Madam," Kemp said. "I shall warm your sheets straightaway."

Alice shook her head. "We still have to report to Phipps, and I want to check on Aunt Edwina."

Kemp's eyes flickered. "According to Mrs. Babbage—"

"Mrs. Babbage?" Alice interrupted.

"That is what the Third Ward's primary Babbage engine prefers to be called," Kemp said. "We have established an excellent working relationship. At any rate, Mrs. Babbage says Lieutenant Phipps is down on the clockworker level."

"No doubt with Aunt Edwina," Alice said. "Let's go."

Against Gavin's better judgment, they headed for the creaking lift. Down in the stony underground, however, they found a pair of guards at the entrance to the hallway. Gavin scrambled to remember their names—Sean Something and Something Donaldson.

"Sorry, ma'am, sir," Sean said. "Lieutenant Phipps left

orders that no one is to enter the clockworker section until further notice."

"But she's my aunt!" Alice protested.

"Lieutenant Phipps?" said Donaldson, puzzled.

"No, I—oh, never mind." She turned to Gavin. "I'm exhausted. Let's go to bed."

Despite the events of the day, the phrase went straight through Gavin's brain to other parts of his body, which too happily responded. "Uh . . ."

"Oh, good heavens." Face flaming, Alice turned and stalked toward the lift. Gavin followed, though not before Sean shot him a small salute. In the lift itself, Alice stared resolutely forward. She was still wearing her cloth cap, though Gavin had taken his off indoors. Should women who wore male clothing remove their hats inside? He had no idea. Maybe some of the rules Alice worried so much about made sense—they told you what to do in a number of situations.

"I don't like lies," he said suddenly. Around them, the cage shuddered and creaked. "It bothers me that you lied to me about what you told Kemp."

"Would you have gone along with it if I hadn't?" she countered.

"No."

She shrugged. "That's why I did it."

"No." He shook his head. "Look, I'm not perfect. When I was little, back in Boston, I lied about all kinds of things so people would give me money, and on the *Juniper* I lied to the pirates, and when I'm on a case for the Ward, I lie to all kinds of people. But I never lied to my family, and I never lied to Captain Naismith, and I never lied to Lieutenant Phipps, and I never lied to you. I can't do this if I think you might lie to me."

She thought about that. "Gavin, I lie to survive. I lied to my father about where I was going and what I was doing in order to sell my automatons or to sneak books out of the subscription library so I could read about science instead of poetry. I lied to Norbert about my feelings for him. And there's more. My title hides who I really am. My clothes hide what I really look like. Even the Third Ward hides its true purpose. Our entire society lies. We give the lie so the truth can live beneath it."

"You can lie to other people all you want," Gavin said. "But not to me. I love you for the real you, for the truth." He took both her hands in his. "I can't do this if you're going to lie."

"Oh, Gavin." Her eyes grew wet. "I've been lying for so long, I'm not sure if I know how to tell the truth all the time. But I'll try."

He nodded, disappointed but understanding. "I suppose that's the best I can hope for."

The lift thumped to a halt, and Gavin opened the gates for them. At the place where the men's and women's dormitories diverged, they kissed and went their separate ways.

Two days later, a tap on wood snapped Gavin awake. Gavin always snapped awake, often with the ghost of Madoc Blue's hands on his body and the first officer's lash on his back. Months gone and he still lived those moments as if they were yesterday. By now, he had forgotten how to wake up like a normal person.

Doves cooed in the barn rafters far overhead. All around him stood a great expanse of space—the building was an empty wooden shell resting on an ancient fieldstone foundation. On the dirt floor nearby squatted a small electric generator. A heavy cord exited one end and terminated at the large, bulbous form that took up a great deal of the barn's empty space. Gavin sat at a carpenter's worktable strewn with drawings and tools, and he remembered deciding to put his head down for just a moment. Sawdust stuck to his cheek. The knock came again, more urgently this time.

"Who is it?" he called.

The barn sported two enormous doors that would allow a piled hay wagon to enter—or a large project to exit—but next to them was a smaller door for more everyday use. It creaked open, and Alice backed in. She wore a dark skirt and white blouse. Her honey brown hair had been pulled back under a small hat, but a few loose tendrils framed her face.

"Alice!" Startled, he leapt to his feet and hurried over to her. "Alice, what are you doing here? I didn't say come in!"

"It's only a barn. Besides, I couldn't wait to tell you. You haven't been to the main house for almost two days now, and—oh!"

Gavin plunged a hand into his coat pocket and found the silver nightingale. He fiddled with it nervously. His sleeves were pushed to the elbows, and bits of grease and sawdust speckled his forearms, and his hair looked like a haystack. In short, he looked a right mess. But her gaze went over his shoulder to the dirigible.

The dirigible was actually small, as such things went. The envelope, longer and leaner than most, was perhaps the length of two cottages and only as high as one. It barely eclipsed its own gondola, which rested on the floor in the final stages of completion while the envelope hovered overhead. Gavin had been about to set the generator in place when he decided to take a rest.

"Are you building this?" Alice asked in wonder.

"Refitting it, actually. Only the envelope is new. I've been working on it off and on for a few months now, but lately the work's been going faster. Has it really been two days since I've been in—?"

"It has. Why didn't you want me to come in?"

He flushed a little. "I didn't want you to see it until it was finished."

"Oh. I'm sorry. Well, since the cat's out of the bag, I may as well have a look." Alice set the tea tray down on the table and walked slowly around it. The dirigible kept its ropes taut, and a fine mesh seemed to hold the envelope's fabric together, a thin, loopy lattice that pressed against the cloth from inside, rather like a lacework skeleton.

Gavin watched Alice in silence, turning the clockwork nightingale over and over in his fingers and feeling oddly unsettled at her appearance. At long last, Alice had left her fiancé for him. The memory of each kiss they had shared clung to his skin like individual talismans. But the ease with which Alice lied still bothered him.

Gavin suppressed a groan as Alice completed her circuit of the airship. It wasn't fair. Everything was supposed to be wonderful now that Alice had joined the Ward and admitted her feelings for him. Did life ever go smoothly?

"What do you think?" he said, and waited for the polite lie.

"I like it. It's very sleek," she said. "Very modern."

"I see," he said neutrally, though his heart was tearing inside. She had lied—again.

She twisted one hand in her skirt. "But," she added slowly, "it'll never fly, Gavin. The envelope is too small to lift a gondola that large."

And Gavin felt abruptly light. "Really?" he said. "You think so?"

"Darling, it's obvious. I don't even have to work out the math. What were you thinking?"

In that moment he could have leapt to the faraway ceiling. "Help me anyway."

Careful not to trip over the cord, he lifted the little generator with easy strength and hauled it up the short ramp onto the gondola's main deck, which smelled of linseed oil and sawdust. Alice snatched up the tea tray and followed. Gavin lowered the generator in place on the deck and set to work with a wrench to bolt it down. Alice laid the tray on the deck next to him. Teapot, bread, butter, jam, sliced ham. Red rose in a vase. His stomach growled.

"When did you last eat?" she asked.

"I don't remember. I'm almost done and I want to finish." He grabbed a piece of bread and butter from the tray and wolfed it down. "What couldn't you wait to tell me?"

"What?"

He reached for another bolt. "When you first came in, you said you couldn't wait to tell me something."

"Ah. I know what to do next."

"About what?"

"Oh," Alice said. "Oh dear."

"What?"

"I was just noticing how handsome you look in the morning, Mr. Ennock, even when you're all dirty and tousled. Or maybe it's *when* you're all dirty and tousled. I think you owe me a kiss for bringing you tea."

Without a thought, he gave her one. It was distinctly odd, kissing Alice with a heavy wrench in one hand and rich bread in the other. It felt decadent, something a prince might do. When they parted, he held the bread up to her mouth, and she took a languorous bite. Her lips grazed across his fingers, and her soft tongue brushed his knuckle. A shudder coursed over Gavin, and he was suddenly very glad to be kneeling.

"I'm in a bachelor's workshop without a chaperone," Alice murmured. "How wicked am I?"

"Very wicked," he said hoarsely.

Her hand ran up the length of his thigh. Blood sang in Gavin's ears. He very nearly threw the wrench aside and snatched her to him. Instead, carefully setting tool and food down, he touched her face, then her hair, then her shoulders. He left a smear of grease on her cheek. She guided his hand lower until it was on her breast, and she gasped as he pressed its warmth beneath his palm.

The barn door snapped open. Gavin snatched his hand

away. Kemp entered the barn and strode up the ramp to the gondola, a largish book bound in leather tucked under his arm. "Madam, I believe this is the volume you were looking for."

Alice recovered quickly and accepted the book as if she and Gavin were sitting in a library. "Thank you, Kemp."

"Shall I clear that tray away for you, Sir?" Kemp asked Gavin.

Gavin shot him a hard look. "I'm still eating, thanks."

Kemp nodded with a faint creak and left. Gavin poured himself some tea to cover his consternation. "What is it you figured out?" he asked.

Alice was already paging through the book. "Just this. Phipps still won't let me near Aunt Edwina, so I don't know for sure how Aunt Edwina is doing at the moment, but she didn't seem to be in the final stages of clockworker madness. That's why it bothered me, the way she kept telling me to play má què with the Queen. So I went down to the library. Mrs. Babbage was very helpful, actually."

"And what did you find?"

"This." She turned the book so he could see a color plate with a series of tiles made of what looked like ivory. Each had an Oriental character painted on it. "It's a game."

"I've never heard of it."

"No one has, really. It comes from China. It has a lot of names: má què, mu tsian, má jiàng, even mah jong. They all mean *sparrow*."

"China," Gavin repeated. "Why would Edwina tell us to play a Chinese game with the Queen?"

"She knew the Third Ward was coming," Alice said. "Those lights on her wall were a series of alarms. She knew you and I were coming, remember? At any rate, she couldn't tell us what she meant outright with the Ward in the room. It's a hint that no one else would get, just like the coordinates puzzle."

"And what's the hint?"

"Mrs. Babbage reads the *Times* every day; did you know that? Every word. She also reads the *Gazette*, *Punch*, the *Examiner*, the *Graphic*, the *Atlantic*, and, well, everything!" Alice's eyes sparkled. "There's a speaking tube in the library, and you can ask her a question and—"

"I know, I know," Gavin interrupted. "I met Mrs. Babbage last year. What does this have to do with Chinese sparrows? What's the hint?"

"According to three different articles in different periodicals, the Chinese ambassador and his son introduced the Queen and the Prince Consort to má què, and the four of them play quite a lot."

"All right. But how could Edwina expect *us* to play má què with the Queen?"

"She doesn't," Alice said. "But who *does* play má què with the Queen?"

"The Chinese ambassador." Gavin fiddled with his teacup. "You think Edwina wants us to talk to him?"

"I do. I think Aunt Edwina knew she was going to be captured, so she's sending us to talk to someone else about the cure. The Chinese ambassador must know something important."

"And where do we find him? We'd never get into Buckingham Palace. Not even with Third Ward credentials."

Alice clapped her hands. "Ambassadors don't stay at Buckingham Palace. They stay at Claridge's hotel. You'll never guess where that is."

Gavin didn't even think. "Near Hyde Park."

"Shall we take a cab or get horses from the stable?"

"Wait just a moment." Gavin tightened the final bolt and tossed the wrench aside with a clatter. "Let's see if this works first."

"I'm telling you, it won't fly," Alice repeated.

Gavin spun a crank on the generator and pressed a switch. It coughed twice, then sputtered to life in a cloud of acrid paraffin-oil smoke. Indicator lights flickered. Gavin reached for a dial on the side.

"Let's see what happens," he said, and turned the dial.

At first nothing at all happened. Then a thin crackle snaked through the air. Soft blue energy threaded through the loops and spirals of the lattice under the skin of the envelope and lit them like threads of sky. A soft hum thrummed under Gavin's feet. Ropes creaked, and the envelope rose, taking the gondola with it. A moment later, it gently bumped the ceiling, as if nosing for a way out.

"Oh my goodness!" Alice laughed. "Oh my goodness! Gavin! What did you do?"

Gavin couldn't stop grinning. "I wasn't sure it would work. That's why I didn't want anyone to come look. It uses wire made from the new alloy Doctor Clef created for his Impossible Cube. The alloy pushes against gravity when you pump electricity through it. The more electricity you use, the more it pushes. So you don't need a big envelope to fly."

Alice balked. "Electricity is running through an envelope filled with *hydrogen*?"

"No, no," he reassured her. "That's something else I came up with. My ship uses helium, which doesn't explode."

"Well! Mr. Ennock, I have to say I find you intelligent and resourceful, and the way you lifted that generator made me truly appreciate how much a man you are."

He laughed again. "How do you always know exactly what to say to a man?"

"I know what to say to *you*." And she kissed him while the gondola swung gently beneath their feet. They parted and laughed.

"You didn't lie about the gondola being too big for the envelope," Gavin said. "Even though you thought it might hurt. Thank you."

Gavin picked her up in one fluid motion, swung her around in a circle, and kissed her again. His tongue slid into her mouth, and she accepted it, smooth and soft. He set her down, and she put a hand up to catch her hat.

"Oh! That was engaging," she said with a laugh. "Should we fly your new ship to the hotel?"

"I have to paint her yet," Gavin said. "Let's hire a carriage."

Claridge's, formerly Mivart's, had gained a reputation as London's only proper hotel for international political travelers. It was five stories of glass and red brick that occupied an enormous section of corner at Davies Street and Brook's Mews. Alice adjusted her hat and allowed Gavin to help her down from the carriage. The afternoon was overcast, but not foggy, so they didn't have to worry about plague zombies—not that even zombies would have dared wander close to Claridge's.

In preparation for visiting an ambassador to the Orient, Alice had spent considerable time in a Third Ward attic searching for a suitable dress while Gavin washed up. She chose an afternoon dress of deep gold silk—and found she didn't like wearing it. No matter how carefully Kemp and her little automatons altered the garment, the restrictive corset and annoying skirts got in the way. But she was calling on the Chinese ambassador, and she could hardly do so in trousers. At first, she chafed at having to follow the rules so shortly after being freed from them, but then she realized the dress was a disguise for a secret agent, which made her feel better.

Gavin's coat and trousers allowed him freedom of movement and made much more sense. He certainly cut a dashing figure, with his powerful build, startling blue eyes, and white-blond hair. He dressed like a gentleman, but moved like a rake, and she saw envious glances from passing women as he offered her his arm outside the carriage to escort her indoors.

The concierge met them inside the lobby doors. Gavin

showed him a silver badge. "We're looking for the Chinese ambassador," he said. "Crown business."

Sometime later, they were ascending in a tiny lift, and Alice was examining a handwritten card the concierge had given them.

"*His Honor Jun Lung, room 310,*" she read. "You'd think he'd have more names than that. What do you know about China?"

"Nothing," Gavin admitted as the lift stopped.

Alice knocked at the appropriate door, and it was opened by a young man in a long blue coat, which was heavily embroidered and had wide sleeves. His black hair was pulled back and plaited in a braid that hung down his back. Gavin showed the badge again and gave their names.

"We need to see His Honor, the Ambassador Jun Lung," he said.

"Sorry. His Honor see no one." The servant's English was heavily accented.

"It's Crown business," Alice said.

The servant bowed. "Sorry. His Honor see no one." And he shut the door.

Alice and Gavin looked at each other, dumbfounded. "That frankly didn't occur to me," Alice said. "Now what? Break the door down?"

"I don't think that would put His Honor in a good mood. Maybe if we left him a note?"

"How do we know he'd read it?" Alice said. "A telegram might—"

The clatter of the lift interrupted them. From the cage emerged another Chinese servant, also in a blue coat. He was pushing a cart with covered dishes on it. Exotic smells wafted from them, and Alice wondered if the ambassador had his own private chef in the hotel kitchen.

"Here's an idea," Gavin muttered. He put a hand in his pocket and approached the man. "I wonder if you could help me, sir. I need to talk to the ambassador." He took his hand from his pocket, and Alice caught a flash of silver. Something dropped to the carpeted floor as Gavin laid a heavy coin on the linen-covered cart. The servant flicked the coin away as if it were an insect and kept going, his expression wooden. Then he jerked the cart to a halt, leaned down, and scooped the fallen object from the floor.

"Where you get this?" His eyes were wide.

"That's mine," Gavin said sharply. "Give it back now."

"Where?" the man repeated.

"It was a present from a friend. Give it back, or I will hit you. Very hard."

The servant dropped it into Gavin's palm and bowed twice. "You come with me, please. Please, you come now." Abandoning the cart, he opened the hotel room door and ushered them inside.

Alice was half expecting the rooms to be decorated in Oriental fashion, with carved dragons and Oriental wall hangings, and silk everywhere. Instead, she found a set of lavish hotel rooms, with generous furniture, thick carpets, large windows, and a marble fireplace. A middle-aged man sat in an armchair with his back to the door, a book in his lap. The servant scurried over to him and bowed, leaving his head down until the man acknowledged his presence with a word. They exchanged several sentences in Chinese before the servant returned.

"His Honor see you now." He brought Alice and Gavin over to the sitting area, and the man rose to his feet. He wore a long, gold-bordered scarlet robe, which was embroidered with dozens of designs. A wide, round cloth hat covered his head, even though he was indoors, and his angular face was clean-shaven. Alice floundered. Should she bow? Offer her hand? Her schooling in etiquette had covered what to do when meeting everything from a priest to a baronet to the Queen herself, but not a dignitary from the Chinese Empire. Gavin looked equally perplexed.

The ambassador solved the problem for them by offering his hand first to Alice and then to Gavin. "I am Jun Lung, nephew of the Guanxu Emperor and ambassador to England."

"Alice, Baroness Michaels, daughter of Arthur, Baron Michaels," Alice said.

"Gavin Ennock, agent of the Third Ward," Gavin said.

"And a friend," Jun added. "Please, sit. My servants will bring food."

Before Alice had time to wonder at the *friend* remark, a servant settled her on a chair and Gavin on a sofa, then quickly set small tables near their elbows while another servant, the one who had brought them inside, trundled the cart up and uncovered the food trays. Three mechanical spiders leapt out from under the cart and climbed to the table. They scooped food onto plates, which they rushed to set on the little tables. But instead of simply leaving the plates there, each spider captured a bit of food between two tendrils. Before Alice could react, "her" spider climbed up her arm, perched on her shoulder, and poked the food at her. She was so startled, she opened her mouth to protest. The spider dropped the morsel neatly between her lips and scuttled down her arm for more. Gavin and Jun received their food in the same way. Jun watched them both for their reaction. Gavin was working to hide his surprise, and Alice quickly schooled herself into an expression of nonchalance. One didn't remark on food or how it was served. It was, though, quite delicious and a bit spicy, with ginger in it.

Jun started with small talk, asking Alice about her family, and then Gavin about his, and she felt compelled to do the same for Jun. She kept a practiced expression of politeness on her face, though inside, beneath the dress, she was prowling like a tiger, wanting to pounce on obvious questions. Jun, however, refused to come to the point. Alice quickly sensed she was in a game, one whose rules she knew well— the first to bring up the real subject would have to tell everything. Gavin started to interject, but Alice caught his eye and gave a slight shake of her head to stop him, and all the while the spiders popped food into their mouths.

"What *do* the ladies at the Chinese Imperial court wear, my lord?" she asked. "I must have every detail."

And when he started to answer, Alice pinned him down further, asking for finer and finer detail. "What color of fan? What shade of scarlet? Do the shoes match the gown or the embroidery?"

Gavin was squirming, and the food plates were empty when Jun Lung finally let out a soft sigh and said, "It is a pleasure to talk to you, Lady Michaels."

"But I must hear more!"

Jun held up a hand, and Alice knew she had won. "I have heard that you, Mr. Ennock, have come into possession of a small object of interest."

"I have," Gavin said with relief.

"May I see it?"

Gavin held up the silver nightingale, and Ambassador Lung let out another sigh. "That is indeed the object."

"What do you mean?" Gavin asked.

At that moment, the front door opened, and into the room strode a Chinese boy of perhaps seventeen, though he was dressed in an ordinary shirt and trousers. Gavin leapt to his feet. "My God!"

"You!" The boy ran over and shook Gavin's hand in both of his. "It is you!"

Alice blinked, bewildered. "What's going on?"

"He saved my life," the boy said. "He saved me!"

"Where have *you* been?" Jun asked sharply, then dropped into Chinese. The boy responded in kind, alternating between looking abashed and stubborn. Jun was clearly struggling to keep his temper under control in front of guests.

"This is Feng Lung, my son," Jun said finally. "And that nightingale he gave you was built by my grandfather, who was one of the Dragon Men."

"Dragon Men?" Alice asked.

"Your empire calls them clockworkers."

"You are unhappy that I gave him the nightingale, Father, but I would be a memory for your sorrow instead of a target for your anger if not for him," Feng said.

"What *are* you talking about?" Alice said.

"It happened in Hyde Park," Gavin began.

"Of course it did."

As Gavin told the story of how he hid a young Oriental man from his pursuers, Alice's eyes went wider and wider.

"I was in the park that day," she said breathlessly. "I heard your music, the most beautiful music since God created the earth, and then I heard the shot. I thought I must have been hearing things."

Feng added, "I gave my brave friend the nightingale as a token to one who saved me with his music. And now he can copy his music whenever he wishes."

"Copy?" Gavin said.

Now Feng looked surprised. He dropped to the sofa next to Gavin. "Haven't you seen? If you press the left eye, the bird listens to sounds until you press that eye again. If you press the right eye, it sings the sounds for you."

Astounded, Gavin held the bird up. Feng pressed the left eye. "Good morning," Gavin said, then pressed the right eye.

"Good morning," the bird said in Gavin's voice.

Gavin gaped. "Is that what I sound like?" he said.

"It's wonderful!" Alice said. "A true treasure."

"Yes." Jun stroked his chin. "But now you must tell me why you came here. I thought it was about the nightingale."

Alice shook her head. "It's about the clockwork plague and clockworkers."

"Ah. Did the Queen send you?"

"What? No!" Alice said. "The Queen has no idea we're—"

"I wouldn't be so sure of that," Jun interrupted. "She's a well-informed woman, and I'm surprised she allows your country to treat Dragon Men—clockworkers—with such deplorable disdain."

"What do you mean?" Gavin asked.

"You Englishmen shun clockworkers as if they carry disease," Feng put in. "In my country, Dragon Men are revered. We gather them up and give them workshops and money and status so they can create their wonderful inventions. A Dragon Man brings any family great honor."

"And what about Dragon Women?" Alice asked.

"They are all Dragon Men," Jun said, "whether they are male or female. Though I suppose China should not complain about the way Britain treats its clockworkers. The balance of power between our empires, as I'm sure you know, is delicate. The British Empire controls the oceans and most of the air, and it has colonies everywhere. The Chinese Empire does not expand its borders, but it does control the tea, silk, and porcelain trades. Europe and the Ukrainian Empire separate us, so we don't come into direct conflict, but the . . . tension is still there."

"Especially over opium," Feng said.

Jun shot him a hard look. "At any rate, our empires are locked in a continual game of má què. Do you know the game?"

"I've only recently learned of it," Alice said.

"It's the best game in the world," Feng said. "Father and I play against the Queen and the Prince Consort all the time. We let them win when Father wants something."

"Does it work?" Gavin asked.

Feng nodded. "Usually."

"What does má què have to do with clockworkers?" Alice interjected.

Jun said, "The players draw ivory tiles of varying value and power, which they meld until a winner becomes clear. The Dragon Men and clockworkers are powerful, random tiles in our little game. They appear when they wish, helping out one player and then the other, but they balance out both sides in the long run."

The world swirled dizzily for a moment. The solution hung there in front of Alice like ripe fruit, and she *knew*.

"Balance out," she echoed. "Good heavens. Dear Lord. Ambassador, thank you for seeing us, but we have to go."

"What?" Feng said. "I want to know my friend better."

"Later." Alice was already on her feet, which forced the men to rise. "Gavin, we have to leave. Now."

Jun Lung caught Gavin's arm. "My son may have repaid you the favor you did, but I have not. Honor still binds me to you, and I hope to see you again, young sir."

With that, they left. Down in the lobby, Gavin turned to Alice. "What was that all about?"

"I understand what's happening with Aunt Edwina and Lieutenant Phipps," she said. "And I want a damned stiff drink before I tell you about it."

A bit later, they were sitting at a corner table in a pub. Gavin had a Guinness at his elbow, and Alice had a very bad glass of wine. She gulped it down without tasting it, and her hands were shaking as she signaled for another.

"Tell me," Gavin said worriedly, "before you get too drunk to talk."

"It's all about balance." Alice leaned across the table, hardly able to believe she was saying these words, but knowing they were true nonetheless. "The Third Ward wants to lock Edwina up because the Crown wants to make sure her cure never, ever gets used."

"What?" Gavin folded his arms. "That's ridiculous."

"Is it? Ambassador Lung reminded us how delicate the balance is between China and England. Little conflicts flare up between us, but never quite escalate into an all-out war. We both trade. We make and break treaties. We negotiate. Why? Because both sides collect clockworkers who build little toys. *Both sides have the same technological advantage.* What would happen if England released Aunt Edwina's cure?"

"Countless plague victims would recover?"

"Unimportant," Alice said, "from the British Empire's point of view. The plague would stop creating clockworkers. Once the current ones went mad and died, we'd have none. An end to clockworkers means an end to world-bending inventions for England, and *that* means China would become the most powerful empire in the world."

"The cure would get to China," Gavin countered. "Their clockworker supply would dry up, too."

"The cure would take quite a while to spread to China," Alice said. "Months, even years. That's all it would take for China to pull ahead, potentially forever. The Crown won't risk that. So they're suppressing Aunt Edwina's cure."

"And condemning thousands to a slow, terrible death," Gavin finished softly. His Guinness remained untouched. "That's terrible."

"Do you believe it?" Alice half hoped he would say she was mad, that he would find some flaw in her theory to prove it wrong, but he only rubbed his palms over his face and sighed.

"I believe it completely."

Alice felt proud of her deduction and absolutely wretched about it at the same time. Gavin reached across the table and took her hand. The gesture made her feel slightly better.

The pub door opened, and Feng slipped in. Ignoring the stares of the other patrons, he dropped into a chair next to Gavin and signaled for a drink. "Found you," he said in his uneven English. "I will not lose you again."

Gavin shifted uncomfortably. "Look, I don't know what you want from me, Feng, but I'm not—"

"I have no friends here," Feng blurted out. "Everyone looks at me; they see a Chinese man. They see a curiosity.

They see a son of the ambassador, grandnephew of the emperor. My father wants me to learn diplomacy, and I try and try, but I'm no damned good at it. If I sneak out to do something fun, it gets me into trouble."

"By fun, you mean women?" Gavin said shrewdly.

"Many times," Feng replied with an unabashed grin. "They think Chinese boys will show them something different. They say there are many things English boys will not do."

"Mr. Lung!" Alice said. "Perhaps this is a conversation you and Mr. Ennock could finish later."

"You see?" Feng said. "This is why I am a bad diplomat."

"Your English is very good," Gavin said kindly.

"I gave you the nightingale because it is meant to carry messages to secret lovers," Feng told him.

"Now look—"

"No, no." Feng laughed. "Boys like you do not please me."

"But others boys do?" Alice couldn't help asking.

"Why not?" He leaned forward. "Have you ever tried them, Gavin?"

"No!"

"Then how do you know—"

"Mr. Lung," Alice put in, "what is your point?"

"The nightingale remembers who held it last and will fly to that person. You can put your voice in it and let it fly away. Then it will return with another message. We can use it to communicate, too, as friends. I had no chance to explain it to you, but I hoped you would figure it out." His Guinness arrived, and he drained it quickly. "I should go, before Father becomes angry again. Good-bye, my friends."

And he was gone.

Chapter Eighteen

"It is finished!" Dr. Clef pushed his goggles onto his high forehead and gave Gavin a wide smile. One of his eye-teeth was missing. "Can you believe? The most difficult thing I have ever created!"

Gavin put out a finger to touch the cube on Dr. Clef's worktable. The cube was the size of a shoebox and made of a frame of thin beams. And it *twisted*. The edges crossed one another in impossible ways, with the front going behind the back, or the back coming before the front. It made Gavin dizzy. When his hand approached it, his fingers seemed suddenly too far away. He pulled back.

"What does it do?" Gavin asked.

"Turn the crank on the generator and you will see," Dr. Clef replied. "Or perhaps I should say you will *hear*."

Gavin turned the crank. Electricity crackled at the spot where the Impossible Cube was connected to the wire. The cube glowed blue and drifted slowly upward. Gavin thought of his new airship. He hadn't tested it in open sky yet.

Dr. Clef picked up a tuning fork from a set on the table and tapped it. A clear tone—G, Gavin noted—rang out. Dr. Clef pressed the base of the fork against one side of the cube. The note roared into full volume, but it was more than just an auditory note. It went straight through Gavin's body, through muscle and bone and into his soul. For a moment he felt as if he had no corporeal self. He had fallen into dust and scattered over the entire universe. Then the note ended, and he was standing in the workroom again. He stopped cranking, and the cube sat inert, though it continued to twist the eye.

"What the hell was that?" he gasped.

"Very interesting," Dr. Clef observed. "Try this one." He struck another fork—D-sharp—and before Gavin could stop him, he pressed the base against one side of the cube and cranked the handle himself. A cone of sound blasted from the prongs of the fork and gouged out a section of stone wall. Chunks of rock crashed to the floor.

"I like that one," Dr. Clef said. "How about this one?"

"Stop it!" Gavin shouted, but Dr. Clef struck an A-flat and pressed it to the cube.

With a *pop*, the cube vanished. It left behind a severed electrical wire.

"*Nicht!*" Dr. Clef exclaimed.

The workroom door banged open, and Lieutenant Phipps rushed in with two agents behind her. It was the first time he had seen her since the Ward had captured Edwina several days ago. "What the hell was that?" she demanded. "I think everyone within a mile felt it."

"Which one?" Gavin said. "The soul sound or the explosion?"

"I'm not in the mood for jokes, Agent Ennock. Doctor Clef? What happened?"

Dr. Clef's wide blue eyes were filling with tears. "My cube! He is gone! Months of work, gone!"

"It's true," Gavin said. "It vanished. Right after it did that to the wall."

"Huh. Maybe it's for the best, then." She turned to leave, along with the agents. Gavin ran to catch up with her.

"Lieutenant," he said, "I wanted to ask you—"

"If it's about your supposedly secret airship, Agent Ennock, you know we encourage our agents to—"

"No." He shook his head as the other agents withdrew and Dr. Clef continued to sob over his worktable. "Nothing like that. I wanted to ask about the clockwork plague. Edwina claimed to have a cure, and—"

"That's enough, Agent Ennock."

"But—"

"Shut it, boy!" she snapped. Then she closed her eyes for a moment with a sigh and put her metal hand on his shoulder, the most human gesture he had ever seen her make. "Listen, Gavin, I know a cure is important to Alice, which makes it important to you. But I've interviewed Edwina extensively and have personally gone through all her research. She's completely mad. There is no cure and never has been. And we can't afford to start rumors of one. You can imagine how the public would react."

Gavin nodded, aware of the weight of her hand on him.

"Good. Don't speak of this with anyone." She straightened and dropped her hand. "Get Doctor Clef calmed down and help him clean up."

"I *am* on holiday, Lieutenant," Gavin said. "I just came down here to check on Doctor Clef."

"There's no such thing as a holiday in the clockworker holding area, Agent Ennock."

When she was gone, Gavin went back to the table, where Dr. Clef remained dissolved in tears. "Months and months of time," he sobbed. "Time flowing like water out of a basket made of gravity. The gravity of my life is pulling me into a sinkhole and warping my space until I can't escape."

Uh-oh. He was moving into a bad phase. He'd be worthless for several days. He'd certainly be unable to help clean up. Gavin picked up the A-flat tuning fork with a sigh and accidently smacked it against the table. The moment the note rang out, the Impossible Cube reappeared on the table with another *pop*.

Gavin jumped, and Dr. Clef instantly snapped to himself. "Wonderful! I should have thought of this myself!"

"Where did it come from?" Gavin asked. His heart was pounding.

"Time, I think," Dr. Clef told him. "The cube is truly unique, you know. Do you remember when Viktor von Rasmussen found a way to bring his parallel selves from other universes into this one?"

"I heard about it," Gavin said, "but that was before my time at the Ward."

"He is dead now. But he started *me* thinking. I built the cube to be absolutely unique. It actually exists in all the other universes, you see, but they are all the same cube. This gives it many strange properties."

"That's impossible."

"Yes. When you give the cube different energies, it changes them. I think that one"—he gestured at the A-flat tuning fork—"has something to do with time. The cube can't travel through time, you see. The cube can't travel at all. I think what happened was that the entire universe—all the universes—moved backward and left the cube in the same place. When you struck the fork again, the cube matched itself to the vibration and pulled the universes back to where they should be, but since we are *in* the universes, it appeared to us that the cube moved, when actually we did."

"That's im— That's not poss— That . . . makes my head hurt."

Dr. Clef waved a hand. "So, so. This is my masterpiece! A wonderful thing, yes?"

"Yes. I mean, I think so." Gavin felt off-kilter, and looking at the Impossible Cube didn't help. "Doctor Clef, you stay here and I'll be back."

"Yes, yes." He waved a hand. "I have more tests."

Gavin locked the workshop door carefully behind him and dashed down the stone hallway and past the extra-heavy door where Edwina was being kept. Her door had three powerful locks on it, and Gavin didn't have any of the keys. Only Lieutenant Phipps ever went in, even with food. He also passed the Doomsday Vault with its four guards, and, deciding not to wait for the lift, hurried up the spiral stairs to the office of Susan Phipps.

"I'm going out, ma'am," he said, poking his head inside, "since I'm still on holiday. But you'll want to check on Doctor Clef again. He found his cube."

"Did he?" Phipps got to her feet behind her desk. "And what does it—"

There was a muffled *boom*. All the lights, including the oil lamps, went out. Shouts went up all over the house. Phipps made an exasperated sound.

"I never liked that thing," she said, fumbling in the dim moonlight for matches. "I think we'll have to put it into the Doomsday Vault first thing in the—ouch!"

"What's wrong?"

"The lamp is still lit. It's just not giving off any light."

"I don't even want to know how that works," Gavin said. "Do you need me? Alice rented a new house with her bonus, and I'm supposed to help her . . . uh . . ."

"Go, go." The lights abruptly came back up. More shouts from the halls and rooms. "But I want you on hand in the morning when we put that thing in the vault. An hour before sunrise. You know the ceremony."

"Ma'am." He fled before she could change her mind.

Alice met him at the front door with a kiss. "You're just in time," she said.

"For what?" He couldn't help smiling.

"For moving furniture. It's too heavy for me, and Kemp is cranky."

This row house was small but newer—well built and free of drafts. The living room had a fireplace and the kitchen had a good stove, which meant the place stayed warm. A sofa, chair, divan, and several end tables were scattered about the front room. Click perched on the back of the sofa, and Kemp was in the kitchen with tea things. Little automatons crawled, whirred, and scampered everywhere, like autumn leaves at play.

"I like this place," Gavin said. "It's very much you."

"I suppose I should hire a maid-of-all-work," Alice said, "but I think it would make Kemp unhappy, and the little ones sometimes get nervous around too many people." She spread her arms. "It's *freeing* to be here, Gavin. I'm renting it with money I earned myself, and that means I can *be* myself. Whyever do you stay in those tiny rooms at the Ward?"

"Most of my money has gone toward the ship, and my family," he said. "But I'm glad you found this place. It's more private."

"That it is." She slid her arms around him, and his heart jumped. "No one to interrupt us here."

"Tea?" Kemp said, entering with the tray. Click chose that moment to leap at one of the flying automatons. It squeaked and shot higher. The clockwork cat missed and crash-landed on one of the tables, which tipped over and spilled him onto the floor. He scrabbled madly at the boards and rushed indignantly out of the room.

"No interruptions?" Gavin grinned.

"Have some tea," Alice said, plucking a cup from the tray.

"Darling? Can you hear me?"

Gavin jumped. Alice dropped the cup and it shattered on the wood floor. It was Edwina's voice, and it was coming from Kemp. The automaton stood completely frozen, still holding the tea tray.

"Hello?" Kemp said, speaking as Edwina. "Alice, are you there?"

"Wha-what?" Alice said. "Aunt Edwina?"

"Oh, good. It works. Listen, darling, I don't have much time, so listen quickly."

"What's going on?" Alice demanded. "Where are you? You're not going to attack another airship, are you?"

"Not to worry, darling. I'm in my cell at the Third Ward. They call it a workroom or a laboratory, but it's a cell, nonetheless. I've been pretending my grip on reality has slipped, but they still give me equipment to play with and I cobbled together this transmitter. Did you talk to the ambassador as I told you?"

"You didn't tell me to do anything, but yes," Alice said, recovering herself. "We figured out what you meant."

"Then you know about the cure and why the Crown wants to suppress it. I realized this would happen, you know, which is why I set everything up the way I did."

"What do you mean by that?" Gavin asked.

"Mr. Ennock is there? Good! This will make things simpler. Have you joined the Third Ward, Alice?"

"Yes," Alice said slowly. "I'm in training, but I'm in."

"Excellent!" Edwina sounded relieved. "I haven't told you everything yet, so I need you to listen closely now. The clockwork plague is destroying the entire world, and not only by disease. One day, a clockworker will make something powerful enough to wipe out all life on Earth. This plague *must* end. Now."

Gavin's thoughts went to the Impossible Cube, and he glanced at Alice. Her face was white. He reached for her hand, but she shook it off.

"The Ward has my first cure, the one that works on one person at a time. They put it in the Doomsday Vault. They're still looking for my second cure, the one that spreads."

"You said it was incubating," Alice interrupted.

"It is. They can't find it because I put it in the one place they'd never look."

"I'll ask," Gavin said with a sigh. "Where?"

"Inside me."

Alice's expression became incredulous. "Inside you?"

"There are places even the Ward can't search, darling.

Now that I have proper facilities again, I can finish incubating it. In fact, it will be done by morning. That's where you two come in."

"I don't understand," Gavin said.

"Both cures must be released. That's why I arranged for the two of you to join the Third Ward. Once I was able to use the Ward's facilities to finish the cure—"

"You would need someone to break you out," Alice finished. "No."

"Darling, you must. The Ward will never let this cure go. You need to break me out of this dungeon, and you need to steal the first cure from the Doomsday Vault."

"Edwina, you've gone mad," Alice protested.

"No. I'm quite sane, though I may not last much longer once the Ward realizes what I'm doing. It's damned hard to work with someone watching. They think I'm growing blue roses. I'm actually quite close, come to that."

"Do you mean all this talk about making me independent was nothing more than a ruse to get me into the Ward so I could eventually break *you* out of it?" Alice cried indignantly. "I'm not a chess piece on a board, Edwina! I'm not a dog to jump when you say so."

"And anyway," Gavin put in, "security is very tight. We couldn't get you out, let alone break into the Doomsday Vault."

"I was afraid you might react this way, darling." Edwina's voice was tight. "That's the real reason I brought Gavin into your life and maneuvered you into falling in love."

Alice gasped, and Gavin's blood went cold. "What do you mean?" he said quietly.

"When I had Gavin asleep in my tower," Edwina continued, "I injected him with the clockwork plague."

Gavin's knees buckled. The room rocked, and he went to the floor with his head between his knees. There had been a bandage around his upper arm when he woke up in the tower of the Red Velvet Lady. At the time, he had been mystified by it. Now he knew what it was for, and he wished he hadn't. His gorge rose, and he threw up on the floorboards between his ankles.

"You're bluffing," Alice said desperately. "It's a lie. He'd be dead by now if it were true."

"No, darling. It was my own recipe, the slowed version, but he does have it. At least he's not contagious yet."

"No," Alice whispered.

"There's good news. You can cure him long before he becomes one of those unfortunates who lurch through alleyways. Just get me out of the Third Ward and break into the Doomsday Vault. And you'd better hurry."

The lights in Kemp's eyes flickered out, then came back on. He turned his head left, then right. "Oh! Oh dear! Did I switch off? Sir! Do you require assistance?"

Gavin stared at the stinking puddle of vomit. The revelation crushed him to the floor, and his back ached anew. A small sore on the back of his hand caught his eye. Was it a plague sore? In a few weeks, he would join the souls shambling through the shadows, hoping someone would throw him an apple.

"I won't let this happen again, Gavin." Alice was kneeling beside him with her arms around his shoulders. Several of her little automatons perched on her shoulders. "I won't. We'll find a way into the Vault, and we'll get Aunt Edwina out so we can cure you. I don't care how impossible it is."

Gavin brought his head up. "I know how to do it."

Moments later, Gavin was sketching madly on a sheet of foolscap at Alice's new kitchen table with Alice leaning over him. Kemp had been banished to Alice's bedroom, however unfairly, and Click perched on the coal stove, heedless of the heat it put out. Several of the little automatons were lined up above the cupboards. Alice kept a continual hand on Gavin's arm or his shoulder or his head, as if he might float away and her touch would keep his feet touching the floor. Thank God he wasn't contagious yet. She couldn't bear the thought of not touching him.

A number of feelings battled inside her—fury at Aunt Edwina for doing this to Gavin and to her, guilt over her role in the entire affair, fear of what was going to happen next, and through it all, a growing and powerful love for Gavin. When he was nearby, she felt his presence, and when he was gone, she felt his absence. When he laughed, she was happy, and when he was upset, she wanted to tear London in two. And right now, she felt ready to destroy the world for him.

"Doctor Clef is the key," he said. "He finished his Impossible Cube earlier today, and Lieutenant Phipps said it has to go into the Doomsday Vault."

"So they'll have to open it," Alice breathed.

"Yes. There's a little ceremony surrounding any invention that goes in. An hour before sunrise, all the clockworkers are locked in their rooms, and the available agents stand honor guard in two lines—like this—while Lieutenant Phipps marches between them. She takes the invention to the Doomsday Vault, which is here. The guards open it, and she puts it inside. Then everyone has a breakfast of kippers and eggs and beer, including the clockworker who invented the device. If he's gone completely insane, he sits at the table in a straitjacket."

"So we somehow sneak in when the Vault opens and hide inside until they all leave?"

Gavin shook his head. "No. The Vault would close on us and we'd be trapped. There's only one way to do it." He put his pencil down and exhaled, long and slow. "Alice, if we go through with this, it'll be a crime against the British Crown. I'll be branded an American spy, and you'll be a traitor. Are you willing?"

And she hesitated. He was right. She tried to set aside thoughts of Gavin and to think of the situation clearly, as would an automaton. This plan went beyond merely breaking a few societal rules. This plan was outright treason. The sentence for that was transportation to Australia at best, hanging at worst, and her title wouldn't protect her. The plan, if it worked, would topple the British Empire and change the course of history for thousands, millions of people. Did she, the daughter of an unimportant, impoverished baron, have the right to make that choice?

Did the Third Ward have the right? They had a vested interest in keeping the status quo. Without clockworkers, the Third Ward had no reason to exist. On the other hand, they were more informed, more aware of the wide world. They knew what was proper.

Alice opened her mouth to answer Gavin just as a brick crashed through the front window and tumbled across the floor. Both Alice and Gavin started, then rushed to the broken frame to peer outside. Norbert Williamson swayed on the sidewalk, just visible in the yellow lamplight. He held a bottle. On the street stood his mechanical carriage.

"You thought you could hide from me, you bloody bitch?" Norbert yelled. "You owe me a child and a title!"

A pang went through Alice's stomach. "Oh God."

"I'll take care of him," Gavin said with clenched teeth.

"No." Alice laid a hand on his arm. "I will." And before he could protest, she was out the door.

"There you are, you whore," Norbert growled. He gulped from the bottle. "Did you enjoy fucking him?"

"Not nearly as much as you enjoyed watching your friends use those machines, you may be sure," Alice replied primly.

Norbert didn't seem to notice the dig. "You're coming home with me. I'll teach you manners and lock you up long enough to make sure the boy didn't pollute you with his spawn."

A crowd was gathering. People opened windows and peered out doors. Alice became aware of every pair of eyes, every judgmental look, every knowing nod. The carriage stood in front of her. It would be so easy to bow her head and climb into it, ride smoothly away from all these unfair, world-shaking decisions, these choices she had never asked to make. All she had ever wanted was a quiet life with a quiet husband.

But that was a lie, too, wasn't it? It was a lie she told herself. She'd been telling herself she wanted these traditional things . . . and why? Because it was her fault the clockwork plague had torn through her family, killed her mother and brother, crippled her father, and wanting traditional things would set everything aright. Except Father was dead, and now the person she loved carried the plague. The tradition, the lie, would cause Gavin's death, and the deaths of thousands more.

"No," Alice whispered.

"What?" Norbert growled.

Alice straightened, standing tall before the neighbors who came to stare. Gavin stood in the doorway. "I said *no*. I am Alice, Baroness Michaels. I am *not* going back with you, Norbert Williamson. I love Gavin and always have. Go back home to your factory and your money and your filthy machines. I hope they rip your cock off."

Norbert flung himself at Alice. Gavin shouted a warning from the front steps, but Alice saw him coming. She stepped aside and gave him a shove that carried him straight into the wall of the house. He smashed into the bricks and staggered backward, dazed and with a bloody nose. Gavin hoisted him by belt and scruff and flung him into the carriage. Alice smacked the emergency switch for home, and the carriage rushed away.

Alice found herself in Gavin's arms. He tipped her chin back and kissed her, right there on the street in front of the little crowd. His embrace was solid as an oak tree, and the kiss electric as a lightning bolt. She gave herself up to it, and to him.

"I do love you," he whispered.

"And I love you," she said.

A smattering of applause broke out, then grew louder. Alice broke away from Gavin. The crowd clapped and cheered. "Great job, love!" someone shouted. "You showed him!" "Wish I had your courage!"

Laughing, she dashed back into the house with Gavin close on her. With the door shut, he kissed her again and pressed his body against hers. She felt his urgent hardness, and her own body responded. "I've never wanted you more than I do now," he whispered.

"We don't have time," she replied with regret. "It's only a few hours until sunrise, and we have to break into the Doomsday Vault."

Chapter Nineteen

Lieutenant Phipps marched past Gavin with the glowing Impossible Cube. As the most junior agent of the Third Ward, he was at the far end of the double line of agents lining the corridor, the end farthest from the Doomsday Vault. Another agent played a military drum. Every beat snapped to Phipps's footsteps. Each agent, and there were nearly twenty, wore a dress uniform of black linen with red trim. Several sported body machinery similar to Phipps's, and all of them, even Simon and Glenda, carried side arms. Alice, who was still in training and not yet technically an agent, was nowhere to be seen, but Gavin knew she was hiding halfway up the stone spiral staircase that led back up to the main floor.

Phipps reached the head of the double line, and the drum stopped. The four agents who guarded the round, two-story door to the Doomsday Vault saluted Phipps and turned to the Vault controls. Each guard knew only one sequence of instructions for opening the Vault, to ensure that no one person could open it alone. The first guard spun a large wheel that reminded Gavin of an airship helm, then spun it backward, then forward. The second guard spoke rapidly into a speaking tube. The third guard turned a series of dials set into the door. The fourth guard took a card from his pocket, punched a series of holes in it with an awl, and fed the card into a slot. A moment of silence followed. Gavin held his breath. With a dull booming sound, the great door swung outward.

Lights inside the Vault flickered to life, revealing a wide, long tunnel lined with shelves. Strange objects, some of them moving, occupied the spaces. Gavin couldn't see into the Vault very well from his vantage point, but he didn't need to. He pulled from his pocket a small object of his own: two glass bulbs connected by a third, like an hourglass with a slight bulge in the middle. The top bulb held water. The small middle bulb held a cube of sugar. The lower bulb held a clear green fluid. Gavin twisted a small brass lever on the side of the device, and the water in the top bulb rushed down over the sugar cube and into the absinthe in the lower bulb just as Phipps entered the Doomsday Vault. The absinthe in the lower bulb bubbled and changed to a milky green.

"What are you doing?" hissed Donaldson, the agent next to him. "Put that away!"

Gavin flipped the glass lid off the device and forced himself to drink, grimacing at the cloying taste of anise. By now, some of the others had noticed. They stared, uncertain what to do about this flagrant breach of protocol. Before they could make up their minds, a fluttering sound came from the stairwell, and a little automaton emerged into the hall, its propeller whirling madly. It held a red ball of the type Gavin had cautioned Alice not to drop in the weapons vault.

"Sorry, everyone!" Gavin shouted.

Phipps, still holding the Impossible Cube, spun in surprise just as the automaton dropped the ball on the stone floor. Pink pollen burst into the air and formed a sweet, choking cloud. The agents staggered as if drunk. Several dropped to the ground.

Gavin was already moving, the taste of absinthe still in his mouth. He sprinted toward the Doomsday Vault and caught Lieutenant Phipps as she slid to the floor. The Impossible Cube had already fallen at her feet. It glowed like a piece of broken sky.

"Wha—?" Phipps said.

"Sorry about this, Lieutenant," he said again. "I really am."

"Why?" Her eyelid flickered. "Why . . . Gavin?"

Gavin hung his head in guilt. Phipps had turned a disgraced cabin boy into a full-fledged agent, and now he had betrayed her.

Alice rushed down the stairs, her lips smeared green. Click and Kemp followed behind her, and the little automaton fluttered down to land on her shoulder. "We have to hurry. You said the pollen wouldn't last more than an hour."

"Alice . . . of course . . . ," Phipps slurred. "You want . . . the cure . . . wreck . . . world."

"It needs to be wrecked," Alice said, "so it can heal. Kemp, Click—you two wait out here. If Lieutenant Phipps wakes up, hit her on the head."

"Yes, Madam."

Gavin snatched up the Impossible Cube. Dr. Clef had charged it, and no one had wanted to drain the charge before the ceremony. It felt springy, as if made of pine boughs. Together he and Alice hurried into the open Doomsday Vault.

The long room inside was crowded with inventions, some on shelves and some on the floor. Some were easily recognizable as dangerous: a bomb the size of a sofa; a glass vial filled with black liquid and marked DEATH; an enormous energy rifle pointed at the ceiling. Others were a mystery: a single automaton with no features; a trumpet; a thick book; five live hamsters in a cage with no food or water. Each object had a small placard in front of it with a name and year. The very first one, closest to the door, was a large iron ball with spikes. The faded placard read RICHARD W., 1829. A chill ran down Gavin's spine.

"Incredible," Gavin breathed. "The power in this room could destroy the world a hundred times, and we walk around above it, living normal lives."

"Our lives are far from normal," Alice said tersely. "We need to find the cure and get out."

They followed the tunnel to the back, where the placards were fresher. The line of inventions stopped, though the Vault itself continued for some distance.

"The Ward means to continue collecting these dreadful things," Alice said. "Look!"

She picked up a largish spider made of polished black metal. Several tubules ran up and down the spider's legs. The placard read EDWINA M., 1858.

"That's the cure?" Gavin said dubiously.

"It's the only Edwina invention in here." Alice snatched it up. "We don't have time for doubt. Let's go!"

They hurried back to the entrance of the Vault, each of them carrying a doomsday device. Gavin's heart beat fast, and his hands tightened around the Impossible Cube. Every move he made changed history, altered millions of lives, and that responsibility frightened him even more than the possibility of being caught and hanged. Maybe this was how Queen Victoria and President Pierce felt all the time.

"Shall I carry that for Madam?" Kemp asked.

"Thank you, no," Alice said, clutching the spider to her chest. "Click! Hurry!"

The five of them, counting the little automaton that still sat on Alice's shoulder, dashed past the sleeping agents down the hall where the clockworkers were locked in their laboratories, and found Edwina's door. Gavin stared at the heavy wood for a moment, surprised at the amount of loathing he felt. Behind that door was the woman who had kidnapped him and infected him with the clockwork plague. He'd been trying not to think about that, to concentrate on the mission; however, now faced with setting her free, he felt disgust and hatred boiling black inside him.

"What are you waiting for?" Alice hissed. "Hurry!"

Gavin clenched his teeth. "She's a monster."

"Oh, Gavin!" Alice put a hand on his arm. "Gavin, I know it's hard."

"You have no idea, Alice. To her, I'm a windup music box, an automaton who'll obey orders. She trapped me in this horrible, filthy city, and now she's dragged me underground and is forcing me to set her free."

Kemp made a coughing sound.

"I know, Gavin," Alice said. "What she did is unforgivable. But you can move on. You're bright and merry and you soar. Your hatred won't change her, or what she did. Don't give her the power to chain you down and ruin you."

Gavin faced her. Every muscle in his back ached, and the cube grew heavy. His throat thickened. "I don't know what to do, Alice. I hate this world. I hate the people in it. A man named Madoc Blue tried to do unspeakable things to me and I killed him. His blood was still on my hands when the first mate ripped my back to shreds. And then the Red Velvet Lady summoned me like a sorceress with a spell and locked me in her round tower so I would do her bidding. She's the figurehead of all the horrible things that have happened to me. To my *world*. I've fallen so far, Alice, and I just want to fly again, be free of all these horrible people."

"Free from me, Gavin?" Her arms went around him, and she kissed him. The warmth of her body went through him, and he closed his eyes, soaking in her presence. Thank God he wasn't contagious yet.

"Can you do this?" she asked when they parted. "Not for me. For you. And for the world."

Gavin bit his lip and nodded. Then he put his hand on the Impossible Cube, took a deep breath, and sang one note. The crystal D-sharp thrummed through him, built in intensity, rushed upward, and roared from his throat. The energy blew the door inward so hard, it cracked in two and the pieces smashed against the opposite wall. Gavin continued to sing. The Impossible Cube glowed blue in his hands. He was aware of Alice shouting at him, but he couldn't stop. Silky anger and disgust poured out of him, slid from his throat in an orgasmic black stream. The badness felt so good, and he felt so bad that it felt good. He struggled against it, then gave in. His body shuddered with the pleasure of it. The cube glowed brighter, and his anger thundered through the underworld until the stones began to crack, and still there was more and more and more. Edwina shouted something at him, and he snapped his head toward her. She dived aside, and the power of his voice shattered the stones behind her. More and more fury tore from him. A hand grasped his shoulder, and he rounded with righteousness.

It was Alice. Her face held no trace of fear, only wonder and concern. Alice, who had also come from the hell that was London. He felt her love, both quiet and fierce, and the music buried within his anger answered it. Before the terrible note could touch her, he tightened his throat and changed it.

The new note rang white and clean as a bell that had only just cooled in the mold and still remembered what it was to be hot and pure. It swept every color of sound along the cracked stone corridors and poured over the sleeping agents, who smiled in their drugged sleep. It rushed over Alice and sheathed her in light, lifting her gently off the floor while sparks flickered about her like snowflakes. The little whirligig on her shoulder clung to its perch.

Gavin's note faded. Alice drifted to the floor, her eyes wide. The glow faded from the Impossible Cube, and Gavin dropped it. As the cube tumbled toward the floor, it changed colors—blue to green to yellow to orange to red. The moment it touched the flagstones, red energy exploded in all directions with a bone-jarring *whump* and a blast of warm air that stirred hair and clothes. The cube was gone.

"Good Lord," said Edwina.

Alice touched Gavin's face. "Are you all right?"

He put his palm on her hand, unable to do anything but nod. Then all the strength left him. His knees buckled, and only Kemp's chilly hands stopped him from dropping to the floor.

"Gavin!" Alice grabbed for him as well.

"I'm . . . all right." His voice was scratchy, and he managed to regain his feet. "Thank you, Alice. For bringing me out of that."

She wrapped her arms hard around him, her face wet with tears. "You're thanking *me*? God, Gavin. I love you always."

"I love you always."

"Heavens, I *am* good." Edwina emerged from the workroom carrying a spider with a large clock built into its belly. "Except for this little toy. Do you know they wouldn't give me the parts I needed to complete—ah! Just the thing."

She set the spider down and plucked the whirligig automaton from Alice's shoulder. It squeaked in surprise, and before Alice or Gavin could respond, Edwina tore open its access hatch and yanked out several bits of machinery. The little automaton quivered and went still. Gavin stared in horror.

"Edwina!" Alice cried. "What—?"

"Shush, dear. Auntie's working." With dazzlingly fast movements, she worked the machine parts—memory wheels, Gavin now remembered—into the clock spider's insides and closed it up. Then she unceremoniously kicked the thing back into her cell and swept the bits of the whirligig aside with her foot. The entire affair took only a few seconds.

"Ready now, darlings!"

"What was that for?" Alice demanded.

"My final project. You wouldn't expect me to leave it uncompleted, would you?"

"But—never mind. We have to get out of here. The noise will bring dozens of people down. Do you have the other cure?"

"I do," Edwina said. "Let's—oh dear."

Some of Gavin's strength had returned, and he straightened enough to glance around. The other doors in the hallway had also been destroyed, flattened by Gavin's voice. Startled faces, male and female, young and old, were peeping into the corridor. Dr. Clef waved to Gavin.

"We should leave now," Edwina said. "In fact, we should run."

They sprinted up the stairs. At the top, they met a group of workers, none of them agents.

"What's going on?" someone shouted.

"There was an explosion in the clockworker laboratories," Alice said. "People need help! Hurry!"

"Halt right there!" barked a new voice. Lieutenant Phipps strode purposefully, if a bit unsteadily, around the lower turn in the spiral staircase. "It's a trick. They've incapacitated all our agents and broken into the Doomsday Vault."

Fear rushed down Gavin's spine. He glanced at the dozen-odd workers, then at Phipps. Her face was pale and grim.

"Do you think this is the first time a cure has been found and repressed?" Phipps said quietly. "You walked right past three others in the Doomsday Vault. I won't let you release any of them."

"I never understood you, Susan," Edwina said. "Even in school, you contradicted yourself. You push the Hats-On Committee into sedition, but balk at this?"

"I won't commit treason," Phipps said. She was bracing herself against the wall for support.

"I left you a present in my cell," Edwina told her. "My final project. In fact—"

"*You have ten minutes to evacuate,*" boomed Edwina's voice from below. Gavin's blood ran cold. It was exactly the voice he'd heard in that terrible tower all those months ago.

"Good God," Alice gasped. "The clock spider."

"You can arrest us," Edwina said, "or you can get all those unconscious agents to safety. You can't do both."

"For the good of the Crown," Phipps replied hoarsely, "I'll make the sacrifice."

"But will they?" Edwina cocked a thumb at the workers. "*You have nine minutes and thirty seconds to evacuate.*"

"I couldn't have said it better myself," Edwina said.

There was a moment's hesitation. Then most of the workers swarmed around the group and out of sight down the stairs to help the agents. The remainder fled outright, leaving Alice, Gavin, Edwina, Kemp, and Click alone with Susan Phipps.

"Five against one, if you count the cat," Edwina said. "And you're still groggy. You can fight and lose, or you can run downstairs and save some lives."

Phipps stared at them for a hard moment. Her eyes met Gavin's, and the disappointment in her gaze nearly pushed him through the floor. Then Susan Phipps turned and marched down the steps.

Outside, they ran toward the barn with Click leading the way. Kemp and Gavin slid the huge doors open while Alice, Edwina, and Click rushed up the gangplank onto the little airship. When Alice arrived, more than a dozen little automatons poured out of a hatchway and surrounded Alice like a cloud of metal fairies. They squeaked with joy.

"And I'm glad to see you," she said, "but we have no time. Cast off!"

The whirligigs and spiders scampered to obey while Edwina glanced around long enough for her plague-enhanced mind to figure out how everything worked. She cranked the generator, which coughed to life in a cloud of paraffin smoke, and pale blue energy crawled up to the envelope, where it swirled and swooped in a fine glowing pattern beneath the skin. The light revealed words painted along the gunwale. Alice read them aloud as Gavin ran up the gangplank with Kemp close behind.

"The *Lady of Liberty*," Alice said with tears in her voice. "Oh, Gavin!"

Gavin grinned and flipped switches. The propellers buzzed to life while Kemp reached for the gangplank.

"Wait for me! Wait!" Gabriel Stark, known as Dr. Clef, puffed up the plank and onto the ship. He was carrying a large lumpy sack. "*Du Lieber.* How could you leave me behind to explode? And where is my Impossible Cube?"

"Er," Alice said. "I'm not sure how to—"

"Oh—you have a clockwork cat. That is very nice. I will forgive you if I may pet the cat."

"Be my guest," said Edwina.

The airship, meanwhile, moved, gliding gracefully out the wide doors into the open air.

"It flies! Gavin. It flies!" Alice clapped her hands with joy, and Gavin's grin widened into exultation.

"*She* flies," he said.

"So this is what for you wanted all my alloy," Dr. Clef exclaimed. "Never would I have thought of this application. Very intelligent."

"*You have four minutes to evacuate.*" Edwina's voice was clear, even outside. People streamed from the house like ants from a hill.

"Why don't they just take the bomb outside?" Alice asked.

"They can't, darling," Edwina told her. "The spider grabs the floor, you see, and it's too complex for anyone but a plague genius to deactivate, and then only with days of study."

The airship coasted past the chaos a bare six feet above the ground. No one seemed to notice them—everyone was busy dragging unconscious agents out of the house.

"You intended to destroy the Ward from the very start, didn't you?" Alice said tightly to Edwina.

"Well, obviously. Look what they've done to us. To *you*. That device will make the one at my country house look like a mousetrap, so let's move along, please."

"I don't see Simon or Glenda or Lieutenant Phipps," Gavin said. He felt sick. "They won't make it out."

"They'd have you hanged, given the chance," Edwina said.

"You have three minutes to evacuate."

Gavin's fingers whitened on the helm. The propellers beat their inexorable rhythm as the ship glided on. An agent Gavin didn't recognize stumbled out the door, helped by a workman, then dropped to his knees on the front steps. He thought about Susan Phipps and the others downstairs, moving through air like molasses while Edwina's voice counted down to doomsday.

Abruptly he yanked the cord from the generator. The dim blue light of the lattice went out, and the airship fell to the ground with a massive thud, though she retained enough buoyancy to avoid a damaging crash. Everyone rocked on his feet. Dr. Clef tipped over with a squawk.

"What are you doing?" Edwina shouted.

Gavin was already dropping over the side. "I have to do something. I have to help."

"I'm coming with you." Alice jumped after him, and Gavin helped her land. Together, they ran inside the house.

Chapter Twenty

An alarm bell clanged as Alice and Gavin charged down the stairs. Partway, they met a group of workmen helping groggy, black-clad agents up the stairs. Alice paused to help them, but Gavin grabbed her arm. "No! Down here!"

"You have two minutes to evacuate."

Alice shut her ears to Aunt Edwina's dreadful voice and followed Gavin down to the cracked and ruined basement. Her heart beat like a snare, and she was only vaguely aware that she had automatically grabbed her tools before jumping off Gavin's ship. Simon and Glenda were on their hands and knees in the corridor, trying to make it to the stairs.

"Gavin!" Glenda slurred.

"Do you hate me that much?" Simon gasped.

Gavin's lips tightened as he and Alice ran past. He called over his shoulder, "I'm sorry! We're trying to help."

"What *are* we doing?" Alice demanded.

"You're some kind of clockworker, Alice," he said.

The words slammed into her like stones. She'd been trying to forget. Her terror of the clockwork plague rushed back at her. Bad enough that Gavin was infected. Now she herself was somehow affected.

Gavin felt her stiffen. "You are! You're not completely like other clockworkers, but you're close. You know machinery. You can defuse the device."

Alice wrestled with fear. "I don't have a diagram!"

"You saw what Edwina did to it, and she used parts from your automaton. You can do this."

"I don't know if I can, Gavin. If I make a mistake, we'll be dead."

"You have ninety seconds to evacuate."

"And the alternative is?"

He pulled her into Edwina's workroom, the one with the door blown inward. Wrecked equipment was scattered everywhere, and for a moment Alice was back in the basement of Edwina's house, the one that had imploded. In the center of the floor crouched the malevolent brass spider, its claws sunk into the stone, and hunched over it was Lieutenant Phipps. She was trying to open it, without success.

"You!" Phipps barked, and launched herself straight at Gavin. She slammed him into the wall with her metal forearm across his throat. "I'll tear your heart out!"

"Gavin!" Alice cried.

"The device!" Gavin choked. He twisted and managed to break away, but only because Phipps was still somewhat groggy from the pollen. She snapped a punch that caught him in the chest and knocked him backward. Alice felt the blow herself.

"You still fight like a pirate, boy," Phipps snarled.

Gavin lashed out with a spin kick, but Phipps ducked beneath it. Her metal hand grabbed his ankle and wrenched him around. He landed on his back. "Alice! The device!"

Alice forced herself to ignore his pain and to turn to the spider. Automatically she unrolled the velvet cloth with its tools inside. Opening the access hatch was no trouble—it was the exact same hatch Edwina put on all her spiders.

"You have sixty seconds to evacuate," boomed the spider in Edwina's voice.

Another crash. Gavin had rolled aside just in time to avoid the heavy pestle Phipps tried to bring down on his head. He managed a one-two rabbit punch to her ribs, but the angle was bad and he didn't do much damage. Phipps pointed her metal arm at him, palm out.

"*You have fifty seconds to evacuate,*" said the spider.

Alice stared at the machinery inside. It was all a complicated mass, and she understood none of it. The wheels and gears and delicate wires snapped with yellow sparks, and she was certain that if she made a mistake, she would die, or the device would detonate instantly.

"*You have forty seconds to evacuate,*" said the spider.

Gavin rolled to his feet just as a wire whipped out of Phipps's palm and wrapped around him. He struggled, but his arms were pinned to his sides. Phipps flicked a knife from its sheath with her free hand and moved toward him. Alice snatched up a half-broken beaker and flung it at the back of Phipps's neck. It scored a red wound.

"*You have thirty seconds to evacuate,*" said the spider.

Phipps whirled, eyes wild. "You snotty upper-class bitch! I'll get you next!"

Gavin lurched into her from behind. They both went down, though Gavin, whose arms were still pinned, was at a clear disadvantage.

"The device!" he shouted again.

"*You have twenty seconds to evacuate,*" said the spider.

Alice forced herself to study the machinery. It still made no sense. She had no diagram and no instructions.

Did she need them?

But operating without them would mean ... what? She wasn't a clockworker—quite. She had been assembling machines for a dozen years, and clockworkers never lived longer than three. Alice had always assumed she was just talented. Theoretically, anyone could do what she did, with careful instructions and enough time. That no one *had* done it meant nothing. If Alice pulled this off, it would mean breaking more than mere societal rules. It would mean becoming truly unique. No rules need apply.

"Ten . . . nine . . ."

Phipps shoved Gavin aside and regained her feet. Alice swallowed. All right. She was unique. Machines answered her touch, and nothing could stop her. And with that thought, the memory of what Edwina had done to the spider came flooding back. She saw how everything fit together and, more importantly, how everything came apart.

"Four . . . three . . ."

Alice reached into the spider with a pair of forceps and extracted a single memory wheel. The yellow sparks died, and the spider released its grip on the cellar floor. Alice tossed the wheel away with a sigh, then stiffened as a cold steel touched her throat.

"Good work, Agent Michaels," Phipps said in her ear. "That deserves a reward."

"We've already released the cure," Alice lied. "There's no point in killing me."

"There's personal satisfaction."

"I saved you just now." Alice's heart beat at the back of her throat. "I saved the entire Ward."

"Susan!" Simon d'Arco was leaning against the doorjamb. "Susan, don't! If she released the cure, there's no point in killing her, and she just saved all our lives. *Your* life."

Phipps turned her head only a little. "She committed treason. I'm just expediting the sentence."

"A man gives in to anger," Simon said. "What would an honorable Ad Hoc woman do?"

A long moment passed, and Alice prayed Phipps would believe the lie. Then the knife went away. Alice found she could breathe again. Gavin struggled out of the wire and sat up.

"You have until sunrise to run," Phipps said. "Then God help you."

*   *   *

The dirigible glowed a faint blue against the cloudy night sky while the gaslights of London slid by below. The stars had fallen to Earth, and the dark ground lay above them. Alice felt a moment of vertigo even as the sight took her breath away. She gave a heartfelt sigh and turned back to the deck. Gavin, lithe and strong, was back at the helm, his injuries only bothering him slightly. A mixture of fear and relief made her hands shake. He was sick with the clockwork plague, which filled her with red fear, but in a moment he would be cured, which gave her relief deeper than a drink from a cool, dark well.

"All right, Edwina," she said, "it's time to give the cure."

"I don't know why I would want to," Edwina said peevishly. "You thoroughly wrecked my wonderful plan to destroy the Third Ward. What am I going to tell the other geniuses at parties? 'My doomsday device *almost* went off. It *almost* destroyed an entire police force.' I'll be laughed out of society."

"Don't make me call Kemp on you," Alice warned.

"Madam?"

"Oh, very well," Edwina sighed. She was holding a large glass jar, and Alice wondered where she'd gotten it. "Set the ship to hover, Gavin, if I may use your Christian name." Gavin obeyed while Edwina set the jar down and took up the spider Alice had snatched from the Doomsday Vault, the one with the hollow tubules running up and down it. "Your left arm, please, Alice."

"Why?" Alice asked suspiciously.

"Because your one true love can't administer the cure to himself, and I need to show you how to do it."

Alice held out her left arm, and Edwina fit the spider around it. Dr. Clef stepped forward with unabashed curiosity. Kemp stood behind Alice, still uncertain what his role in all this was. Alice had banished the little automatons belowdecks for fear they might get swept overboard or otherwise lost. Click stood on his hind legs and peered over the gunwale, intent on something that interested only him. He popped his phosphorescent eyes alight to see better.

The spider moved cold and heavy against Alice's skin. Its legs wrapped around her forearm, and its body flattened against the back of her hand, forming a sort of gauntlet that left Alice's palm bare. It also put little claws at the end of each finger. A quick pain pierced her arm, and Alice yelped. The tubules ran red with her blood. Instantly, Gavin was at her side.

"What have you done?" he barked.

"Don't strain yourself, darling. Everything is going according to plan. The spider creates a curative serum from her blood. It's quite harmless, though the spider will never come off. It's quite fashionable, don't you think? Much better than a corset."

"What do you mean it won't come off?" Alice shook her hand, then pulled at the spider, but it clung like a tiny demon. Gavin pulled at it as well, but to no avail. The spider's eyes glowed scarlet.

"If you're finished fiddling," Edwina said, "we can get on. The spider's eyes glow red when it touches someone who's infected with the plague. You're touching Gavin now. Scratch or poke him with the claws to inject the serum. The lights will then glow green to indicate that it worked. Go ahead—you've earned it."

Gavin silently held out his arm. Alice set her mouth. If this was what it took to cure Gavin, she would do it without complaining. She took a tentative swipe at him, but failed to pierce the skin. Gavin flinched, then held himself more firm.

"Don't be shy," Edwina instructed. "You're saving his life."

"You endangered it," Alice retorted, and swiped harder with her new claws. This time she drew blood, four parallel scratches on the inside of Gavin's forearm. The claws sprayed a bit of bloody serum over the wounds. Gavin winced but held firm.

"That should do it," Edwina said. "Kemp, let us know when sixty seconds have passed."

"Yes, miss," Kemp said.

Edwina arched an eyebrow. "What happened to Madam?"

"Madam is currently occupied with Sir," Kemp said.

"Ah." Edwina actually looked flustered and a bit disappointed. "Yes."

The longest minute of Alice's life passed. She looked at Gavin, his blue eyes and silver-blond hair lit by the dim light of his new airship. He managed a smile, and suddenly she was glad to be here on this ship, as long as he was here.

When Kemp announced the minute was over, Alice grabbed his hand with her new gauntlet. Everyone looked at it.

The spider's eyes glowed red.

"Wait a moment," Edwina said. "Wait."

Alice held her breath. Everyone watched. Even Click turned his head. But the lights glowed red. A ball of hot lead formed in Alice's stomach, and Gavin's face went still as a block of ice.

"I don't understand it," Edwina said. "The cure works. I know it works. I tested it extensively. Why . . . ?" Her expression changed. "Oh! Oh dear. There's some bad luck."

Alice rounded on her. "What are you talking about? What do you—?" And then Alice knew. She turned back to Gavin and saw the same realization in his eyes. The strength of it rushed at her with a physical force and drove her to her knees. Gavin went to the deck with her.

"You babbled at the symphony," Alice said. "About math and the universe. I thought you'd gone mad."

"I couldn't stop myself," he whispered. "I didn't know why. And the *Jupiter* Symphony swept me away until Simon snapped me out of it. I was born with perfect pitch, so no one thought of that as a symptom."

"Increased physical coordination," Alice said. "Going for days without sleep. Building an airship that not even Doctor Clef would have considered. It was all there."

"I'm sorry," Edwina said again. "I didn't mean to make you into one of us."

Alice was crying again. "Cure him! You said you can cure him!"

"I can't cure people like us."

"Say it!" Alice grabbed Edwina by the collar and shook her like a rag doll. "Say the damned word!"

Edwina whispered, "I can't cure a clockworker."

Alice let her go and ran back to Gavin. The world was swallowing her up, crushing her between stones. Gavin had been infected for a year. He might live another year, if they were lucky. Or he might go mad tomorrow.

"I won't," she sobbed, running her hands over Gavin's face. He took her fingers and kissed them. "I won't watch it again, Gavin."

"I won't die," he said. "Not yet."

Edwina stepped forward with the jar. "We need to release the other cure, Alice. *You* need to release it."

"And how do I do that?" Alice felt drained.

"I have finished incubating it." Edwina tapped her own chest. "Here. Where no one would look for it, just as I told you."

She handed the jar to Gavin, who kept his free arm around Alice. "What's this for?"

"You'll see in a moment. That's more warning than Pandora had."

"I don't understand. If the cure is inside you, how can it help anyone else?"

"I gave Alice the means to release it, darling." Edwina glanced meaningfully at the metal gauntlet. "That's the final stage."

Alice held up her metal-encased hand. The claws gleamed like knives in the blue light. "No. No, Edwina. I never want to see you again. But I'm not going to—"

"Darling, please! I'm so tired." Edwina passed a hand over her face. "I've been holding the plague at arm's length longer than anyone else in the world, but I'm starting to lose. I can feel my mind slipping. Please, darling. Destroy England, and save the world."

"Why must it be both?" Alice cried. "Why is it everything or nothing?"

"I'll ask God when I see him." Edwina spread her arms and raised her chin.

Alice, pale and trembling, stood before her aunt and thought of the thousands of children dying of plague below their feet. She thought of her father and mother and brother. She thought of the way Edwina had manipulated her from childhood, of how she had signed Gavin's death warrant. With a low scream, she raised her left hand. The claws glittered. Edwina held her breath. Alice pulled her hand back—

And dropped it.

"I can't," she whispered. "Not even to save the world."

And then Gavin was behind her. He took her gloved hand in hers and raised it again. "All right?" he said.

Alice bit her lip and nodded. Her gaze met Edwina's, and Edwina shut her eyes, her arms still spread. Together, Gavin and Alice pulled her hand back, and together they slashed down.

Edwina's clothing and flesh parted like a ripe strawberry. A dark and terrible gash opened up, and Edwina fell backward onto the deck. She thrashed and convulsed. From the wound poured not blood as Alice expected, but millions of insects. They buzzed upward in a cloud, their tiny bodies blinking phosphorescent green.

"Fireflies," Gavin said in his hoarse voice.

"The jar!" Dr. Clef shouted.

Gavin reacted. He swept the open jar through the cloud

and caught a small section of the cloud inside the glass, then clapped on the lid. They flitted around inside.

Click batted at some of the free-flying ones, then backed away, back arched. Dr. Clef slapped his arm. "Ouch!" he said. "They bite!"

"It's how they spread the cure," Alice said. "And each person they bite will spread it to other people when he coughs or sneezes, until the cure goes through the whole world. A disease to cure a plague. It just doesn't work on clockworkers."

Gavin held up the jar. "Why did she want us to keep some?"

"So we can take them to Europe and elsewhere, I think," Alice said. "It'll spread the cure faster."

Edwina's body fell still. It lay, small and shriveled, on the deck. Alice knelt by her as the fireflies descended into London. For better or worse, this single woman had just changed the entire world, and no one would ever know who she was. Alice tried to close Edwina's empty, staring eyes, but they remained stubbornly open. A piece of canvas descended to cover the body.

"I hope Madam doesn't mind," Kemp said.

"Thank you, Kemp," Alice told him. "You always know what to do."

"Madam," Kemp said.

Gavin took up his place at the helm again. "Where should we go?"

"China," Alice said. "We need to go to China."

The propellers started up again, and the airship glided forward. "Why China?"

"Phipps said the cure had been discovered and suppressed more than once, and China has its own clockworkers— Dragon Men. They may have a cure for clockworkers." She managed a smile, though it came out sickly. "We must remain optimistic."

"I can do that," Gavin said, "if I'm with you."

"How will we go to China?" Dr. Clef asked. "I do not think even I can learn Chinese so quickly."

"We have a friend." Gavin produced the silver nightingale from his pocket. "Feng Lung was the last person to touch this besides me. I hope it works." He pressed the bird's left eye. "Ambassador Lung and Feng Lung, this is an emergency. I need to invoke the favor you owe me. Meet us where Feng Lung and I first became friends."

Gavin tossed the nightingale into the air. The tiny messenger angel fluttered its wings and skimmed away.

"To tell you the truth, I find myself relieved," said Ambassador Jun Lung. "Your difficulty solves a problem for me."

They were standing at the crossed pathways where Gavin had first rescued Feng from trouble all those months ago. Alice and Gavin faced Jun and Feng while Kemp busied himself with a shovel near Edwina's canvas-wrapped body. For once, he didn't complain. Click stayed on the airship, which had landed on a nearby field. Dr. Clef stood a few feet away, clutching the sack he had salvaged from the Third Ward. He had offered to stay on the ship as well, but Alice didn't trust him enough to leave him alone. Night was lifting like raven wings, revealing soft light beneath. The chilly air rang with traffic sounds from the distance. London was nearly awake.

"What kind of problem, sir?" Alice asked.

"I have come to the regretful conclusion that my eldest son is unsuited for statecraft." Jun bowed his head briefly, his hands folded within his sleeves. "He is talented at language, but often fails to choose his words wisely."

"My father is correct," Feng said without a trace of embarrassment. "I would start a war between our countries."

"So you would like us to escort him home," Gavin said.

"Precisely." Feng winced and slapped his neck. A bit of green came away on his fingers. "I do not remember London suffering from biting insects at this time of year. Is this normal?"

"We would be pleased to take Feng home, Ambassador," Alice said, ignoring the question. "Can he leave—"

"Immediately, yes," the ambassador said. "I believe certain people of ill repute are already seeking him, and diplomatic immunity would not be helpful."

"We should go ourselves," Alice said. "I'm sure Phipps is rallying the Third Ward to look for us once the sun rises, and it's still dark enough for plague zombies to—"

"Look!" Dr. Clef pointed.

Half a dozen plague zombies, possibly those once controlled by Edwina, shambled toward them over the grass. Their arms were outstretched, and thin skin hung in tatters ragged as their clothes. One of them was a child, perhaps six or seven years old. Alice and the others backed away, toward the ship. Then the first bright beams of sunlight came over the horizon and struck the zombies full on. They flinched, but, instead of fleeing for the shadows, they stopped. Identical looks of wonder crossed their mottled faces as the sun slipped gold slowly over their bodies and faces. They faced the dawn and let the light wash over them. Even as Alice watched, some of their sores stopped weeping, and their bloody tears ceased. The child jumped once, then twice. Then he smiled.

"It's working," Alice whispered. "Oh, Aunt Edwina! Oh, Father! It's *working*!" She hugged Gavin, who whirled her around with giddy joy. "It's working!"

"I do not understand," Feng said. "What is working?"

Tears were streaming down Alice's face. "I didn't think I could be happy again, but I am! Can you forgive me, Gavin?"

"What for?" he asked, laughing.

"For being happy, even when you're . . ."

"Sick? Alice, I never want you to feel sad or guilty. I love you always." He kissed her. "Let's fly."

*   *   *

The *Lady of Liberty* skimmed steadily over the English Channel. Gavin stood at the helm, feeling every creak of the ropes, every movement of the deck. The fresh, clean air washed over him, and the sun shone overhead. His back bothered him not at all. He should have been tired, but he wasn't. Alice was sleeping belowdecks, as was Feng. Kemp was in the galley attending to lunch, and Click, perched on the tiny bowsprit, was pointedly ignoring the seagulls that screeched at him. Gavin should have felt frightened or unhappy about the disease rampaging through his brain, but he didn't. He was back where he belonged at last, Alice was with him, and they were heading off to explore a new land. What more did he need? He tipped back his head and sang:

> With a host of furious fancies whereof I am com-
> mander,
> With a burning spear and a horse of air to the wilder-
> ness I wander.
> And still I'd sing bonny boys, bonny mad boys, bed-
> lam boys are bonny,
> For they all go bare, and they live by the air, and they
> want no drink nor money.

A hatch opened, and Dr. Clef climbed out with a machine under one arm. He stumped over to Gavin and pushed his goggles up to his forehead in a way that reminded Gavin of Old Graf.

"That workshop you have below is primitive and dreadful," he spat. "How am I going to re-create my poor Impossible Cube without a decent laboratory?"

"You're lucky to have a laboratory at all, Doctor," Gavin pointed out. "What is that?"

"My first attempt. I have tried to find ways to stretch across to other universes to find my cube, but all I did was reach back to old hypermagnetic frequencies. Look at this nonsense."

He twisted dials on the machine. Two parabolic reflectors spun, and a square of glass lit up. The machine made eerie pinging noises, and bits of light danced across the glass.

"What am I looking at?" Gavin said.

"Sources of power for automatic machinery," Dr. Clef said impatiently. "You see? This one is Kemp. It is very close. And this tiny one is the clicky kitty."

"What's this one?" Gavin pointed. "It's a different color."

"That one has a different power source than the others."

Gavin studied the glass a moment. His brow furrowed. "Is it . . . following us?"

"Yes, of course."

The connection clicked instantly, and a feeling of dread came over Gavin. He knew the answer, but he had to ask the question anyway. "Why is it a different power source?"

"This kind of machinery demands it. It is what happens when one grafts machine parts to human flesh."

"Like the machine parts grafted to Susan Phipps?"

"Yes, exactly."

Dr. Clef shut off his machine, and Gavin pushed the *Lady*'s engines harder, speeding them toward the Orient.

ABOUT THE AUTHOR

Steven Harper Piziks was born in Saginaw, Michigan, but he moved around a lot and has lived in Wisconsin, in Germany, and briefly in the Ukraine. Currently he lives with his three sons near Ann Arbor, Michigan.

His novels include *In the Company of Mind* and *Corporate Mentality*, both science fiction published by Baen Books. He has produced the Silent Empire series for Roc and *Writing the Paranormal Novel* for Writer's Digest. He's also written novels based on *Star Trek*, *Battlestar Galactica*, and *The Ghost Whisperer*.

Mr. Piziks currently teaches high school English in southeast Michigan. His students think he's hysterical, which isn't the same as thinking he's hilarious. When not writing, he plays the folk harp, dabbles in oral storytelling, and spends more time online than is probably good for him. Visit his Web page at http://theclockworkempire.com, and his Twitter feed at http://www.twitter.com/stevenpiziks.

Read on for an exciting excerpt from
the next novel of the Clockwork Empire,

THE
IMPOSSIBLE CUBE

Coming in May 2012 from Roc.

Gavin Ennock snapped awake. His temples pounded, his feet ached, and his arms flopped uselessly above his head. Far above him lay green grass strewn with twigs. It took him several moments to understand he was hanging upside down by his ankles. At least he wasn't naked this time.

"Hello?" he called.

Below him, nothing moved. He shifted in confusion, and the iron shackles around his ankles clinked like little ghosts. How the hell—? The last thing he remembered was walking back to the inn from a much-needed trip to the bathhouse and hearing someone call his name. Now he was hanging head down amid a bunch of trees. Most were little more than saplings, but a few were full sized. Gavin didn't know trees, but these certainly didn't seem ... normal. Their branches twisted as if with arthritis, and the leaves looked papery. Two or three bloomed with bright blue flowers, with bees bumbling among them.

The forest itself was contained within a domed greenhouse, three or four stories tall. Gavin's head hung fully two of those stories above the ground. Glass walls broken into geometric designs magnified and heated angry summer sunlight. The whole place smelled green. Water trick-led somewhere, and humidity made the air heavy. Breathing felt almost the same as drinking.

Poison ivy vines of fear took root and grew in Gavin's stomach. "Hey!" Blood throbbed in his head, and his voice shook more than a little. "Is someone going to tell me what's going on?"

A man limped from around one of the trees. His back was twisted, and his sparse brown hair clumped unevenly against his skull. This and his scarred, gnarled hands gave the initial impression that he was old, but Gavin quickly realized he was barely older than Gavin, who wasn't yet twenty. The man was a clockworker, and the plague had left him with both physical and mental scars.

"Shit," Gavin muttered.

"Is he awake?" The man had a French accent. "Yes, he is awake."

"I'm an agent of the Third Ward," Gavin called down to him, lying. "When I don't report in, they'll send a team to see what happened to me. You don't want that. Let me go, and—"

The twisted man threw a lever Gavin hadn't noticed, and Gavin dropped. The ground rushed up at him. His stomach lurched, and Gavin yelled. At the last moment, the twisted man threw the lever again and Gavin jerked to a stop five feet above the ground. His ankles burned with pain, and the headache sloshed hot lead inside his skull.

"I think he has no idea who I am." The twisted clock-worker pressed a scarred hand to Gavin's upturned cheek in a strangely tender caress. The gesture created an odd convergence of opposites. Gavin's captor stood firmly on the ground. His body was as twisted and warped as his trees; his face was scarred beneath greasy sparse hair, and he wore a filthy robe that looked like it had once belonged to a monk. Muddy hazel eyes peered at his captive. Gavin had even features, white-blond hair, and blue eyes. His black shirt and trousers contrasted sharply with his fair skin and hair, and his fingers were straight and strong.

The clockworker cocked his head, as if hearing a voice—or voices. "Then maybe he should look around and try to remember who I am. Maybe he should."

Gavin considered socking the clockworker, but discarded the idea—he had bad leverage, and even if he managed to knock the other man unconscious, he would still be trapped in the shackles. His earlier fear gnawed at him again, mingling with the pain.

Now that he was lower, he could see a nearby large stone worktable littered with wicked-looking gardening tools, a large control panel bristling with levers, dials, and lights, and, incongruously, a brass-and-glass pistol. A power cable trailed from the stock and ended in a large battery pack.

"Listen," Gavin said with growing desperation, "I can help you. I can—"

The man turned Gavin, forcing him to look at the trees. "I don't know if he remembers. Maybe he will if I point out that the forest is old but the greenhouse is new. What do you all think?"

"What are you talking about?" It was useless to argue with clockworkers—the disease that stoked their brains also lubricated their grip on reality—but Gavin couldn't help himself. "You aren't making—"

One of the trees moved. It actually leaned down and in, as if to get a closer look at Gavin. The blue blossoms shifted, and a glint of brass caught the light. Long wires and strips of metal ran up the bark. Gavin's breath caught in his throat. For a moment, time flipped backward, and he was fleeing through a blur of leaves and branches that were actively trying to kill him. A tall, bearded clockworker in an opera cloak rode one of the walking trees, steering it by yanking levers and pressing pedals. His partner, Simon, shouted something as Gavin spun and fired the electric rifle attached to the battery pack on his back.

"L'Arbre Magnifique," Gavin whispered. "This is his forest. But the greenhouse wasn't here before, and you aren't him."

"I heard him mention my father, L'Arbre Magnifique," the clockworker said. "But I don't believe he asked *my* name." He paused again. "Yes, that was indeed rude of him. He should know my name is Antoine."

Gavin's mouth went dry. Fantastic. What were the odds of two clockworkers showing up in the same family, or of Gavin running into both of them in one lifetime? The shackles continued to bite into his ankles with iron teeth.

"Look, Antoine, your father is alive and well," Gavin said, hoping he was telling the truth. "In London. We gave him a huge laboratory and he invents great . . . uh, inventions all day long. I can take you to him, if you want."

Antoine spun Gavin back around and slugged him high in the stomach. The air burst from Gavin's lungs. Pain sank into him, and he couldn't speak.

"Ah," Antoine said. "Do you think I hurt him? I do." Another pause, with a glance at the trees. "No, it was not as painful as watching him kidnap my father." He turned his back to Gavin and gestured at one of the towering trees. "That is true. My father only taught me to work with plants. I will teach myself how to work with meat. Slowly."

An object flashed past Gavin face and landed soundlessly on the grass where Antoine couldn't see. It was a perfect saucer of glass, perhaps two feet in diameter. Startled, Gavin looked up toward the faraway ceiling in time to see a brass cat, claws extended, leap through a new hole in the roof. The cat fell straight down and crashed into some bushes a few feet away. Antoine spun.

"What was that?"

It took Gavin a moment to realize Antoine was talking to him and not to the trees. "It was my stomach growling," he gasped through the pain. "Don't you feed your prisoners?"

A string of saliva hung from Antoine's lower lip. "Yes. I feed them to my forest."

The leaves on the lower bushes parted, and the brass cat slipped under the worktable, out of Antoine's field of view. It gave Gavin a phosphorescent green stare from the shadows. A ray of hope touched Gavin.

"Your father is a genius, Antoine," he said earnestly. "A true artist. Queen Victoria herself said so."

The trees whispered among themselves, and a storm crossed Antoine's face. "You are right! He should never mention that horrible woman's name, not when her Third Ward agents took my father away from me!"

"Simon and I captured a tree with him, remember? The tree turned out to be really useful," Gavin continued, a little too loudly. The pain from the punch was fading a little, but his ankles still burned. "It helped us track down a clockworker who hurt a lot of people."

Another glance at the trees. "Ah, yes. I miss Number Eight, too. What? No, I have definitely improved your design since then. Look at yourselves. I can make you blossom and create seedlings that grow their own metal frameworks, if only you have enough minerals in your roots. The entire forest will walk at my command! I only need more money. Money to buy more metal for my hungry trees."

Through the hole in the roof flew a small whirligig, its propeller twirling madly to keep it aloft. It trailed a rope. The whirligig zipped down to a support beam close to the ground and grabbed it with six spidery limbs, leaving the slanted rope behind it. Two of the trees creaked and leaned sideways, as if they were searching for something. Antoine, sensitive to their moods, started to turn. The unnatural position of his arms started new pains in Gavin's shoulders. The aches made Gavin's concentration waver, and he had to force himself to speak up and divert Antoine's attention.

"Where are you going to get money?" he said. "You live in a forest."

Distracted, Antoine turned his attention back to Gavin. "He doesn't know that I will collect a reward for capturing him. Yes, I will. But will I play with him first? Also, yes."

Gavin froze. "What reward? What are you talking about?"

"Is it a large reward? Enormous!" Antoine began to pace. The cat watched him intently, and when Antoine's twisted back was turned, it bolted out from under the table and took a flying leap onto Gavin's back. His claws sank into Gavin's skin, and Gavin sucked in a sharp breath at the pricks and stabs of eighteen claws.

"Ow! Click!" Gavin gasped.

Antoine glanced sharply at him, but the cat was hidden from view behind Gavin's body. "Click?"

"I said I'm sick," Gavin managed. "Who could be offering a reward for me? I've only been in France a few days."

"That would be Lieutenant Susan Phipps."

Gavin's blood chilled. "No," he whispered.

"Ah. Did you see the way I frightened my new subject?" A pause, and his expression turned churlish. "But I should be allowed to play before I turn him over to Lieutenant Phipps. Just a little. Just enough."

"What about Alice?" Gavin couldn't help blurting. "Is there a reward for her, too?"

"Would I like to double the reward?" Click the cat climbed higher just as Antoine snaked out a hand and pulled Gavin closer by his hair, which gave Gavin an excuse to yelp in pain. "Where is your little baroness?"

At that moment, a woman in a brown explorer's shirt, trousers, and gloves slid through the hole in the roof and down the slanted rope. Her hair was tucked under a pith helmet, and her belt sported a glass cutlass. Her expression was tight, like a dirigible that might explode. Alice Michaels. Oh God.

"We split up," Gavin gasped, too aware of the cat on his back. What the hell was the damned thing doing? "Right after we left England. The Third Ward was chasing us and we decided it would be safer. You'll never find her."

"Do I believe him? No, I do not. Do I think his Alice is somewhere nearby? Yes, I—"

"*MON SEIGNEUR!*" boomed one of the trees. "*MON SEIGNEUR! ROCAILLEUX!*"

Everything happened at once. Antoine snatched up the brass pistol from the worktable. Click scrambled up Gavin's legs to his ankles and extended a claw into the shackles. Alice whipped the glass cutlass free with one hand and sliced the rope below her. Clinging to the top piece like a liana vine, she swung downward. With a *clack*, Gavin's shackles came open and he dropped to the ground, barely managing to tuck and roll so he wouldn't hit his head. Antoine fired the pistol at Alice. Yellow lightning snapped from the barrel. Thunder smashed through the greenhouse. A shout tore itself from Gavin's throat. The bolt missed its target, and four windows shattered. Alice landed several yards away from the circle of trees, stumbled, then regained her feet in waist-high shrubbery. Click dropped to the ground in front of Gavin. Antoine took aim at Alice again.

Gavin tried to come to his feet, but his legs, chained for too many hours, gave way. Instead, he snatched up Click and threw him. Click landed on Antoine's head with a mechanical yowl. Antoine's arm jerked. The pistol spoke, and thunder slammed the air as the yellow bolt tore through the top of one of the trees. Another window shattered.

"*ROCAILLEUX,*" the tree cursed.

Alice crashed through the bushes toward Antoine, who was still struggling with Click. Blood flowed from a dozen tiny cuts on his face and head. He finally managed to fling the cat aside and bring the pistol around on her.

THE ULTIMATE IN
SCIENCE FICTION AND FANTASY!

From magical tales of distant worlds to stories of
technological advances beyond the grasp of man, Penguin has
everything you need to stretch your imagination to its limits.

penguin.com

ACE
Get the latest information on favorites like
William Gibson, T.A. Barron, Brian Jacques,
Ursula K. Le Guin, Sharon Shinn, Charlaine Harris,
Patricia Briggs, and Marjorie M. Liu,
as well as updates on the best new authors.

ROC
Escape with Jim Butcher, Harry Turtledove, Anne Bishop,
S.M. Stirling, Simon R. Green, E.E. Knight, Kat Richardson,
Rachel Caine, and many others—plus news on the
latest and hottest in science fiction and fantasy.

DAW
Patrick Rothfuss, Mercedes Lackey, Kristen Britain,
Tanya Huff, Tad Williams, C.J. Cherryh, and many more—
DAW has something to satisfy the cravings of any
science fiction and fantasy lover.
Also visit dawbooks.com.

*Get the best of science fiction and fantasy
at your fingertips!*